I0827060

PRAISE FOR THE CORRIGAN BROTHERS SERIES

"Hard-eyed characters and six-gun action."

— PUBLISHERS WEEKLY

"Characters are placed in realistic emotionally driven situations, bringing with them souls filled with concern, fear, joy and desire."

— TRUE WEST MAGAZINE

"Solid writing and superb storytelling."

— AMERICAN COWBOY MAGAZINE

"The traditional Western doesn't get much better..."

— ROUNDUP MAGAZINE

PLAY FOR BLOOD

PLAY FOR BLOOD

CORRIGAN BROTHERS
BOOK SIX

SCOTT F. SMITH

Play for Blood
Paperback Edition
Copyright © 2026 by Scott F. Smith

Wolfpack Publishing
1707 E. Diana Street
Tampa, FL 33610

www.wolfpackpublishing.com

All rights reserved. No part of this book may be reproduced in any form or by any electronic or mechanical means, including information storage and retrieval systems, without express written permission from the publisher, except for the use of brief quotations in reviews. Any use of this publication to train generative artificial intelligence (AI) technologies is expressly prohibited.

This book is a work of fiction. References to historical events, real people, or real places are used fictitiously. Any similarity to real persons, living or dead, is purely coincidental and not intended by the author.

All brand names and product names used in this book are trademarks, registered trademarks, or trade names of their respective holders. Wolfpack Publishing is not associated with any product or vendor in this book.

Editing by My Brother's Editor

Paperback ISBN 979-8-89567-275-4
Ebook ISBN 979-8-89567-274-7
LCCN 2026938224

For my biggest fan, Cindy.
She wears many hats...
my favorite golf partner and world traveler...
my story editor...
my best friend...
and, oh yeah, my wife.
Thanks for saying yes to all of it.

PLAY FOR BLOOD

CHAPTER ONE

Thwaakk!

A devastating left hook crashed unexpectedly into the riverboat captain's jaw and snapped his head around. Out cold, he teetered briefly on his feet before toppling over like a felled tree.

The ship's two mates and clerk standing in the midst of the morning assembly were absolutely stunned, rendered motionless when the hulking pilot turned his attention to them.

A huge right fist to the first mate's heart landed like a battering ram and forced all the air from his chest. He folded into a large blue-coated ball. A thunderous left cross to the man's jaw drove him to the floor.

A ferocious side kick to the second mate's stomach doubled him over. A vicious blow to the nape of his neck did untold damage.

Texas morning shadows cradled the large steam-driven boat as its sternwheel churned gracefully up the Colorado River. The serenity provided a stark contrast to the brutality taking place in the perch on top of the ship.

The massively built pilot had not even broken a sweat in his attack. Like a predator wary of his territory, he now assessed his surroundings. His daunting physical presence matched his fierce, menacing eyes. They locked onto the final prey still standing inside the pilothouse.

The administrator, wide-eyed in terror, tried to back away from the imposing assailant closing in on him. "Why are you—" He stretched his arms out, pleading desperately to thwart the advancing savagery. "Wait, wait, wait…"

The attacker, wading toward the terrified purser, launched an overpowering uppercut to the defenseless clerk's chin, snapping the man's head back. He crashed against the floor like a ninepin.

In a matter of moments, Shane Foley, the pilot of the steamboat *River Dreamer*, had single-handedly taken control of the ship. In addition to being a giant of man, Foley was equally skilled with a gun and in hand-to-hand combat, utilizing Oriental judo and karate.

"You there!"

The owner of the boat, a white-jacketed Southern man with hair to match, had suddenly appeared in the doorway, brandishing a drawn cane sword.

Foley eyed this new threat with an almost sympathetic gaze. The older man waded through the bodies on the floor, holding the sword in front of him as he cried out, "I trusted you!"

A rattler-quick blow from Foley chopped into the Adam's apple of the cotton-haired man, leaving him gasping and choking frantically. He dropped the blade and the cane shaft, his hands pawing at his throat, trying to coax breath that would never come. The *River*

Dreamer owner's struggle was brief, perishing as he hit the floor.

Foley began to move toward the speaking tube connecting the pilothouse to the engine room when the final two of the captain's crew members appeared in the doorway. Each brandished a pistol.

The taller of the two shouted, "Foley! What the hell have you done?"

The other crew member tried to gather his courage, even with the loaded gun. "What's the meaning of this?"

"Seemed like a nice boat." Foley grinned ominously. "Thought it needed new management."

"You can't—"

In an eye blink, a masked figure concealed on the deck outside the pilothouse stood without warning.

Booom! Booom!

Through an open window, blasts from both barrels of a sawed-off shotgun blew the two men out the door onto the floor of the hurricane deck outside. Their bodies sprawled in odd contortions as their guns thudded to the floor.

The *River Dreamer* continued its steady journey through the Texas morning.

The masked assailant walked slowly around the outside of the wheelhouse and calmly stepped inside, handing the smoking shotgun to the enormous Foley. The silhouette of this invader was that of a man, but as a wide-brimmed hat was removed, long, brunette tresses shook out. A kerchief draped around the face was pulled down, revealing delicate features.

No man, this was a dark-haired, green-eyed, deadly woman.

CHAPTER TWO

"Looks like the ship has a new captain," the woman said, continuing to shake her hair free. Even dressed in black canvas trousers, a black shirt with a high-stand collar, an unbuttoned black vest, and black traveling boots, she was dangerously beautiful.

"Yes, Miss Thorne," new Captain Foley said.

"You must *never* call me that! Ever!" she snapped, then paused. "It is best you forget you ever heard it." Isla Thorne was the name she used as an alias, protecting her when dealing with politicians, businessmen, and the like.

Foley nodded.

Her tone was deadly. "This is a mistake you only get to make this one time. Are we clear?"

"Yes, ma'am." He gulped in dread.

"I am Calista Theriot, the Bayou pirate. Daughter of the feared raider, Cyprien Theriot."

"Yes, you are. My apologies, Miss Theriot." He bowed. "It will never happen again."

She gathered herself and looked around the pilothouse. "Is the engine room under control?" she asked quietly. Her lightly wrinkled eyes were like emeralds, surrounded by dark, long lashes that pulled and pushed a man in a single blink.

"Chapman's down there."

"Maybe you should let him know your mission is complete up here."

"Yes, ma'am." He moved to the speaking tube. "Lewis? Lewis! You there?"

"Yeah, Foley," came the confident reply. "Going well down here. What about those gunshots?

"There were some extras to clean up," Foley replied. "The ship is ours."

"I heard those booms," Lewis continued. "I stayed put. I stayed put like the boss said."

"And you did well!" The dark-haired woman joined Foley at the speaking tube. "I like men who can follow orders." Her hand rested lightly on Foley's shoulder. Her voice was commanding. And alluring.

"Thank you, Mizz Theriot." Came the voice up the tube. "Thank you."

"Half speed for now, Lewis," Foley ordered. "I'll be sending Zack and Owen your way."

"Yessir."

Calista had already moved away from the tube and was strolling through the wheelhouse, inspecting the collection of bodies.

She nudged her boot against the downed form of the former captain. Moaning and movement came from the body. She pulled the large kerchief from her neck. "He can't have any more marks," she intoned, handing Foley the scarf. "But take the rest of his breath."

Foley stepped over his former boss and held the cloth tight against the man's nose and mouth. His other strong hand kept any fight left in the officer at bay. The end was not long in coming.

"This one's still breathing, too." She pointed to the second mate. Foley moved with agility, like an animal. He grabbed the man's head with a bear-like grasp. With a sharp, unsparing twist, he snapped the former mate's neck.

"Here's another one," she observed. Foley started to approach, but she stopped her new captain. "My turn," she purred as she pulled a pearl-handled dagger from her boot. Razor-sharp, the blade sliced through the first mate's neck like butter. Gasps and struggled gargles emanated from the man's final living moments.

A look of gratification crossed her face. Wiping the blade on the man's sleeve before returning it to her boot, she spoke softly, "Take his coat. Wrap all that up. We can't have any more blood spilling all over your pilothouse."

New Captain Foley dutifully obeyed. After finishing up swaddling the gory mess, he returned his focus to his boss, the notorious pirate queen herself.

Not taking his eyes off her, he was reminded of all the tales he had heard of *Calista Theriot*, since even before the war. Feared plunderer. Bold assassin. Ruthless poker player. Shrewd businesswoman. Voluptuous temptress.

He quickly glanced at her chest and considered that last tale. Right now, dressed in wrangler trousers and a dark work shirt, she looked like any number of men in his gang. Her womanly build was well concealed.

Her voice snapped him out of his reflection. Pointing

to the bodies on the floor, she ordered, "Your new officers have work to do. Only your men will clean up this blood, not the chambermaids. Have the maids find you some new uniforms instead." Gesturing to the stilled bodies, she added, "Tell the maids that the captain and everyone else is down in the engine room. There is trouble there."

"I'll have them look in the quarters' closets for new suits," Foley responded.

She nodded agreement and added, "Put Mr. Chapman in charge of cleanup here. He seems efficient."

Foley made sure the coat wrapped around the head and neck of the recently dispatched man was preventing further burbling of lifeblood across the floor. Into the tube, he summoned his man, Chapman, up here to the pilothouse.

"If any passenger asks, tell them the same," she instructed. "The officers are down with the engine. If they heard those shotgun blasts, they're to be told it wasn't a gun, it was noises from the boiler."

"Yes, ma'am."

She moved to the front of the pilothouse and ran her hands slowly across the wheel, admiring the look of the boat, the view of the river. She reached to open a window, letting the coppery smell of blood be replaced by the scents of a new day. Her attachment to the water was apparent in her longing gaze.

She had heard it was difficult to tell her age. God had bestowed many gifts on her. She was beautiful and knew it well. Her looks had given her opportunities. But it was her mind that allowed her to be successful, and feared. She knew that as well and smiled at the thought.

Standing here in the triumphant aftermath was like

raking in a big pot after a winning hand. Invigorating. Exhilarating. It wasn't fate or luck. It was knowing that you had outplayed your adversary. "The day is ours," she said softly as she caressed a small silver-and-brass amulet under her black shirt.

She thought of her father. At war's end, his boats worked the contraband trade along the Mississippi, from New Orleans to St. Louis. A thriving flotilla. Yes, he had been a prosperous raider in his own right, but she had made the Theriot name formidable, imposing. Today, Calista Theriot's boats and crafts menaced the waterways up and down Louisiana, Texas, and beyond. She spoke again quietly into the morning, "It's damn near a fleet, Papa."

She breathed deeply. The wrappings keeping her bosom restrained were doing their job, but were beginning to be uncomfortable. The suspenders holding up her trousers weren't helping either. She was ready to remove herself from this outlaw garb and truly revel in today's success. A grand meal. Rich wine. The touch of a bold, ambitious man. Soon…in Austin…a young man she had her eyes on…from whom she expected big things.

Her eyes closed, and she bit her lip slightly at the tantalizing vision. But now she must wait. There was time for all of that, but not now…the sound of nearby movement dissolved those sensual thoughts instantly.

Around her, Foley's men, under the supervision of Lewis *Grapeshot* Chapman, were starting to remove bodies and clean up blood.

"Captain Foley, after you have stowed all this mess and gotten your men squared away in their new roles, you are to cut the engine back and begin spreading the word to all on board that you are having trouble with the engine. Tell them there is no danger, but continuing to Austin will be out of the question."

"We'll put in up ahead at Bastrop, yes?"

"Yes. At Bastrop. When all of the bodies are hidden, cut the engine to quarter power. That should make your arrival in Bastrop near suppertime. Everyone who is not part of our crew will get off there. Passengers. Stewards. Even the chambermaids."

Foley nodded.

"Once everyone has disembarked...*with ALL their belongings*. Do you hear that, Mr. Chapman? Now is not the time to be grabby." She turned her sole attention back to Foley. Her emerald eyes intense. "You will wait for sundown." She gestured in the direction to which the bodies were being taken. "Have your men ready to take all of that...*excess freight*...to the Bastrop hog pens." She paused. "The bloody ones especially, and old Bedford the owner, in particular. We don't need *that* story to bust us."

"Yes, ma'am."

"Do it quickly. Dump them all but this one, understand?" She pointed to the final body remaining, the former captain. She stood with one booted foot on the dead man. He had not been shot nor cut, on purpose. "He does not go to the pens. Keep him on board, but ready to travel."

Foley nodded, not sure about this last instruction, but it was an order that would be followed nonetheless. He could wind up in a hog pen, too, he noted to himself.

"While the hogs are being fed," Calista continued, "back here at the ship, you will break off two good-sized pieces of the nameboard. Break, not saw," she reiterated, holding her hands wide apart, indicating the size of the pieces. "The rougher the pieces look, the better. While you're docked in Bastrop, you'll give those pieces to the chief of my snag boat, the *Watershield*."

Foley's look was serious and attentive. He knew any lapse in this plan would trigger fiery anger from his bewitching boss. The one thing that matched her beauty was her capacity for unbridled wrath. He need not rely on tales—he had already seen the fury for himself—her shooting a loudmouth across a poker table for accusing her of cheating, poisoning men for transgressions real and imagined, as well as audacious raids like the one they just pulled off.

Such temperament in a man might get him called loco or mad, but Calista Theriot? He would never say such a thing. Crazy men had hair-trigger tempers, their rage a barricade to thinking or acting wisely. Calista was not so volatile. No, her composure was unnerving, a weapon. Instead, she was a bombshell that, once her fuse had been lit, would detonate deliberate retribution and revenge on her quarry. Foley knew what actions, what things, would bring a match to his boss's fuse.

Foley turned from his boss and called to the men, "Keep the captain separate. Put him in his chambers for now. Dump all the bloody ones on the same tarp. Same with Bedford."

Old man Bedford, the recently deceased owner of this boat, had tried to bring the law's attention to other large paddlewheels Calista operated here in Texas and in Louisiana. Two ships in particular, the *Calluna* and the *Bluestar,* caught Bedford's vexation. Both of her steamships hosted high-stakes gambling games in addition to smuggling extensive amounts of cotton, sugar, tobacco, practically anything that could make a profit.

Everything but human beings. Calista would have none of that. In her mind, human trade was an abomination. She had turned in fellow marauders after discovering they operated in such activities.

Both the *Calluna* and *Bluestar* enjoyed unsullied operation up and down the Red and Mississippi Rivers. Old Bedford tried to interfere. He would now be dumped in what used to be his cargo hold, soon to be pig swill.

Her eyes took in the face of her newest boat captain. She never had to worry about him following orders. His loyalty to her was long-standing. Years ago, she saved him from a St. Louis lawman's noose.

The slip-up with her name would not happen again. Foley was thorough and took her instructions without question. He was also not at all unattractive. He had eyes that, to her, were both predator and prey. All coupled with his incredible brute strength. She gave herself a moment to imagine his naked torso. Taking instruction without question? It made her lips curl up at the thought. Such a man would be fun sport for an afternoon, a snack. But there was no way she would mix pleasure with business. Not with one of her crew. This line must always be drawn. His face gave no indication of what he was thinking. She liked that in him.

"Don't worry. The snag boat chief will come to you," she continued. "His name is Mr. Shrewsbury. Best damn boatman I've got." She paused and cocked her head slightly, running a light hand affectionately down his arm. "Next to you." She smiled. "You will give him the pieces of the name board—and the captain's body."

Foley looked a bit perplexed.

She ignored his look and continued, "The moon will set about midnight tonight. When it sets, you'll quietly push off, turn the ship around, and head downriver. Let the current work. Don't fire up unless you absolutely have to."

"Yes, ma'am." Foley was still uncertain, but not going to object now.

"Tomorrow morning, after you're well gone from Bastrop, word will have reached Austin about a large paddlewheel exploding," she explained matter-of-factly.

His face mirrored his uncertainty.

"I've long done business in Austin. I have a wharf master in my employ and a constable or two who will always look the other way. Plus, I'll be dining with a…an official…who is an *acquaintance* of mine. Word will get out."

Foley began to understand.

"When my snag boat reaches Austin, Mr. Shrewsbury will be carrying proof that the *River Dreamer* met a ruinous end."

The new captain now grinned his comprehension. "You sure like to run a bluff."

"What bluff? The pieces of nameboard wood and a body are *evidence*. A snag boat is supposed to keep the river clear. Two pieces of the doomed *River Dreamer* and its captain, all fished out of the river. Mr. Shrewsbury will report that the rest of the ship was blown to bits and carried to oblivion."

Everything made sense now. Foley had to nod in appreciation.

She continued, "All of the passengers you debarked in Bastrop will be abuzz about the crew discussing engine troubles—"

"So no questions—" Foley interjected.

"Or investigation." She paused. "Besides, you'll be

far away, steaming along the Sabine or over to Atchafalaya."

"*What* River Dreamer?" he said.

They laughed together.

The new captain shook his head and grinned at his boss's meticulous coordination. Her taste for deception was as dangerous as it was impressive. He would never sit at the same card table against her.

Her instructions continued, "Tonight, after you've pushed off from Bastrop, you must work quickly. While it's dark, get new nameboards that change the name of the ship to the *Hollyhock*. What's left of the old name-boards goes into the firebox. As does any paperwork or artifact on board that references the *River Dreamer*. Burn it all."

"Chapman is good at finding that stuff."

She nodded and continued, "Get your men to paint the outside of this pilothouse, whatever color you can find. Blue would be nice. Anything to cover up this white. She needs a new look, a little spruce-up."

Foley nodded acknowledgment. "So, downstream... our next stop is...LaGrange or Columbus?"

"LaGrange, so you'll have to get your decorating accomplished quickly."

"Yes, ma'am."

"You'll moor outside LaGrange. You know the spot. Just past town. Take on no passengers or freight...other than our men departing LaGrange—"

"In a big hurry." Foley chuckled. "We'll use the engine trouble story if anyone wants to know."

"Good. Get those arriving men and their horses under cover on the main deck. The cargo hold should be plenty big. Don't let them dismount until you're out of sight rounding that sharp bend."

Foley nodded. "Too much noise and commotion."

She gave a slight nod of affirmation. "You have your orders. Captain."

"Yes, Miss Theriot!"

CHAPTER THREE

Two days later, farther down the Colorado, the paddlewheel *Hollyhock*, was moored just outside the growing town of LaGrange.

Resting at a slip often used by Theriot boats and other marauding craft, the surrounding water and bank was chosen for its ability to handle surreptitious activity. Live oaks, colorful lantana bushes, and other vegetation lined a serene riverfront. A craft, even one this size, could come and go relatively quickly and easily.

It was why Captain Shane Foley and his boss, Calista Theriot, preferred these sternwheelers. Yes, sidewheelers were faster, more maneuverable for some. Everyone knew about the *Natchez* and the *Robert E Lee*. But you really only needed only one person to manage a sternwheel, and those sidewheelers needed two. Sidewheelers were wider and could not navigate narrow channels like this sternwheeler could. Sternwheelers like the *Hollyhock* had a lighter draft and could operate in shallower waters. Plus, the body of a boat like the *Hollyhock* could protect the wheel at the rear from most of the debris it encountered.

Captain Foley smiled at the thought of the discussion he had with Calista when figuring out which boat to commandeer. She knew exactly what she wanted.

Captain Foley calmly called down to the engine room via the brass speaking tube with the funnel mouth, “It shouldn’t be long now, make ready.”

Twenty minutes later, five riders galloping flat-out, appeared in the open bottom land leading to the river. Signs of their approach were observed before they were. However, the plume their mounts were kicking up was not as large as the ominous dust cloud billowing behind them.

“Here they come,” Captain Foley thundered. “Let’s get this right!”

The five masked riders were eating up the open green land and barreling hard toward the leafy bank.

The last of the five outlaws glanced back over his shoulder and turned to holler to his companions, “Ride! Don’t let that posse catch up!”

The bandit next to him yelled back, “Don’t worry! Minutes are all we need.”

Another called out over the clamor of the pounding hooves, “There it is, the *Hollyhock*!”

“Just where we were told it’d be!”

The awaiting steamboat was moored silently, defying the current, its stacks puffing impatiently. The outlaws slowed their pace as they neared the ship.

“Head for the bow!” their leader hollered.

Reaching the bank, the riders did not allow their horses the opportunity to think. The men urged their lathered mounts onto makeshift stages that bridged land to the bow of the boat. The animals did not hesitate, stepping briskly onto the wide enough wooden planks that led onto the ship's main deck. When the final horse and rider completed their hasty embarkation, several crewmen pulled the wooden stages on board.

Foley's right-hand, Lewis *Grapeshot* Chapman, had stood on the main deck as the bandit group clattered aboard. "Stay mounted!" he called out as he threw a few banknotes into the lapping water's edge. He then latched onto the lead horse's headstall and reins, coolly leading it into the huge covered cargo hold on the main deck. The rest of the bandit horses followed without complication.

Observing all this from the pilothouse, Captain Foley gave word to the engineer to get the *Hollyhock* underway immediately at full speed.

In the enclosed darkness of the large hold, Chapman ordered, "Stay in the saddle. Keep 'em quiet." Before he headed back outside, he smiled at the tense, winded group. "I'll be right back. Gonna make sure that posse doesn't try anything."

He stepped out onto the deck and casually watched the bank and its surroundings. The watery clearance between land and the *Hollyhock* was growing. Soon, the boat would reach the deep channel. There, the engine and the current would take hold.

And they would be too far away for any posse to intervene.

Just in case, all of Captain Foley's men not involved with boiler and engine operation were readied. Most ducked down along the LaGrange side of the ship, all along the hurricane deck and crew quarters—each crouching just out of sight. Rifles had been passed down the line.

Standing next to a huge wooden chest, Lewis Chapman stood calmly on the main bridge. Inside the chest was a small swivel gun. If necessary, *Grapeshot* Chapman would quickly pull a pin, dropping the sides of the crate, and be the first to open fire with an already loaded artillery piece. His specialty.

Silence prevailed on board the *Hollyhock*. Only the rhythmic *splashsha-splashsha-splashsha* of the paddle-wheel thumping its way through the murky water could be heard.

Long minutes later, a dozen armed citizens and their sweating horses reined up at the open part of the bank next to the wide, churning water.

A rider closest to the river turned and yelled to the marshal as he pointed at the water with his drawn Winchester. "Their tracks end at the river!"

Another LaGrange citizen hollered, "They must've tried to cross it!"

"Anyone see 'em in the water?"

The marshal dryly shook his head. "No way they made it. River's too wide."

"Filled with undercurrent, too," came another observation.

Uneasiness spread through the men and their horses.

"Look! At the riverbank! There's money!"

The bills that *Grapeshot* Chapman tossed into the water floated easily against the bank.

The marshal shook his head again. "Fools. Serves 'em right, drowning like that—"

"But they took our money with 'em!"

"You're more'n welcome to go swimming, Dawson," the marshal said resignedly.

Grumbling reality spread through the posse.

"Hey! Lookit there! Down at the bend! You don't suppose they made it onto that riverboat?"

The marshal scoffed, "In this territory? Filled with outlaws? There ain't a boat captain around that'd risk picking up strange riders in mid-river."

Back aboard the *Hollyhock*, Captain Foley held the posse in view with his spyglass. He smiled as he watched the marshal and fellow citizens turn glumly back to town.

Collapsing the glass, he told his pilot he was going down to the main deck. "We're headed to Bay City, Mr. Allen. Keep her safe."

Reaching the cargo hold, he joined his second-in-command, "Lewis, let's tell our guests the good news."

Peering inside the cargo hold, Foley announced to the outlaws, "Well done, men. The posse's turned for home. You can dismount and see to your horses."

Chapman added, "We'll have nosebags of grain brought in for your mounts. And buckets of water once they've cooled down enough."

Captain Foley stepped inside and shook hands with the outlaw leader, who was mopping his head with a kerchief that had served as a mask. "Nice work, Colter." The huge captain grinned.

Colter Jones smiled in return and untied a set of large saddlebags. "There are three more of these," the outlaw noted as he handed them to the captain. "One on each horse, stuffed with gold and certificates. Bobby on the last horse over there, has two sacks of money. Big bills, too."

"LaGrange was ripe for picking." Foley grinned.

"Yeah, but we never could have made it without this floating hideout," the leader said. "The extra weight was tiring these boys out." He chuckled and patted his horse appreciatively.

The bandit next to them overheard and cut in, "Ya ain't kiddin'. That posse was breathin' down our necks. They'd have caught us fer damn sure."

Another called out, "Slickest damn operation I ever saw."

"Can't go wrong with Calista Theriot," Chapman boasted.

"Yes, Miss Theriot is pleased with your work," Foley said. "Once your horses are squared, get yourselves some grub. Your jump-off is Bay City. We'll divvy up the splits then."

CHAPTER FOUR

Across the state, not quite three hundred miles to the northwest, in the growing town of Wilkon, Texas Rangers Holt Corrigan and Orion Higbee were enjoying well-earned peace and quiet.

They had been colleagues for about a year, but in that short time, they had been through more action than most would face in a lifetime.

The two had been paired together by Ranger Captain Laird McCoy. Their first mission had been to hunt down a brutal killer known as *The Angel*, an evil priest on a murderous rampage. That rugged assignment had thrown them into a tangled web to reveal just who was pulling the preacher's strings—a vicious businessman by the name of Meden Taliff, who fancied himself the next governor of Texas. The two Rangers brought his campaign and his life to an incendiary ending. With only a brief lull, Holt and Orion were then ordered to the cattle country town of Stebbins to help capture a band of ruthless rustlers, a local family named the Viklunds.

The mission to bring down the Viklund operation had

been harrowing. The cold-blooded Swedish family stopped at nothing to get what they wanted, including harnessing the support of a lawless sheriff and his brother, an Army quartermaster. In the process, Holt had been shot, and Orion had sustained a nasty rapier wound. Another Ranger was also wounded by outlaw bullets. All three lawmen withstood the onslaught and were able to bring the outlaws to justice.

In the few weeks since the showdown with the Viklunds, time finally slowed down enough for Holt to return to Wilkon and acquaint Orion with the Corrigan family. The young Ranger now had reason to stick close to home. He had found Laudie Kate Hart, a woman possessing a spirit as fiery and indomitable as his.

Suppertime had arrived at the Black Hat Saloon, a favorite spot. Laudie Kate was the manager at the recently opened tavern.

Holt and Orion commanded a table in the middle of the brand-new establishment. Holt, a young man who radiated a formidable presence, and Orion, lanky and approaching middle age, paid no attention to what was happening around them, yet knew the position and scenario of everything in the large room.

Holt's dog, Tag Along, lay sleeping at their feet under the table, his head resting between an emptied bowl of beef stew and a bowl of fresh water. The Rangers knew the placement of everything under there, too, and minded their boots and spurs accordingly.

The two friends were nursing beers and Irish whiskey while discussing the idea of expanding the Corrigan family ranches into the horse business. The brothers operated two ranches: the original family spread called the Rafter C, and the Bar 3, a ranch that became part of the family via tragedy.

More than a year ago, a New Mexico outlaw named Agon Bordner fancied himself a cattle baron. He moved to Texas and began acquiring thousands of acres in and around Wilkon. His strategy to achieve this goal was simple, brutal—and, for a time, effective. Gaining control of that much land was easy for Bordner. He murdered ranch owners and their families, blaming Comanches for the attacks. The Corrigans, their godfather Silka, their neighbors the Sanchezes, along with James Hannah, banded together to put a stop to Bordner's evil plan.

In the aftermath, Bordner's largest illegal gain, the Bar 3, was ruled by a judge to be divided between the Corrigan brothers and Jeremy Regan, a young boy whose family had owned the ranch originally and had been murdered by Bordner's gang. Jeremy was now officially an adopted member of Blue Corrigan's family. It was decided that the three Corrigan brothers would run the Bar 3, as well as their own Rafter C spread, until Jeremy was old enough to officially become a co-owner. Deed and his family had become caretakers of the Bar 3 until that day.

The cattle herds at both ranches were doing fine, but the region and the state always needed quality horseflesh. The Bar 3 was large enough to accommodate both horse and cattle operations.

Holt had always been fascinated with the idea of raising horses. Adding such an enterprise at the Bar 3, with Orion to help him and his brothers, made sense.

The part not settled was turning in their Ranger badges first.

"We can add numbers by combing the chaparral and

scrub," Holt said. "There are still some smaller mustang herds patrolling there."

"That'll add numbers. But best to grow good stock through breedin'," Orion noted. "Get a coupla more sturdy, muscular stallions an' some strong, intelligent mares."

"We've got a good studhorse at the Rafter C, been doing his job well." Holt nodded. "If we jump into this, we'll definitely need one or two more uncut colts. We'll train 'em young so we can manage 'em when they become stallions. A lot of posturing and aggression among those rascals."

Orion nodded at the plan.

Working her way around the main room of the Black Hat was Laudie Kate, a petite brunette, warm-faced with sparkling blue eyes. She stopped to watch a table that had a serious card game in progress. Holt immediately halted his conversation to gaze at her. Her normally luxuriant hair was now upswept into a bun. She wore a white Louisa blouse with billowy sleeves and a tan skirt that flared wide at her knees. It was hard not to notice her proud figure. She was every inch a woman, but as tough as she was attractive.

Holt smiled. He had never seen someone so captivating without making any attempt at it. Her eyes locked on to his. For that brief moment, Holt and Laudie Kate were the only two people in the room.

She walked away from the card game and approached Holt's table. She pulled a chair and sat next to him. He found her hand under the table and took it in his. He leaned over to whisper something and took in the smell of her hair. Lavender. Even in the middle of the smoky Black Hat.

They met when Holt busted into another saloon she had managed, the Blue Sky, in Stebbins. Holt was attempting to arrest a gunman, the first move in the operation against the Viklunds. Laudie Kate did not hear Holt call out that he was a Ranger. Thinking he was someone trying to rob her place, she shot him.

Holt smiled at her. "Busy already."

"Busy, I can handle," she said over the din of the packed room. "I hope it stays quiet."

"Do you have time for supper?" Holt asked affectionately. "I'll buy you a steak."

"Probably not." She smiled in return. "But I can set you boys up with two of our best."

"No, sit here for a while. The company just got better," he teased, glancing at Orion.

Orion smirked and jerked his thumb at Holt. "I been searchin', but for the life of me I can't see what it is you see in this…this no-good frog squatter here."

Laudie Kate laughed and leaned in closer to Holt. "He's a work in progress," she deadpanned. "But he's got possibilities."

Holt blushed slightly as Laudie Kate and Orion chuckled over their favorite Ranger. In this light, the long scar running down the right side of Laudie Kate's face, from cheekbone to jawline, was more noticeable.

In that moment, Orion flashed on the accumulated memories since meeting Holt. He admired his confident bearing. The young man seemed like a cougar, all coiled strength—silent and cautious—yet ready to strike with ferocity. The impression was compelling. Holt's matching pistols carried an ivory silhouette of a panther inlaid into each black grip, a tribute to Holt's belief in reincarnation. He was convinced that in one of his lives he had been a jaguar in South America. An Apache holy man had counseled him that the spirit of a panther walked beside him.

Orion had not known Holt very long, but he thought about how his life had changed these past months and not just because the young Ranger and his dog had twice saved his old Navy butt. But because in this short time, he had come to look upon Holt like a brother. He was happy to see his friend find a woman so perfectly meant for him.

The mood broke as a roostered drover seated a table over, hollered at Laudie Kate, "Sweetheart, wutever he's payin' ya ta sit thar, I'll dubble it. A mighty fine filly ya be."

Neither Holt nor Laudie Kate looked over at the man.

"C'mon, honey, I got good money to give ya a spin you'll never forget."

Holt slowly readjusted his coat so that the grips of both Russian Smith & Wesson pistols in his shoulder holsters were more visible and therefore easier to draw. A silent, but lethal, signal.

Holt was an imposing figure, even though he was only of average height. His long brown hair swept along the shoulders of his new shirt and trail-worn vest. His rugged face was highlighted by light-blue eyes with high, bronze cheekbones. A trim mustache and days-long overgrowth of beard added to the aura. A long scar on his right cheek from a long-ago cavalry battle—a mark surprisingly similar to Laudie Kate's—was a prominent testimonial to his intimidating presence.

Still not glancing at the interloper's table, he caught Orion's gaze. The young Ranger's peripheral vision found the drunk drover seated there with two other cowboys, a bottle of cheap whiskey mostly gone.

Orion drawled at the cowpuncher, "There ain't a sportin' woman in this entire place." Orion looked like a Ranger: black coat and vest, tall, confident, and rugged, but generally not threatening. Except in the din of battle, when he became a six-foot-two wolverine. His dark brown eyes were usually genial and pleasant, but burned lava hot when trouble unfolded. "Perhaps you best move along." His smile was not neighborly. His statement was not advice.

Holt finally turned to face the loudmouth. "And apologize. To the lady." Holt's light-blue eyes were anything but easy-going. His glare seared with predator-like intensity.

Fear shot through the drover. It was only then that he noticed the two Ranger badges on these rugged men. "S-S-Sorry," he mumbled as he stood and threw some coins from a vest pocket onto his table. He hustled the two friends seated with him up and out the door.

Without moving his head, Holt's eyes followed the group as they left.

"You said somethin' 'bout bein' quiet, I think." Orion grinned at Laudie Kate.

She chuckled in return. "Can you be here every night?"

"I'm sorry, Laudie Kate," Holt said. "That doesn't happen very often, does it?"

She smiled and kissed his cheek. "Only when you're around." She stood, smoothing her blouse and skirt. "I'll have some steaks with all the trimmings sent out. And more beer and Irish." She moved toward the kitchen, holding his hand until their two arms couldn't stretch any more.

Holt watched her walk away toward the bar.

"She can handle herself," Orion said. "She handled you, remember?"

Holt mumbled, "Yeah, just wish it didn't seem like we're always in the line of fire—"

"Should be used to it by now." Orion raised his eyebrows and his glass. Holt lifted his whiskey in a return salute.

Though Orion and Holt had fought on different sides of the war, they were able to look at their experiences with appreciative contemplation. They often needled one another about their post-war activities, riding on the other side of the law—Holt as a Rebel desperado who ignored the surrender and Orion as a Federal turned plundering buccaneer.

Just then, their good friend James Hannah, the owner of the saloon, appeared out of the crowd. Tonight, Hannah was wearing his other hat as the owner of the Wilkon newspaper.

"Hey, you two, I got a wire here that the sheriff told me to share," was Hannah's way of greeting his friends.

"Look, it's our favorite former marshal! Why are you here?" Holt inquired with a grin. "Laudie Kate's working tonight because you were supposedly at home."

Hannah chuckled and shook his head.

"I've got half a mind to take her home with me right now," the young Ranger teased.

"Imagine what you could do with a whole mind," Hannah retorted.

Orion laughed and slapped his Ranger partner on the shoulder.

"I think you're going to be interested in this," Hannah said. The former gunslinger turned lawman turned saloon owner had been through a lot with Holt and his brothers. The crucible of their upholding the law in this yet-to-be-tamed land had made them good friends. "Sheriff Wheeler gave it to me. The rewards of being the former sheriff and now newspaper publisher." He tapped the paper in his hand.

"Let's see it," Orion said, reaching for the paper first. His brow furrowed as he read.

"Well…?" Holt wondered.

"A note from our buddy Moose Elkins." Orion glanced at Holt, handing him the note in the process. "He's sent Linus Carmichael an' Christer Viklund to Fort McKavett for safekeepin'."

"Those the two prisoners from your rustling mission in Stebbins?" Hannah asked.

"Yeah, they are." Holt exhaled deeply. "Seems Moose is worried about the town taking matters into their own hands."

Orion nodded. "Yep. That's 'zactly what's happenin'."

"Sending them there is as good as any place, I guess," Holt noted wearily. "Lynching's been known to happen."

Orion bobbed his head in silent agreement. Their investigation into *The Angel's* rampage had been severely compromised when the evil priest was lynched by the citizens of Sweetclover. It took time the two Rangers could not afford to find out just who was pulling the madman's strings.

"Moose is findin' out a sheriff's badge is just as tricky as wearin' a Ranger one," Orion said.

Hannah chimed in. "He's probably overconcerned

about the possibility. If an execution like that happens on his watch, it might look like he was asking for it to happen. Some could say he didn't do enough. I think we'll send out an article that says he's done plenty. He sure didn't have to go to all this trouble."

Holt grimaced. "I don't know…"

"Those sonofabitches shot him, right?" Hannah continued. "And kidnapped his woman. Your woman, too. You don't think he wants to see them swing?"

Holt nodded grudgingly.

In a last-ditch effort, Lars Viklund and Linus Carmichael, the leaders of the Stebbins rustling operation, had kidnapped two women from town, one of them Laudie Kate. During the rescue operation, Holt and Laudie Kate, shot Lars dead, and Holt had beaten Carmichael within an inch of his life with his bare hands. The memory of Laudie Kate in that much danger galled Holt and simmered the blood of his inner panther spirit.

Holt shook his head to clear the imagery. "Something about all that Stebbins business has stuck with me," he said. "And now those two being sent to Fort McKavett…"

Orion's eyes were a question.

Holt numbered with his fingers. "They rustled cattle. They brought it to the McKavett quartermaster. The quartermaster arranged to sell the herds to a broker. The broker loaded them onto boats. The broker shipped 'em down the Guadalupe to Matagorda."

"Yep, that's 'bout right," Orion agreed.

"Somewhere, there is a lot of money unaccounted for. That had to be a pretty lucrative operation, right?"

Orion mused with a smile, "It sure would."

"Well, you were in that army for a while, *Captain*

Higbee. Could a seemingly lowly quartermaster run that kind of deceptive operation without anyone further up the chain of command not knowing?"

"Why my army? Whatta 'bout yours?"

"Hell, Orion, we were nothing but skulkers and scroungers," Holt shook his head. "We needed too much. We had nothing. There were no secrets. Whatever we made off with got shared, spread around. No one was running any kind of private game."

"If you put it that way, yeah, there was lots've shenanigans bein' run." Orion shrugged. "You know good'n well what I know."

"*Shenanigans,* you call it. Is that why I needed a pardon and you didn't?" Holt smirked.

"To the victors go the spoils." Orion grinned back. "So you're thinkin' there was more to that Viklund operation?"

Holt scratched at his beard. "I know Captain McCoy looked into the affairs surrounding the fort—"

"He said the evidence appeared like it was an independent operation," Orion noted. "That quartermaster they hung was all there was to it, Army-wise."

Holt's thoughts continued to grind on the information they had. "That damn scarecrow-looking sheriff and his brother. Linus and Porter Carmichael. What a pair to draw to."

"Yep, the Carmichaels." Orion nodded. "Sergeant Carmichael was all the cap'nCap'n could connect. The Army was rebuildin' that fort the entire time. That butter lickin' pumpkin roller apparently could hide a lot of *shenanigans*."

"A sergeant did all that?" Hannah asked.

Holt shook his head. "Seems odd, doesn't it?"

"Well, yeah, at least the ones I knew." Hannah retrieved the wire message from Holt and asked, "What do you make of this Sergeant Carmichael hollering that a major at the fort was in on everything?"

Orion was about to finish his glass of Irish before stopping. "What major?"

Holt chimed in, "Yeah, what major? Where did you hear this?"

"I read it," Hannah said. "In the New Braunfels paper. Just got a copy."

Orion repeated, "New Braunf—"

"The town near McKavett," Holt said. "If the stolen herds didn't go to Fort McKavett, they went to New Braunfels."

"Yeah, the New Braunfels newspaper, it's printed in part English, part German," Hannah continued. "They had an article about the hangings. First, they strung up the Viklund son and their riders. Then, a week later, they hung the sergeant, that Carmichael fella. It was quite a detailed article. Viklund yelled something Swedish as the hood was placed over him, and apparently, soiled himself quite prolifically when the trapdoor dropped. Then, a week later, at Sergeant Carmichael's hanging, he hollered about a major being in on everything. Guilty as sin. Hollered all that until the rope shut him up."

"Ho-lee damn," Orion uttered.

Holt shook his head. "We haven't heard any of this."

"The article said that the sergeant's outburst was just the rambling of a desperate man. There was no more mention in the article or the rest of the paper about it. I've still got the paper in my office if you want to read it." Hannah watched the two Rangers. They were already engrossed in what this new information might mean.

Orion finally spoke up, "The cCap'n is mighty thorough."

"Yeah. I don't want to question that," Holt said. "But this whole mess has been chewing on me."

Orion gulped the remainder of his glass.

Holt continued, "Whoever was buying those cattle just disappeared into the wind. That guy somehow had the boats and the resources to move a lot of beef clear down the river to the coast, and no one has any idea who that was?"

"You think pirates gonna rat out other pirates?" Orion smirked.

"Thick as thieves," Hannah joined in.

"And what about Stebbins?" Holt asked. "All that land being grabbed by the Viklunds? Did no one in town or at the bank even raise an eyebrow to what was happening?"

"We're justa bunch of Rangers," Orion said. "Can't solve 'em all."

"I guess so." Holt paused. "Regardless of where the trial is held, we know what's going to happen. Do you think we should go to the hanging?"

"Only if I'm still wearin' a badge." Orion laughed.

"Speaking of the captain," Holt continued, "I'm going to make sure he knows about this Sergeant Carmichael's outburst on the gallows."

CHAPTER FIVE

Not quite halfway between Wilkon and LaGrange, near a different Texas river—the San Saba—stood the windswept post of Fort McKavett.

The fort had only recently been reopened and rebuilt by the U.S. Army. Important structures like the headquarters, officers' quarters, storehouses, commissary, and hospital already existed or were relatively new. Not all of the barracks for the troops were finished, and some soldiers still had to live in temporary structures. Not-so-jocular wisecracks among the enlisted grumbled whether the stables would be completed before their housing.

In a far corner of McKavett's drab military hospital, prisoner Linus Carmichael was propped up on pillows in a small bed. The legs of the simple metal cot were bolted to the floor. A heavy shackle clamped around Carmichael's ankle, chaining him to the bed. A prison orderly had helped prop him up, readying him for supper.

Next to Carmichael, blond-haired Christer Viklund tried to nap despite a heavily bandaged shoulder. He was manacled in the same way to a similarly secured cot. The young Viklund and the disgraced former lawman both found themselves recuperating here following the violent finale of a murderous rustling operation that engulfed the ranches surrounding the previously tranquil town of Stebbins, Texas.

The scheme was fueled by the insatiable greed of Lars Viklund, Christer's father. The evil Swede was the patriarch of a ruthless family that stopped at nothing to get what they wanted.

Viklund would target a ranch, then, in order to bleed the owner dry, he sicced his sons and hired riders to steal portions of its herd. It would not take too many of these rustling hits before the Swede would have convinced the rancher to sell, at a reduced price. The ranchers who were targeted never got far away with their proceeds before they and their families were murdered. Viklund would recoup his money and keep their property.

Although the land would become part of the Viklund empire, the stolen cattle needed a place to go. This is where the fort entered the operation. Utilized as a front, McKavett was an unfortunate hub that provided a smokescreen for the clever and elusive thievery.

While former Sheriff Linus Carmichael cleared legal paths for the Viklunds and acted as their financial courier, his brother played an even more crucial role in the venture.

Sergeant Porter Carmichael was Fort McKavett's quartermaster. The small herds of rustled beef were quickly driven to the fort or to New Braunfels, a town just to the southwest, without much attention. Porter would take possession of the stolen herds, and through a broker, have the cattle sent via rivercraft down to

Matagorda. The poached herds brought good money to all involved.

The quartermaster was an easy mark to become embroiled in the scheme. He had amassed a great deal of riverboat gambling debt and was being pressured to settle his obligations. It was through these floating card games that an ambitious and unscrupulous broker came forward, someone who would buy all the livestock Carmichael could provide.

The operation was working smoothly until Texas Rangers stepped in. With two Rangers secretly working on the inside for the Viklunds and two more Rangers investigating the rustling activities in the territory, the operation came to an abrupt halt. The Viklunds and the Carmichaels' reign of aggression and plundering was brought to a ferocious end.

Sergeant Carmichael and the eldest Viklund son, Baldur, were caught red-handed bringing a herd of stolen beef to New Braunfels. They and three other Viklund riders were arrested and brought to the fort. A quick civilian trial followed. With additional evidence supplied by the Rangers, all of the thieves were found guilty of cattle rustling. Baldur and the three Viklund men were hung immediately. A week later, Porter Carmichael faced a military tribunal with the same verdict and sentence. After their executions, all five of the outlaws were buried in unmarked graves down the hill from the fort, outside the installation compound.

As all of this was going on at McKavett, the Rangers sprung a trap at the county roundup outside of Stebbins. Lars Viklund and Linus Carmichael were chased from the roundup. In an attempt at escape, they kidnapped two women, but were cornered in a shootout. Lars was killed, and Linus was beaten severely and taken into custody. Christer was shot at the roundup and also jailed. The women, girlfriends of Rangers Holt Corrigan and Moose Elkins, were returned safely.

In the aftermath of the bloody Viklund/Carmichael showdown, Ranger Elkins volunteered to become the new sheriff of Stebbins and found himself with two very unpopular prisoners. The possibility of a lynching concerned him, so he had recently sent both prisoners to the fort, which had the ability to provide better security, not to mention putting distance between them and the angry citizens of Stebbins.

The prisoners' injuries required them to be detained in the fort's infirmary, manacled to their beds. The youngest Viklund, Christer, was recuperating from the bullet wound to his shoulder. Carmichael was burdened with various wounds, including a broken nose, a fractured cheekbone and jaw, and three missing teeth. All of those injuries were inflicted by Holt Corrigan. Carmichael's face was swollen *almost* beyond recognition. His eyes and face were severely bruised, and his lips were busted up. A mess.

Tonight's supper, like all his meals, would be administered to him by a prison matron. Sitting on a stool, she tried her best to hand-feed him a meal of soup and a soft roll with honey. The simple broth and bread were prescribed, not only due to his busted-up mouth and jaw, but also because he had been complaining about everything, including stomach distress and dizziness.

"When doesh da judge git here?" Linus Carmichael asked with painful difficulty. "Or a lawyer? I need ta shpeak wif one."

"I do not know of such things, sir," the matron said. "I only know you are to eat supper and get stronger."

"Da law needsh ta know." Carmichael's swollen mouth and face struggled to form words. "Da major here wuz helpin' ush. He mos' shertainly wuz. I'ma lawyer, I know my rights."

After a few mouthfuls of soup and a couple of gingerly chewed bites of a honey-laden roll, he suddenly sat up in a panic, grabbing her wrist. The force sloshed the bowl of soup in her other hand, spilling it everywhere. The small plate on his chest holding the bread and honey fell to the floor.

The former lawman was wild-eyed. "Oh gawd! I can't..." *Cough.* "It hurts...unhhh..." *Cough. Hack.* "Ughhhh..." Gasping violently, Carmichael struggled momentarily, then fell back, silent and motionless.

CHAPTER SIX

At the same time, across the fort compound, the highest-ranking officer currently on the post, Major Merriman Wooster, and his wife, Celinda, were readying for their usual evening meal.

The major, at one time, had designs on becoming the commander of the Fifth Military District overseeing Texas and Louisiana, and all the perks and promotion that came with it. He was routinely passed over.

They were joined by the major's brother, Ames Wooster. He was the president of the bank in Stebbins, a town located square in the middle of good cattle country. And the town from where the fort's two newest prisoners arrived.

The mood in the dining room was awkward and somber, much like the major's comportment.

"I think you'll find this satisfactory." The major only half-smiled as he handed a goblet of wine to his younger brother.

"Why, thank you." Ames nodded to receive the glass,

but kept his attention on the friendlier, much better-looking Celinda.

Ames raised his glass. "Here's to sunny skies."

"Sunny, indeed," gushed Celinda.

The major broke the moment, almost hollering in his typical bluster, "Surely you jest! I don't know what there is to celebrate—"

Ames raised a hand to silence his brother. He looked behind him, making sure the door to the dining room was closed. "Orderlies," was his one-word admonishment. Moving closer to the major, he declared in a soft voice, "Keep your voice down. The Stebbins rustlers have been dispatched. The Rangers have moved out of St. Clair County." In an even quieter voice, "And the only direct connection to Fort McKavett—and us—has been silenced by a rope."

Celinda smiled. "Well, *à ta santé*!"

"And *here's to you*, my lady," Ames replied.

Celinda's eyes flashed at the sobriquet, quickly clinking her glass with her brother-in-law and taking a large sip from her goblet.

The grim countenance of Major Wooster did not acknowledge the toast nor take a drink, his visage taking on a stern look, even more dour than usual. He asked stuffily, "Have things truly quieted in Stebbins?"

"Yes, Merry, they have," his brother answered quickly.

The look that shot from the major's eyes made it clear he did not like the childhood moniker.

"What? Mother used to call you that," Ames teased. "When you weren't such a stick-in-the-mud."

"Recent events were not so childish," the major observed. "We were too exposed, here. I never liked the arrangement with those Swedes and never cared for dealing with…" He caught himself before finishing. "Her."

Celinda's lowered head could not hide the look she shot at her husband. A look that did not disguise hostility.

"Aw, Merry," Ames coaxed. "That's no way to talk."

Ames was the silent partner in Lars Viklund's rustling scheme, which was based in Stebbins. He saw to it that ownership of the small ranches overrun by the evil Swedish family was transferred discreetly to a secret company owned by Lars Viklund. He also served as the operation's accountant, keeping track of all the cash raked in from the stolen cattle. He and Celinda had convinced her husband to look the other way when his quartermaster became involved in the stolen beef venture.

Thanks to the Viklund and Carmichael operation, there was a lot of money for Ames to keep track of. Much of it found its way into a private account set aside for the major and Celinda.

The major hissed, "I thought this all would die away when that sergeant was finally strung up and the Rangers dispersed. And why didn't the Rangers kill his brother? They killed everyone else!"

"C'mon, dear, it's done," Celinda coaxed her husband. Ames grinned impishly and raised his glass, trying to get a response from his brother.

The major thundered, "Done?! Hardly so!" Catching himself, he lowered his tone. "First, that sergeant hollered my name from the gallows. Screamed that I was involved. Now, the youngest Swede and the sergeant's brother, that foul Linus Carmichael, have been sent here to await trial. Here! How can the mission be accomplished with them still around? Right across the compound! Right here in my installation!"

Suddenly, the door to their dining room flung open. The table candles flickered wildly.

Calista Theriot breezed through the door, a force of nature that announced itself with no spoken introduction. One of the major's orderlies had tried to control her arrival, but could only hustle behind her to keep up.

Celinda reacted first, a huge smile beaming across her pretty face. "Callie!" She set down her glass and swept across the room.

"My dear, Cee, you are a vision," Calista enthused in return.

The two sisters rushed together and hugged enthusiastically. Finally, they stepped back to arms-length, hands still held, beaming at one another. After a long moment, they wrapped each other again in a truly affectionate embrace.

Separating, but not releasing hands, Celinda smiled tenderly. "You are lovely as always, Callie. I must say, though, you look a bit tired. You have to admit. You work too hard."

Her baby sister being the only person alive who could use that nickname *and* say such a thing, Calista responded to the caring statement, and said, "The past week or so has been robust to say the least…business on the Colorado…then dealings in Austin…a phaeton dash from Menard…to be here."

Celinda cocked her head mischievously. "Business?"

"As usual." Calista shrugged with a knowing smile. The sisters chuckled.

Several years older than her sister and an incredibly beautiful woman, Calista was worldly and cultured.

Dressed for travel in a two-piece day dress, its scoop-cut revealing ample decolletage that was enhanced by a striking silver-and-brass amulet. Her bewitching sensuality felt out of place in austere Fort McKavett. Celinda was equally as lovely, a match in charm and elegance. Like her sister, she appeared more suited for an opulent receiving room in a New Orleans Garden District mansion than a stark Army outpost.

The sisters were of Cajun-German descent, sharing glorious dark brunette hair. Calista had her mother's emerald-green eyes and Germanic complexion. Celinda got her father's deep brown eyes and Acadian skin tone. The two women had always been very close.

Finally turning attention to the others, Calista deadpanned, "Merriman, always a pleasure." The major did not reply, a slight look of derision on his face.

Sauntering over to Ames, Calista gave him a beguiling look that spoke its own hello and gently took the goblet from his hand.

Sipping the ruby-red liquid, she noted, "Rather impressive." She threw a surprised look at Merriman. "A claret. From *your* stock?"

The major continued his silence. Celinda filled in her husband's reticence with a sweet smile. "We have a few bottles remaining from one of your barge deliveries a couple of months ago."

Though not as cunning or wicked as her older sister, Celinda was definitely not innocent. Although not involved in the family *business*, she had helped Calista dispatch several beaus and at least one lover of her own. She herself believed she was marrying into a strong military family, but instead discovered that her husband, the major, was ineffective and a bit dense. She has had to rein in her sister's dislike of her husband—the kindest word Calista had found for him was *obtuse*—while weighing her life's ambitions.

Calista's fuse for the major had grown short. She had been in her sister's ear for some time, urging her to leave him or have him *leave her*.

"I couldn't help but overhear your lamentations, Merriman," Calista said. "What are you whining about now?"

CHAPTER SEVEN

"Now see here," the major snapped. "The troubles are plenty—"

Calista stomped her foot. "Plenty?" Her glare stopped the major. A glare that could stop a roomful of men.

"Plenty?" she repeated. Her eyes and her words brandished like a saber. "Now that's an interesting word, Merriman. Plenty."

The major shuffled uneasily, unable to look her in the eye.

"*Plenty* was the work Ames did. Plenty were the risks *I* took. Plenty, oh my god, *plenty* is the amount of patience my sister has for your—"

"Callie." Celinda stopped her sister.

Without pause, Calista continued, "*Plenty* is the amount of money in your account."

She held out her glass for Ames to refill.

Calista's exasperation and contempt for her sister's husband was never far from the surface. He was one of the few things in her life that was at odds with her patience and plans. There were two kinds of men she had no use for: those who were stupid and those who were arrogant. She knew Major Merriman Wooster to be both. In her tactful estimation, the major was not worthy of Celinda. It was times like this that proved—to her—that, despite his want to achieve and advance, Merriman was not shrewd enough nor savvy enough to navigate the churning political waters of the Army and the state of Texas.

"I hear the general is moving on and the colonel will be taking his place." She sipped at her refilled wine.

"Lieutenant Colonel," the major replied.

"What?"

"Lieutenant Colonel. Entriken is a lieutenant colonel," he noted.

"That's your concern? Command here at the fort is shifting, and you correct me with a trivial detail?" Calista was incredulous. Shaking her head with a chuckle, she sneered, "My god, Merriman, what you need to concentrate on is making sure my sister is happy. Because you don't—"

"Callie!"

Calista stopped and took another sip. The sisters locked eyes. Silence enveloped the room.

Orderlies suddenly burst into the room bearing a supper of beef tips, potatoes, and fried okra.

"Come, let's eat," Celinda chirped, trying to defuse the rough start to the evening. "You both must be famished!" She indicated to Ames and Calista where they should sit, giving her sister a *let it go* look in the process.

Ames pulled out the chair for Calista, and she rewarded him with a smile that hinted of intimacy.

Seated, she tried to smooth out her tone. "In all seriousness, Merriman, what are the plans for the two prisoners? I mean, don't we know any trial is just a formality for the inevitable hanging?" Watching Ames retrieve another glass of wine, she offered her goblet for a refill as well.

"They being civilians, we must wait for a circuit judge," the major said. "I wasn't pleased to say the least, when they were sent here. It was not my decision."

Calista let that remark slide. Of course, the McKavett commanders would not consult him.

Ames spoke up, "Our new sheriff, a former Ranger who posed as a Viklund rider, knew that the good folk of Stebbins would likely not wait for a trial but would take matters into their own hands. I can't blame him, but then, why not let it happen? A lynching, I mean."

The major was still gruff. "Is that the only reason they were sent here?"

Ames was confused. "I-I'm not sure what you mean…"

The major growled, "Damn it, Ames, did this other Carmichael say anything about me?"

Ames shook his head calmly. "No, Merriman. I have not heard anything like that. I wouldn't have held back news like that."

Silence again enveloped the room.

Celinda finally spoke, "So, the dust has truly settled in Stebbins?"

"Yes," Ames replied. "It has. I will give Sheriff Moose Elkins credit. He has restored a sense of security. The town has settled back down."

"*Moose*, what a delightfully Texan name." Celinda giggled.

"And he is all what his name suggests." Ames smiled. "He is a large man with a large presence."

The mood lightened slightly, and they began to enjoy supper.

"I've been tending to my affairs, making sure the Colorado, Guadalupe, Sabine, and the others are still flowing, so I'm out of touch," Calista remarked. Unsaid in the evening's lively discussion was that it was her boats that transported the Viklund's stolen beef downriver to be sold in Matagorda. She smiled sweetly and turned to Ames. "Is it true that Stebbins and St. Clair County are making news in other ways?" As always, her line of questioning seemed to suggest that she already knew the answer. "Stebbins is one of several towns I hear mentioned quite often in Austin," she added.

Celinda listened intently but noticed her husband's bland expression. It was not clear whether he was understanding or even listening. She looked over and saw that her sister had made the same observation. A look of exasperation and contempt briefly shaded Calista's face. She caught her sister's eyes and shook her head slightly.

Ames responded earnestly, "The recent *activity* in Stebbins not only hasn't cooled the opinion of business interests on the town, but it has, in fact, increased general awareness of and interest in the entire county."

"So, it's not viewed as *just* cattle country?" Calista asked.

"On the contrary," Ames said, enthusiasm in his voice. "Word has it that the potential line and lands of railway corporations include Stebbins and the territory surrounding it."

"We've heard the same here at the fort," the major added staidly. "St. Clair County is among the many areas under discussion to be reserved for proposed railroad development. Lots of localities are being bandied about, all across the state, including Morita and Granbury." He cleared his throat authoritatively. "No rhyme or reason to the locations. Just speculation."

Calista tilted her head back, a slight grin on her face. Celinda watched and could tell her sister's curiosity with railroads was more than small talk. A new project, perhaps? She watched, fascinated, as her sister grilled the brothers further. She could tell Calista's line of questioning was gauging their actual knowledge of what was happening in regard to railway expansion, with what she already knew.

Ames, in his capacity as a bank officer, was privy to a great deal of information and speculation. His circle of clients and associates were very much hearing that the Stebbins region was quite possibly in the crosshairs of such a major windfall. "Well, Stebbins and St. Clair County is definitely under consideration," he added. "At the very least, for being part of a spur arrangement."

The major leaned back in his chair, looking at his sister-in-law with disdain. "Surely *you* aren't considering playing the land acquisition game." He shook his head dismissively.

"Don't be a fool. Of course, *Calista* is not making the purchases," she said.

"Good." Merriman was blunt, not realizing Calista's distinction. "Besides, the state will be donating open, unused land to those developers. Not buying property. Such expansion will only benefit those heading the railway corporations."

"*Couillion.*" Calista growled softly before speaking, "Look beyond the obvious for once, you *fool.* Where there is railroad track, there will be growth. Progress. New businesses. New towns even! *That* land will not be donated! *Right there* is where the money and power will be. Knowing where the railway corporations are looking is called hedging your bets. You can be assured I'm looking to get into that game."

The major had no response.

Calista rested her chin against her chest and exhaled in frustration for her sister.

Just then, the doors opened, and the prison matron quickly entered and quietly reported to the major.

"This is terrible! Most unfortunate," the major blurted out. "I've been entrusted—"

"What's happened?" Celinda interrupted calmly.

The matron repeated her report to the group. The prisoner Linus Carmichael had been stricken. "He is not dead. But is very, very sick. The doctor is most concerned," the matron said.

The sisters glanced furtively at one another.

Ames dismissed the matron. "Thank you, ma'am."

"Yes, please keep me informed," the major added. He leaned over and spoke in muted tones to his brother.

Celinda whispered to her sister, "I don't know what happened. There should have been enough wisteria seed in his broth to finish the job. The azalea honey should have done the trick, too."

The collective concern of the four people in this room was that Linus Carmichael might talk—or worse, escape and be on the run. Fortunately, his brother's screams from the gallows were ignored, deemed the desperate protestations of a condemned man.

Until Linus could be similarly dispatched, there was significant worry as to what he might say. Did he know what his brother knew? Surely he did, making him a threat as long as he drew breath. If either of the Carmichael's claims were taken seriously, they knew the major would buckle under the pressure, and the Theriot enterprise would fall like a house of cards.

Merriman stood to leave and announced, "I must look into this at once."

"Perhaps we can help," Calista offered. "Our *tante* taught us about the powers of the world around us. Come Cee, let us look to your garden for a way to *remedy* this."

The major glared at Calista. "You sit right there. You've done enough, *Isla Thorne*." He tried to make the statement humorous and looked to his brother for support.

Calista slammed her fist on the table. Utensils rattled, and glasses of wine splashed. She stood and snarled, "*Fils de putain!*" She matched glares with the officer. "You miserable *son of a bitch!*" She stepped around the table toward him. No one saw that she had drawn her razor-sharp dagger as she stood. Now, the steel blade glinted in her hand. "That name protects you, your wife, and your phony career. What would the United States Army and the Fifth Military District think of you marrying into the Theriot family?"

The major couldn't speak, only gulped for air.

"Don't you ever make light of Isla Thorne, and don't you dare think you can order me around!"

"Don't…" Merriman found his words. "You can't speak to m—I am an officer—"

"You preening dandy," Calista interrupted. "You say one more word, and I will gut you like a fish." Her voice was savage. She was now close enough for her blade to do damage to the major if she wished.

"Calista." Both her sister and Ames spoke her name in a cautionary tone.

In the blink of an eye, she flicked her knife. The second gold button from the top of Merriman's tunic clattered to the floor. Her snarl was now just a hushed growl. "Don't you dare meddle, *Merry*." Her eyes never left his as her foot propped onto a chair, and she returned the blade to her dress boot. "It was a stroke of luck that Linus Carmichael was brought here." She leaned up into the major's face, smirking. "*To keep him safe from the people of Stebbins,* you *imbécile*."

"Wh-What d-do you mean?" Even though Calista had put away the knife, Merriman tried not to show his fear.

"Are you that brainless?!" Calista continued. "*J'en ai marre*." She shrugged and looked at her sister. "*I'm fed up*."

Celinda looked pleadingly at her husband. "We can't take the chance Carmichael will talk at his trial. And we can't just *kill* him."

The major still did not comprehend.

Calista shook her head. *This man*. "Your wife has been making sure that the voice of Linus Carmichael will be silenced forever. By means no one will suspect."

CHAPTER EIGHT

Alone in Major Merriman Wooster's private officer's quarters, the two sisters stood outside on the tiny back veranda. The small patio was fenced in, surrounded by lush vegetation planted and cared for by Celinda.

Her older sister fumed, "I've had enough of your husband's idiocy." Celinda was silent, tending to a few selected plants with a watering can. "I'm serious, Celinda. He *cannot* go throwing that name around." She made sure no one else was around and gained her sister's complete attention. "*Isla Thorne* doesn't just protect me. It protects you—"

"I know, I know—"

"We've come too far. If he meddles in this and does his usual stupid—"

"He won't," came Celinda's quiet reply.

"He cannot joke around with that name. Isla Thorne can move in circles that Calista Theriot never could. If anyone ever knew I am—"

"Isla's true identity will never be known."

"Good," Calista continued. She joined her sister in admiring the selection of plants, including azalea, oleander, lily of the valley, and foxglove. All beautiful to look at, but when necessary, deadly.

Just like the Theriot sisters.

Excellent pistol shots, both women were proficient in inflicting damage. The two possessed an extensive knowledge of plants, those that could heal and those that could kill. This know-how had been administered on numerous victims.

"You have foxglove here," Calista noted. "Brew a strong tea, it's time to finish this."

The younger sister nodded. "I agree. The matron will continue to be my unwitting assistant." She reached for gloves and shears to snip a few of the purple and pink leaves and petals. "When she first arrived, I gave her some plantain sap for bee stings. I taught her how to make yarrow poultices, too. She thinks I'm trying to help with him."

Calista smiled, admiring her sister's garden. "You know, some of this bounty would do well for that husband of yours…"

"Callie!"

"I will only have a short time to pull off this latest maneuver. Deals need to get done and contracts signed before others get wise. Everything here at the fort needs to be behind me. I can't be bothered with a troublesome prisoner. Or your annoying husband." She absentmindedly rubbed at a bump along her temple hairline. A permanent reminder of a close call.

"He's just on edge," Celinda shrugged. "The general's going on assignment and may not return."

The rumblings around the compound were true. Soon,

General Headly was departing on a wide-ranging tour of the western and northern Texas forts, and Lieutenant Colonel Entriken would be going on extended leave in Washington. Even if temporary, the fort's replacement commander was a coveted post.

Calista could not help but show her disdain. "Do you *really* think Merriman is in line to be considered?"

"You have your stakes game, I have mine." Celinda smiled sweetly.

"My game is winnable."

"I think mine is worthy."

"He does not deserve you." Calista hugged her sister and kissed her on the cheek.

Ames Wooster later heard Calista return to her room in the fort's civilian quarters. He knocked softly, and she let him in.

He smiled slyly as he reached for her. "We never had dessert."

Calista cooed, "Not tonight, my dear."

Although they had carried out a discreet, on-and-off affair for nearly a year, Calista really only saw Ames as a means to an end. She did not need money—she could buy his bank many times over. She looked to Ames for his generosity in the bedroom as well as solutions to finance obstacles, both producing desired results. In addition to hiding and protecting her money, Ames had helped keep his brother, the major, under control. With her new railroad objective, she had big ideas for which she could use the expertise Ames offered, as a banker and a lover.

"I've got a plan," she blurted, sliding away from his advances. "We must move quickly."

"Will it involve my brother?"

"Heavens no, I'm done with him. This is too big for his small mind."

Her beauty overwhelmed him. He forgot to whom he was talking and let his guard down. "After you and your sister left, Merry let out that he was tired of the games."

Calista met the remark with silence. Ever the domineering and conniving figure, she possessed a brilliantly wicked mind. She enjoyed life to the hilt, filling it with powerful men, good wine, and rich food. Navigating in such circles demanded she be clever and shrewd.

Trying to fill the awkward void, he continued, "The major said he wants no more of Calista's—or Isla's—games."

She had had enough. "*The major*? Would that be *your brother*?"

Ames knew he had said the wrong thing. Chastened, he looked away.

"Games?" she said mockingly. "Is the size of his bank account a game? It's certainly larger than a *Major* of his deportment should have." She turned and faced Ames. "And this I can promise…if he continues to be a thorn in Isla's side, *I* will slit his throat."

At first, Ames thought the pun was meant to be humorous, but then was shocked to realize it was an unblinking threat. He did not want this confrontation. His anticipation of an evening of lovemaking had now vanished into a hope she would not throw him out on his ear. Or worse.

She walked briskly to the dresser in the sparsely furnished room. Finding a flask in her handbag, she filled two drinking glasses with aged rum, her favorite. She handed Ames a glass.

He accepted the drink and quickly took a sip to steel himself. "How is our patient?" he asked, trying to move on.

"*Our* patient?" Her tone was derisive. "In addition to being a former lawman, Carmichael is an attorney. As long as he breathes, he is absolutely a threat." She took a good-sized slug of the gold liquid. "Don't you agree?"

Ames bobbed his head as he followed her lead, taking a large swig. He had never drank rum until he met Calista, finding the taste as complex and intoxicating as her.

"Well, your brother, *the major,* needs to agree as well. Quietly," Calista snapped. "Because if he can't stay out of the way and be quiet…" She let the remark trail away, ominously.

"I don't think we need to go that far—"

"Of course *we* don't," she hissed. "But *I* do…and will if need be."

Ames listened carefully and finished his drink. He would not make any more mistakes tonight by saying the wrong thing. She added more rum to his glass.

"Remember, you and your friends from Stebbins needed a buyer for your stolen herds. The quartermaster here was your go-between, and your brother made sure no one found out." She did not wait for a response. "Sound familiar?"

Although related by marriage, Calista and Ames had only met after her men squeezed Sergeant Porter Carmichael for payment on a sizable debt he had racked up playing cards on her boats. Carmichael's sheriff brother had come to Ames for help. It was the banker's idea to meet with the person running these boats. It was then that Ames presented an opportunity to Calista: a Stebbins family had a steady amount of stolen cattle to unload, and would this beautiful entrepreneur consider using her resources to funnel the plunder elsewhere? For a profit, of course.

The audacity of the banker had always intrigued Calista. To gauge Ames's worth, she took him on a raid of a steamship—a forced grab of sugar and cotton from a northbound packet ship. She had tightly wrapped her breasts to hide that she was a woman when they stormed the boat. In the post-raid celebration, taking off her wrap had been Ames's favorite part of the adventure.

Now in the quiet of the fort's civilian quarters, she was focused and matter of fact. The storm cloud that was Calista's brow lightened. "The threat will be over soon. Carmichael won't be alive much longer."

Another slug of the rum gave Ames the confidence to look her in the eye and nod.

"We must talk of what's ahead," she said. "It's vital we move as urgently as possible." She gestured for him to sit. "Even before this Viklund mess blew up, I had been formulating a plan. One that required an alias. The one you helped set up." She eyed Ames closely to see that she had his attention. "And Isla Thorne was born!"

Ames acknowledged he was following along.

Calista explained, "After orchestrating my way—Isla's way—into Austin's backroom poker games, the legislators and businessmen unknowingly taught me the machinations of railroad development."

It stood to reason she was an expert poker player. Her devastating looks added to her card-playing wiles, plus she could read men like a book. Armed with these formidable advantages, *Isla Thorne* had gained favor, and sometimes grudging respect. No one knew they were seated across from the infamous pirate Calista Theriot. During these games, some she purposefully lost, she quickly grasped the cluttered tapestry of Texas politics. There was as much going on under the tables of power as there was aboveboard.

"It was just like navigating a river," she continued. "Where the undercurrents were often more dangerous than anything on the surface."

It was during a dinner with a visiting financier from back east that got her calculating mind set on this course. His bragging about cutting shady deals was meant to impress her out of her undergarments. All it did was create a humorous cat-and-mouse as she fended off his advances with teasing and more questions. During his amorous swaggering, he mentioned the resumption of railroad development, especially a significant east–west line spanning the whole of Texas. Calista left him wanting as she moved on to tease other men who tried to seduce her with their boasting.

As usual, her smile could fell most men. A long kiss promised. The hint of a delicious night together. They received nothing, but craved more. She recognized opportunities and took them. As a result, she received more information than she bargained for.

"There's no diplomacy in the capitol, just money, influence, and promulgation." Her eyes were glowing, far away, as if viewing the cards dealt around her, knowing what each hand held. "Information is as valuable as finances or control. It's like currency! Unconfirmed reports can influence huge decisions. There are actions and reactions to facts as well as rumors. Think about it!

Even fabricated information can manipulate men and money." Her eyes gleamed. "The deceit at that level is astounding. I can play that game. I *will* play that game."

Her eyes still blazed, but now they focused on Ames. "This is where my attention must be. I'm going to be dealt into the railroad development game and win by any means possible!"

Her scheme required figureheads, both in Austin and in Stebbins—frontmen who could at least appear to have greater strength or resources than they actually possessed. She had begun grooming her Austin candidate on these recent trips to the capitol. He had what she needed, for her plan and for her bed. Her Stebbins candidate stood in front of her now, with the same abilities.

"Those congressional foreheads in Washington may have readmitted Texas to their union," she said. "But all the formal requirements for readmission have yet to be met, like doing away with this military district rule. They haven't dismantled it, even though the district has always been a joke. Austin is a mess, it's in chaos. No one knows who's in charge. Decisions are being made by the developers and brokers. They could hear that the sky over El Paso is green now and there would be people believing it. I have to act *now* before a real Texas government takes hold!" She poured more rum, her enthusiasm taking over.

"A-Act now, to do what?" Ames was in awe and a little unnerved.

Her passion was forceful. "I want land! As much as I can get. But it's got to be in territories the railway speculators are looking at. With land, I'll either be brought into a railway corporation as an investor, or I'll have land to sell them for new farms, new businesses, new towns!" Her voice soared. "Land is the game, and Isla Thorne is going to deal herself in! Understand? Starting with Stebbins." She raised her glass for effect and downed its contents. Ames did the same.

He couldn't help himself. The rum was having its effect as he blurted, "That's crazy. A bluff at best."

This time, Calista did not erupt. "Of course it is," she smiled wickedly. "What have I been saying? Bluffing doesn't have to be reckless. It's a calculated risk. It's convincing others you have the strongest hand and inducing them to follow along!" She looked Ames square in the eyes. "I may not have the best hand, but Isla Thorne is going to force people to *think* she does."

"I take it I'm part of the calculated risk," Ames asked quietly.

She ignored his statement. "First thing, I want that rustler's ranch. Immediately. Isla Thorne will be the new owner of the Viklund place. You can tell me about the Stebbins newspaper later."

She set her glass down and took his as well.

"That's enough business for tonight." She reached behind her back and unbuttoned her dress, stepping out of it. Her husky voice purred, "You mentioned something about dessert."

CHAPTER NINE

"It's time, *mi amigo*. Time for someone else to live on the edge of a knife." Orion admitted to Holt that his mind was made up, that he would be turning in his Ranger badge. He had done his duty. It was time to enjoy life.

The two friends were leaving the Howard's Real Estate, Insurance & Telegraph Office on the main street of Wilkon. A daily check-in, with the hope that Texas continued to remain quiet. They enjoyed their chats with Mr. Hayes, the meticulous telegraph operator. Today, the wires had been silent. Nothing for the two lawmen.

"I can't say that I'm surprised, peckerhead." Holt made no effort to attempt a poker face at his partner's announcement. "Happy for you. Sad for me." The young Ranger's wry grin bore his bittersweet feelings. They had been through a lot together.

Holt's thoughts flooded with their first mission—to track down and capture the killer known as *The Angel*. He remembered the long trail-eating discussions they had about the war.

He had once asked Orion, "What was he like? General Sherman. I always wondered if he was as big a son of a bitch as we suspected," he had said, laughing.

Orion had laughed his response. "He was somethin' else. Actually, he was a pretty scary peckerhead, if you ask me. The man was intense. Had no tolerance for fools."

"That sounds like everything I've heard."

"He was about your height. Had a real presence. If he was nearby, you could feel him. Red hair, grizzly beard, he didn't care as much about his appearance like a lotta generals did, but he wasn't as grubby as Grant could be."

"Strutting peacocks, most generals," Holt had interjected.

"Fools, on both sides," Orion had added. "Too many politicians an' rich chuckleheads playin' soldier."

"And pissing matches between each other that got too many good men killed."

From there, *peckerhead* had become kind of a watchword for the two Rangers. A shared acknowledgment and warm-hearted banter between warriors.

"So, what's your plan, *former* Ranger Higbee?" Holt said. "Still interested in helping us start our horse herd?"

"That definitely has my attention." Orion smiled as he scratched his beard. "But first, I'm thinkin' of ridin' back to Stebbins. Mebbe look in on Lilly."

"The widow?"

"I can do some horse research there, too."

"Research?" Holt teased.

"You've got no room to talk, Mr. Mellifluous," Orion teased back. Holt had always struggled with talking to women. For a man who had faced all kinds of challenges and danger, it was unexpected that he would act so uncomfortable around them. It was also a great source of humor and teasing for Orion and James Hannah.

"I'm gonna send a note to Moose," Orion said. "Take the town's tempature."

"Temperature?"

"Yeah, an' the people in it."

Holt just grinned.

"Alright, alright," Orion admitted. "I'm gonna ask Moose to see if she still remembers me. He an' Evie will tell me what's what."

"Well, you're not leaving right away. You have to come out to the Bar 3. You've never looked it over. Seeing it may help with your *research.* Besides, the family will want to say goodbye."

CHAPTER TEN

Days later, Holt stood shirtless in the doorway of his in-town quarters. The room was stuffy and needed fresh air. Wilkon's main street was empty and quiet, the sun yet to fully present itself for duty.

Since returning home to Wilkon after the Stebbins rustling mission, he had been staying in this small office-apartment next to the jail. A few years earlier, the county had turned a tiny former tailor shop into a sheriff's office and sleeping quarters. The space contained a bed, a dresser, a desk covered with wanted bulletins and telegrams, and a struggling wood stove. At times, it also served to store extra ammunition or equipment. Deputy Bradley Cooke even used this place as a secret staging area for evidence that helped crack the mysterious puzzle that surrounded *The Angel* killings.

Neither Bradley, nor the new sheriff Logan Wheeler, nor the new marshal Lear Freeburg, used this housing, so Holt got their permission to bunk here temporarily. He had rearranged the interior so the bed was oriented in a north–south manner. Prior to leaving for the war, he had heard that it was healthier and luckier to position your head toward the north at night. He had slept that way ever since.

He could stay at either of his brothers' ranches, but this place felt dear to him. This had been his home after he was pardoned for his Confederate post-war conduct. The pardon came with the pact that he would serve as county sheriff. Holt smiled at the memory of Judge Oscar Pence, the man who gave him that new life. He sighed. All of that seemed so long ago.

He knew the best reason to stay here now was that it was in town. Close to Laudie Kate and her bungalow.

He tossed his pan of bath and shaving water onto the dusty street. His furry buddy, Tag, trotted out to investigate and sniff at the new muddy swash in the dirt.

Stretching and yawning, Holt spied a button on the sidewalk outside the door. He leaned over and picked it up, immediately identifying it as neither his nor Laudie Kate's. That's good luck, he noted to himself as he slid the tiny piece into his pants pocket. His two brothers had long known of his superstitious nature. Now his Ranger partner, Orion, and Laudie Kate were learning as well.

Leaving the door open, he went back inside to finish dressing. He sat on the bed and fastened his old Rebel cavalry spurs with the small rowels. Standing, he gave his knee-length boots a couple of good stomps, carefully re-tucking his pants into the tops.

He moved to the scratched dresser to retrieve his medicine pouch. In the pouch was Holt's personal sacred medicine—a small red stone with a white star-like spot in its center. The stone was a spiritual support, a belief he had embraced from the very same Indians he sometimes had to fight.

It was during a fierce battle against a Kiowa war party in the early days of the war, when Holt and four other Confederate guerrilla fighters had been surrounded by eighteen warriors. He saw the stone lying at his feet and decided to put it in his pocket.

All the Rebels survived the fight, and Holt had kept the rock ever since. He knew that Indians believed in the strength of personal *medicine*, usually something of nature, an item that gave them courage, strength, and protection. Who was he to question the idea? It was the reason he also carried a panther's claw in his pocket—a gift from his mother when he was a boy.

He credited these special tokens with getting him through some tough times. Only his brother Deed knew about them. His brother, Blue, being a preacher, would frown on the native belief. Holt was certain the pebble was actually something that belonged to him in another life when he, too, was an Indian. The stone had waited for him to find it again.

The pouch had been a recent gift. One night along the trail, at the beginning of Holt's original journey to meet Orion and track down The Angel, he had been visited by an eerie Apache who seemed to appear out of nowhere. The holy man, Four Shields, told Holt that there were many spirits following the young Ranger, spirits that were all around him and in him.

"Your spirit, the *ndołkah*, has served you well in times of difficulty," Four Shields had said.

"*Ndołkah*?" Holt had questioned that night.

"Big cat," the medicine man had said. "The mountain lion is a warrior. It carries with it energy, power, and strength. This spirit is what gives you the skill, cunning, and stealth you have. It has led you through great turmoil and strife. Although…it almost left you when you struggled with choosing the proper path to travel."

He counseled that Holt now had new spirits walking with him as well. "These are protector spirits. They are those who looked upon you highly in life. They are your *tsét'soyé*, your bear spirits. Your *ndołkah* helps you fight, but your *tsét'soyé* will help you fight for what is good and true. Listen to them well."

Four Shields then reached into a medicine bag at his side and pulled out a small elkskin pouch with a lanyard of twisted elk rawhide. The pouch had a painted circle on it. The circle was colored with plant and vegetable pigments in equal quarters of blue, white, red, and yellow. He told Holt that these colors were sacred, symbolizing a balance of life and spirit. Inside the pouch was cattail pollen.

As he decorated Holt's neck with the pouch, the Apache had pointed at Holt's shirt pocket and instructed, "Your medicine stone belongs inside the pouch too."

Holt had wondered ever since how the medicine man knew about his sacred stone.

The pouch was now treasured, a revered comfort to him. Its gentle weight was an affirming presence that always settled just near his heart. He had since added an owl feather to the pouch as well, believing that his mother now visited him as an owl spirit.

Shaking his head back to today, Holt decorated himself with the pouch, reverently placing the pouch's thong around his neck. Then he pulled on a faded blue wing-tip shirt and added a canvas rancher vest over it.

He held the precious pouch under his vest and shirt,

giving thanks to the spirits for this day and all his days, and asking for guidance on his daily journey. Tag, finished with his initial morning rounds, was back inside patiently watching this familiar routine.

Next, Holt moved to the lopsided mirror that hung over the scratched dresser. His hand served as a comb to straighten brown hair laying over his ears. He rubbed his just-shaved chin and smoothed out his trimmed mustache. The long scar on his right cheek was fading into a mark that some said made him more handsome, more mysterious. Most men who encountered Holt sensed the warrior within him—a rawboned gunfighter—and were intimidated, whether they admitted to it or not. Women were drawn to a hidden gentleness.

He slipped on his twin shoulder holsters that lay on the scarred desk. As he checked the loads in his two Russian Smith & Wesson .44 revolvers, he quickly eyed the ivory panther silhouettes inlaid in each black grip. Four Shields's pronouncement of a panther spirit within him only made his belief in reincarnation stronger.

Tag's tail really began to wag when Holt grabbed his narrow-brimmed hat from the dresser. That meant it was about time to go.

He tugged on the brim of his hat and ran his fingers across the cardinal feather in the hatband—another silent ceremonial tradition. He took a last swig of old coffee sitting atop the cranky stove and grabbed his trail coat.

"You ready to go see Cooper?" he called to his brown-and-gray buddy with the floppy ears. Tag leaving the door first was the enthusiastic answer.

Walking down a quiet street just being touched with the first glimmers of light, led Holt to continue grinding on matters that had been keeping him awake. Fort

McKavett. The Viklunds. The rustling operation. Although he and the Rangers had brought down the Viklunds and the Carmichaels, something did not seem right. Was there unfinished business?

Coupled with that, Orion's retirement weighed on his mind. It wasn't so much losing a partner—that was a separate issue. Orion leaving the Rangers was challenging Holt to face where his own life was headed. It all made him feel restless, older than his years.

Three days had passed since Holt had sent the wire to his captain about the newspaper article describing the Fort McKavett hangings. He had not yet received a response, which made him anxious. That was unlike Laird McCoy. The captain was usually efficient and prompt. Holt was not aware of any action involving the captain—it had been quiet for McCoy and his patrol. For a change.

The young Corrigan was troubled that his message had offended his boss. Asking if the captain had heard about the condemned sergeant's accusation from the gallows might have gone too far.

No, he told himself, *I did what I had to do. The captain would answer in due time. And let me know if the notice was warranted or unwelcome.*

The ride today was an endeavor to show Orion the Bar 3 homestead, the location where the family was thinking of expanding its horse operation. They truly could use Orion's help. Holt did not think it would actually keep his partner from leaving, but it might be worthy enough to draw him back.

As he rode, thoughts of Holt's own life and family filled the familiar trail.

Holt's own name was Holton Jefferson Corrigan, named after their mother's father. Dedrick William Corrigan was his youngest brother's full name, but everyone called him Deed, except their mother. Blue's birth name was Bluemont Wade Corrigan, a combination of the names of their father and paternal grandfather. They had a sister, Calliope Rose Corrigan, whom they all called Poppy.

All three brothers looked a lot alike, even down to their once-broken noses, courtesy of each other. Holt was two years younger than Blue and two inches shorter. Deed was eight years younger than Blue, an inch taller, fifteen pounds heavier, and definitely wilder. Deed and Holt resembled each other the most in looks and temperament, even down to their long hair and mustaches. Their older brother, Blue, kept his face clean-shaven and hair clipped short.

Both of their parents had died when the boys were young. Their mother and sister succumbed to pneumonia when Blue was eighteen; Holt, sixteen; and Deed, ten. Their father had died six months before their mother from a broken neck when thrown from a horse. The boys —and their ranch—were saved by the appearance of Nakashima Silka, a former samurai, who took them under his wing. The Corrigans grew to look upon Silka as their godfather.

Three years later, Blue and Holt left to fight for the Confederacy while the much younger Deed stayed with Silka to keep the ranch afloat. While the older brothers were gone, Silka honed Deed's fighting skills. Blue returned from the war with his left arm missing. Holt rode the outlaw trail after the surrender and came home only after Blue convinced him the war was truly over.

Distinctly, the three brothers had elements of their mother's approach to life within them. Deed cared about all things of nature, from snakes to birds to deer. Holt had picked up their mother's fascination with superstition and reincarnation. Blue's beliefs were more pious, serving the Wilkon church as a part-time minister.

Deed had built a reputation for fighting, but only when cornered. He married a widow almost a year ago. Atlee, the manager of the Wilkon stage station, had two children, Benjamin and Elizabeth.

Blue was just as intense as his two brothers, but after losing an arm in the war, he directed that energy toward building a great ranch—the original Corrigan spread, the Rafter C. He and his wife, Bina, a full-blooded Apache, had two children, Mary Jo and Matthew. They had recently adopted an orphan, Jeremy, whose family was murdered by outlaws.

Holt knew he was more than welcome to move in at either ranch. He had a room at both places. Blue and Deed had repeatedly encouraged him to build something permanent on the properties. With Laudie Kate and a future together now occupying a place in his heart, Holt knew the rambling life of a Ranger was not the trail he should be on for very long.

CHAPTER ELEVEN

"My, my, my, I see why you're so proud of this place." Orion smiled into the late morning sunshine. The glorious expanse of the Bar 3 ranch spread out in front of him as Holt, Holt's brother Deed, Deed's son Benjamin, and ranch foreman Travis Dean stood with the tall Ranger. Tag Along alternated between running wide circles in the yard and returning to do happy figure-eights among their legs.

"Plenty of territory to run cattle *and* horses." Holt beamed, slapping his partner on the back. "We sure could use the help."

"Yessir, we could make this operation the envy of the entire state," Travis said. "We got some top horses to build from. Easy mouths. Good ways too. We got them all…morning horses, all-day horses, ropin' horses, night horses, river horses. Got some top-notch peg horses too. Turn on a button, they will." The pride for the Bar 3's remuda shone in the black man's voice. "Ranchers need savvy horses with lots of leg, that's for sure."

"Room for another house or two as well," Deed

noted. "I'm trying to get Holt out here myself. As soon as Laudie Kate can tie him down." He winked as the others laughed.

Orion looked at Holt and continued chuckling. "I walked right into a trap, didn't I? You got the full sales pitch cued up."

"Guilty as charged, my friend." Holt smiled. "I couldn't let you leave without it."

"I 'preciate it, Holt. I really do." Orion nodded. "I ain't said no, but you know I've gotta go look in on Lilly."

"I know, horse research." They laughed.

"Well, let's go on in and say hello to Atlee," Deed said. "Boody's got dinner waiting for us too."

Inside the spacious Bar 3 ranch house, Atlee greeted the men. Her daughter, Elizabeth, also made sure everyone said hello to the family dog.

"This is Cooper," the little girl said. "He's been naughty. He caught a rabbit, but I don't think he hurt him. Mr. Boody said he'd braise it, so I guess that means he'll be okay."

"Okay, Elizabeth." Atlee smiled. "You and Benjamin take Cooper outside to play with Tag Along. He's been inside long enough."

Deed called to Benjamin, "Maybe take a look at Uncle Holt's and Ranger Higbee's horses for them. I'm sure they'd be obliged if you took a quick hoof check." Benjamin looked more pleased at this assignment than the one to look after his sister and the dogs.

The seven-year-old trundled off, following her teenage brother and Cooper. With a dolly under her arm, the little girl sang something that sounded like "Mary Had a Little Lamb," but she traded *rabbit* for the lamb.

"Please, have a seat. Our cook, Boody, will have dinner right out." Atlee smiled again.

Travis leaned over to quietly tell Orion, "Boody Barreto's a chef, from Louisiana, although there are whispers that he may have been something of a pirate or at least an outlaw somewhere. It was explained to me that he told everyone to call him *Boudin* when he first got here."

Deed chimed in. "Well, that was too big a mouthful to say, so the boys shortened it to *Boody*. He didn't take a cleaver to anyone, so the name stuck."

"*Boo-dan* Barreto, you say?" Orion said with raised eyebrows. "Boo-dan. Hmmm," he repeated, slowly nodding his head in contemplation.

Momentarily, Boody entered the dining room, bringing a large steaming tureen of rice, meat, and vegetables to the table. The olive-complexioned man was focused, yet pleasant. His ageless face neatly shaved. There was a refinement to his nature, an enthusiastic spirit, that set him apart. He seemed to have a darker side, too, which kept people on their toes.

"I'll be back wit' da bowls an' cornbread," the stocky Cajun said, in a tone that conjured the rues and alleys of New Orleans.

Orion eyed every move the dark-haired man made and grinned ever so slightly before calling out, "What kinda *tataille* are you feedin' these good people?"

Surprised, the cook blurted back, "*Tonnerre mes chiens*?! *What da hell—*"

"An' *Boudin*? Ain't that a sausage?" Orion continued. He followed the cook into the kitchen. "Seriously, what kinda liver-loafin' name is that? One they give a *canaille* like you, I bet."

"What'd you call me?"

"*Kah-nie*. A *sneak*. Ain't that what you are?"

This happened so suddenly, Holt and Deed were shocked. Holt had never seen this in his partner before. The two brothers followed Orion into the kitchen. Atlee and Travis sat at the table, equally stunned, not sure what to do.

Orion did not let up. "Do these fine people know just what kinda *sauvage* been hidin' under their roof?"

Finally, the cook had had enough. He turned on Orion. "*Couillon*!" Boody's brown eyes hardened. "Not in dis house! Not in my galley!" He pulled a cleaver from a carving rack and chopped it threateningly on the counter as he took a fighting stance. "Come for it, *brigand*, taste steel you will."

Orion and Boody closed the gap between each other, circling menacingly.

Holt hollered, "What the hell is this?"

Boody said calmly, "Dis is no way to greet a friend, *cher*."

"You're right, *darlin'*." Orion smiled. "I jus' wanted to make sure you remembered me."

"You too *cheum* to forget." Boody cocked his head. "*Ugly man*, you always be my friend."

"Ahh, Boo-dan, you apple-knockin' pig thumper. You are a sight." Orion grabbed Boody in a giant bear hug, kissed the Cajun on his head, and threw his head back in hearty laughter.

The cleaver in Boody's hand clattered to the floor as the stocky cook embraced the tall Ranger in return, howling with his own mirth, "*Pauvre bête*, ya *poor little thing*." They rocked side-to-side in an embrace that melted years.

The Corrigan brothers looked at each other, not sure what to make of what just happened. Atlee and Travis had cautiously entered the kitchen as well. Holt threw up his hands and shrugged. "I guess they're friends?"

"Yeah, very friendly," Deed answered warily and took the time to ease the cleaver out of reach from the duo with the toe of his boot.

Orion and Boody released each other and turned to everyone, arms around each other's shoulders.

"I take it you know each other," Holt smirked.

"What jail was dis *boucanier* in?" Boody asked.

"I like the word, corsair, if you please," Orion corrected. "Sounds more gentlemanly."

Holt murmured quietly to the others. "Damn bluebellies," he said with a wink. They all snickered a sigh of relief and headed back to the table.

Orion was enjoying the moment with his old friend. "Ensign Barreto?"

"Yes, Capitaine Higbee."

"Before we eat, might there be a dram of your best for this distinguished group to savor?"

"I have such a bottle," the Cajun grinned. He disappeared into the kitchen and soon came back with a beautiful-looking carafe sitting on a tray with five glasses.

"Jamaican rum. A lil' *lagniappe*, from home. A lil' some-ding *extra*, only special occasions." Boody beamed as he poured drinks for everyone.

He raised his glass. "*A la santé*, my friends."

"Indeed. An' *to your health*, Boo-dan." Orion responded. Everyone sipped at the aromatic, golden liquor.

Glasses poured and bowls filled, the group sat at the

table to enjoy a midday meal that had begun rather unexpectedly.

In between mouthfuls, Orion grinned. "Were y'all aware that this man has been known to use gunpowder in his recipes?"

"Dat was wartime necessity when sometime we had to eat beef tongue. Or worse." He paused, then looked at Atlee. "Never here, Mizz Corrigan. Never."

Atlee grinned. "That's a relief." The rest of them chuckled through mouthfuls.

"So you Yanks weren't eating steaks every night," Holt teased.

"Really, it's not dat bad," Boody defended. "Gunpowder is jus' sulfur, charcoal an' saltpeter. Trow in a lil' treacle an' let pickle for awhile—"

"Then throw the whole dammed thing out!" Orion bellowed. Everyone joined in the hearty laughter.

Talk eased, and the peaceful meter of spoons tinking into bowls took over as the group enjoyed the hearty concoction from Boody's kitchen.

Orion broke the silence through a mouthful, and said, "I haven't seen you since—"

"Our days of da United States Navy," Boody replied.

"Galviston. Atchafalaya. New Orlins. That was a time," Orion said almost wistfully.

"Dat it was, Capitaine."

"But then you left—"

"I left dat lil' enterprise for a kitchen an' a *catin*." He threw a roguish smile at Orion. "I left to open a lil' gatherin' place on da New Or-luhnz riverfront." Boody nodded wistfully. "A café for all da souls plyin' der trade along da wharf."

"*Plyin' their trade*?" Orion joked, eyebrows raised.

"Aye, dey be pirates. Like you."

"Corsairs, Boo-dan. Corsairs." Orion gave a short, seated bow in acknowledgment.

They all chuckled. Holt smiled at Deed. They had heard very little of Boody's history.

"An' this *catin*...you left us for a *woman*, too." Orion smiled. "Very pretty, as I recall. In a dangerous sorta way. Loved a card game. A noted corsair in her own right..."

A shadow passed over Boody's countenance, but disappeared just as quickly. A tight, grim smile accompanied a brief nod.

Orion continued. "Calista...wasn't it?"

"Yes. Theriot. Calista Theriot. She...she was *une belle femme. Very beautiful.* Truly so."

"That she was. Smart too," Orion added. "Could make a man not think straight an' pay dearly."

Boody shook his head. "You know, memries of her haven't visited for a long while." Boody stared off into another time. "She had dis way 'bout her. Got it from her father, a pirate, too. Gambling. Pillaging. Hijacking. Craved danger, an' high stakes, she did. Navigated all of it like no man I ever knew...'cept maybe me...or you." He gestured at Orion.

"A heart blacker than coal..." Orion responded.

"Dark as deep water..." Boody uttered.

"Calista Theriot," Deed said quietly. "Heard of her. She's notorious. The *Bayou Pirate*."

"Dat she was," the cook said reflectively.

In a near-whisper, Orion said, "Is she..."

Boody was staring off into his memories. He was quiet for a moment, then said, "Always said I'd die in bed, wit' her," he mused. "I was mostly right. We had been at odds wit' each other for awhile. Our life game was folding as dey say." He stopped and stared into his glass of rum. "I woke up wit' her dagger at my throat…I hit her wit' a wine bottle. Here." He pointed at the hairline above his temple. "She out like a light. I set everyting ablaze. Da upstairs aparttement. Da galley. Da whole café."

No one said a word, strangely fascinated by the horrific tale.

Boody looked up from his drink at the others around him. "My café burned down da night she…died." He drained his glass. He looked almost apologetic as he turned toward Deed and Atlee. "I came to Texas after dat. T-to…g-get awa…to forget."

Quiet took hold of the room. The Corrigans had not heard this part of Boody's story either. Not that it mattered to them.

Orion shook his head. "I'm sorry, Boo-dan. I did-n't di'nt mean to poke into your back trail."

"No matter. Better for it I am, an' happy now in life." He cleared his throat. "I hear a woman has entered your life."

"Well, mebbe so. Been waitin' on word 'bout that very matter." Orion smiled. "And speakin' of which… lookit what arrived jus' this mornin'." He pulled a wire message from his vest and shook it in the air before handing it to Holt. "Whattaya think, my friend?"

Holt read only a few lines before stopping. "A speller Moose is not."

Orion snorted good-naturedly. Holt read it for the table.

OHRYUN

STEBBINS IS CHANGIN. YOU KIN FEEL IT.

BANK PREZIDENT SOLD VIKLUND RANCH.

TO A NEW ORLEENS WOMAN. ISLA THORNE, WITH AN E.

WEARS A VOODOO TRINKET AROUND HER NECK.

INJUN SENSE TELLS ME SUMTHIN AINT RIGHT.

OH YEAH, MISS LILLIAN ASKS ABOUT YOU OFFEN.

MOOSE.

When he finished the note, Holt saw a strange look on Boody's face.

"You okay, Boody? You look like you saw a ghost," Holt asked quietly, concerned.

"It's…it's…nothing." Boody shook his head. "Can I see dat?" He reached for the telegram and stared at the paper. The strange look reappeared on Boody's face.

The cook shook his head to chase away his thoughts. "Calista hated Texas. Thought cows smelled funny." He continued to mumble softly, "I never did find that *gris gris*."

"*Gree gree*?" Orion heard his friend and wondered.

"A charm I gave her. For luck," Boody explained. His hand drew from his throat down to his chest. "Silver with brass, hanging from a chain, between her…" He stopped to collect his thoughts. "She believed it protected her. From evil. Brought luck."

"An' more lives than a cat as I recall," Orion said.

"Yes, you an' I both know da times when all of us, including her, should've had our lights go out."

Orion's eyes widened. "Do you think this—"

"No!" Boody's response was immediate.

Orion kept at it, and said, "Did you ever see—"

"See her dead body? No." Boody rubbed at his brow. "I almost di'nt get out myself."

Everyone sat in silence for a few moments.

Holt broke the quiet. "So, Moose said that a woman from New Orleans bought the outlaw Viklund ranch."

"Sounds like a setup to a joke," Deed quipped. "She isn't a cattle person, is she?"

Orion spoke up, "Yeah, what's she—"

Atlee interrupted. "Listen to you two. Deed, you know better." She eyed her husband sternly. "Maybe she is going to raise cattle. Seems there's another woman we know up there doing the same thing." She raised her eyebrows at Orion. Their joking stopped.

"But…" she continued. "What if it's the railroad?"

They halted their banter and looked at her.

"It could explain someone from Louisiana who's not a cattleman wanting land around there." She looked each of them in the eye as she spoke. "Look at a map. Draw a line from Shreveport to Dallas to Fort Worth to El Paso."

"Well, hobble my lip, Missuz Atlee. That makes too much sense," Orion said sheepishly.

"In case you didn't know…" she continued. "The capitol is in shambles. Somehow, the bureaucrats have managed to anger ex-Unionists *and* ex-Confederates."

Her husband, Deed, wanted to understand. "But, railroads—"

"Among the many hard-to-fathom pronouncements coming from Austin is a proviso that might actually make sense," Atlee explained. "It ends the granting of public land to anyone but an actual settler. When, not if, there is an east–west rail line across the state, this will be huge."

The men listened intently. Atlee, being an owner of a stage relay station, had examined the progress of railroad development with a studied and wary eye. She had even written a couple of newspaper articles. In a recent editorial, she had used the words, *corrupt officials*, *fast-buck profiteering*, *shoddy ethics*, and *unscrupulous behavior* to describe the men in Austin and in railway speculation.

"Railroad developers look to acquire free land. Speculation is expensive. Now? With no governor in place? Who knows what happens? It's all about grants and charters and currying favor among the fat men in back rooms with back slaps and cigars," she continued. "It sounds to me like this Thorne woman wants to be dealt into a very high-stakes game."

Her words sunk in around the table.

Holt smiled at his sister-in-law. "That's good stuff, Atlee. Can you find out more? Maybe sniff around Hannah's out-of-town newspaper people, see what else you can find out about railway development and contracts. Especially around Stebbins."

"Maybe I can find out some more about this Isla person, too…" Atlee added. She glanced briefly at Boody before returning her attention to Holt.

Orion stood. "This news is all the more reason I've gotta get to Stebbins. Sooner than later." He pulled his Ranger badge from a coat pocket and looked at it thoughtfully. "Mebbe not a good time to be gettin' rid of this thing either."

"More than horse research now," Holt said.

CHAPTER TWELVE

Back at Fort McKavett, Linus Carmichael had been removed from the hospital clinic. He died without a struggle. Major Wooster ordered the fort's doctor and hospital matrons to keep quiet and dispose of the body in secret.

Calista had pressing matters waiting for her in Austin—Isla Thorne business—but something told her that, this morning, her presence was required here. Her intuition, whether on the river or at a poker table, had always been reliable.

In recent days, the clinic's other prisoner, Christer Viklund, had become increasingly anxious. His nerves were fraying. A judge was due any day, and the young man realized that his sentence would soon be carried out…at the end of a noose. And now, his accomplice, Linus Carmichael, had disappeared. Yesterday morning, while Viklund slept, soldiers had silently carried out the former sheriff and his bed.

Throughout all this, the clinic's head matron had become a friend of Celinda and Calista. This older nurse did not suspect the sisters of preparing toxic food and drink for the unfortunate Carmichael.

Today, the matron kept watch as Calista entered the infirmary to visit the young Christer. She had given Calista a nurse's outfit so she would not attract attention.

In disguise, Calista now approached Christer and sat on his bed. He was confused. This nurse was younger than all the others and had a hint of French perfume about her, not a musty wool or antiseptic odor like the others.

Calista Theriot leaned forward. Her dark green eyes bore deep. She spoke softly, "How would you like your freedom, Christer Viklund?"

Christer could only gape wide-eyed and open-mouthed.

Calista repeated, "Tell me, would you like to get out of here?"

He stammered, then found his voice. "Y-You m-mean, a pardon or a stay? Linus says—"

"Forget about Linus," she interrupted sharply. "He has no future." She paused. "Answer me, do you want to get out of here?"

"Y-Yes."

"Good. I can make that happen for you."

This *nurse* had the young Viklund's full attention. He blurted what had been on his mind. "Could I get my father's ranch back?"

Calista looked at him with a touch of pity. "Do you really want it back?"

"Well…y-yeah…"

"The Windmill V."

"It was my father's…"

"Christer." Her beautiful looks turned dark. "Listen to

me. Do you really want every sheriff, Ranger, and bounty hunter to know where you're hanging your hat?"

His face betrayed that he had not considered such a thing.

"No, young man, that hand has been played. Even if you ride to Stebbins, you cannot stay."

He looked her in the eye, not sure whether to cry or be angry, but he was intrigued.

"You have another game ahead of you." Her smile was assuring.

He said nothing, though his youthful face brightened.

"Ever been to Baton Rouge? New Orleans? St. Louis?"

Christer swallowed hard. His immaturity was crashing hard against a new reality.

"Prove yourself," she whispered. "You can come work for me."

"Wh-Who are you?"

"A friend, if you want one."

The young man breathed deeply before lowering his voice. "C-Can I p-pay back the men who did this to my family?"

Calista raised her eyebrows ever so slightly. She had not expected this response.

The young Viklund continued, "Moose Elkins, the Ranger who shot me. The Ranger captain who hung my brother. The man who killed my father, Holt Corrigan." His voice got more heated as he listed the names. "And the others who hurt us. I want…I want them all dead."

Calista smiled. "I want that too." She softly pulled her hand across his jawline. "All in good time, my dear Christer. All in good time. Rest now and wait for my word."

CHAPTER THIRTEEN

Holt waited with his dog, Tag, inside the Silver Spur Café for the arrival of Laudie Kate. She had worked late at the Black Hat. Holt told her he would take her for breakfast when she woke up. It was the Corrigan family's favorite restaurant, not only because of the food, but also because the owner had no problem serving their Mexican neighbors, the Sanchezs, and when he was alive, their Japanese godfather, Silka. The proprietor, a German immigrant himself, had felt the sting of prejudice and had no room for it in his world. To show his allegiance, when he became sheriff, Holt made sure to order official county food from the Spur. James Hannah, and now Logan Wheeler, had continued the routine once they each served as sheriff.

With time to think, Holt's thoughts wandered. His partner's talk of retirement from the Rangers got Holt thinking about his own future. Laudie Kate was his forever blue sky—he felt that clearly, but how could he even think of marrying her if he had to run off and be a Ranger every time the captain summoned him?

He knew the answer, and it made him uneasy. Turning in his badge would be a big step. Outlaw Holt Corrigan had become *Texas Ranger Holt Corrigan*. It was who he was now. Had he outrun his past? Was he worthy of a quiet, happy life?

His memories jumped to the day of Judge Pence's murder.

Holt and his brothers, plus their godfather Silka, and James Hannah, had the judge's belongings and saddlebag contents spread out on a desk in the jail. They were looking for clues, anything that might explain the magistrate's gruesome murder.

"I hate this part." Hannah had sighed, looking at the judge's writing journal. "Going through what someone left behind."

"Never stopped to think about it much…*before*…" Holt had reflected. "This isn't like wartime when you quickly rifled through a dead man's things, looking for maps, ammunition, or food. You took what you needed. For survival. This is different. This is an accounting of a man's life." The distinction had hit Holt as hard as a fist, and he paused a moment before continuing. He gestured at the items spread before them. "*This* is Judge Oscar Pence." He shook his head and touched the medicine stone in his pocket. His voice got husky. "Damn. This is all that's left…of him."

Silka put a hand on Holt's shoulder. "Not all. There more to a man, if worthy."

"That's why you build ranches, create families, and make memories," Deed had acknowledged. "You leave important pieces of yourself behind, not just stuff. Right, my teacher?" He smiled first at Silka, then at Holt.

"That is most good." Silka nodded and touched the *Bushido* medallion around his neck, then tapped his right fist across his heart. "Judge gave new life to Holt. Never forgotten."

Recalling this and reflecting on the lives his brothers were carving out, Holt realized his godfather Silka had left a lot behind, too.

"It is so, my friend," Holt acknowledged quietly to his gone, but not forgotten godfather. "I will *never* forget. I will leave behind something important."

Tag heard his master's vow and sat up to nestle his head on the young Ranger's thigh.

Just then, Holt was snapped out of his musing by Mr. Hayes, the telegraph operator at the Howard's Real Estate, Insurance & Telegraph Office, bustling up to his table.

"Ranger Corrigan, this came for you," said the meticulous, out-of-breath clerk. "Although…" He worriedly scratched at his brow.

"What is it, Mr. Hayes?"

"Well…although it just arrived here, I believe it was sent days ago. Maybe even a week." He paused. "To our south and east, there has been trouble with the wires being down. No explanation why."

"That's okay, Mr. Hayes, it's here now. I appreciate you bringing this to me." He started reaching for a coin in his vest but was stopped by Mr. Hayes.

"Oh, thank you, sir, but no. It seemed official, and it

was late. My pleasure." The nervous man took quick leave.

Holt opened the note and began reading the message.

HOLT,

BEEN IN AUSTIN. NIECE'S WEDDING.

CAPITOL A MESS.

CORRUPT. UNETHICAL. VENAL.

NO ONE IN CHARGE.

NO COMMUNICATION. RUN BY SECRETS & RUMORS.

BEEN THINKING ABOUT FORT MCKAVETT.

GLAD YOU SHARED INFORMATION.

I SAW VIKLUND & CREW HANG.

NOT THE SERGEANT.

GOING TO FORT NOW TO ASK QUESTIONS.

WILL KEEP YOU INFORMED.

MCCOY.

Holt exhaled and nodded. That explained the silence from the captain. A wedding and wires down. So, when had he sent this? How old was it? Was he at the fort now?

And the captain did not include Orion in the message.

"He still thinks Orion is turning in his badge," he muttered quietly to Tag, waiting patiently for an order to ride or sit.

Just then, Laudie Kate and James Hannah walked up.

Hannah was smiling brightly. "Ahh, Ranger Corrigan, look who I found!"

Holt was still immersed in his telegram.

Hannah continued, "This kind of beauty shouldn't be walking around alone, no telling who might—"

Laudie Kate gave her boss, Hannah, a good-natured, but not gentle, elbow. "Hush yourself, James Hannah, or

I'll tell Rebecca you've been stalking women at the dress store. Again." She laughed heartily before leaning over and kissing Holt on the cheek.

Holt, for a change, did not immediately light up at her presence. He was deep in thought.

Laudie Kate stayed bent over, still leaning into Holt's face. "Are you okay?" she asked quietly, as Tag did friendly circles around her long skirt.

Holt finally realized Laudie Kate was there. "Oh. Hi!"

"*Oh hi*? I got a better greeting from Tag."

Holt stood quickly, grabbed her shoulders, and pulled her close. His kiss was one he meant.

"That's more like it."

"I'm sorry, I just got a wire from the captain and was chewing on it."

"Uh oh…"

Holt still couldn't get his mind away from the message. "Hey, what's *venal* mean?"

Before Hannah could speak, Laudie Kate answered, "Corrupt. Susceptible to bribery."

"Venal?" Hannah said. "Sounds to me like a word your sister-in-law would use in her article about Austin or someone there."

"As a matter of fact, the captain was talking about the capitol," Holt replied.

Laudie Kate's brow furrowed. "Something new?"

"No, still this Fort McKavett thing," Holt said. "Something's just not right about all that."

"What'd he say about the hanging?" Hannah asked.

"He was only there for the hanging of the Viklund son and Viklund riders. He was not there for the sergeant's hanging." Holt paused. "I should've remembered that. He was in Stebbins when the military tribunal would have been held. He was with us at that roundup and wouldn't have heard if the sergeant accused anyone else at his hanging."

Hannah nodded. Laudie Kate's face was full of concern.

"He said he was going to the fort, to ask questions." Holt's thoughts raced from McKavett to Stebbins and back again. "There's been trouble with telegraph lines in the region. I don't know when he was—"

"You'll hear soon enough," Laudie Kate soothed. "Not much you can do about it. Right?" She rubbed his shoulder. "How about that breakfast you promised?"

CHAPTER FOURTEEN

A thin, bespectacled man with a scrubby goatee presented himself at the headquarters of Fort McKavett. "I'm Laird McCoy, captain of the Texas Rangers. This is Ranger Dal Frantze. I need to speak with your commanding officer, right away."

"Commanding..." The young lieutenant was obviously giving the request some thought. The lawman in front of him seemed nearer a minister or bookkeeper and not a rough-and-tumble Ranger. The man with him, yes, but not this *captain.* But that was not what gave him pause. With so many officers gone, he was trying to think of who the ranking officer on base would be.

He finally cleared his throat. "Uh, that would be Major Wooster, sir."

"Major Wooster?"

"Yes, sir. Major Merriman Wooster. I will have him summoned right away."

McCoy's closely held suspicions about the goings-on at Fort McKavett were never completely abated. It was obvious that the quartermaster sergeant was the linchpin to the rustling operation here, but how could he have done it alone? Yes, there had been much turmoil here, changes in command, a rebuilding of nearly the entire fort. But a lowly sergeant? Hundreds, if not thousands, of heads of cattle moved through here and New Braunfels? Not to mention a patrol of troopers assigned to ride guard with a civilian sheriff?

No, Captain McCoy had now surmised, those affairs could not have been accomplished by just one man, even a resourceful sergeant.

After he and Dal Frantze had arrested the oldest Viklund son and the three Viklund riders in New Braunfels, they were brought here. The evidence gathered back in Stebbins by the Rangers and the fact that these four were caught red-handed with a stolen herd, was enough to convict all the Viklund men. They were hung shortly thereafter.

Back then, Captain McCoy did not have much time for interrogations or evidence gathering. He needed to get back to Stebbins to spring the rest of the trap on the remaining Viklunds. He did, however, have a lengthy conversation with the general in command at the time. General Clark, no longer assigned here, had described how an enterprising sergeant could have pulled off such a crime without anyone else knowing. Details of how Sergeant Carmichael could conceal records, cover up patrol movements, and generally operate as an independent contractor, were convincingly explained to McCoy by the wizened old officer.

"The officers and men are simply too busy, too occupied with the duties of an Army and reconstructing a fort to have the time for such treacherous moonlighting," General Clark had said. "The only one who could operate so uncontrolled would be Sergeant Carmichael, our superintendent of supplies. And look what he got himself into."

At the time, the general's explanation was plausible enough for Captain McCoy. However, it was his nature to be thorough, and he had always wondered if there was more to the McKavett story. Holt Corrigan's telegraph about the gallows accusation by the doomed sergeant reignited his uncertainty into action.

The Rangers did not have to wait long before a somber, ramrod-straight officer appeared before them. By all appearances, Major Merriman Wooster was the epitome of a U.S. Army man-at-arms—taller than average, close-cropped auburn hair, freshly shaved, crisp uniform.

"Major Merriman Wooster?"

"Yes, I am Major Wooster."

"Laird McCoy, Captain, Texas Rangers. This is Ranger Dal Frantze."

"Good to make your acquaintances, gentlemen." The major managed a stiff smile. "I am familiar with Ranger Frantze. Your eyepatch is, er, memorable, if I may say so. He was instrumental in the apprehension of, uh, those Swedish rustlers. A spy of sorts, yes?"

"That's correct, Major Wooster." Captain McCoy nodded, as did Ranger Frantze. "In fact, that's why we're here. Trying to tie up some loose ends on the Viklund case. May we talk, somewhere, quiet?"

"I'm afraid there is construction everywhere here, Captain. Quiet is hard to find. The trees out back might provide us with shade."

Captain McCoy smiled. "We'll follow you, sir."

Stepping behind the headquarters, McCoy and Frantze could see a lot of the fort's layout. Many brand-new buildings had emerged since they were here not long ago.

Concealed in a lush garden from the officers' quarters, two pairs of eyes watched the three men intently.

"Quite a bit of activity going on, Major, even for a military installation," Captain McCoy noted. "Must be hard to keep track of everything, what with all this construction and the daily burden of overseeing a sizable force."

"No, not at all." The major looked around proudly. "Everything is organized and supervised, from nails and horses to training and operations."

McCoy glanced at Frantze before returning his attention to the officer. "I'm wondering, then, Major, how a sergeant in charge of the quartermaster department could become so embroiled in a rustling operation with a Swedish family from a county roughly 150 miles away. Would the sergeant not be supervised, closely supervised?"

"Of course, he would." The major looked down at his brightly polished boots before returning his gaze to the Ranger.

"This post sure had its fill of beef over the past year. Was that a normal allotment?"

"I'm not sure what you mean?" The major cocked his head slightly.

"Hundreds, if not thousands, of cattle came here. That couldn't have gone unnoticed—"

"Not unnoticed, but sure appreciated." The major tried to chuckle away the seriousness of the conversation.

"How do you explain that? Surely the herds were larger than standard issue and more frequent, not to mention from outside the normal supply chain."

"This is Texas, sir. Are we not known for cattle?" The major again tried a weak attempt at humor.

"Doesn't the Army have supply records? Inventory? A budget?"

"Well, er…uh…yes. Sure." The major was getting fidgety. "But that's often changed, improvised."

"Improvised?" the captain asked, a slight needling to his voice. "An outfit so *organized and supervised*?"

The major stiffened at the reproach. "What are you getting at, Captain?"

"Just curious, Major. We're just talking." McCoy let the moment sink in, then continued. "So how does a hard-working sergeant have the time to involve himself in such activity? Was he not gone from the post often?"

The major was still composing himself.

Captain McCoy repeated himself. "Sergeant Carmichael was often off post, to New Braunfels, yes?"

The major fidgeted a bit more, his mind churning for an answer slow to come. "Well, er…uh…a great many of our supplies come from…from New Braunfels."

"Is that so?" The captain knew all this, but wanted the major to walk him through it.

"The r-river…" The major stammered slightly. "Yes, the river is there. A lot of our materials come from the river."

"Yes, the river. Of course." Captain McCoy paused his questioning. The major appeared to relax. "But, then, a lot of materials leave from there, yes? Like stolen cattle?"

"See here, now, Captain McCoy, I've—"

Captain McCoy raised his hand to stop the major. "My apologies, sir." He looked the major in the eye. "Why was there a patrol often assigned to Sergeant Carmichael's brother?"

"A-A patrol…?"

"Yes, a full patrol. A dozen troopers, a scout, a lieutenant, a full complement. They were seen escorting your current prisoner, former Sheriff Linus Carmichael. From eyewitnesses, this occurred often. From the fort, through Overfield, to Stebbins. And back. Often," Captain McCoy repeated.

The major squirmed from the heat of the question. He almost divulged that Carmichael died just a few days ago, but caught himself. "I-I-I have n-no idea. This is the f-first I've h-heard of it."

"Hmmm, organized and supervised," the captain muttered. "And what about one of these patrols getting ambushed on their return from Stebbins? By Comanches."

"Ambushed?" The major gulped heavily before his answer. "Unfortunately, we suffer occasional losses from Indian activity. There would be a written record of such an action."

"We'll look into that," the captain said. "Is there a record of shipments from New Braunfels?"

"New Braunfels?"

"Yes, you know, the river. Would there be a written record of what the quartermaster received? And the dates?"

"Yes, there should be…"

"We'll look into that too." The captain looked over again at Frantze before continuing. "I appreciate you taking the time to talk to us, Major Wooster. I've got one more question…"

"Yes?"

"Why would your quartermaster, Sergeant Carmichael, scream your name from the gallows? Why would he accuse you of being in on his enterprise?"

The major got red-faced and shouted, "That's despicable—"

"Why not accuse the general? Or the lieutenant colonel? Or anyone else?"

The major looked down, muttering under his breath, "That no-good pirate…"

Only Frantze caught the utterance. "What pirate, Major?" he asked.

Major Wooster looked up. "Well, surely you suspect that Sergeant Carmichael had to be dealing with a pirate. Why would you ask?" He was seething now. "Who else would do that?"

Captain McCoy joined in. "Do you—"

"NO!" the major hollered. "I do NOT." He calmed himself. "I do not…I did not…know."

The captain ignored the retort. "Major, if you have—"

"No! I do *not* have any more information for you. I wasn't involved. I don't know anything!" He composed himself back to his original ramrod-straight bearing. "Gentlemen, I have rounds to make. We are finished here."

As the Rangers turned to leave, Major Wooster called

out. "I know what you're thinking. Leave my brother out of this. My wife, too. Leave us alone."

Rangers McCoy and Frantze continued their departure. Dal watched the horses while the captain went inside the headquarters to request a look at the supply records and action reports from the past year.

Captain McCoy returned shortly. "I have to come back to look at their paperwork. Not quickly retrieved, and someone needs to authorize. Hopefully not that major." Then he looked at Dal. "Did we even know he had a brother?"

Dal smirked. "Or a wife. Why warn us?"

The captain asked, "What do you think, Dal?"

"He's guilty. He knows exactly what went on."

The captain shrugged. "Maybe he's just dumb."

"Or both."

They did not chuckle as they rode away.

From their concealed position in the lush garden of the officers' quarters, the two Theriot sisters looked frustratingly at each other.

"I don't think that went well," Celinda frowned.

"Don't let him talk to anyone," Calista growled. "I don't care what excuse you give. No more interviews."

She murmured something under her breath as she gripped the silver-and-brass amulet concealed by her clothing. "The first steps of my plan are in motion. It's time to ante up. Cee, I need you and your pen to take action." She smiled gleefully. "Have we got stories for the newspapermen in New Braunfels and Stebbins!"

Celinda listened with fascination.

Finally, Calista pulled out the amulet from underneath her dress. "Soon, that Ranger captain and his little band will be hit by a tornado the likes of which they've never seen." She fixed a lock of hair that had come astray and smoothed it over the bump on her head.

"Isla Thorne is at the table, and the stakes are do-or-die."

CHAPTER FIFTEEN

Late morning found Holt leaving the Wilkon blacksmith's forge holding a large canvas bag. A friendly voice called from across the street, "Oh, Ranger! Ranger, dear? Can you help a poor soul?"

Tag Along reacted first with a friendly woof. The dog knew better than to charge across the street without his master. Holt looked over to see his good friend, James Hannah. "Let's go, boy. Let's see what this miscreant is up to now." The two trotted across well ahead of a freight wagon just starting to make its way down the thoroughfare.

James Hannah gave the two a regal bow. "Good morning to you, fair and gracious friends!"

"Morning, Hannah."

"Have I thought long to see this morning's face, And doth it give me such a sight as this?"

Holt smirked. "A bit early for a taste, James?"

"For wisdom cries out in the streets, and no man regards it."

Holt looked down to address Tag. "I don't know, buddy. Think we ought to lock this chap up? He's clearly not right in the head."

"Shakespeare, my friend. I was reading it last night. Always makes me think of you and your brothers."

"Alrighty then."

"I always said meeting you Corrigans has been like living Henry the IV. Gawdamighty, Shakespeare would have loved you three." He clapped Holt on the shoulder with a grin. "So, what have you got there?"

Holt held up the canvas bag. "Our Bar 3 foreman was wanting some old cavalry bits. They only had some discarded Shoemaker's at the forge. Hope Travis can use 'em." He gestured at the package Hannah was carrying. "What are you up to?"

Hannah patted a stack of thin, brown paper-wrapped packages and smiled. "Newspapers! From all over. Just came in on the stage. Pay a pretty penny to get 'em here. Helps me not miss out on anything." The former gunman had recently decided to hang up his sheriff's badge, choosing to make a difference with words and information.

Holt nodded, thinking with a grin. "How like you, ever curious. And nosy."

"Me and my fellow publishers try to use telegrams to keep up, but that's not always practicable." James continued. "Hey, Laudie Kate's busy overseeing some deliveries. But I guess you knew that. How 'bout some coffee at the Silver Spur before you go? I'll buy."

"You? Buy? In that case, I'll have some pie too."

"I never see thy face, but I think upon hell-fire."

Holt chuckled. "C'mon, *Henry*, let's go."

Seated at the Silver Spur, Hannah thumbed through the stack of his newspapers while Holt dug into a piece of pecan pie to accompany his coffee. Tag was finishing a bowl of scrambled eggs at their feet under the table.

Suddenly, Hannah exclaimed, "Hey, listen to this… Christer Viklund has escaped from the jail at Fort McKavett."

"What? Viklund escaped?"

"Yeah, says right here in the New Braunfels paper—"

"Wonder why we…wonder why Sheriff Wheeler wasn't informed. You would think they'd want help, to keep an eye out for him."

"I don't know. Seems odd." Hannah continued reading out loud, "*Christer Viklund, youngest son of Lars Viklund, the deceased cattle rustler, has escaped from the military jail at Fort McKavett.*"

"Any word on Carmichael? Was he with him?"

"Says here that Carmichael is dead."

"Killed in the escape?"

"It doesn't say. Just says that Christer is on the loose and former St. Clair County Sheriff Linus Carmichael, in prison with Viklund, is dead."

"Does it say when?"

"No. This edition is about three weeks old."

Silence. Holt's mind rifled through a myriad of thoughts and questions. What was missing here? Details. Details were missing, like how and where.

"You think he'd head for Stebbins?" Hannah wondered, interrupting Holt's deliberations.

"He's just a kid. He threw up on his boots when we caught him."

"I dunno. Kids do dumb stuff." Hannah said,

eyebrows raised. "At that age? I'd go back. In a heartbeat. Wouldn't you?"

Holt's face was covered with concern. "If he does, Orion is going to be right in the middle of it."

CHAPTER SIXTEEN

"A*aeeeeee!"*

A woman's scream shrieked like a missile into the calm Stebbins, Texas morning.

Crrissh!

An instant behind the scream, a billiard ball whistled out through a plate-glass window in the front of Bellinger's, leaving a neat hole in the pane. The 9-ball came to a rolling halt at a young boy's feet. He gathered up the deep red ball as though it was found treasure.

Bang!

Bang!

Bang!

From inside, one errant shot blistered into the front window, finishing the job started by the billiard ball as the pane exploded into a shower of shards. People along the walkway outside had been unswayed by the scream and the thrown ball through the window. The gunshots, however, touched off alarm and frantic scurrying for anywhere but the front of the pool hall.

A melee had erupted inside the smoky watering hole,

the result of a combination of cheap whiskey, a soiled dove's attention—or inattention—and angry words. There were three combatants, but everyone in Bellinger's, the seediest establishment to operate in the main part of town, was involved, whether they liked it or not.

Inside the pool hall, a brawny drover with a huge red beard held the saloon girl with one hand and a pistol in the other. The drover was big enough to handle the other two combatants with his bare hands, but decided to escalate the matter and settle it all with his gun.

A squatty man with a bald head and scraggly mustache had taken cover under a billiard table while his friend, a stringy-haired teamster with large buck teeth, dove behind a pile of chairs. Both were only chatting with the painted woman when the drover took issue with them talking to *his girl*. The first shot embedded in the pool table above the bald man's head. In response, he had drawn a gun and fired at the drover, missing everything but the window. The red-bearded man fired again, tearing the felt on the pool table.

Suddenly, more shots were fired. From behind the chairs, the teamster joined the fray and fired through the openings in the chair rails, hitting the drover twice in the stomach. The large cowboy fell forward, his red-bearded face slamming against the floor planks like a dull axe. The saloon girl screamed and ran for the safety of the area behind the bar. A friend of the fallen drover took up his cause and began firing at the teamster who was still hiding behind the chairs. The squatty man under the pool stable returned fire as well.

More shots were squeezed off, wildly, not hitting

their targets, but causing damage to walls and lamps. Two bystanders were hit by errant rounds.

Booom! Booom!

Abruptly, the roar of a shotgun detonated from the front of the saloon.

"Drop them guns!" came a shout from the doorway. "Drop 'em, I say, or I'll kill ya all dead," Marshal Baxter Hollings yelled. "Ya hear me? Drop 'em now, dammit!" The doughy, older marshal quickly ejected the two spent shells and smoothly replaced them with new loads.

The pool hall patrons now realized Hollings was accompanied by a deputy. Deputy Gus Brooks had fanned out off to the left, covering a great deal of the barroom with his own double-barreled Greener. His eyes surveyed the scene for any movement that did not fit.

Another voice hollered into the chaos, "Briggs! Johnny! Drop those guns!" A heavyset man with a groomed mustache and tailored suit shouted the order from a five-handed poker game. "You know better, damn it!"

"Sorry, Madig…er…boss." The stringy-haired man from behind the chairs stood now and spoke, pointing at the no-longer-moving drover. "He started it, though."

The well-dressed gambler turned back to his game. "You do what the marshal says. No question, got it?" The man's immense belly appeared to have a life of its own, but his clothes, nonetheless, fit his rotund frame without strain. He appeared entirely out of place in Bellinger's.

The silence in the room indicated that everyone understood the law had arrived and that the fireworks were over.

"My apologies, Marshal." The fat man smiled.

"These two men here will cooperate fully. I am quite certain their story will check out."

Marshal Hollings nodded briefly at the portly gambler, then turned his attention to the combatants. "Okay now, y'all drop them pistols rite where ya stand. No more fightin' or shootin' or we'll cut ya ta pieces." He took the time now to re-seat the dirty bowler hat atop his head.

Deputy Brooks gathered the three uninjured fighters and herded them outside toward the jail.

The little parade was crossing the street when the deputy noticed a lanky rider in a black trail coat riding up slowly on a big bay.

"Orion Higbee!" The deputy waved without losing his focus. "Welcome to Stebbins! Sorry, I can't stop for a chat."

"Mornin' Gus. I'm just ridin' into town," Orion smiled. "Looks like the fun started early."

"All in a day's work." The deputy continued with his march to the jail.

Orion looked down the street toward a crowd gathered outside a saloon, the flock straining for looks inside. Must be the party Gus came from, he surmised.

Ambling further down the street, away from the commotion, he reined in and dismounted. As he was tying up his bay, he saw a huge man in a checkered shirt approaching the onlookers. This familiar figure was a bear of a man with a voice to match, one Orion could hear all the way down the street.

"Alright, people. Time ta go be somewhar else." Moose Elkins commanded attention and was given it. The shirt he wore could easily have been a horse blanket. "Git, I say! No need ta be here a-gawkin'!"

The townspeople were dispersing as he reached the pool hall entrance. A doctor followed closely behind him, carrying a medical bag.

"C'mon now, go go go!" Moose continued. "Got the doc here, people're hurt." He stopped to let the doctor move past him and hurry inside. Looking at the remaining curious citizens, he hollered, "Alright, last ones standin' here help clean up blood!"

Orion had to shake his head and grin. His friend—Sheriff Moose Elkins—was a giant who had a way with words.

Just as conspicuous as Moose, the tall Ranger also stood out. Even in the midst of directing unwanted onlookers away, Sheriff Elkins easily spotted his old pal, Orion, and comically doffed his hat.

Orion pointed at the entrance to the Blue Sky Inn, silently telling his friend where he was headed.

Just then, Marshal Hollings exited the pool hall, taking Moose's attention.

"Doc's in there now. Coupla bystanders shot. I think they's gonna be okay," the marshal reported. "Undertaker's on th' way. Gus locked up th' three doin' all th' fightin'. We's gonna sort through their stories now."

Moose nodded. "Bar fight. More'n usual these days."

"Say, Moose, d'ya have any idear who that big gambler is? Th' fat one in th' 'xpensive suit."

Moose peered through the broken window. "No, cain't say that I do."

"Oh well, I'll see if'n me an' Gus can git ta th' bottom of it all."

Because it was a town incident, Sheriff Elkins was not really needed, so he took his leave and headed toward the Blue Sky to find his Ranger friend.

Inside the Blue Sky's main room, Orion was seated alone at a table when he saw Moose come through the inn's batwing doors. "You ol' hog-kickin' saddle blanket!" Orion hollered as he stood. They both shook hands and thumped each other's shoulders.

Moose beamed in response, "An' how might Range-uh Oh-ryun be doin' on this lovely day?"

"Finer than frog hair, my friend. Been helpin' out at the W Bar L for a few days. Decided this mornin' seemed a good time to visit town."

"Ya picked a banner day." Moose chuckled. "Used ta say this diddent happen offen. Cain't say it no more."

"Seems like you're workin'. Got time for coffee?"

"Wish it could be sumthin' stronger, but coffee sounds good." He looked around the large lobby that doubled as a saloon. "Evie should be aroun'. Don' see her tho."

"We've said our hellos. She got me my coffee."

"So, ya bin in my county a few days, but haven't come in ta say howdy?"

"Yeah, like I said, I been out at the W Bar L. Helpin' Lilly get her ranch back in order. I figured a low profile is always best. Besides, there's been plenty of work."

"She still operatin' short-handed?"

"For now."

Lillian Whitman and her ranch were still recovering from the effects of the Viklund plundering. What was left of her herd was slowly being recovered, and there was damage to her house and buildings, but it had been only the widow, her foreman, Big Jeff, and four riders doing all the work. She had been happy to see Orion for lots of reasons.

The lanky Ranger kept his badge tucked away in a

pocket. He had decided not to fully commit to turning it in, figuring the outcome of his visit to Lilly would be the deciding factor. He had a feeling his badge would be needed before all was said and done.

"Moose, somethin' 'bout Stebbins seems off," Orion said. "I ain't been here long, but there's an odd sense somethin' ain't right."

"Ya hit that one on th' head," Moose responded. "Even wit' th' Viklund attacks settled down, sumthin's changed. Sumthin darker's afoot, I'm afraid."

"If we were out on the trail, I'd be expectin' Comanches, or worse," Orion acknowledged.

"Me too, my friend. It's like a blanket bin thrown ov'r th' entire place. Ya kin feel it, ya know?"

"Like the weather."

"That's th' feelin'!"

Just then, Evie appeared with a tray holding a coffee pot, extra mugs, and three pieces of apple pie.

"Hi, darlin'." Moose's grin was as big as he was.

She leaned over and kissed his head. "Heard Bellinger's had a bit of an altercation."

"Yeah, seems like a drover an' sum newcomers were in a dispute ov'r Hazel."

"Hazel? Men fightin' over Hazel? She had to love that."

Moose nodded at Evie's remark, then smiled to let her know he was talking about something else. "Somethin' peculiar's goin' on here, Oh-ryun. It ain't right. Like even that bar fight. Like th' ownership of ranches aroun' here now."

Evie caught on. Moose leaned in to speak quieter. "Even people we thought we knew have changed. Like

Ames Wooster, at th' bank." Evie nodded silently in agreement. "He's always bin friendly enuf, but now…"

"Grumpy. Even nervous," Evie added.

"Seems like Ames is gone all th' time, too. Secret-like, ya know? Like thet scary damn sheriff Carmichael was. He's never here. An' when he is here? Kinda jumpy, like he's guardin' sumthin." He stopped as a town couple passed, smiling at them as they walked by. He leaned in again. "One rich-lookin' stranger came ta town an' tried ta buy th' River D spread. Wooster tolt him it wasn't fer sale, it was already bought. Had th' feller escorted from th' premises."

Orion scratched his head under his hat. "Big Jeff said Lilly looked into how much the Half Moon 6 might be. You know, couldn't hurt to add onto her land. Big Jeff said she was told someone had already purchased it. Said the bank wouldn't tell her who. I didn't think then to ask her who she talked to at the bank. Di'nt know it was somethin' to be suspicious of."

Moose raised his eyebrows and shrugged his shoulders. "Yeah, now ya know."

It was Orion's turn to lean in so no one could hear. "So *no one* knows who bought those places?"

"I dunno. Nobody knows." Moose sipped his coffee. "An' now, Wooster's bin made mayor. By a secret meetin' of th' town council. Jus' like that." He snapped his fingers. "An' we suddenly got a new town judge. Th' old one up an' left." He snapped his fingers again.

Evie blurted, "It's that Thorne woman."

"Thorne? Whattaya mean, Evie?" Orion asked.

"I know for a fact she's moved into th' old Viklund place. I mean, it's a nice place an' all—"

Moose interrupted. "She's from New Or-leens. Got

all that juju aroun' her." He shivered. "Ya know, that voodoo crap."

Just then, Baxter Hollings arrived at their table. Evie stood and hurried to the bar for another mug and more coffee.

Moose greeted the marshal. "That diddent take long."

"Strangers." Baxter shook his head. "An' we're gettin' more n' more of 'em all th' time." He pulled a chair and sat down. "Lik' thet gambler in Bellinger's. Th' big, fat one."

Moose nodded. "Mighty fancy fella fer Bellinger's. For that matter, he's mighty fancy fer Stebbins."

Baxter agreed. "Looks lik' he belongs on a riverboat. An' two of th' fellas in thet dust-up answer ta him. He an' several people who witnessed th' fight, includin' th' gal in th' middle of it, came to th' jail. They all said th' two acted in self-defense. Said th' dead drover started it all. I had ta let 'em go. Judge is gonna lissen to th' other guy's story. He di'nt have ta join in."

Moose harrumphed. "Go figger."

"You talkin' 'bout that fat gambler? Fancy suit?" Evie returned and leaned in, lowering her voice. "Heard 'is name is Madigan Sanders, from sumwhere in Loosiana. Word has it he's lookin' to hire men. For what, I'm not sure."

Orion raised his eyebrows in surprise. "Louisiana? A bit far off his mark, dontcha think?"

"'Xactly, Oh-ryun." Moose rubbed at his mop of brown hair. "I ain't likin' it much. First th' Thorne woman an' now this Sanders fella."

Orion was curious. "Isla Thorne?"

"I ain't met her yet myself," Moose answered first. "Lotsa talk tho. She's made quite th' impression."

"I saw 'er at th' fabric shop," Evie said. "Didn't meet 'er. She's beautiful. Prettiest gal I ever seen. Dark hair, green eyes, big…" She gestured at her chest with her hands. "Likes to give everyone a peek at 'em too. She ordered three dresses from Dory, each of 'em"—she gestured again at her chest—"cut low. People say she's nice enough, but…"

"But what, Evie?" Orion asked.

"Somethin' about her, seems like she makes people nervous or afraid. Or bewitched."

Baxter remarked, "I heard Isla Thorne is who bought th' River D an' th' Half Moon 6. Heard it for a fact."

"Where'd ya hear that? From who?" Moose asked.

"Hogan, one of th' bank tellers. Heard it from him. He oughta know." He nodded, proud of his information, then added, "No word on whether th' ranch brands is changin'."

Orion broke in. "They were the spreads stolen by those damned Swedes, right?"

Baxter nodded. "Yep, sure were."

"The timin's a bit unusual, I'll give you that. But is there anythin' illegal goin' on?" Orion asked.

Baxter continued, "Who kin tell? Wooster ain't sayin' anythin'."

The table got quiet before Moose spoke again, this time in a whisper to Orion, "Are ya shure we got all them Viklunds? Or Carmichaels? Is that hand still bein' played?"

"We sure thought we got 'em all," Orion said. "Maybe we could've missed a player. Or, it's a brand-new game an' a brand-new dealer."

With that, Orion announced he needed to go to the

general store, then get back to the W Bar L. He gestured with his eyes for Moose to follow him out.

Once on the street, Orion spoke in a hushed tone, "Moose, you gotta keep this under your hat. Swear? Not even Evie."

Moose nodded in serious agreement.

"Holt an' I got information from his brother's wife. She's a newspaper writer, knows her stuff. She thinks this Thorne woman could be here to acquire property ahead of the railroad."

"*Day-um*."

"That's right," Orion said.

"Nothin' against th' law there."

"Well, not that we can see anyways, but like we agreed, Stebbins has changed."

Moose inhaled in acknowledgment. "It jus' don' feel right, Oh-ryun. Ya know that feelin'."

"I do, you'll just have to keep an eye on things, Moose. An' keep an eye on her," Orion cautioned.

"Feels like waitin' on a storm ya cain't see."

"Holt an' the Cap'n are lookin' into this. We'll hear what's goin' on an' what we need to do. Okay?"

"That sounds better," Moose acknowledged.

"For now, I'm keepin' my Ranger badge hid away. Understand?"

Moose nodded.

"I'll be out at the W Bar L with Lilly," Orion said. "I just might look in on Mr. Frederick at the 5 Star an' say howdy, if you know what I mean."

"Yeah, heard Mr. Fred-rick's dun hired hisself extry riders an' turnt that place inta a fortress."

CHAPTER SEVENTEEN

Days later, early traffic made Stebbins seem busier than usual. At the Rising Goose Café, townspeople breakfasted and got a start to their days.

Two of the diners were County Sheriff Moose Elkins and his sweetheart, Evie O'Neill. Their relationship blossomed when Moose, then a Texas Ranger, rode undercover as a rider for the wicked Viklund family. After taking down the evil Swedes—including their crooked partner, Sheriff Linus Carmichael—Moose had turned in his Ranger badge and became the popular choice to replace the wayward lawman.

At an out-of-the-way table, Moose and Evie lingered over their finished meals. Moose needed to get to the jail, and Evie would soon have to report to her job at the Blue Sky Inn. With heads bowed together, Evie shared a discussion she had with a friend at the bank. "Hogan says that a bungalow near th' doctor's is goin' to be vacant. Soon."

Moose smiled. “Are ya suggestin’…are ya thinkin’ what I think yer thinkin’?”

“Well, it’s a promise I’ve heard from you many times, Michael Patrick Elkins. If we get married, we could live right there.” She smiled, letting her statement sink in.

“Aw, Evelyn Grace O’Neill, nothin’ would make me prouder.” He paused and reached into a coat pocket. “I wuz wantin’ to make this more special, but ev’ryday is special if yer in it.” He handed her a simple gold band. “Ya have my gramma’s locket. This wuz my mother’s.”

He hadn’t even finished his sentence before Evie melted in tears of joy.

“Ya kin wear it now,” he continued. “We’ll do all th’ churchy stuff when we kin get the preacher an’ ev’ryone put together.”

“I love it!” was all the words Evie could muster as she leaned from her chair and wrapped her arms around the large man.

At a nearby table, Marshal Hollings saw the joyful laughing and crying, and couldn’t help but saunter over to see what his friends were celebrating.

As Moose returned a teary Evie kiss, screams punctuated the morning bliss.

Christer Viklund, his flowing blond hair now shorn to closeness, suddenly loomed in the Rising Goose doorway, pistols in each hand. Two other men, one clad in cavalry trousers and a leather tunic, the other wearing a dirty duster trail coat, spread out on either side of Christer. The man to the left of Christer brandished a Winchester rifle. The gunman to the right shoved a waitress to the floor and drew a pistol.

Christer looked directly at Moose. “This is for me and my family…”

Moose pushed Evie down under the table and stepped to the side, instinctively trying to draw the attack away from her.

Christer and his men opened fire.

Moose overturned a nearby table and pulled his revolver, directing his shots at Christer. Marshal Hollings drew his gun and only got off a few shots before being cut down in a hail of fire, the attackers' bullets struck Moose's huge body repeatedly.

Behind the bar, the Rising Goose bartender leveled a Greener and fired one barrel at Christer and the other in the direction of the closest attacker, missing them in his haste. He bent down to the safety of the bar and reloaded, then re-emerged and fired both barrels, dropping the man to Christer's right.

Seeing his colleague fall, the gunman to Christer's left hollered, "Let's get out of here!" He ran out the door, with Christer following.

At the first sound of the gunfire, Deputy Gus Brooks hurtled from the jail, not exactly sure where the shooting was coming from. Bystanders outside the Rising Goose crouched down and huddled as the attack commenced. Several were screaming as two men bolted outside and jumped onto waiting horses.

Gus quickly aimed his Henry rifle at the two fleeing gunmen, squeezing off shots as rapidly as he could. Dust popped from one rider as Gus's bullets found their mark, toppling the man in a heap onto the street.

Christer Viklund, unhit and still riding fast, turned for one last look and disappeared into the broken terrain.

CHAPTER EIGHTEEN

Back in Wilkon, the wire from Deputy Gus Brooks with news of the attack in Stebbins hit hard. A runner from Mr. Hayes at the Real Estate, Insurance & Telegraph Office found Holt at the jail having coffee with Marshal Freeburg.

RANGER HOLT CORRIGAN:

MARSHAL HOLLINGS IS DEAD. SHERIFF ELKINS IS HURT BAD.

ATTACKED BY CHRISTER VIKLUND AND 2 MEN.

VIKLUND ESCAPED.

ISLA THORNE OWNS STEBBINS NOW.

NEW MAYOR, NEW JUDGE ANSWER TO HER.

WORD IS SHE HAS 40 GUNMEN. ASSUMING VIKLUND IS ONE.

STEBBINS IS IN TROUBLE.

DEPUTY GUS BROOKS.

"Stebbins is where you helped bust up that Swedish

rustling ring, isn't it?" Marshal Freeburg asked as he handed back the wire message Holt shared with him.

The young Ranger stood to grab the note and clicked his mouth to wake a sleeping Tag Along. "Yeah, it's also where Orion went to help that widow put her ranch back together." Holt nodded grimly.

"You think he knows what happened?"

"I don't know, he was planning on being inconspicuous." Holt adjusted his hat and coat to leave.

"Ride careful, Holt."

With a nod of acknowledgment, Holt stepped outside. His immediate destination was the telegraph office to send the information he had just received to Captain McCoy.

His next stop was Laudie Kate's bungalow. He had to ride to Stebbins and was not looking forward to telling her.

The mid-morning found Laudie Kate just waking up. Her tousled hair and sleepy blue eyes made Holt smile all over. Her rumpled just-out-of-bed look or a sparkling gown, it did not matter to Holt. She was the most beautiful woman he'd ever seen.

"Can I make you some coffee? Eggs?" He offered.

"Coffee's already on," she said, as she splashed her face in a porcelain basin. "I'll settle for a towel."

His smiling face was right next to hers when she finished drying and pulled down the cloth. "Good morning, Sunshine." He kissed her forehead, waiting to see if she wanted more.

She reached to grab his face, and they kissed, once,

twice, more. Finally, she smiled and said, "G'morning, Holton Jefferson Corrigan. You're much too bright and shiny. What's going on?"

Holt chuckled briefly. She knew him all too well. He immediately told her about the telegram from Stebbins and its bad news. He apologized and said he needed to leave right away. "This looks bad, Laudie Kate. This feels like my hunch about Fort McKavett was correct."

Laudie Kate now wore worry all over her face. "Did the deputy say anything about Evie? Is she okay?"

"Deputy Brooks didn't say." Holt gave her the message to read for herself. "He knows she's a friend. I think he would have said something if she wasn't."

"When do you leave?"

"Soon. Now. I'll grab the saddlebags and gear in my quarters. Pick up some food at Jorgenson's store, and get my horses.

"I'll go to the store for you. What do you want?"

"Canned beans and peaches, one of their big packages of jerky, a little salt pork, a sack of dodgers, and a small bag of coffee. I've already got grain for the horses."

"You're easy to please." She laughed. "Anything else?"

He grinned in return and gave her a kiss. "Two or three apples, if they look good. Orion got me in the habit of having some on the trail." His face turned serious. "I need…I need some…ammunition too." He really did not want to bring it up. This was not just a visit.

Her countenance turned solemn as well, a reminder that he was not going on a picnic. "How much?"

He was doing a mental check of what he already had.

"Three boxes." His superstitious nature reminded him that was an odd number. "Make it four."

".44's, correct?"

He nodded. Something in the back of his mind was sad that his special lady knew what kind of bullets he used. "I have a Ranger account set up with them. They'll know."

They kissed and hugged again before departing to complete the tasks for his departure.

CHAPTER NINETEEN

Holt didn't take long at his quarters to gather his gear and extra clothes for the ride to Stebbins. Most of it was already loaded into his saddlebags and pack. Experience had taught him to be ready to ride at a moment's notice. He called to his furry friend, "What do you think, Tag? Are we ready? Have I forgotten anything?"

Holt's bay and buckskin were at the livery. He knew they were trail-ready. With things being quiet, they had enjoyed their own period of rest, getting good grain and new shoes. As usual, he would prepare two horses so he could ride harder and cover ground more quickly. Both mounts had their own saddles and bags. Each would carry a canteen, water bag, and rifle. The horse that Holt wasn't riding would be outfitted with a small set of panniers, a specially made pack that would tote the bulk of the food and any extra gear. Tag could lie on top of the pack if they weren't riding full out or needed a rest.

He was re-checking the saddle cinches and lashings on the pack when Mr. Hayes burst into the livery.

"Miss Hart said you would be here." As always, the fastidious clerk was intense and matter of fact. "I knew you would want this right away." Mr. Hayes presented the paper message and briskly strode back to his office before Holt could respond or offer a tip.

As Holt led his two mounts back to Laudie Kate's bungalow, he read the message:

HOLT:

RANGER FRANTZE WILL MEET YOU IN STEBBINS.

LOOK INTO THE ATTACK ON ELKINS.

ALSO, FORT MCKAVETT CASE MIGHT NOT BE CLOSED.

DAL HAS INFORMATION.

MCCOY.

Laudie Kate was waiting for him. He handed her the new message as he stowed the provisions in his saddlebags and pack.

Worry and determination filled her eyes. She would not allow tears. "Find out what happened to Moose. Take care of Evie, too. She has to be frightened."

His nod was solemn. He checked his cinches one last time. "All right, Tag, go do your business. We need to ride."

The dog didn't move, having already visited plenty of scrub bushes and posts while his master got things squared away, so Holt hoisted the dog up onto his saddle. He patted Tag to reinforce sitting still. "We'll be riding hard to start, boy. You're going to hang on with me."

In spite of the moment, Laudie Kate smiled. It was endearing the way the man she loved would talk to his dog as though he was a person. Her smile deepened, knowing maybe Tag could understand.

Holt turned, hat in hand, to Laudie Kate. Her kiss lingered, as did her embrace. She did not want to let him go. It was the feeling she dreaded when she first fell for him. She shook her mind of the thought. “You return to me in one piece, Holt Corrigan.”

He smiled and touched her face. “Of course I will.” His thumb softly traced along her scar. “You’re my forever, Laudie Kate.” Tears started to well in her eyes, but she would not let them fall.

She knew her voice would crack and could only mouth the words, “I love you.” She kissed him once more before he put on his hat and ran his fingers across the cardinal feather in the band. He stepped up into the saddle and adjusted Tag’s fit in front of him. He smiled one more time at Laudie Kate. “I love you too,” he called out, as he spurred his horse into a hard run.

CHAPTER TWENTY

It was well into the evening when Holt decided they had covered enough ground for the day. Having the two mounts and being able to swap, kept both horses from becoming overly weary. Even so, it was time to stop. He was familiar with this territory and knew he could find a suitable spot for the night. His mind churned, eager to get to Stebbins as soon as he could, but his heart was uneasy. Once again, he would be dealing with an adversary who had made deceit and violence a way of life. Why were there people like that?

A tiny, sometimes creek huddled up against a steep embankment. Nestled among bedraggled cottonwoods and gnarled oaks, this camp would provide shelter and good cover for defense as well as sufficient forage for his mounts.

After rubbing down the horses and checking their hooves, he dug into the pack for a fireless supper of corn dodgers and jerky. Dessert would be an apple. Tag was not overjoyed with the meal offering, but still happy to eat next to his master.

“If you don’t like the menu, maybe you can go catch something,” Holt teased his furry friend.

The young Ranger was about to begin his nightly ritual of wiping down his guns and touching them with the cardinal feather in his hat when the singers of the night changed their sound. His keen ear told him this was no warning of danger. The night world had not hushed, which would foretell of menace or threat. Rather, the tone of the sounds transformed, like a choir just changing its song. One of the horses blew softly and stomped once. Not agitated, but aware. Tag was quiet, no growling rising within him. The dog just sat and stared intently into the congregated darkness as though he was listening to a beckoning voice.

Holt was embraced with a feeling he was not alone. He had felt this inner sensation of peacefulness before.

Across the camp, an Apache stepped silently out of the shadows and into the moonlight. His perceptive gaze locked firmly on Holt.

Four Shields.

Like his previous encounters, Four Shields appeared to Holt with his hands open, arms stretched out at shoulder level, indicating a welcome and that he was weaponless. Holt knew now there was no need to react defensively. Even if he was a threat, Holt would not know—he would already be dead. No, this man possessed an otherworldly quality, an aura. Holt was sure he was some kind of priest or holy man.

If he was even a man at all.

Holt stood slowly, in a similar pose. Like Four Shields’s previous visits, he was experiencing familiar senses. He was calm. Untroubled. Fascinated.

The Apache was dressed as all the other times, with

deerskin leggings and high-topped boot-like moccasins tied at the ankles for support. He wore a long, fringed deerskin shirt that was dyed a shade of indigo with a dark belt fastened around his waist. A weathered medicine bag was at his side. His long, black hair hung loose with no braids and a simple, faded blue strip of cloth tied about his head.

"*Da'anen,*" Four Shields said.

"*I see you,* my teacher," Holt responded, not sure where he found those words.

"*T'agodel. It is good.*" He gestured for both of them to sit. "You have come far, Holt Corrigan. Following your *ndołkah*, listening to your *tsét'soyé.*"

"I am grateful to have them with me."

"As with all men of this world, the road ahead is filled with chaos."

Holt sat up straighter, listening fully.

"The path you are on, though, is filled with even more hardships and tests. The shiny star circle you carry makes it so. You are choosing to be a light that draws darkness to it."

Holt nodded in agreement.

"Important are your tasks. This is why the turmoil and strife you often face on your journey can be greater than most."

Memories turned Holt's face skyward in reflection.

"The darkness that you draw is filled with liars, thieves, and outlaws. Spirits walk closely with those who dare to meet those challenges." The night drew closer, as if everything in it leaned down to listen. "The spirits watched as you were challenged by *Ba'*, the *coyote.* The trickster is not necessarily evil, but in this case, it was, and there were three of them. *Dił táágí*. You would say, *blood trio*."

Holt nodded silently. The months spent tracking and fighting Meden Taliff, the very personification of evil, and his two stepbrothers—the brutal Kane Barlow, and Miguel Beltran, and the murderous priest known as *The Angel*, were indeed a dark journey. It took a toll, costing the lives of people dear to Holt, including his godfather Silka.

"You were not broken in spirit by those coyotes who dared try to tear you asunder. Nor were you undaunted when new tricksters crossed the paths of you and your star circle friends. The danger of your path was realized when bullets sent you to the shadow lands, drifting between worlds. A dangerous time. Before you could come back, your spirit had to decide which path to take."

Holt closed his eyes. The vividness of the clash with the Viklunds and the Carmichaels stormed through his memory. Getting shot and the tormented dreams that followed as he struggled for life exploded in his mind to an abyss he had struggled to forget.

The calm voice of Four Shields brought him back. "As a shadow, you asked the Creator to allow you a sense of purpose and to continue your path set by the spirits. You asked for all that is good and light to help you to be true. Your courage was rewarded with renewed life and the gift of a new spirit, this one chosen to truly walk beside you forevermore."

Laudie Kate, Holt thought.

Four Shields smiled, eyes gazing intently at the young Ranger. He leaned forward slightly. "There is another trickster to which you must now pay attention."

"Yes."

"Our Earth Mother is a nurturing and life-giving force. Yet, she can become angry, with power all should fear. Women who journey with us in this world have powers to embrace as well as to fear. They are able to bring life into this world—and to take it away. Their minds work in ways that men of your world can never understand. The miracle they have been bestowed with, the ability to carry life within, is what makes this so." The holy man paused, his countenance now becoming stern. "Which is why a trickster with a woman's heart can be especially vicious."

Holt gritted his teeth with comprehension.

"As you know, coyotes like to mix their goodwill and warmth with fear, chaos, confusion, and menace. These are all easily within her reach, like the others you have faced," the Apache affirmed. "But, because she can add beauty, passion, temptation, and lust, she becomes harder to detect and fiercer to fight."

I can resist, Holt thought.

Four Shields's eyes squinted ever so faintly to go with a slight tilt of his head. "Do not make the mistake of overconfidence. Or underestimating. The result could be devastating."

Holt wondered just how this holy man seemed to know what he was thinking.

"I cannot say how you will fare because I cannot see down your path," Four Shields said, sweeping his hand and arm to indicate the wide world around him. "The spirits can guide, but they cannot offer the full vision of the road ahead."

He paused for a moment before speaking again. "You must take care. A coyote does not respect the values of your world. This one appears to be a master at causing confusion and convincing people to believe her. Her lies are bigger, unlike any you've seen. The chaos is meant to further her gain at the expense of all others. Remember, doing battle with such an adversary requires both your strength and your cunning. The ability to think without confusion must always be close at hand."

He stopped to gaze at Holt, to make sure everything was sinking in. "Remember, a trickster lives to deceive others but is always fooled in the end."

Four Shields's eyes locked onto Holt's chest, where his medicine pouch laid under his shirt. With a nod of his head and a point with his lips, he indicated that he wanted Holt to bring out his medicine pouch. The Apache dipped his hand into the large leather pouch at his own side. From it, he removed a smaller bag. He dipped his fingers inside and from it drew out a pinch of cattail pollen. As he sprinkled it into Holt's medicine pouch, he spoke again, "I tell you of these things because you are not of *the people*. I tell you of these things because you are special. I tell you of these things because you need to know that you are on a difficult journey," he advised. "Give thanks that the spirits have looked upon you in this way. The measure of a warrior is the size of his test."

Holt wanted to ask more but knew his moment with the holy man was ending.

Four Shields then raised his right hand in a blessing. "I pray that you keep your eyes open and your ears open. But most of all, keep your heart and your mind open. Your spirits will guide you if you listen."

He departed into the darkness as quickly and silently as he appeared. Tag was still calm and came to Holt for a head scratch. Holt listened hard for the sound of movement or a horse being ridden away. Nothing reached his ear. Only the night chorus returning to its original symphony.

Holt exhaled. As before, the Apache's counsel was helpful, but troubling. He wished Four Shields and the spirits following him had suggestions on trapping and subduing such a trickster—without costing the lives of his friends or himself.

Starting to bed down, he checked the sky, gauging that his head would be pointed north. He once again began the nightly ritual of wiping down his guns and touching each one with the cardinal feather from his hat. The holy man's words resonated through his soul. He knew enough about traditional Apache religion to know that it was mystical in its belief and based around the power of the living world. Nature explained everything in life for their people. That made sense to him and gave him comfort.

He did not know why he had been chosen by spirits or why he was deemed worthy to receive counsel from Four Shields. He was grateful, but the words he had heard were not at all comforting. He could feel chaos dawning in his personal horizon.

CHAPTER TWENTY-ONE

At first glance, the town of Stebbins appeared the same, but to Holt, there was a noticeable difference. Plenty of people were out along the boardwalks, hurriedly moving among stores and businesses, but heads were bowed and smiles were few. Everyone seemed focused only on themselves, eager to be done with their errands and move on.

One good thing, Holt noted, was that no one seemed to notice or care that a stranger with two horses and a dog just rode in. He had hoped he could remain inconspicuous, keeping his Ranger badge tucked away in a coat pocket. His coat was buttoned around him, keeping his deadly Smith & Wessons out of sight.

He rode through the main part of Stebbins, headed for the part of town where his old bungalow hideout was located—the tough and gritty part. Hard work and hard drinking were done at this end of town. Genteel folk were generally not found here after dark.

The livery, post office, telegraph station, and doctor's office were established nearly in the center of Stebbins.

The bathhouse, too. This middle area—situated as it was—with all the services required by all the denizens, unofficially separated the rough side from the rest of town.

During the Viklund operation, the bungalow allowed him to remain unnoticed and unidentified. He doubted he could use the little cabin again, but being down here, he hoped to blend in. This was also the eastern end of Stebbins, the direction from which Ranger Dal Frantze would likely be arriving.

No one appeared to be inside the cottage at the moment, so Holt tied the horses up out front. With a grain mill, lumber mill, wool factory, and even a mill for making barrel staves up and running nearby, plus several warehouses and three rowdy saloons, there was enough activity that he could hide in plain sight.

Near the bungalow sat one of those seamy drinking establishments, Grainger's. Late morning was not yet a busy time for the saloon, so Holt grabbed a plate of beans and tortillas and asked for a small ham steak as well. He hurriedly ate the beans and tortillas, wrapping up the ham to give to Tag, who was waiting patiently outside.

As he was leaving, he spied a folded-up issue of the *Observer*, the Stebbins newspaper, sitting on a table under crusty plates and empty mugs. The crumpled paper turned out to be two issues—the two most recent. He looked around. No one seemed to notice or mind if he took them.

As Tag enjoyed his ham steak, Holt sat on a bench outside and thumbed through the issues. He flipped through each edition twice and double-checked to see that he had all the pages. There was no article about the attack at the Rising Goose, and no mention of the shooting of their Stebbins lawmen. He checked the publication dates. Both had been printed since Moose and Baxter had been shot. He mumbled to his floppy-eared friend, "You'd think the murder of their marshal would be big news, huh Tag?"

With no sign of Ranger Frantze, Holt decided to visit the Hanson Livery. He left his bay tied up at the bungalow and gave Tag the rest of the ham steak to keep him with the horse.

The man operating the stable today was not the man Holt remembered. A good thing. The previous employee would surely recognize the young Ranger.

"G'mornin'!" Holt donned his best Orion drawl as he greeted the filthy stableman. "I was wonderin' if ya might have time ta take a look at this buckskin. Heard sum funny clinks comin' from his back shoes. Might be loose." He tossed a coin into the man's calloused and grubby hand.

The man looked at the coin and pocketed it. "New ta town." He nodded, his words not a question.

"Jus' rode in. Wanted ta get 'im checked an' then find sum grub."

"Darn nice horse. Yer rig too," the stableman noted, still not moving to look at Holt's mount.

Holt did not respond to the man's observation. His eyes and presence could wait this little game out.

Momentarily, the man spat a stream of tobacco, wiped his hand across his dirty overalls, and shuffled to the back of Holt's horse. He bent over and gathered up one of the buckskin's legs so he could take a closer look at the hoof and shoe. "Ya here on bizness?"

Holt did not respond right away, gently rubbing the side and neck of the buckskin. "Nah, jus' passin' through. Got sum work in Overfield."

"Hmm," the man grunted. "This one looks fine. Good 'n' tight." He repositioned himself to look at the other hoof. After several moments, he declared it to be in good shape as well. As he stood, he loosed another thick stream from his chaw. "Some folks from bayou country is lookin' for men." He presented the information casually, not looking at Holt, still studying the leg structure of the buckskin.

Holt let the man's information sit hanging in the air without a reply.

The liveryman gestured at the Winchester in Holt's saddle scabbard. "Well, if'n yer inclined, there's some hirin' goin' on, especially if ya know how ta use that."

Holt waited a few moments to respond. "Bayou country? Workin' riverboats?"

"Not 'ntirely sure. I've gotta job, so I'm jus' passin' along what I've heard."

Holt stepped in to check the cinch on his saddle, again waiting to answer. Finally, he stood and smiled at the stableman. "I 'preciate th' information, my friend, but I really am movin' on. Do I owe ya anythin' else?"

"Nah, ya dun took care've it."

Holt nodded with a forefinger to his hat brim and led his buckskin away.

The livery operator called out as Holt walked away, "Big man in a fancy suit. Plays cards at Bellinger's. If'n yer so inclined."

The afternoon crept slowly. There was still no sign of Ranger Frantze. Holt wasn't concerned, just restless. He had wandered into a couple of the bars on this end of town. There were still not many customers, and those he did make small talk with were not the types to glean information from. The ones he did speak with did not want to talk about the attack on the sheriff and marshal, acting as though there were others listening in.

It was getting close to end of day. Holt figured that anyone staying in the bungalow might soon be coming home and wonder about the horses tied out front. One of the close by storehouses had several horses outside, so he moved his mounts to blend in and be with them. A carpentry shop sat next to a lumber mill. Two people were sitting on one of the benches outside. With another bench free, Holt and Tag made themselves comfortable.

The young Ranger pulled the folded Stebbins newspapers from a coat pocket and began thumbing through them again. There were articles about the bank president becoming the new mayor and even a follow-up piece about Christer Viklund escaping from Fort McKavett. Both stories reported the essence of the headlines, but were short on details.

Holt leaned over to scratch Tag's ears. "It doesn't make sense, boy. I thought this town liked Moose. Baxter too. I wonder if they even sent a posse after the attack." Tag's eyes and tail were appreciative of his master's touch. The dog's answer was that he thought it was time for supper again.

"You hungry, boy? Me too. Let's go find something."

As Holt stood and tucked away the newspapers, he spotted Dal riding into town. He watched as the dusty Ranger trotted past. Although the image of this rider was striking—Comanche-long hair, midway down his back, an eye patch, and a sawed-off shotgun slung around one shoulder—no one seemed to take notice of him or even care as he entered town. Holt was fairly confident no one recognized the one-eyed Ranger riding a dirty, nondescript horse. Back during the Viklund operation, Dal had posed as one of the Swede's ranch hands and was rarely in town.

Wh-eeet cheer cheer cheer. Holt whistled his version of a simple cardinal birdsong and repeated it.

Dal picked up the sound and casually glanced in the direction from where it came. He gave a slight smile and guided his horse toward the lumber mill where Holt had just been sitting.

Holt stood and began checking the headstalls of his mounts at a storehouse hitching post. Dal eased his sorrel into the same rail. Someone else's horse stood between them.

The one-eyed Ranger did not look at Holt, but said quietly, "Good to see you." He took off his flat-brimmed, open crown hat, and slapped it against his arms and chest in an attempt to knock away trail dust. Dismounting from his horse, he stamped some life back into his feet and knees.

Dal smoothed his hair back and donned the hat. The strap of the black patch over his left eye helped keep his long, dull auburn hair in place. The eye patch, like Holt's scar, was a physical record of war's cost. Looking in an entirely different direction, Dal asked, "How long you been here?"

Holt inspected a fleck on a saddlebag and shrugged. "Not long. Late this morning. Just about to go grab some supper. You hungry?"

"Absolutely. I'm sure this guy is too." He patted the neck of his leggy chestnut.

Holt gestured with his head. "Livery is as good a

place as any for your mount. The hostler's a character. He was eager to tell me there were *bayou folks* around looking to hire men."

"Is that so?" He reached to loosen the cinch on his saddle, not completely, but enough to give his horse relief. "I'll go get a little grain for this guy an' see what he has to say."

Holt gestured inconspicuously with his head. "Meet me at Grainger's when you're done. It's out of the way until we're ready to be seen."

A half-hour later, Dal joined Holt in the rough-looking saloon. He ordered tequila, and Holt nursed a beer while they waited for plates of beans. For supper, the cook had added barbacoa to the pot.

"Heard anything so far?"

Holt looked at Dal. "Not much yet. The only thing new came from the livery. He tell you about any jobs?"

Dal nodded. "Yeah. Only he din't say it was *bayou country* folk. He flat-out said that a fella from New Orleans was lookin' for men. He din't specify the job, only that someone needed to be willin' to use a gun an' take orders. Told me a fat man wearin' a fancy suit could be found at Bellinger's." He sipped at his tequila. "I don't remember, that somewhere further in town?"

"Yes. A bit higher-class than this place, but not much. Billiards and poker there."

Their meals arrived. Instead of eating in silence like most, the two lawmen quickly shared what they knew.

"You weren't in town as much during our Viklund

work," Holt began. "But Stebbins is different now. It's not as friendly. People seem guarded."

"I hear there's a new mayor an' a new judge."

"I haven't talked to anyone about that, but the wire from Deputy Brooks and the newspaper both said so," Holt affirmed. "A woman from New Orleans, Isla Thorne, is buying up all the ranches east of here."

Dal filled Holt in on the details of the suspicious interview with the Fort McKavett major. "He had to have been in on it, even if it was just to shield that crooked quartermaster." Dal sneered. "If he isn't guilty, I'll eat my horse."

"I wonder about the bank here, too. A lot of ranch land changed hands, forcibly. And no one there spoke up?"

They both paused to finish eating.

"Here's something odd, Dal, no one I've talked to will comment on Moose's attack. Their newspaper didn't report on it either."

"That's more'n odd." Dal glowered, angry that his friend, Moose, was hurt and that no one seemed to care.

"I haven't really dared to go into the main part of town," Holt acknowledged. "I don't even know where Moose or Evie are staying. Or Deputy Brooks, for that matter."

"Sounds like we need to fan out an' find some answers."

Holt agreed. "Why don't you visit the Blue Sky Inn? I'm too well known there. I'll go to this Bellinger's place. Let's meet behind the Blue Sky in a couple hours."

"All right. We used to say, 'Keep your powder dry.'"

Holt grinned. "Be careful yourself."

As the day gave in to dusk, Holt departed for Bellinger's. He crossed the street, walking between his horses to stay relatively unnoticeable. Tag followed just behind. He eased down a side passageway to the alley behind the Blue Sky. He was familiar with this route, having used it to stay out of sight during the Viklund operation.

Holt did not have to wait long before Dal made an appearance and spoke up first. "For one thing, this whole town is afraid of this Isla Thorne," Dal said. "An' no one knows much of anythin' about Moose, like he never existed. You said it, people seem nervous, as though they're scared someone's listenin'." He went on to report hearing rumors that this Thorne woman had brought gunmen here from Louisiana.

"Makes sense, she is from New Orleans," Holt said. "Deputy Brooks's wire said she had forty gunmen!" He paused. "We got trouble, Dal."

"What's happened?"

"I never saw the fat guy in Bellinger's who was supposed to be hiring guns. But I did sit next to a couple of whiskey-soaked chuckleheads wearing fancy new pistol rigs. Bought after *the bayou lady* hired them."

"Isla Thorne?"

"Yes." Holt continued. "They were talking about their friends striking Lillian Whitman's ranch. Tonight. They were drinking their relief that they didn't have to go."

"That's the widow's place," Dal grimaced. "Damn, that Thorne woman moves fast."

Holt nodded. "Orion's there. I doubt he knows what's about to hit 'em. We gotta ride. Where's your horse?"

"Out front."

Just then, the owner of the Blue Sky Inn, Migual Navarro, opened the back door. He threw a big pan of greasy water before noticing the two men and a dog standing there.

Navarro noticed Tag first. Then Holt. "Señor Holt! Tag Along!" he blurted happily.

Holt put his finger to his lips to shush the friendly man. "Howdy, Miguel. We really don't want people to know we're here, understand?"

"*Sí. Sí.*"

Holt explained they were here to look into the shooting of the sheriff and the marshal.

The diminutive hotel owner shuddered. "Eet was terrible about Marshal Baxter and Sheriff Moose. Terrible."

"You should say nothing. To anyone. You haven't seen us. You haven't seen a Ranger in weeks. Got it?"

The little man bobbed his head in understanding.

"There's one more thing you can do for me, Miguel."

"Anytheeng, Señor Holt."

"We have business tonight, riding hard. I'm going to leave a horse here. Will you take Tag too, and keep him here until I return? We might not be back 'til morning."

A broad, happy grin crossed the hotel owner's face. "*Sí*, Señor Holt! I can do so."

"Thank you, my friend. I can ride easy knowing he's here with you." Holt smiled. "Let me get him coaxed inside before I duck out. You know he'll want to follow me."

"*Sí*. I know there's some stew and beeg soup bone in my keetchen for your brave Ranger dog! I make sure he stays."

Holt nodded and shook Navarro's hand. "*Gracias*, my friend."

CHAPTER TWENTY-TWO

The ghostly shapes loomed before Texas Ranger Holt Corrigan in the darkness. Before being spotted himself, he had spied the two gunmen and reacted, silently launching himself like a puma into the grama grass surrounding the right side of the W Bar L ranch shed. The little shack was on the far side of the large barn, too far from the ranch house for him to know what exactly was going on. He knew enough, though, to know that these were not Lillian's riders. They were hired gunmen.

He crawled in the grama grass and underbrush until he was lying on his chest in a marshy gully twenty feet away. His hair swept along the shoulders of his trail-worn duster, the long coat keeping the random puddles of water from completely soaking his clothes.

He laid his Winchester on a small bank of the gully. Moonlight shivered on the spotty pockets of water that laid in scattered patches along the shallow ravine. Despite efforts to stay dry, his right trouser leg was wicking up some of the dark water.

He would hide here until the gunmen got close.

Carefully, he reached inside his coat for one of the Russian Smith & Wesson pistols nestled in his shoulder holster. His hand found the black grips, inlaid with an ivory jaguar silhouette. If he was discovered, the short gun would be better than his rifle. He drew the revolver with one hand. The other hand's fingers ran across the cardinal feather in his hat band. For luck.

Holt's powerful inner panther spirit was bristling, coiled for attack. As the men drew nearer, he froze. Not surprisingly, stalking prey came naturally to him. He was certain they were not aware of his presence. A good thing. A shootout now would likely prove devastating for the people inside the ranch house, especially his Ranger friend, Orion.

The *ndołkah* in Holt wanted to attack. The *tsét'soyé* in his heart convinced him that lying in wait was the right play. A smart move. Determine exactly what was going on. And where. And who.

Holt hoped that Ranger Frantze was on the other side of the ranch yard, waiting for his signal to advance. Although they had both been deeply involved in bringing down the Viklund/Carmichael operation, Holt had not directly worked with Dal. He did not know the man's heat-of-battle tendencies, but knew that Frantze had seen plenty of action during the war in a squadron under General John Hunt Morgan. Morgan's Raiders laid waste to federal supply lines from Tennessee to Kentucky to Ohio. Besides, he knew that Captain McCoy, Moose Elkins, and his own partner, Orion Higbee, held Dal in high regard. That was good enough.

So far, he had not heard any shots fired. A nagging thought toyed with Holt's emotions that the widow and

Orion had been captured, or worse. However, as he observed the two men, it was clear they were not keeping watch—they were searching.

Holt and Dal had no idea how many gunmen Isla Thorne had sent tonight. He guessed it would be eight to twelve. They would not know for certain until this was all over.

The two assailants he had been stalking were now standing above him on the overgrown bank. Holt noted that these were not alert sentinels. Their rifles were not at the ready. Both had no interest in the ground surrounding them, including Holt's gully hideout. Their attention was fixed on the ranch house. Less danger there.

Holt did not lift his head. War had conditioned him how to remain unseen while out in the open. No movement was required. Complete patience was essential. Avoiding staring directly at the person was absolute, as eye contact would often make the man feel like he was being watched. He knew in his heart that he had learned these instincts from a previous life.

The wire from Gus Brooks said this New Orleans woman had forty men in her employ. They wouldn't all be here, would they? Or could forty include the men working at the ranches she now owned? At least two weren't here, Holt tried to humor himself—the drunk cowboys who told him of tonight's attack.

On their ride here, Dal said the rumors he heard were that Isla had hired Louisiana gunslinger Monroe Guidry and likely more outlaws from across that border. Word was that Guidry had already been sent to the W Bar L at least once to persuade Lillian Whitman to sell. It was apparent that Isla was rapidly trying to gain control of this part of Texas by any means she saw fit.

A darkness that was on edge was interrupted by casual conversation from the two Thorne men.

The young gunman, who looked like he wasn't even shaving yet, broke the stillness. "Still think the boss is gonna cash in tonight?"

The other intruder was older, more grizzled. "Yup. This widow's land'll make it four of a kind. The Windmill V, the Half Moon 6, River D, and now the W Bar L."

"Sure thought it was gonna be easier. Monroe said he'd make that widow sign over her place an' hang ever'-body who got in the way."

"Seemed like a lotta effort. Shoulda just shot 'em all an' got it over with."

The younger man let that observation go without comment.

The older gunman continued, "I'm sure Monroe had orders from Mizz Thorne. You know, sendin' a message an' all that. Besides, we did shoot the first guy tryin' to protect the widow."

"Guess that's why we brought all've us, huh?"

They both casually peered across the ravine, toward where Holt was concealed.

The youthful one asked another question. He was showing himself to be inexperienced and nervous. "I heard Monroe was suppos'd ta give the widow a thousand dollars so it looked all legal like."

"Yup, heard that too. The bank wants it that way, I suppose."

"It's worth more'n that, ain't it? This place?"

"Whattayou think?"

The two took a few steps. Holt could tell they were just giving cursory glances at the inky blackness around them.

"So, how did the widow an' that big damn leprechaun get away?" The young outlaw couldn't help but ask what was on his mind. "Did she really take the money too?"

"I dunno about the money. It's Talbert's fault. He let the old lady visit the outhouse, and the big sumbitch jumped 'im. Took 'is guns."

"Think either of 'em is any good at shootin'?"

"I doubt it. She's a woman, he's a cattleman. Don' really wanna find out though."

The young man snickered restlessly. "If they're even still aroun'."

"Well, they've been smart enough 'bout stayin' quiet. If they had any sense, they'da high-tailed it outta here."

The fresh-faced outlaw wanted to ask why, with the plan falling apart, they all hadn't retreated and left the widow alone. He thought better of it and tried a different question. "So, now Monroe is in a standoff with the tall, lanky guy an' one of her riders?"

"Yup, 'till we find the widow an' bring her back."

The young gunman exhaled. This was not what he expected to do tonight.

The older one spoke up. "You jus' look alive, Jimmy. She's fought off ev'rthing to this point. I think she's still here, figgerin' out what to do next."

The youthful Jimmy grunted his agreement.

"Here, hold this." The older gunman handed Jimmy his rifle. "I've gotta take care of somethin'." He walked a few steps to a cottonwood and began unbuttoning his trousers.

"Dang, I've had to do that forever." The young man propped both their guns against a large, gnarled post oak and stepped around it to relieve himself as well.

They were so intent on doing their business, the two

did not hear Holt rise from the concealment of the gully and skulk toward them. By the time they became aware of any threat, the shadowy presence exploded upon them. Holt's gun barrel hammered against the older man's head, crumpling him into the undergrowth. The young intruder tried to make a grab for his gun, but he was too slow. Holt's pistol whipped across his face, and he reeled backward, buckling into a heap. A soft groan was the only response as Holt hit him again in the head.

He immediately looked around, determining whether his charge had alerted any others. The surrounding darkness was still silent.

Fortunate.

He holstered his Smith & Wesson and drug the two bodies down into the gully, throwing their weapons in the opposite direction. Deciding he could probably move unobserved down in this ravine, he retrieved his Winchester and began making his way slowly, careful not to splash in the creek bed.

Holt still did not know how many men he and Dal were facing, but at least he knew why Thorne's gunmen were prowling around the ranch. The widow and her foreman, Big Jeff, had somehow escaped. He also was relieved to hear that Orion was still alive inside the ranch house.

He quietly levered a round into the rifle, but did not cock it.

Leaving the area of the shed, Holt recognized another building, the bunkhouse. From the vantage point of the creek bed, he could see two sides. No one there. He decided to chance leaving the relative safety of the gully and make his way up to the side of this building out of his sight.

Reaching the top of the bank, he quickly trotted into position. No one here either. The absence of lights inside the bunkhouse and its open door told him the building had been searched and found abandoned.

He continued on, gliding stealthily through the night, all his panther senses alert. Any night sounds had completely disappeared. Definitely a confirmation that Thorne's men were still lurking. Yet, only the shadowy shapes of rocks and trees revealed their locations. This darkness could easily hide armed men, but it gave Holt good cover as well—a deadly quandary in whoever showed themselves first.

His stalking had shifted the medicine pouch under his shirt. He reached to reset it back to its rightful spot near his heart. The move was also a natural way to give tribute to his special medicine—an appreciation and request for guidance.

To his far left, a stirring near a patch of skinny cedar elms became the gray silhouettes of gunmen. Holt took a deep breath, drawing in murky, cool night air, and slowly crouched. About fifty yards away, the silhouettes came into focus. With his rifle aimed in their direction, he quickly determined how many there were.

Moonlight washed stingily across the intruders. Five. There were five. Obviously searching for the two W Bar L prisoners who got away. Shadows way across the property and disjointed voices borne through the darkness told Holt that more men were probing on the other side of the ranch. His inner voice admonished, *Eight to twelve? There's closer to twenty here.* He grimly refocused his attention on the gunmen.

A tall man with ammunition bandoliers belted across his coat gestured his rifle in the direction of Holt's position. "Fox, go look over there, check that bunkhouse again." He turned to another man and ordered, "Clete, you go over there. They gotta be here somewhere. Remember, they've got Talbert's guns."

Holt watched the outlaw named Fox creep toward the bunkhouse. He wore a beat-up Confederate forage cap and a filthy barn coat with two guns belted at his waist. Even at this distance, he could see that the man was uneasy, stepping slowly, cautiously.

Holt watched him approach, mindful to not look him in the eye. Even in the low light, Holt could see that this gunman's pistols were tied down. As the man moved further away from his friends, he became more spooked. Seeing sounds and hearing shadows, he swung his rifle back and forth at every imagined onslaught. If Holt charged him now, it was highly likely the jumpy man's finger would squeeze the trigger the instant Holt hit him. What if he didn't charge, but just walked up to him…

Noiselessly, Holt propped his Winchester against a large tree, then circled to the outside and skirted around the back of the gunman and in line with the bunkhouse. It would appear he had just come from there.

The ploy was risky, being exposed like that, but he was counting on no one paying attention to another man walking freely, out in the open.

Holt ran his fingers across the cardinal feather in his hatband and pulled the brim lower to help cover his face. He drew one of his Smith & Wessons and walked toward the man.

The brown-haired gunman still had his back to the bunkhouse and had not heard Holt's stealthy advance.

"If you even breathe loud, I'll blow your head off." Holt snarled. The barrel of his pistol lifted the nervous man's chin to attention as the young Ranger's left hand grabbed at the receiver of the outlaw's rifle, sliding his hand between the rifle's cocked hammer and the readied bullet in the chamber. Holt's pounce was a blur. As expected, the man reflexively pulled the trigger. The rifle's hammer hit the fleshy part of Holt's hand between the thumb and first finger, pinching it hard. It was what Holt anticipated, his lightning-quick action keeping the strike from reaching the cartridge.

His hand held in place on the rifle, Holt commanded, "All right, Fox, let go of this gun, real easy like." His words were a growl as he tugged the rifle from the scared man's grip, his hand still blocking the hammer. "Now, move over to the shadows. Do it naturally… There you go."

Tucked into a safer pocket of darkness, Holt holstered his Smith & Wesson, then carefully removed his hand from the rifle. He recocked the weapon and stuck its barrel to the outlaw's head.

"Listen up, I'm a Texas Ranger and I won't hesitate to shoot you. Understand? As quiet as you can, tell me what's going on. I'll know if you're lying, and I hate liars."

"D-Don't…d-on't…d-don't," the man whined. "I-I'm jus' doin' what the boss says."

"Quieter, damn you." He jammed the rifle barrel into the man's neck for emphasis.

The man's whisper was fearful. "I-I do wh-what I'm told. P-P-Please Ranger. I-I-I'll tell the truth."

"First, how many of you no-good bottom feeders are there?"

"I-I d-dunno. I-I d-didn't count. Sixteen? Seventeen? I-I-I dunno for sure."

In terrified fragments, he went on to tell Holt that Monroe Guidry had led this attack on the W Bar L. Isla Thorne had ordered Guidry to force the widow to sign over her ranch to her. They had ambushed her when she was out in the barn doing chores. A tall, lanky man was with her. He had been walloped in the head. A ranch hand had been shot as they all left the barn. They used both prisoners to get inside and capture two more men in the kitchen.

Holt exhaled. "So why hasn't she signed? Why are you all still here?"

"T-Two of them escaped. The widow and a huge red-haired guy." The nervous man shook his head. "Monroe's gonna make Talbert pay for lettin' 'em get away."

The man did not know much about Isla Thorne, saying he had only seen her once or twice, but never spoke to her. He did say that Monroe Guidry was from New Orleans and was a friend of Isla's right-hand man, Madigan Sanders.

Satisfied that this man was no more than a lackey and could not provide more information, Holt whacked him over the head with the barrel of the rifle, dropping him to the ground.

Holt quickly scanned the surrounding area. No one observed what had just happened. He breathed a sigh of relief. The Thorne men were spread out, most searching away from the yard and the outbuildings. He dragged the unmoving body behind the bunkhouse and into a shallow drainage ditch.

He quickly stripped the man of his guns, shoving one of the revolvers into his own belt and throwing the other pistol and rifle into the dark field beyond the ranch yard. As he was doing this, he weighed the idea of systematically disposing of the Thorne attackers as he had done with these first three.

No. That would be nearly impossible given how many there were. He would run out of nighttime, too. No, he scolded himself, that plan ends in discovery and a shootout, the odds of which were not in his favor.

He heard someone coming through the brush. He crouched in preparation for a fight.

It was Dal.

The one-eyed Ranger pointed at the downed body with his sawed-off shotgun. "Saw you dispatch this fella."

"Yeah, that's three now. Plenty more, though."

"Thought I'd show you who I found." He turned and waved. A huge creature with a mop of unruly red hair and matching beard lumbered noiselessly out of the shadows. A few steps behind, Lillian Whitman materialized from out of the darkness. Taller than average, square-shouldered with a proud bearing, the widow's light brown eyes looked weary, yet her expression was resolute. Her smoky silver hair was pulled back into a long, broad braid.

"I think you know these two," Dal whispered. The enormous mountain of a man was Jeff Clark, *Big Jeff*, the W Bar L foreman, fiercely dedicated to his boss.

Holt acknowledged Big Jeff but spoke to Lillian. "I'm glad to see you're all right, Mrs. Whitman."

"Seems like whenever I see you, Ranger Corrigan, all hell's breaking loose." Lillian managed a somber smile. "But I'm sure glad you're around when it does."

Big Jeff explained, "I tried ta git her outta here fer safety but she wuzn't havin' any of it."

"I'm not leaving. This is my house."

Holt nodded his understanding.

Big Jeff continued, "There's three invaders at th' house, holdin' vigil ov'r Orion an' one of our hands, Tooley. Orion got whonked on th' head purty good, but I think he's alright."

Lillian spoke up, "One of the three intruders is on the porch by the front door, another is out guarding the back door. The third one's inside, but he's the leader."

Holt nodded. It matched the number Fox gave him—the gunman he just clobbered.

Big Jeff said, "There were four of 'em at th' house ta begin with. One less now." He grinned. "Mizz Whitman pretended she needed to visit th' outhouse. I convinced 'em she wasn't goin' out alone. When she went inta th' little house, I worked 'im over an' he provided us these guns. They all deserve ta die fer whut they did ta Brody."

"They shot Brody when they brought me and Orion from the barn," Lillian added. "He hollered stop and stood his ground with a pitchfork. They just shot him and moved on." She held back tears, swallowing them into anger and grim determination.

Holt watched the widow and gritted his teeth, knowing the work ahead of them this night.

Dal rechecked the loads in his sawed-off shotgun. "How're we gonna play this, Holt?"

"Even with the three of us, two more if you count our friends inside—"

Lillian cut in on Holt's observation. "Don't leave me out, Ranger Corrigan. I've been shooting and fighting a long time."

Big Jeff spoke up as well. "We gots two more riders, Sammy Lee an' William, but they's out in th' line cabin. Bet they don' even know we's in trubble."

Lillian continued, "The one they call Monroe, the leader, has a shotgun trained directly on Orion. Plus, all his men are spread out around the property. We can't just rush in."

She had a long-barreled Colt revolver, and Big Jeff held a Henry carbine, the guns they had acquired.

"Whatever we do, this Henry only has twelve ca'tridges in it. Mizz Whitman's gotta half belt of .38's fer that Colt. Not a lot."

Holt envisioned a plan now. One that could work. He hoped.

He looked at his fellow Ranger, a wry grin on his face. "Dal, you were one of General Morgan's Raiders. We always heard about the shenanigans you pulled on the Yanks. You up for running another bluff?"

Dal's wide grin matched Holt's. "I ain't scared."

CHAPTER TWENTY-THREE

Holt walked toward the house with Big Jeff posing as his prisoner, his huge arms held behind him as though he was tied up. The young Ranger had grabbed the Reb forage cap from the last downed gunman and pulled it low on his head in an attempt to keep his face covered. His rifle was cocked and readied. Big Jeff trudged in front of Holt with two pistols stuffed into his back waistband within easy reach.

Dal Frantze and the widow, Lillian Whitman, were headed for the back door, using the same strategy, with Frantze appearing to bring in the owner of the W Bar L. Frantze had his sawed-off shotgun as well as his usual complement of two snub-barreled Webleys and two throwing knives. Lillian had the commandeered pistol tucked into the back of her worn denim trousers.

As they neared the house, Holt gathered himself and lowered his rifle for a more casual approach. For this to work, he needed to get close without being discovered. Pretending to be one of Isla Thorne's men made the most sense to get inside, within reach of this Monroe Guidry.

At least he hoped it made sense. Part of a successful bluff was believing in it.

He said a silent tribute to his *tsét'soyé* bear spirits. It helped quiet his insides. His *ndołkah* panther spirit wanted to strike hard and fast.

"Well, lookit who you got there." A stringy-haired man with large buckteeth saluted them at the front door. "Thought you could get away, huh? You big damn goblin." The gunman, who looked more like a wagoner, moved out onto the porch to get a better view.

Holt and his prisoner kept walking, getting nearer the porch and the guard.

The gunman eyed the approaching prisoner. "Hard to hide a big ol' bastard like that. Where's the old lady?"

"I don't know. Just got this one." Holt growled his response, hoping the hoarseness sounded like someone in the gang. "Got any makin's? I'm out."

"You bet." The stringy-haired gunman reached for his vest.

As Big Jeff tromped up onto the porch, Holt stepped out from behind the huge man, his rifle leveled.

Holt quietly but firmly ordered, "Keep your hands right there where I can see them."

"Wh-What? Who the hell are you?" Surprise registered on the guard's face. His hands, filled with a tobacco sack and papers, were now held chest high.

"I'm Ranger Holt Corrigan, and your little game is over." He pulled the outlaw's pistol from its holster. "Turn around."

"Why?"

"Because I said so." Heat started to rise in Holt's intense face. "Got any more stupid questions?"

The stringy-haired man licked his oversized teeth and

tried to put on a brave front. "You're gonna regret this night. This is Isla Thorne's business."

"When I see her, I'll be sure to tell her you warned me like a good little flunky. Now turn around." He jabbed his Winchester into the man's belly.

The man slowly complied. As he did, Holt handed the man's pistol to Big Jeff, who emptied the gun of cartridges and placed it back in the man's holster. He pocketed the bullets. "Might need 'em fer later," he winked.

Holt stepped close to the guard and growled into his ear. "Now, you're going to lower your hands and walk inside. Tell your boss that the big foreman's been found." He pushed his rifle into the outlaw's back. "Say anything else and your brains will paint the room."

The W Bar L ranch house was easy to navigate. Holt had been here before on the chase to capture Lars Viklund and Linus Carmichael.

The huge one-story structure was a dog-trot design, probably left over from two big log cabins that eventually had a common roof thrown over them. Holt knew the foyer opened into a wide main hallway that led directly to the back of the house, where the kitchen and rear door were.

On the far right side of the house, a large doorframe marked the threshold of a parlor that gave way to two large, separate bedrooms. The showdown with Viklund and Carmichael had happened there.

The other side of the house contained the huge central room just inside the door to the left. Dominated by a large, stone fireplace, this main area contained sofas and wingback chairs, and included a big wooden dining table at the rear of the room.

Orion and the W Bar L rider, Tooley Barnes, sat on wooden, plain-backed chairs near the table. They faced away from the front door, their hands tied behind their backs but not to the chairs. A bloodied cloth around Orion's head was evidence of the ambush that opened the night's raid.

Seated back at the table, a lean man with copper-brown hair and a matching goatee played solitaire. His black cutaway coat was splayed open. His two pistols, holstered over a dark-gray silk vest, were visible, but it was the double-barreled shotgun placed next to his card game that was ominous. The cocked gun's barrels were aimed directly at Orion, seated just a few feet away. A steaming mug of coffee sat next to the weapon's trigger. It would take more effort to raise the mug for a sip than it would to cut the lanky Ranger in two.

Holt guessed this man had to be Monroe Guidry. The well-dressed man in the tailored coat had a presence that commanded the entire house.

Holt gritted his teeth. A killer from Louisiana. Isla's handiwork.

"Yes, Briggs?" Guidry's demeanor was smooth, composed. His free hand moved easily to rest on the butt of one of his matching revolvers. His other hand calmly set down the deck of cards. His quick glance confirmed the shotgun next to him still covered his tall prisoner.

"M-Mr. G-Guidry, h-he found that big damn foreman, the one who laid out Talbert," the stringy-haired guard replied woodenly as they left the foyer and entered the main room. He accompanied the answer with a thumb over his shoulder, motioning toward Big Jeff. Holt brought up the rear, purposefully staying hidden as much as possible.

A broad grin came to Guidry's face. "Very good! And the widow?"

"N-No sign yet, sir."

"Well…she'll turn up. This hothead was the one to worry about anyway." He slapped his hands good-naturedly on the table. "So, big'un, what do we do with you?"

A voice rang out from behind Big Jeff. "The question is, what do we do with *you*?" Holt stepped out from around the huge W Bar L foreman and swung his rifle at Guidry. "Hands where I can see them, or this ends right here." He took three more steps into the room, closing the gap between the barrel of his gun and the Louisiana gunslinger's head.

Instantly, Big Jeff raised his huge fists overhead and brought them thundering down onto the guard, Briggs's neck, crumpling him instantly. He then moved to quickly untie Orion, then Tooley.

The tall Ranger reacted by standing and swiftly grabbing the double-barreled shotgun that had been aimed at him for far too long. He trained it on Guidry with a barked order. "Here's two more reasons to stay real still-like."

Big Jeff pulled the two pistols from his back waistband and gave one to Tooley.

From the morning room table, Guidry grinned as though they had just presented him with a cake. "Well played, sheriff…er…marshal…?"

"Texas Ranger Holt Corrigan."

"Nicely done, Ranger." Guidry's untroubled demeanor remained. "You know, though, if you shoot, a lot of men with guns will come running."

Holt matched the outlaw's grin. "A few less than you think."

"Even if you don't shoot," the gunslinger continued, "my boys know you're here. Let's skip the bluffing, Ranger, before you get called."

Holt raised his Winchester. "How about we skip to the part where I shoot you in the head? A rattler usually stops being dangerous when there's no more fangs to back his play."

Guidry went silent as if waiting for something to happen.

Orion motioned with his head. "There's 'nother of these bastards through the kitchen, out the back door. Gotta long gun of some kind. Don' know if it's a rifle or scattergun."

"You know that man is getting help as we chat, Ranger Corrigan." Guidry's eyes now had a different smile than his mouth.

"Count the guns pointed at you, Guidry." Holt started with a smile, but ended with a hiss. "Whatever goes down, the first thing to happen will be that you will be shot. Your boys may get us in a rush, but not before that fine suit of yours gets riddled with holes."

Just then, Dal and Lillian burst through the back door, momentarily startling everyone inside. For an instant, Guidry flinched like he thought of going for his guns.

"Stupid thoughts make for stupid decisions, boy," Orion drawled. "Don't make that mistake."

Bolting the door immediately behind them, Dal announced, "Got the rear guard." A Thorne-hired gunman, bald-headed with a full, bushy beard, was shoved in front of them, hands over his head.

The prisoner started to speak, but Lillian slammed the

butt of the big Navy Colt into his head, dropping the outlaw to the floor in a silent heap. She smirked. "That's going to hurt even more when he realizes it was his own gun that turned out his lights."

"How're we doin' in here?" Dal asked.

"Small talk and advice," Holt responded. "You can help us gather up his guns." He turned to the captured leader. "All right, Guidry, get rid of those guns. Slowly." The lean, Louisiana gunman complied, unholstering one converted Remington Army revolver and placing it carefully on the table, followed by a second matching pistol. Dal swiftly moved to gather up the two weapons.

"Nicely done," Holt growled. "Now get rid of the gun behind your back. Pull it and drop it." Guidry's eyes and smile turned hard. He reached behind him, under his coat. A third Remington revolver thudded to the floor.

Orion motioned with the shotgun. "Time for you to stand up, pretty boy, and step out where we all can see you."

The gunslinger trudged his way into the main room. Holt's tone was deadly serious. "All right, Guidry, you and the rest of your vermin are under arrest. Ranger Frantze and I are charging you with murder, attempted murder, assault, and rustling." He purposefully did not identify Orion as a Ranger. "Tooley, is there any rope in the kitchen?"

"You betcha."

Tooley soon returned with rope and rags. He stepped in to tie Guidry's arms tightly behind him. To make sure he was trussed enough, the gunslinger's belt was added as a restraint. Big Jeff slapped the other two guards awake, then helped Tooley tie them up, securing both in a similar fashion with rope and their belts.

While that was going on, Lillian walked to the table. A document, a bill of sale, sat with Guidry's solitaire game. She crumpled the paper and moved to the fireplace. Her eyes locked onto the outlaw as she spat on the document and threw it into the fire.

"This will never work," Guidry intoned coolly. "Our men are everywhere out there. But I'll tell you what… you two are Rangers. I will let you go. We have no fight with you. We've only come to offer this woman a way out."

Dal couldn't help himself. "*A way out*? Is that what you crawfish call an attack like this?"

Guidry ignored the one-eyed Ranger and continued, "The widow and her men have been rustling cattle. Isla Thorne has made a generous cash offer for this ranch. Mrs. Whitman can accept the money, and she and her men can ride on."

"*Ride on?*" It was Lillian's turn to explode. She rushed from the fireplace to confront Guidry. "Rustling? That's a lie!" she shouted, her anger erupting. Unexpectedly cat-quick, she slapped him heavily across the face. "I should shoot you where you stand. I have never stolen anything in my entire life! You and that unholy bitch have threatened my life repeatedly! You killed Brody, you bastard!"

"How dare you strike me!" Guidry roared. "I should have killed you right off." He gathered himself. "There is time," he smiled serenely, evilly. "Yes, there is time. I will kill you. You and all your men."

His diatribe ended suddenly when Lillian drove her knee into the man's groin. He doubled over in instant pain and nausea. She raised the pistol in her hand, all set to pull the trigger and fire into Guidry's head. Orion hurried to her side, placing a firm but gentle hand on her arm. His smile was calming. "Not now," he whispered. Then he turned to Holt. "Jus' what *are* we gonna do with these flea-hopped frog butts, Ranger?"

"Seems the majority in the room would just as soon shoot 'em all," Holt surmised. "But we're going to take them into town. To jail. They'll stand trial."

Big Jeff blurted, "Th' new judge is bought 'n' paid fer by that no-good witch!"

Holt answered with conviction, "Then we'll wait for a *real* circuit judge, like Elsher Nash."

Big Jeff continued, "But…they's all hired by her—"

"Jeff, we're taking them to town. All of them." Holt was determined. "To be locked up and held for trial. We have to follow the law, even if it isn't easy."

Orion's brow was furrowed deep with concern. "So how're we gettin' the rest—"

"Guidry here is how." Holt smiled at the outlaw, who was still bent over, his breath slowly returning. He grabbed the back of the gunslinger's collar and stood him up. "You're going to stand on the porch and call in your men. Just like calling supper."

"That'll never work," Guidry sneered in between waves of pain and nausea.

"You'd better hope it does," Holt said simply.

Guidry's discipline and comportment left. "Isla will reward you. She's an impressive woman. Dangerous too. Got that voodoo behind her. She's got the ear and the bed of the lieutenant governor. He'll do anything she says. Anything. She is going to be a very powerful woman around here when the railroad comes. She has more guns around her than you can imagine. You'll be dodging bullets from here to hell and gone—"

"Guidry, I've had enough of your prattle." Holt indicated to Big Jeff and Tooley to tie a rag across his mouth. "Nothing more out of you until we're on the porch and I tell you to talk." He motioned for Orion to give Lillian the shotgun. "Mrs. Whitman and this scattergun will be the first to fire on you if you don't follow directions."

CHAPTER TWENTY-FOUR

It was not long before the two door guards were seated on the floor against the kitchen wall. Their hands were securely bound behind their backs, each with rags stuffed into their mouths to keep them quiet.

Holt, Orion, Dal, and the rest of the W Bar L defenders inventoried their weapons, including the confiscated guns. Orion retrieved his own guns from a bedroom.

"Everybody got enough guns and ammo?" Holt asked the group. The oil lamps inside the house had been dimmed but not extinguished. Dim light washed on the Reb forage cap that Holt wore, then drifted along his shoulder-length hair.

Orion stared at his partner and quietly asked, "Where'd ya get that damn Reb hat?"

"Borrowed it. Helped me get up on the porch with Big Jeff. The original owner is lying somewhere out by the bunkhouse."

Orion thought about mentioning Holt's real hat and the cardinal feather in the band, but thought better of it.

Everyone gathered around. Tooley stayed with the prisoners.

Holt laid out the plan. "Orion…you, Dal, and Big Jeff will head out the back door. Orion, bear left, take the side of the house closest to the bunkhouse. There were four in a group moving through there earlier. Dal, you take the other side. Big Jeff, you cover the back. Tooley guards the two already tied up. I will accompany their leader onto the porch." He looked at each of them for their understanding. "Lillian, position yourself by that front window, out of sight. Guidry is your only target. If this goes sideways, he dies, right away."

The enormity sank in.

"When we've got them all," Holt concluded, "Tooley brings rope, and we start tying up these sons of bitches."

Orion spoke up, and said, "How many, Holt?"

"Based on what the owner of this Reb cap said, they started with sixteen or seventeen, he wasn't sure. I got three early on. There's these three from the house. That leaves at least ten more. Assuming he told the truth."

Orion grinned. "So, plenny to go 'round." He grinned at Dal and Big Jeff.

"I'll give you guys five minutes to get in position and get cover," Holt said. "Try not to pop the first thing that moves. We need Guidry to call 'em all in."

Orion looked at the widow and smiled. "Stay low, darlin'. We've got some fun times ahead of us to cut loose on." Then he and Orion looked at each other and nodded. No words needed between warriors.

The three crept out the back door. Tooley braced it from inside.

Holt looked at Lillian. "Glad you fought back?"

"This is my entire life. I'm not giving it up." Her light-brown eyes glowed fiercely.

"I hoped you'd say that. Got enough shells?"

"A whole bagful. My carbine is right there, too."

Five minutes seemed an eternity. Holt told himself Orion and the others should have found their spots by now. It was time. He approached the well-dressed gunman seated at the front door and pulled the cloth from his mouth. "All right, Guidry, time to call in your men."

They stepped through the door and out onto the porch. Guidry first, followed by Holt, the Reb forage cap he wore pulled low. The young Ranger touched the medicine pouch under his vest and shirt. He wished he had his real hat with the cardinal feather. This was a bluff that required the assistance of all the spirits.

"If you say anything that sounds like a signal or a warning, you won't know how this ends." The *click* of the hammer on his already levered Winchester punctuated his promise.

Guidry called out into the darkness with a strong, loud voice. "All right, men…time to come on in! It's over. You hear? Come on in, it's over. The widow gave up. We're riding out." Holt was surprised he added the bit about the widow. Guidry made no attempt to start anything. Yet.

From across the property, Holt could hear voices muffled and clear, close and far, passing along Guidry's command. He tucked himself a little more behind the gang leader.

"This is a good start, Guidry," Holt whispered. "No shenanigans when they get closer. Remember, you make a good shield."

As they watched dark shapes move from the darkness and materialize into men, Holt rasped into the gunslinger's ear. "You needed all these guns to offer a widow cash for her land?"

"Business is business, Ranger."

"This isn't business, you bastard. This is murder and plunder."

"What's the difference?" Guidry sneered.

"How many of you river rats are on Louisiana wanted posters?" Holt growled.

"I don't know what you're talking about, Corrigan," Guidry responded, then called out again. "Come on, gentlemen. It's over!"

From the left side of the yard, two well-armed men approached from between the corral and the bunkhouse.

The shortest of the two wore a beat-up mariner's cap. He stopped to peer at the porch. "That fella wearin' the Reb hat up there with the boss. That ain't Fox."

"What's goin' on?"

"I dunno, and I don't like it. The boss's acting funny."

"Let's get closer. We can take 'im out if we need to."

They walked toward the porch, trying to look relaxed, untroubled. Other Thorne men were appearing from various locations all over the property.

Holt was relieved no one had seen or mentioned the three men he had downed earlier.

The two men from the corral and bunkhouse halted thirty feet from the porch. Suddenly, they swung their rifles into position.

Off to Holt's left, Orion shouted, point-blank to the two men, "Drop 'em, boys!" Another outlaw who had already made it to the porch was startled enough by Orion's order that he dropped his rifle.

The two men pointing their rifles did not comply. The short man in the mariner's cap aimed his gun toward the sound of Orion's voice.

Crack! Crack! Crack! Crack! Crack! Crack!

Six shots, as fast as Orion could chamber a bullet and squeeze the trigger, fired at the two men, dropping them both.

At the sound of the shots, Guidry threw himself to the deck of the porch. Holt knelt behind his body for cover.

Gunfire erupted in the darkness.

Two men appeared suddenly from the right, pistols drawn, running and firing at the porch. Holt levered and fired his rifle four times, sending both men sprawling. Holt fired once more at the body that continued to move.

Shots spat at the front of the house and the porch's wood flanks, finding their mark, sending ricochets and pieces of wood flying.

Lying there on the open platform, Guidry was helpless, his hands tied behind his back. Unable to take anymore, he sat up and cried out, "STOP! Stop! Stop this! Hold your fire! This is Monroe! Put your guns down! Come in. These are Rangers. They will kill me!" Holt heard the desperation in the man's cries. Real tears flowed down his cheeks.

Shots out front continued. Guidry dropped back down. Holt fired twice at a running shape that sprawled onto the ground. A rifle in the back yard barked four or five times. To his right, Holt heard Dal's sawed-off shotgun detonate twice.

Then, as quickly as it started, silence abruptly took over.

The night had changed. Thorne's men lay dead and injured. Slowly, the remaining attackers—two of them—approached the porch, arms in the air.

Tracking in from his cover on the left, Orion hollered to the surrendering outlaws, "Drop your guns an' step away. Do it now!"

Holt took the time to reload and check on the still-prone Guidry. Blank, lifeless eyes stared back at him. The defeated leader was bleeding from a slice on his cheek where a chunk of porch wood had ricocheted. But the real damage was elsewhere. Guidry's tailored coat and vest were riddled with holes. His starched white shirt now blossomed red. His own men had cut him down.

The first of Isla's gunmen to make it to the porch and surrender his rifle, was also lying motionless, having been caught in the hailstorm of bullets.

Before long, Dal emerged from the right side of the house, announcing, "Big Jeff an' I got two. They won't be bullyin' women or anyone else for that matter." He looked at Orion, who was guarding the unharmed prisoners. "Gimme those bogholes. They can carry bodies."

Under Dal's watchful eye and brandished sawed-off shotgun, the two surrendering gunmen made an organized display of dead outlaws in the front yard. Big Jeff himself carried the body of Brody Bennett, the W Bar L ranch hand, to be laid out in the bunkhouse. Lillian had instructed him that's where Brody should go for now.

Holt pointed out to Dal's body-gathering crew where he had stashed the three men he coldcocked earlier. They would be fine except for massive headaches. The young Ranger also retrieved his hat, tossing the Rebel forage cap at the man from whom it was appropriated. Dal had the captives deposited next to the array of their dead compatriots.

Bodies gathered, Big Jeff and Tooley immediately began tying all the captives up. Lillian also asked that the two tied up inside her house be removed at once. They were added to the collection against the porch.

Although all the surviving outlaws appeared to have dropped their rifles and unbuckled their handguns, both Holt and Orion checked each man for hideaways while Dal stripped the dead men of weapons. Soon, they had acquired an impressive mound of firearms and knives.

As all of this was happening, the sounds of galloping horses in the night reached the yard. All of the W Bar L defenders instantly raised their weapons.

Big Jeff hollered, "Hold yer fire! That's Sammy Lee an' William!"

Jumping down from lathered horses, the last of Lillian's riders were as breathless as their horses. William, a young black man, declared, "We heard the shooting from the line cabin! Came as quick as we could." He, Sammy Lee, Brody, and Tooley were the remaining W Bar L riders who had endured the hardship of the past year at the ranch. The intimidation and violence from the Viklunds and Sheriff Carmichael had not run them off. Nor had the recent threats from Isla Thorne. They, like Big Jeff, were devoted to their boss.

"If ya don' have a gun, get one from that pile," Big Jeff ordered.

Holt walked up. "Mighty glad to see you boys. Somewhere fairly close by, there's going to be horses that belong to these bastards. Find 'em and bring 'em here."

In the blanketing darkness, while the W Bar L

defenders were preoccupied with all of the post-fight tasks, one gunman watched from a hidden vantage point. When the two riders arrived from the line cabin and held everyone's attention, the figure in black clothing slipped away into the night.

CHAPTER TWENTY-FIVE

False dawn would soon flirt with the darkness. The W Bar L defenders worked quickly and quietly to tie up all their hard-gained prisoners. The Thorne horses that Sammy Lee and William discovered were being brought into the yard.

"These are all you found?" Holt asked, indicating the outlaws' horses.

"Yassuh," Sammy Lee said. "In two groups. Eight behind the barn and eight more by the haymow."

Holt nodded. They had seven prisoners and nine dead outlaws. That added up. Something inside him still wondered, though, if that had been all the Thorne men here tonight.

Big Jeff and the three W Bar L riders tied dead bodies on the saddles of retrieved horses, then concentrated on putting prisoners onto mounts. Dal kept a heavily armed watch as the captives, arms already bound securely behind them, were hoisted up and tied to saddles. Earlier, he had suggested to Holt that they make these survivors walk all the way back to town. They decided it would be impractical and slow.

Inside the ranch house, Holt conferred with Orion and Lillian about the remainder of the plan. The night's conflict had been settled, but the fight with Isla Thorne was far from over. It was decided that Orion, Big Jeff, and Sammy Lee would stay behind to protect Lillian and the ranch. The two Rangers—Holt and Dal—plus W Bar L men—Tooley and William—would escort the Thorne men to town.

Eerie pre-dawn light dappled the ranch yard's peculiar assemblage. Horses blew and stamped. Captured men muttered and swore. Before they were lifted onto a mount, all of the tied-up gunmen had their bindings double-checked and their belts used as additional restraints. Additionally, their ankles had been lashed together under the horses' bellies. No one was getting loose or free.

Before mounting up, Holt retrieved a small pouch of shredded tobacco from his trail coat. He took some of the tobacco and sprinkled it in all directions, a ceremony he had adopted from Indians. "Spirits of the land…" he began, speaking to the sky. "Thank you for walking with us…for leading me on my journey…and for continuing to watch over those we care for."

The grim caravan soon made its way into town. The seven surviving Thorne prisoners led the macabre parade. Even the horses were secured from running away. Each man's saddle horn was connected to the next with rope. Holt rode off to their side, his Winchester across his saddle, aimed at the men. Even though it was on the trail, his Ranger badge was prominently displayed on his coat lapel.

Tooley Barnes, the W Bar L wrangler, rode on the opposite side from Holt, a double-barreled Greener brandished openly.

Dal followed immediately behind the prisoners, sawed-off shotgun at the ready, his Ranger badge also conspicuously worn. Then came a string of nine horses, each with a body slung over the saddle. The tail-end of the caravan was under the vigilant glare of W Bar L rider William Kemp, who guarded this silent crew as well as observed the entire procession.

Holt would not let the dawn reach into his weariness. The exhilaration of battle and a night without sleep had left him drained. He fought to stay alert during the two-hour ride. Calling out to his fellow guards to ask what their favorite desserts were was an effective way to help keep them attentive.

The sun had not yet made its appearance, but light was softly bathing the town of Stebbins when the column of tired men and horses arrived. The town was still waking up, and only a few citizens were out beginning their day.

As the caravan neared the jail, a lone figure emerged to confront the procession.

The sandy brown-haired man with similarly colored eyes was slump-shouldered but muscular. He wore a nice dark-gray sack suit that did not quite fit him properly. The trousers were a little too long and the coat a bit too short. His gun belt with one pistol was easily observed. He carried a double-barreled shotgun nonchalantly in one hand.

Holt halted the column. Dal and the two W Bar L men herded the tired horses into a large knot around the jail hitching rack.

"What do we have here?" the man in the baggy suit asked cordially.

"A state law matter," Holt said. He had casually eased his rifle to a more ready position. "Need the marshal's help to lock some of these men up."

"I'm the new law around here. Sheriff and Marshal." He opened his jacket. A badge was pinned to his shirt. "Sheriff Chapman at your service." He smiled.

Holt muttered, "That was quick."

Dal answered, "Money buys a lot of vermin."

It had been about a month since Christer Viklund and two men brutally ambushed Sheriff Moose Elkins and Marshal Baxter Hollings inside the Rising Goose Café. The marshal died on the spot. One gunman was killed inside the restaurant. Another was shot in the street while trying to escape. Viklund got away. Witnesses swore that Elkins had caught lead, but in the chaotic aftermath of the shooting, his body was not found. No one in town knew whether he had survived because his body had disappeared. His fiancée, Evie O'Neill, was also nowhere to be found. Deputy Gus Brooks had vanished as well. In the hushed pockets of town that had not bowed to Isla Thorne, it was fervently hoped that the three were somewhere safe, waiting to reclaim their jurisdiction.

In the meantime, the evidence that Isla had positioned her own hand-picked hireling to be the town's law stood in front of them.

Holt addressed the Thorne-placed lawman. "These are our prisoners, Chapman. We're going to need your jail for a while."

"Who might you be?"

"I'm Holt Corrigan, Texas Ranger, but I bet you already knew that."

"Hearda you." Chapman's pleasant demeanor faded.

Holt noticed the change. "These men are under arrest for the murder of Brody Bennett and the attempted murder of Lillian Whitman and her men at the W Bar L. They're charged with rustling and assault as well."

"That can't be." Chapman quickly scanned the column for Monroe Guidry.

Holt saw the look but let it go. "What can't be, Chapman? The charges or the fact they were caught?"

Dal kept his sawed-off shotgun deliberately laid across his saddle, aimed directly at the man wearing the town badge. His eyes slitted as he spoke up, "If Holt an' I hadn't been there, the Widow Whitman an' her men would be dead."

The man with the badge shook his head and peered again for Monroe.

Dal and Holt both looked at each other, knowing what this meant.

"Searchin' for someone, Chapman?" Dal continued. "If you're lookin' for your pissant friend, he's bringin' up the rear." Dal gestured with his thumb at the string of prisoners and dead bodies. "These dumbasses shot him."

"That can't—"

"Do we get the jail or not?" Holt demanded.

Chapman was at a loss. "I don't—"

"Are you questioning our statements or our authority?" The ferocity in Holt's eyes and voice was intense.

The Thorne-bought lawman rubbed his chin before responding. "I reckon neither." He kept his eyes on Holt as he raised his free hand slowly, then moved it to retrieve the cell keys from a pocket. He tossed them to the young Ranger. "Guess I'd better fetch the undertaker."

Holt added, “Chapman, the state of Texas isn’t going to pay to bury a bunch of Louisiana bottom feeders. Have your boss, Isla, pay for it.”

CHAPTER TWENTY-SIX

With their guns drawn, Holt and Dal watched as the two W Bar L riders dealt with the surviving Thorne men one at a time. First, the ropes lashing the prisoner's ankles together were cut, as were the restraints binding them to the saddles. Then, each man was pulled off the horse and steered inside the jail, not untying their hands until they were placed into a cell.

Across the street, a small group of citizens were drawn to the proceedings and gathered in a small flock. A tall, well-dressed man in an expensive suit announced that the group should go and arrest those strangers who were marching tied men into the jail. Murmuring flowed, but no one moved to act.

In the past few months, a cloak of unease had enveloped Stebbins. Intimidation fostered uncertainty and apprehension, which kept people hesitant to speak out. Avoiding trouble had become the business of the town.

The chatter continued as the nosy throng watched the

string of men being led into the jail. The tall man who started all the nattering hurried off.

Above it all, a lone figure stood undetected in a window above the bank.

The dark-haired, green-eyed woman fumed as she observed the unfolding scene below. One hand toyed with a silver-and-brass amulet at her neck. The other hung at her side, a fist slowly opening and closing.

For one thing, Calista Theriot did not like staying in town, for another, she detested failure—and the previous night had been an absolute disaster. She had witnessed for herself the waste of money that was Monroe Guidry and his men. The gunslinger had come highly recommended, too. He and his dandies from Chalmette had been whipped, easily, by two Rangers and a sprinkling of ranch hands.

"Pathetic," she grumbled into the shrouded quiet of her chambers.

Calista stood undressed except for an unbound dressing gown. She generally enjoyed being naked and all the sensual feelings it aroused. But not this morning.

To avoid being seen returning from the W Bar L, she had raced back to town before it got light. Leaving her worn-out horse in the bank's alley for Ames to deal with, she slipped up the back staircase to the private apartment above. The process of getting out of her black canvas trousers, black shirt, and black vest was an exercise in controlled fury.

She had quickly loosened the tight cloth wrapping that bound her chest, releasing her ample bosoms—the only relief in her fit of agitation. Naked, she quickly stashed the black outlaw clothing in the back of her closet. The long, dark cattleman's coat, streaked with permanent dirt that helped cover her bound breasts and hide her hips, was placed on a hook over the clothes. Her wide-brimmed hat went on the hook over the coat. Only then had she retrieved her robe.

The amulet was becoming warmer as she angrily rubbed its surface. This round of her plan had been nearly complete. She was one ranch away from owning thousands of acres! She did not care that it was prime ranch property that came with large numbers of cattle. This would have secured all the land she needed in St. Clair County. Land that, before long, would hold train tracks, and all the growth and construction that came with it. The railroad movers and shakers would pay attention, and deal her in. The meeting was set up. Developers Thayer and Emery were coming here to meet with her. With the magnate, Isla Thorne.

And now this.

Instead of calling the W Bar L ranch her own, she watched as a dead Monroe Guidry was cut from his saddle and flopped to the ground.

In her mind, she could hear the voice of her sister, Celinda, telling her to be calm.

Her mind whirled. *Where did those Rangers come from? How did they know… Why were they out at that widow's place?* When it came to her business, she hated surprises. The charade of a military district running the state would not last forever. Neither would her handpicked *lieutenant governor*. She fumed. There will be a legitimate government and governor before long, and every advantage and charade will be gone!

She needed to bathe, but decided she only had time for a quick birdbath. She would put on a nice dress and meet with Madigan, her right-hand man. If he wasn't awake, she would send Ames after him. She needed answers. And breakfast. Her mind needed to be free to think, but not on an empty stomach.

She had become wealthy at a young age, even before she inherited her father's thriving river enterprise. Poker enriched her coffers back then. So did well-to-do lovers who enjoyed taking care of her and her voluptuous charms. She enjoyed men. Always had. Using her body to get what she wanted came easily and early in life. She drew a line at actual prostitution because she could acquire more assets through seduction or marriage.

Her first husband, an old Missourian rich with gold, had died of water hemlock poisoning, leaving her a trove of bars and coins. A second husband, wealthy from inheriting his family's St. Louis shipping company, mysteriously vanished on a business trip down the Mississippi. The family had fought to retain the business, providing her a widow's settlement of a sizable sum of gold certificates and two new packet boats.

The latest husband was a former war privateer who had become a chef and owned a prosperous New Orleans restaurant. He wanted her to give up her plans to follow in her father's wake and raise a family with him. She was not about to give up her father's raiding and plundering interests. Passions turned into hostilities that manifested in her trying to slit her husband's throat. He defended himself with a wine bottle. When she came to, the entire building where they lived—the restaurant, their apartment—was completely ablaze. She barely escaped and never looked back. She had only stray thoughts of him.

In that fiery aftermath, she had made the name Calista Theriot formidable and imposing. Her boats and crafts navigated and marauded up and down the waterways of Louisiana and now Texas. This new venture was not rivers but rails. It was a high-stakes game that could not be played fairly. She knew setbacks were always a possibility, but not on a hand she should have already won.

Abruptly, Calista broke off her chain of thought, yanked the curtains together, and prepared to clean herself up.

A knock at the door was timid. Was it Ames? Another knock. Had to be him. She grabbed a double-barreled derringer from her nightstand, one that usually was carried in a special holster strapped to her leg. It wasn't the only weapon she regularly carried. A razor-sharp, pearl-handled stiletto was always in one of the stylish boots she wore.

She checked through the tiny peephole and confirmed the visitor was Ames. She slid the gun into her housecoat pocket and pulled the door open.

The tall, well-dressed man smiled and entered.

Slamming the door behind him, Calista hissed, trying valiantly to keep her voice down, "Where the hell have you been, you stupid idiot? What the hell is going on?"

Ames's face tightened, and he took a step backward, halfway thinking he was about to be attacked.

"Calista, wait, you've got it all wrong…" He reached for her, mostly to keep her from charging or striking him, but also because her pleasing, naked figure was on display through her open dressing gown.

She pushed him away and quickly tied up her gown.

"Tell me why last night failed!" Calista's voice was quieter, but her eyes still cut into his face.

"Monroe wasn't my fault..." he stammered. "Your man, Madigan, vouched—"

Before he could finish, there was another knock at the door, this one more robust.

She looked through the peephole. "It's Ridgely." She said the words as though they tasted bad.

As she opened the door, Dugal Ridgely, Stebbins's newly appointed judge, immediately began reciting the morning's news. Events Calista had already witnessed.

Ames Wooster, Stebbins bank president, had been having an affair with Calista for nearly a year. Ridgely was new to town and not aware of this liaison, as were most people. As such, he desperately manufactured every possible excuse to be near and gain favor with the alluring woman.

He also had no idea this was the infamous Calista Theriot.

Sensing Dugal was amorously motivated, Ames's insecurity took over. He stepped in to disparage the newcomer. Dugal sensed a potential opportunity to make an impression. Both began talking at once, like schoolboys trying to be noticed, escalating over one another with stale information, unsubstantiated rumors, and half-baked advice. All of it wearying and exasperating to Calista.

She was having none of it. "Enough!" She took a breath.

"Ridgely, go see what the hell Chapman thinks he's doing. Do something a real judge would do... Set a hearing? Get my men out of jail?" She shook her head. "And, *Judge*, expect a telegram from Austin. The lieutenant governor will be sending directives for you to follow post-haste."

"Yes, Isla. Right away." His legal knowledge told him Texas was currently without gubernatorial leadership, causing Ridgely to wonder about this lieutenant governor. Her eyes signaled it was time for him to leave, and he left the matter unquestioned.

Hearing Dugal's footsteps receding down the hallway, she turned to Ames. "First, get ahold of yourself. Don't blow my cover arguing with that insignificant gnat. Next, you need to get our thousand dollars from Guidry's saddlebags. Then have those rebranded cattle from the Half Moon 6 brought here. Fast. Got it?"

Ames nodded vigorously.

"Also, find Madigan and Malo," she added. "Have them meet me at the Blue Sky. Now. We're through wasting time playing nice with that widow."

Ames tried to linger, hoping to soothe her tension with a long, intimate morning. But Calista wanted nothing of the sort. Her eyes burned into him like a loaded gun. "You're the mayor. And the banker. Act like it."

She shut the door forcefully in his face.

Toying again with the amulet, she spoke to herself, "Rangers want to play, hmm? Time to raise my edge."

CHAPTER TWENTY-SEVEN

With all of the widow's attackers locked up, Holt and Dal's primary concern was getting her W Bar L riders, Tooley and William, out of town as soon as possible. It did not take the prickling sense of Holt's *tsét'soyé* bear spirits to realize the vulnerability of the situation. Some might even say it was folly. With a Thorne man carrying the town badge, would the prisoners really remain locked up? Likely not, but Holt felt he had to follow the law nonetheless.

What was certain was that they all definitely needed to get back and protect Mrs. Whitman. Equally certain was the nagging feeling that none of them were safe here. Holt and Dal could depend upon their Ranger badges and battle experience, but the two young ranch hands had no such advantages.

Holt quietly took Tooley and William aside. "While everyone is preoccupied with all the horses here, I want the two of you to walk your mounts down the street. When you get near the edge of town, high-tail it back to the ranch. Tell Orion that we'll be along as soon as we think things are squared away here. Don't stop for anyone. Got it?"

They both nodded without question.

While the Rangers were having their conversation with the two ranch hands, Ames Wooster hurriedly visited the jail and left just as quickly.

Knowing the W Bar L attackers were secured in the Stebbins jail cells and the young W Bar L riders were safely away, Holt and Dal led their horses from jail toward the Blue Sky Inn. They paid no attention to Thorne's Sheriff Chapman and his deputy rifling through the prisoners' saddlebags. The two Rangers were purposefully staying in town and being visible. At least until their telegrams to Captain McCoy and the federal magistrate went out, and they were notified about a hearing for these Thorne men.

Chapman called out to the departing Rangers, "What about these horses?"

Holt did not stop, hollering over his shoulder, "They belong to your boss. Ask her."

"Yeah, but the mess?"

Dal hollered back, "She can buy a shovel. With you around, I'm sure she's used to dealin' with it." He chuckled at himself.

The Rangers decided that treating themselves to a well-earned breakfast was a good idea. It would feel good to sit on something besides a saddle, too. Most of all, being seen was important. State law still carried significance, even here.

They were just getting seated in the quietest corner of the very busy Blue Sky tavern when its owner, Miguel Navarro, spied them and hurried over. "Ahh, Señor Holt! There eez someone who weel be so happy to see you!"

He quickly disappeared to his back office and returned promptly, Tag Along in tow.

Holt beamed. "There's my buddy!" The floppy-eared dog practically leaped across the lively room, greeting his master with his paws up in Holt's lap and his tail furiously wagging. Holt chuckled as his dog persisted in his enthusiastic reunion. "Thank you, Miguel. Much obliged!"

"Your brave Ranger dog eez always welcome here." Miguel beamed. "Your horse, the one with the *paquete,* is at the stables."

"You're too good, Miguel. Thank you so much." Holt grinned.

Soon, the two Rangers were brought ham steaks, eggs and potatoes, and steaming mugs of hot coffee. Tag was served his own bowl of ham and eggs under the table. They had not taken particular notice of anyone in the crowded establishment, but there were quiet whispers among the clientele about the two state lawmen and their dog. Especially interested were three patrons seated at the largest table in the back of the room, men who observed the two lawmen with great awareness.

Suddenly, without fanfare, the huge room hushed. Everyone, including the bartender and waitresses, stopped to watch the entrance of Isla Thorne. Her presence brought the entire place to a standstill—except for Holt and Dal's table in the corner. They noted the interruption was not threatening and continued with their meal. Only Tag paused to briefly look and sniff at the movement.

Miguel Navarro sped immediately across the room to welcome Isla with fawning exuberance. She was what now passed for royalty in Stebbins. It wasn't that he considered her worthy. He had heard the rumors that she might try to purchase the Blue Sky. She would only buy it if she felt it was a nuisance or a threat. Because of this, he believed it advisable to remain in her good graces. The generally genteel man was more lavish with his hospitality every time she visited.

He led Isla to the largest table in the back of the room, reserved especially for her. Miguel was given notice of her impending arrival when her three companions had shown up before she did. As usual for her visits, Miguel had laid out his own crisp, embroidered linen tablecloth. His family's best china was set just for the occasion.

Her three men interrupted their observation of the Rangers to watch her grand entrance. As she neared the table, the heavyset man with a groomed mustache and tailored suit stood first. Ames Wooster stood an instant later, chagrined that the large man was quicker with the courtesy. The third man had been reading a copy of Edgar Allan Poe's *Murders in the Rue Morgue* and got to his feet almost as an afterthought.

The fat man pulled out the chair nearest the rear wall in a grand gesture, allowing Isla to sit, then pushed it back in after she was seated. Ames gave the man, and his courtesy, a quick glower, before smiling at Isla.

The rotund man's immense belly appeared as if it was capable of splitting every button as he settled back down, but his fine-tailored suit still fit his frame without strain. A golden watch chain stretched across his mountainous stomach and vest. Notably, two pearl-handled pistols were visible from inside his sizable coat.

The other man seated with them was a peculiar-looking individual with extremely pale skin and icy-blue eyes. A man who would stand out even in the dark. The hair on his head was more white than blond, with an equally fair-haired wispy beard and mustache that were touched with tinges of red. A black, low-crowned John Bull hat with a flashy silver concho band perched on the ear of his chair. The handle of a Navy Colt protruded from one side of his open dark-gray sack coat. A bulge over the coat's pocket indicated the presence of another gun.

All three of these men knew that Isla's real name was Calista Theriot. They were paid handsomely for their trust and services. They were here to see to it that their boss's plans for being a part of the Texas railway expansion were successful. Calista the pirate would never get a seat at the table where such commerce was transacted. *Isla Thorne* and her money, however, would be invited to just such a game.

Holt finally looked up to take in what had captured everyone's attention and was surprised at what he saw. A woman with glorious dark brunette hair and deep emerald eyes. The brilliant green silk dress she wore seemed more suited for the evening, its scoop cut revealing an almost-scandalous amount of her rounded decolletage. She ruled the room with her regal presence and engaging charm.

Miguel Navarro would not let anyone else attend to Isla, promptly serving her table fresh coffee and biscuits. After ordering a stack of pancakes, she asked him about the dark-haired man in the corner with the dog, her tone haughty yet syrupy. "Am I to understand that animals are allowed to frequent this establishment?"

For a moment, Miguel did not know what she was talking about. He followed the gesture of her entrancing eyes to a table in the corner. “Ohh! That eez Señor Holt, madame. Holt Corrigan. He eez Texas Ranger. So eez thee other one. The dog eez Señor Holt’s. It eez honored guest. They all are heroes in town.” He smiled and nodded, seeking her approval.

She ignored the answer and tilted her head, eyeing Holt and his silky hair just brushing his shoulders. Even from across the room, his presence was palpable. She noticed his light-blue eyes and high cheekbones. *Mmmm. Is that a scar along his cheek?* she thought. Drawn somehow to this young Ranger, a wry smile came to her face, her eyes gleamed—a blaze that was at once predatory and seductive.

“I would like to talk with him, Mr. Navarro. Both of the Rangers. Would you be so kind?”

With a quick nod, Miguel hurried to where Holt and Dal were eating. At the approach of his friend, Tag sat up, swishing his tail happily back and forth along the floor.

“Señor Holt? The lady, Mrs. Thorne, would like to speak weeth you. Both of you.” His hands fidgeted with the crisp, white apron he wore only for her visits. He had an uneasy feeling about this unfolding situation and did not like being in the middle. “That eez her, at the back table.” He leaned closer to Holt. “She eez very rich, very powerful. There are those who say she eez very dangerous too.”

“So I’ve heard,” Holt said, casually forking another bite of his ham.

“That’s some dress. Quite the display.” Dal chuckled. “Seems more suited for a riverboat soiree, don’tcha think?”

Holt chuckled slightly in return.

"Please, Señor Holt, I do not want trouble. Weeth her. Weeth you. I am asking, please."

"I'm sure you don't, Miguel. I don't want any trouble either. Please tell her we'll come over after we're through eating."

Migual stood for a moment, not wanting to deliver that news, but instantly calculating a way how. He hurried off, dreading the next few moments.

Dal focused hard on not looking at her table for her response. He spoke quietly, and said, "Whattaya think she wants?"

Holt took a deep breath. "To size us up. Probably flex her muscles. Her dining companions aren't choirboys." Noticing without directly looking, he could tell Miguel notified Isla without incident.

"Thank you, Mr. Navarro," she said pleasantly enough. She leaned over and quietly spoke to her companions. Both the fat man and his pale colleague stood. Only Ames remained seated with her. The two left the restaurant, neither of them glancing toward the Rangers' table.

Holt watched their departure and muttered, "Our exit out of here could get interesting."

CHAPTER TWENTY-EIGHT

Finished with their meals, Holt and Dal had another mug of coffee. Finally, they stood and dropped some coins on the table. Holt left extra money for his friend, Miguel's help looking after Tag Along.

Holt flagged down Miguel with a quick nod of his head. "Can you stay here with Tag? I know you're taking care of your special guest, but we won't be long, I promise."

"Sí, Señor Holt, I weel watch Tag Along." The diminutive hotel owner tried to smile through his worried look.

The two Rangers made their way to the back of the room. Holt nodded and smiled at patrons at a few of the tables, not sure if the responses he got were fearful or forced. The room was different now that Isla Thorne had arrived.

He approached her table, holding his hat in his hand. As he got closer, what he saw was startling. Before him was the most beautiful woman he had ever seen. Light and shadows in the room danced to embrace her stunningly attractive features. His earlier glimpses of her from across the room were but a taste of the vixen now just an arm's length away.

The woman's cheeks were touched with a rosy glow that was natural, not powder. She had thick black lashes, which accented her emerald jewel eyes and which seemed to burn with a secret that dared further discovery. Her luxurious dress did not hide much, and she knew it, keeping her shoulders back and straight.

The air around her smelled like a bouquet of fine flowers.

Her appearance rattled his mind for a moment. When he discovered his voice again, he found himself literally standing next to her. "Ma'am, you asked to talk to us?"

"Oh yes! Yes, I did, thank you." She looked over at the man still seated with her. "Do you know Ames? He is the banker and the mayor here in Stebbins." Holt gave him a perfunctory nod. Dal, being closer, offered a quick handshake. "He was just leaving," she continued. "Important matters at the bank." The look on Ames's face indicated he was surprised by her announcement, but he complied nonetheless and took his leave.

"Please, won't you sit down?" She gestured for Holt to sit at the chair closest to her, then included Dal in the invitation to sit at one of the chairs previously occupied by the well-dressed—and well-armed—men she sent away.

"I'm afraid we'll have to stand, Miss Thorne." Holt smiled. "We appreciate the offer—"

"But we have work to do." Dal completed the thought.

"Oh, that's too bad. I was looking forward to a chat. I

would love to meet your friend, the one with the big ears."

Holt was caught a bit off guard and chuckled, "Tag Along? Señor Navarro is nice enough to let him stay, as long as Tag behaves himself. Not everyone likes that he's here, so we left him in the corner."

"Tag Along! What a delightful name!" She smiled, her magnetism and charm on full display.

Holt waited a polite moment before declaring, "Well, Miss Thorne, it was nice to make your acquaintance, but we need to—"

She didn't let him finish. "Your choice, Ranger Corrigan."

Holt was not surprised that she knew his name, but hearing it from her mouth gave him a jolt of desire or concern. He wasn't sure which.

She continued, "Perhaps you have time to hear the truth." The look from her eyes intently locked both men into place.

"There's always time for that." Holt looked at Dal, who nodded, then returned his gaze to Isla.

She smiled, but the warmth no longer reached her eyes. "Lillian Whitman and her men have stolen beef from my land. Those men you just brought in…I ordered them to bring her in for trial."

"You ordered them…to bring her in for trial?" Dal choked on his guffaw and scratched at the side of his scruffy, unshaven face. "In your capacity as, what, justice of the peace? We can see there's no place to pin your badge." His leer at her cleavage was derision, not lust.

Holt cleared his throat and tried to smooth the waters churned up by the one-eyed Ranger. "You know, we talked with several of those men we brought in, including the departed Monroe Guidry, and not one of them mentioned anything about a trial. They were quite clear their orders were to buy out the widow, run her off, or worse. Besides, taking the law into your own hands is generally frowned upon, even here in Texas."

Her voice was now cold and exact. "If you check with Sheriff Chapman, he will tell you those men were acting with his authorization."

Thinking clearer now, Holt envisioned the sight of Lillian fighting for her land and Orion standing bloodied next to her. The images stirred his *ndołkah* panther spirit. "Interesting. We already had a conversation with your minion."

Her head tilted slightly. She did not care for the jibe.

Holt continued the point, "If they were acting on Chapman's behalf like you say, they should have been deputized. A real lawman would know that."

For a brief moment, Isla looked as though she had been slapped. Her unexpected response was a cozily warm smile that disarmed the two lawmen. But Holt noticed the sweet glow did not come from her eyes, which remained cold and aggressive. Or was that a flicker of madness in them? Those eyes searched Holt's, but he couldn't read her intentions.

She abruptly changed the subject. "How much do you make? Your salary, I mean, as Rangers." Her eyes measured Holt's. The intensity of her stare made him uncomfortable.

Holt shook his head. "I already have a job."

"I'll triple whatever you're making. As you can see, I could use some good men."

The two Rangers turned to leave. Her hand touched Holt's arm. He sensed it was calculated, not spontaneous as if she knew well the effect it would have. The same impact her touch had on all other men, he suspected. Even so, the close attention of such a beautiful woman played with his emotions, sending shafts of red up the back of his neck. He halted his departure.

Her gaze invited him closer. She knew she was irresistible.

In words no one else could hear, she said, "You might find me most interesting, Holt Corrigan. Some men do, you know." Her smile was laced with arousal. Her manner changed to one of not-so-subtle seduction. "Your wages would come with extra benefits, bonuses you would never forget."

It was difficult for Holt to concentrate with her eyes caressing his face. A tiny message in his brain tried to assure him that she was actually attracted to him. Worse, it was a message he wanted to believe. Yet, he knew it wasn't true.

He closed his eyes and sought the image of Laudie Kate actually caressing his face, not only with her eyes, but with her hands. He breathed in and could feel and smell Laudie Kate's lavender presence. Her spirit filled his heart.

When he opened them again, Isla saw a different light anchored in his light-blue eyes. A look that was steadfast and immune to her allure.

"You have a good day, ma'am." Holt placed his hat on his head and headed for the door. Mouth clicks from Holt that Tag Along heard above the clamor of the room, brought the dog trotting to his master's side.

Isla's beautiful face twisted into a smile that was more of a sneer, and her eyes glowed with an animal look that burned with intensity. "Enjoy your taste of power, Holt Corrigan," she growled under her breath. "It's nearly over."

CHAPTER TWENTY-NINE

Bright sunshine and a heated day greeted the Rangers and Tag as they stepped out onto the planked sidewalk in front of the Blue Sky. Remembering the earlier foreboding when he watched Isla's men leave the restaurant, Holt was uneasy at this distinct disadvantage. One hand grasped the lapel of his coat—near one of his shoulder-holstered pistols—while he squinted his eyes to hasten their adjustment.

"I don't like not knowing where that woman's heavies are," Holt said quietly, his warning implied. "They weren't dandies like that banker."

"Yeah, but they're all dressed real nice like him." Dal smirked.

He had a point, Holt thought. All of Isla's main gunmen had nice, brand-new suits. Something to remember.

They made their way down the street to the telegraph office. Inside, the banker Ames Wooster and a spindly clerk with slicked back hair and thick eyeglasses were huddled over the counter in a deep, whispered conversation.

Dal murmured to Holt, "Speak of the devil."

The arrival of the Rangers appeared to startle the clerk. He hastily ended his conversation with the banker. "What can I help you with, gentl…er… Rangers?"

Ames acted awkwardly as he moved past the two lawmen on his way out the door. "Morning, gentlemen. Seems we meet again." A feigned chuckle followed his greeting.

Holt took the opportunity this time to shake the banker's hand in passing. "Ames," was all he said. Dal just put a finger to the brim of his hat. They waited until the door closed behind him before responding to the man's query.

The clerk wrote down their messages to Captain McCoy and Judge Elsher Nash—a report of the current situation: *W Bar L attackers, questionable local law, and an immediate need for a circuit judge.* The operator promised to deliver any response or other messages right away.

"We'll be at the Blue Sky," Holt informed the spindly clerk, as Dal placed coins on the counter.

Not seen by the Rangers was the real telegraph operator, seated in the back office, eyes wide with fear. One of Ames's tellers, resplendent in a new black suit, held a large Griswold & Gunnison revolver to the man's head.

On their return, Holt swung by the livery and retrieved his second horse before visiting the general store. This horse carried a specially crafted pack that fit over the saddle. Holt had it created when he became a Ranger and set out to track down the deranged killer known as *The Angel*. The special carryall was not like the large, full-sized panniers that packhorses carried, but bigger than saddlebags. Soon, he was stuffing both sides of the holdall with small sacks of flour, jerky and coffee, a bundle of salt pork, plus several cans of beans and fruit. Another extra box of ammo, too.

Although he planned to stick around long enough to hear back from the captain or the judge, he could not ignore an unease deep inside him. He did not want to admit it, but he might need all of this soon. To escape.

Walking both his horses toward the Blue Sky, Holt spied the two men who had been seated with Isla. They were at the jail. The fat man was standing on the planked walkway, talking with the man wearing the badge, Chapman. His pale colleague was also outside, seated by the door, reading. Holt's panther sense prickled as he tied up his horses outside the hotel.

Holing up in the Blue Sky would give Holt and Dal temporary sanctuary until their telegraphs were answered. And give them a chance for a quick cleanup and nap.

Miguel set them up with the largest room he had, actually, the only one vacant. Holt suggested to Dal that they take turns resting.

Dal agreed. "Never thought I'd be *night owl* in a hotel, but it makes sense. I don' trust anyone in this town except you an' maybe little Navarro."

Both took turns cleaning up in the basin, washing some of the night and its skirmish away. Holt offered to take first watch for the drowsy one-eyed Ranger.

Later into the day, a persistent knock at the door and Tag's answering woofs woke them both up. Dal had gotten a couple hours of rest before taking over the watch, but had fallen back asleep in the chair he had jammed against the door, his sawed-off shotgun on his lap. Holt was not aware how long they both had been sleeping. A situation they were supposed to be avoiding.

The knocking persisted. "Dammit!" Dal hissed. "Who is it?" he hollered through the door.

A young-sounding voice responded, "Telegram for Ranger Corrigan!"

Gun in hand, Dal opened the door slightly. A lad's fresh face peered back and asked, "Are you Ranger Holt Corrigan?"

Dal opened more of the door and peered outside into the hallway, both ways. "I'm Ranger Dal Frantze," he finally answered.

"Here's a wire for you. Mr. Templeton said to deliver it right away. Downstairs said you were up here."

Dal reached into his vest and gave the lad a coin. "Thanks." As he closed the door, he rubbed at his face. "Sorry, Holt, I fell asleep. That wasn't good."

"Can't worry about that now," he offered to Dal. Holt got out of bed and poured fresh water into the basin. A quick face splash would help wake him up.

Dal suddenly blurted out in a thunder, "What the hell is this load of crap!" He handed the unfolded message to Holt.

RANGERS HOLT CORRIGAN AND DAL FRANTZE:

LIEUTENANT GOVERNOR HAS ORDERED ME TO REMOVE YOU AS RANGERS.

COMPLAINTS THAT YOU ARE DEFENDING RUSTLERS,

EXCEEDING YOUR AUTHORITY.

HE IS SENDING NOTICE AROUND THE STATE.

EXPECT LOCAL LAW TO TRY TO ARREST YOU.

REGRETFULLY,

CAPTAIN LAIRD MCCOY.

Dal shook his head. "Think that Isla woman knows about this?"

"I'd bet on it," Holt responded grimly, as he slipped on his twin shoulder holsters. "We need to warn Orion and Lillian. They're next." He checked the loads in his matching Russian Smith & Wessons and tucked the guns into place.

"What about the hearing?"

"The only hearing likely to happen is ours."

"Shouldn't we stay an' fight this crap?"

"Until we know what's really going on, we can't win. Not with the local judge and the law in her pocket. And any gun battle… We're outnumbered. By more than we know. No, Dal, you need to ride for the W Bar L. Now."

"What're you gonna do? I can't leave you alone."

"Yes, you can. Go and warn Orion. I'm going to make a mess here. Hold things up. Delay whatever posse they send."

In moments, they were down in front of the Blue Sky. Holt watched Dal adjust his horse's cinch and ride off. He did the same with his own horses. That feeling that had been nagging him was becoming real. He would be escaping. Soon.

"Come with me, Tag. This could get sideways in a hurry."

Ignoring the wire message, Holt decided he would honor his oath and responsibility as a Ranger. He tugged at his hat brim, ran his fingers across the cardinal feather there, and led his horses toward the jail to tie them out front. A brief sense of relief came with not immediately seeing Isla's breakfast gunmen.

Instead, her hand-picked hired sheriff stepped onto the planked walkway outside the jail. "Well, well, well, if it isn't Holt Corrigan." Chapman smirked. "You're right on time. Judge Ridgely's hearing is going to dismiss the cases against those men you falsely arrested. They're about to be let go."

Holt reacted. "What kind of hearing takes place without the prosecution present?"

"Huh? What kind…? The kind that happens when the right people run things around here. Those men?" He gestured with a thumb over his shoulder. "When they're out, they're gonna be deputized, too. Under my authority. We're gonna send 'em after the Widow Whitman. She and her men are wanted for stealing cattle."

"That's not true, Chapman. Lillian's not a thief. Neither are her men."

"You calling me a liar?"

"What do you think?"

Chapman hesitated, not sure what to do. The conversation was not going like he thought it would. What he did know was that he would die if he tried to match guns with Holt Corrigan.

Holt dismissively waved this excuse for a lawman aside and stepped the rest of the way into the jail, followed by Tag Along. "Bring that judge here now," Holt ordered.

He slammed the door shut in Chapman's face, leaving the dumbfounded sheriff outside, and braced the entry from the inside.

Jeers and hoots came at Holt from the locked-up Thorne men. They had heard of the hearing and could sense their freedom was coming soon.

"Whattaya gonna do when we're let go?"

"We'll be comin' after ya, law dawg!"

"You're going to die, Corrigan!"

Laughter followed the taunting. Holt ignored it all.

Before long, Chapman returned to the jail and banged on the door. "Open up, Corrigan! In the name of the law."

Holt took the brace off the door and opened it, a loaded Greener shotgun in his hand, derisive tone in his voice, as he said, "That's a good one, Chapman. *The name of the law…*" The barrels of the gun pointed directly at the man's face. Only a few steps behind Chapman were Judge Ridgely and the two men who had dined with Isla Thorne.

"Come on in, boys!" Holt grinned. "Let's have a talk."

He stepped back to allow the four men inside, but only far enough to keep them in a small group just inside the door. He kicked the door shut. "You boys don't mind, do you? This is going to be a private meeting." Although he smiled, he was far from cordial.

"This is ridiculous," Dugal Ridgely stormed. "I've made my ruling. These men are innocent. I issued a warrant for Lillian Whitman's arrest. She's a rustler." He folded his arms. "Matter of fact, *you're* under arrest, Corrigan. For the murder of nine Thorne employees."

The young Ranger said nothing, but eyed the group in front of him. Ridgely was not armed, and Chapman was too scared to act. But Isla's breakfast partners were well-dressed rattlers, poised to strike. Holt coolly kept the Greener pointed at them.

Ridgely continued to bluster, "You don't have any authority, Corrigan. The lieutenant governor had you and that one-eyed bastard removed as Rangers."

"At the moment, all the authority I need is right here." Holt's eyes briefly indicated the cocked and readied double-barreled shotgun in his hands.

"Come on, Madigan, Malo. Do something!" Judge Ridgely urged, desperation in his voice.

"Ridgely, you're a sorry excuse for a judge. And for that matter, a sorry excuse for a man," Holt declared, his face and voice deadly serious. "In addition to not knowing anything about the law, you also don't know anything about guns." He took a breath. "Ridgely, *you* think you see two hired guns versus one Texas Ranger. What *they* see is a scattergun that, at this distance, will blow a pattern that cuts both of them in two before they even clear their holsters."

Ridgely appeared to shrink in size. His bluster now gone.

"Now, here's what's going to happen," Holt continued. "Big man there, in the pricey suit… You've got some fancy pearl-handled revolvers on either side of that gold watch chain. Get rid of 'em, one at a time. Slow and easy." The fat Louisiana gunman complied, unholstering one revolver and dropping it onto the planked floor, followed by a matching pistol that also tumbled to the floor.

"Nicely done," Holt growled. "Now get rid of the hideaway I know you've got. Pull it and drop it." The heavyset man's eyes turned hard. He reached behind his immense body, under his coat. A third Remington revolver thudded to the floor.

"And you…" Holt now focused his attention on the second hired gunman. A pasty-skinned man with snow-white hair, and an odd-looking low-top hat with a flashy silver band. The guns this man wore were not those of a slick gunslinger. *No*, Holt thought, *this is an assassin, a cold-blooded killer*.

This man followed Holt's orders just like the first. His large Army Colt pistols joined the collection of guns on the floor. "All right, that's good. But it's time for you to get shut of the rest of your weapons. You've got another Colt. Get rid of it. Now." An easy-to-spot blush of anger rose in the pale man's face. He produced a third revolver from his coat and dropped it with the others. "Now, your boots." Holt motioned.

For the first time, the white-haired man hesitated.

Holt barked, "There's a knife in your boot. If you don't want to wear it somewhere really uncomfortable, draw it out now. Nice and slow." The assassin bent over slowly and pulled a Bowie knife from his left boot and dropped it with a clatter. "Now, get rid of that pistol in your other boot. C'mon. I'm getting really tired of this."

Suddenly, Isla's corrupt sheriff decided to be brave and flinched for his gun. In a split second, Holt took a side-step and mashed the butt of the Greener into Sheriff Chapman's face. The man and his gun fell harmlessly to the floor.

At the same time, the ghost-white man grabbed at a fourth gun, a converted snub-nosed Pietta, from his polished boot and started to raise it.

In an instant, before anyone could react, Tag pounced. His snarling and clamping startled everyone, but the attack stopped whatever the pale man had in mind.

The dog's furious grip was relentless, teeth clenched hard onto the killer's wrist. The assassin screamed in fury and pain, "Get him off! Get him off! Get him off me!"

The fat gunslinger quietly uttered, "You've had your fun, Ranger. Make him stop."

"I'll call off my dog when you call off yours."

The well-dressed gunman nodded. "Drop it, Malo." The pale assassin finally dropped his gun.

Holt slapped his thigh, one hand still aiming the shotgun. "C'mere, boy." Tag trotted over to him as though nothing had just happened. "Good job, boy. Good job."

Holt returned his focus to the matter at hand. "Ridgely, help that idiot up," he ordered. Calista's freebooter judge pulled up the woozy Chapman by his coat collar. Blood gushed from the man's busted nose all over his new suit. Holt continued, "Now, hand me the keys from his pocket." Ridgely obeyed, handing the ring of cast-iron keys to the young Ranger.

Next, Holt motioned with his shotgun. "Now, everybody move over this way." He followed them to the cell that had the fewest men, hollering at the prisoners inside, "Back! Everyone to the back wall!" Opening the cell door, he ordered the four Thorne men to join them. "Don't think. Move! Go!" He prodded them into the cell and slammed the gate shut.

Holt viewed his handiwork. Nearly a dozen pairs of angry eyes, their owners pressed up against the bars of the cells, glared at him right now. Blinking and burning, like blinking coals in a fire. The image made him laugh.

Holt was still tickled at that thought as he stuffed all the guns on the floor into a gunny sack. The cell keys went into his coat. As he left the jail, he hollered from the open door, "Once you get out of here, send for a state marshal or Federal Judge Elsher Nash. Bring in real law, and we'll give ourselves up. We're not surrendering to you Isla Thorne puppets."

CHAPTER THIRTY

Holt hurried and jumped onto his bay outside the jail. As he had done before, he arranged Tag on the saddle in front of him and ponied his second horse on a lead rope. He would be riding hard, so the dog needed to be with him and not atop the second horse's pack. When he reached the outskirts of town, he stopped at the holding corral pond and threw the gunny sack of outlaw guns into the murky water.

Then he spurred his horse and rode from Stebbins as though as was already being chased. He constantly looked over his shoulder to see if he was being followed. He would not push the horses, galloping full out only for brief stretches. He kept to a steady pace of lopes and trots in between. With water up ahead, they slowed to a walk. He would let the mounts have a little drink and take a brief break. These were good horses—no need to tear them up.

At the creek, he decided no one was following him. No dust coming from the direction of Stebbins. Something was kicking up ahead of him, though. This was cattle country, not necessarily trouble.

Watching Tag take a drink, a notion hit the young Ranger. He was an outlaw. Again. He shook his head with an exasperated snicker. No, he *is* a Ranger. And he would act like one despite what this lieutenant governor said. He had meant his declaration when leaving the jail. They would surrender to real law. Sort everything out then.

It might take a while, though, for all those locked-up men to be discovered. Who knew how many sets of cell keys they had? Maybe just this one? He patted at the ring of keys in his pocket and snickered at the thought of a blacksmith having to free that motley crew.

Holt and his small group moved out at a trot. Still no sign of anyone approaching from town, but the dust cloud ahead was large and drawing nearer.

Whoever this was, he would let them pass before continuing on to the W Bar L. Now was not the time to be spotted. He peeled off to the right, the rolling terrain providing a number of rises and hills. He loped toward a knoll harboring a stand of gnarled post and blackjack oaks, mesquite shrubs, and other brush.

Soon, the dust cloud appeared alive, rising and growing. The sounds of cattle were unmistakable. A herd, a smaller one, came into view. Out of curiosity, he glassed the cattle with his battle-worn Reb binoculars. The brands caught his attention. Each steer carried what looked like a rough version of Lillian Whitman's W Bar L brand! He did not recognize any of the men driving them though. No Big Jeff, no Tooley, nobody from her ranch. The brands weren't exact, sloppy in fact. But close enough.

The realization of what this meant hit Holt like a fist.

This beef was being delivered as proof that Lillian Whitman was a rustler.

This would be all the justification the Thorne gang would need to have the widow arrested. There would be no investigation. No checking to see how the brands were altered. No trial. Now they would have their excuse to go after Lillian, Orion, Big Jeff, and anyone at the ranch.

And hang them.

Holt's mind reeled. An idea struck that he should charge the herd and pick off the men. There weren't that many, he could do it. He shook his head. That would be murder. The telegram said he no longer had the law of Texas riding with him. He really would be an outlaw. Plus, it would only prolong the inevitable. These steers or others would be rounded up and brought in as false evidence.

He needed to ride hard to the W Bar L.

After the herd passed, Holt and his four-legged companions were once again on the move, giving time for him to think, starting with *What the hell is going on?* His mind grinded on a myriad of questions: "What was going on in Austin? What was this new lieutenant governor doing? Why did he take action against him and Dal? Why now? What would he do next?" The only answers that came clearly was that someone had to be pulling this politician's strings and that person had to be Isla Thorne.

Holt was so deep in thought that he neglected to notice another cloud of dust approaching ahead. A small one, but bigger than a single rider. Whoever it could be was already too close for him to find cover. This would be a fight he could not avoid.

He drew one of his Smith & Wessons and ran his finger across the cardinal feather in his hat.

It was not long before a small, one-horse wagon came into view.

Holt's eagle eyes realized who the driver was about the same time the man recognized Holt.

"Gus Brooks?" Holt was astonished.

"Mighty glad to see you, Holt." The Stebbins deputy nodded at Tag. "I see you still gotta good partner there."

"Yeah, he's hard to leave behind. I'm here with Dal Frantze, another Ranger. Hope he's already back at the Whitman place, meeting up with Orion."

"I remember Frantze. With the eye patch, right? He an' Moose spied on the Viklunds. Helped bring 'em down."

"That's him." He took a quick look back for dust. Hard to tell now with the herd behind him. "I heard Moose—"

"Yeah, shot up. Pretty bad for a reg'lar man. But he's so damn big an' ornery." He wiped at his mouth and his bushy mustache. "He's with us at the Flying G. Evie's there too. Moose saved her. Pushed her under a table before…"

"We were wondering what happened. No one in town is talking."

"That damn Christer Viklund did it. Probly hired by Isla Thorne. They cut down Baxter. Tried to kill Moose." His voice found a mixture of sadness and anger. "Bartender got one of 'em, I got 'nother. Missed Christer, though." He spat, trying to force the memory away.

"I'm sorry about Marshal Hollings. He was a good man."

Gus sniffed the emotion away and changed the

subject. “I brought Moose’n Evie to the Flying G. My brother’s the foreman there. Owner wanted to help. He hates this Thorne woman. I don’t think anyone knows we’re there.”

“Word around Stebbins is that you all disappeared. No trace.” He checked his backtrail again. “Aren’t you all worried about this Isla woman?

“We’s apparently on the wrong side of Stebbins. So’s the Triple S. She wants everythin’ in the county south an’ east of town. Supposedly somethin’ to do with a future rail line. She’s livin’ at the old Viklund place. Word is she’s grabbed the River D an’ the Half Moon 6. Lillian’s W Bar L is next.”

“What about Harold Frederick’s 5 Star?”

A wide grin game to Gus’s weathered face. “Even if she wanted the place, she won’t mess with him. Foolish if she tried. He’s turned his ranch into a damn fortress. Got more riders than the Fourth Cavalry. Word is, he’s bought himself one of them new-fangled Gat-Ling guns.” He paused to acknowledge the thought. “I know for certain he’s got an old Reb smoothbore. Baxter hisself saw the crates of cannon balls.” His face turned solemn at the mention of his marshal friend.

“Good to know. So, why are you out this far?”

“Gotta go into town occasionally. Supplies. Lil’ Navarro at the Blue Sky an’ the Scotts at the general store help keep my secret. My racin’ buggy here makes it easier.” He chuckled. “It don’t carry as much as a buckboard, but can move a helluva lot quicker. Important these days. Helps I got these too.” He held up a wig and bowler hat. “Not as many Thorne riders out this way. Yet.”

“Well, that’s going to change. Fast. Thorne’s new judge has charged Lillian with rustling. That dust cloud you were following is Isla's men with a small herd that's been running-ironed with her W Bar L brand."

"No! That vile harridan—"

"And I just locked up Isla Thorne's new marshal, new judge, and two hired guns. A fat guy in a nice suit and a man who looked like an albino—"

"Wait, a fat gu… Madigan Sanders? Looks like a riverboat gambler?" Holt nodded affirmatively. "An albino, too? Dammit to beans, Holt! That's Malo Johnson." He whistled in awe. "Them two is bad, Holt. Real bad. They's wanted all over Looziana an' Texas. Figgers that Thorne woman brought 'em in." He allowed himself a short snicker. "Locked 'em up, you say? Jerusalem crickets! That sure is somethin'."

"Well, the conversation dried up, and I couldn't afford the stakes if shooting got involved." He paused. "Listen, tell Moose I said hello. Evie too. You should know, some new Texas lieutenant governor forced Captain McCoy to remove me and Dal as Rangers. They'll be coming after all of us."

"Damn. That woman don't mess around. You know they won't be lookin' to arrest you." Gus paused as the implications hit him. "Maybe you shoulda shot that Madigan. An' Malo."

"Yeah. Maybe so. We're going to get Lillian somewhere safe. Then we'll figure out a counterattack." He looked behind him again for approaching dust. Hard to tell with that moving herd. "I gotta go, Gus. You should, too. Her riders may not be too far behind me. Everyone'll be glad to hear about Moose."

"You ride careful now, Holt Corrigan."

"You too, Gus."

CHAPTER THIRTY-ONE

It was near nightfall when Holt arrived at the W Bar L. Shadows revealed themselves and crept across the land, creating all kinds of strange-looking shapes. The encroaching darkness would create a veil masking movement both essential and ominous.

Holt neared the now-familiar configuration of the ranch. Near the front of the house, he spied a man lying on the ground, arms tied behind him. Even his ankles were tressed.

"Who's he?" Holt called out to the figures seated on the porch.

Orion answered from a comfortable rocking chair, "He works at the bank. Gotta nice suit."

Lillian was seated next to him with a carbine in her lap. "You mean he works for that Thorne woman. He dared to bring me a *final offer* to buy my ranch." She glared at the prisoner. "Lars Viklund, even with his indecent suggestions, at least offered more money." She looked like she wanted to spit. "It's in the fireplace where all the other offers went."

Holt exhaled with exasperation at the news. "Can you get some relief guards out here? We need to talk."

Orion gestured with his rifle. "Big Jeff's out back, Tooley's on the roof, keepin' watch. Dal ain't been here long. He's in the barn arrangin' some horses. We was fixin' to come after you."

Lillian's riders, Sammy Lee and William, took over the watch from the porch. Both of them were heavily armed with guns confiscated from the other night.

"I'm going to leave Tag with you," Holt said in a loud voice. "He'll bite this guy if he moves wrong." The Thorne man's eyes widened with worry. Holt winked at Sammy Lee and William as he followed Orion and Lillian into the house.

Around the table in the morning room, Orion brought three mugs of hot coffee. Holt spoke quietly as though even the shadows were listening.

He eyed both Lillian and Orion. "I suppose Dal already told you about the warrants for your arrest."

"Yes, and that's absolutely crazy." Lillian's eyes were on fire.

"I know. This world has turned upside down." Holt explained. "We have to make the right decisions now so our counter-moves later will be effective."

Holt went on to explain his brief encounter with Gus Brooks, confirming that Marshal Hollings was dead, but that, although Moose was shot up, he was going to be okay. He went on to tell them that Evie did not get hit and was with Moose. "They're all laying low at the Flying G. The foreman there is Gus's brother."

"Sawyer Gates is good people," Lillian remarked, referring to the owner of the Flying G.

"Gus said that Sawyer absolutely hates Isla Thorne.

He also said that she isn't interested in the land north of town, like the Flying G. Just the territory east and south. Said it's all due to railroad concerns." Holt looked at Orion. "Where have we heard that before, peckerhead?"

Orion nodded in realization. "Ho-lee damn. Atlee was right on the nose."

Holt cautioned, "There's more trouble directly ahead, too." He handed Orion the telegram from Captain McCoy.

Orion scowled as he read. "Heard we all were wanted an' the two of you weren't Rangers anymore."

"Wanted for rustling and murder, Orion. You know what that means."

Just then, Dal breezed through the door, with Tag following.

"Fellas out front said Holt was back." He slapped Holt on the shoulder. "Damn glad to see you, hoss."

Holt smiled. "Good to be standing here. You need to hear this, too, Dal. Each one of us should have all the information. Chime in if you have something to add." He glanced at everyone before continuing. "Gus Brooks filled in some blanks for us. Remember the fat man, dressed like a riverboat gambler? That's Madigan Sanders—"

Dal blurted, "Madigan Sanders…from Shreveport?"

"And New Orleans. He's Isla's right-hand man," Holt explained. "And the albino-looking guy? That's Malo Johnson."

"Hearda Malo. He's a hired killer, a back shooter," Dal said. "Damn, Holt, those were th' two eatin' breakfast with her."

"Yeah. I'm a little surprised our leaving the Blue Sky wasn't contested."

Orion spoke up, "I di'nt know 'im, but I heard've Madigan. A report or two of him bein' connected with Calista Theriot way back when. Di'nt seem to fit, he's a gunslinger, not a river rat."

Holt got things back on track. "There's someone new installed as the town judge—Dugal Ridgely. Even Tag here knows more about the law."

Lillian spoke up, "That means they ran off Judge Lagrasso."

"Or worse," Dal noted.

"We have a new mayor too, but he isn't new to town," Lillian added. "The banker, Ames Wooster, was suddenly appointed. Our old mayor fell ill."

"That's right handy," Orion said.

Holt nodded. "Ames…we met him—"

Dal suddenly cut in. "Wait…Ames…Ames *Wooster*? The idiot major at Fort McKavett is a Wooster."

"An officer at McKavett?" Holt asked.

"Yeah, Major Merriman Wooster. About fourth in command. A real blockhead. When Cap'n McCoy questioned him about th' Viklunds, he got all agitated an' angry. Warned us to leave him an' his brother alone…an' his wife."

"Well, that's odd, don't you think?" Lillian remarked.

Holt and Orion both looked at each other and said, "Pretty thin coincidence."

"I always wondered about the bank situation in this town," Holt declared. "Viklund built the size of his spread pretty quick and easy. Two ranchers were run off and their lands taken in by that damn Swede? With no questions? He had to have help."

"There's your connection," Orion observed. "That scary-damn Stebbins sheriff an' his brother the McKavett quartermaster were runnin' stolen cattle an' th' Woosters were takin' care of th' money an' th' fort!" The lanky, older Ranger locked eyes with Holt. "Now we know."

"The brothers Carmichael and the brothers Wooster," Holt mused. "Makes sense now."

"Gotta get more evidence than *it makes sense*," Dal cautioned.

Lillian broke in, "Should you wonder about this major's wife? Why would he warn the Rangers away from her?"

No one immediately answered. The realization of this full Fort McKavett connection was still sinking in. Holt finally spoke, "Yes, we probably should, but there's a lot to concern ourselves with right here." He stood up. "Mrs. Whitman, we need to act. Now. You should leave. Tonight." He looked at Orion.

The lanky Ranger stood as well. "First, we get you somewhere safe, Lilly."

"Then we return and stir up trouble until a real judge arrives," Holt said determinedly. "This Thorne woman is going down. Hard."

CHAPTER THIRTY-TWO

Storm clouds ruled the midnight sky. Thunder grumbled, and lightning turned darkness into day. A wagon, six riders, three extra horses, and a dairy cow made up the forlorn W Bar L group preparing to move out, headed west toward the 5 Star ranch.

While they were packing, the Thorne prisoner was allowed to overhear them speaking of their plans. "We'll be safe in Wilkon," Holt had declared for all to hear.

Before they mounted up, Big Jeff gave one last look around. The widow would not walk with him—it was too sad. When the huge red-haired foreman returned, he strode over to the prisoner laying in the yard and administered two hard kicks to the man's ribs and a rifle butt to the head, knocking him out. "Let th' bastird nap while we git far away. Someone'll find 'im," Big Jeff growled. "If they don't, then ta hell with 'im."

The murky blackness matched the mood. Squeaking saddle leather, occasional thudding hooves, and the creaking and groaning of a wagon added to the deep rolls and sharp cracks of looming thunder.

Lillian sat with Orion as he drove the wagon. She had to leave her beloved W Bar L once before to help trap the Viklunds, but that was not the same. This departure felt like she was not coming back. Tonight, there hadn't been much time to pack all the precious and valuable belongings. Silent tears flowed from her as the W Bar L fell further behind them.

With a rifle across his saddle, Big Jeff took the point. He knew this land well. Dal rode next to the wagon. The other three W Bar L riders fanned out to keep an eye on their flanks. Holt, with Tag in front of him in the saddle, brought up the rear. Whether it was the approaching storm or an unseen threat, his panther spirit was on edge.

Big Jeff was pushing the group to keep a brisk pace in order to reach a small river a few miles ahead. The waterway rambled from 5 Star land through W Bar L property before meandering south out of the county. With the brewing storm about to unleash itself, the stream—which flowed strong most of the year—could become a raging torrent in a heavy downpour.

Thunder that had been rolling ominously now crashed deafeningly as lightning spidered overhead. The increasing bursts of light gave the group flashes of their surroundings. Pounding rain was not far away.

Suddenly, a simultaneous crack of thunder and lightning revealed the entire panorama around them. Three men on horseback stood on a ridge to their right!

Holt kneed his horse and loped to the wagon beside Orion and Dal. "We've got company. Gotta be Isla's men."

Lightning flashed again, but the riders had disappeared.

"What do we do?" Lillian exclaimed.

"I'm gonna ride straight at 'em," Holt announced. "Dal, take my extra horse. I'll try to keep 'em busy."

"I'm goin' with you," Dal declared.

"No, if they get past me, you're going to be needed here." He looked at Orion. "Head south now, just like we planned. We'll meet back up right here after she's safe." He handed the lead rope for his extra mount to Dal and spurred his horse.

"Wait! What about Tag?!" Orion hollered, but thunder drowned him out. Frustrated that there was nothing he could do, he snapped the wagon's reins and turned the caravan south.

As he galloped away, two realizations hit Holt like lightning bolts—one, he had Tag on the saddle in front of him, and two, he had no idea what he was going to do. All he knew was that he needed to delay these attackers, maybe thin a few of them out if he could.

Holt figured the riders had to have come to the W Bar L, discovered it was empty, and sped after them. It would not have been hard to trail their caravan, even in this storm.

Ahead of him was the ridge where the riders had appeared. Lining the narrow hilltop were boulders, trees, and scrub grass, all perfectly good places for someone with a gun to hide. He kept charging, certain in his belief that the Thorne riders were paralleling his group of friends and not expecting a crazy man charging directly at them.

He urged his horse into a lope up and over the crest. Ahead of him was the small river Big Jeff had warned about. Black water was already running and bubbling furiously, warning of the deluge battering the land upstream. Holt guessed Isla's men would use this waterway as a guide as they wended their way to set up an ambush.

Another huge bolt of lightning cracked its way across the clouds, revealing six riders down the ridge ahead of him. They were concentrating on picking their way along the trail and did not see or hear him approach.

As he guessed, they were following the land banks in an attempt to get in front of his friends. He reined in and quickly dismounted next to a large rock outcropping. The craggy escarpment was a good place to protect Tag and his horse. He tied up the horse and placed Tag under a large mesquite bush. Tag did not care much for the thunder and wind, so this snug hiding spot was fine by him. A chunk of jerky from Holt's pocket sealed the deal.

Getting into a firefight with six gunmen wouldn't be the smartest thing Holt had attempted, but he needed to delay the would-be attackers in order to give Orion and the others time to get away. What he needed was an edge. With the attackers focusing on the terrain and imminent storm, they were not even contemplating the notion that someone could be trailing them. The next burst of lightning gave him an idea. The stream where they were traveling was littered with a snaking line of big, round boulders.

Moving away from where he tucked Tag and his horse, he levered his Winchester and fired at the attackers three times, intentionally missing them. Even with the rumbling thunder, there was no mistaking the sharp cracks of a rifle. They reacted as he hoped—jumping down from their horses and seeking cover. To make them think there was a second attackers, Holt drew a pistol and fired three times at random boulders surrounding their mounts. Bullets spat and ricocheted, sending already skittish horses dashing in all directions. He emptied the gun to ensure the horses kept running.

The rain arrived, heavy and cold. Holt had accomplished his first goal: delay the attackers. Now he would shoot to stop them completely.

An extended bolt of lightning illuminated an exposed shoulder and arm. One shot from Holt's Winchester spun the man from his cover. Now out in the open, the assailant became Holt's first victim as his second shot found its mark. Reacting to Holt's muzzle flash, another rider stood and fired, wildly. The young Ranger fired two quick shots at the rider's own muzzle blasts and dropped the man where he stood.

Instinctively, Holt knew it was time to move. In between thunderbolts, he ran crouched to a large scrubby oak. Four Thorne riders concentrated their fire on where he had just been. Quickly reloading his rifle, he waited patiently. At the next stroke of lightning, one of the ambushers was revealed, sneaking between boulders. Three rapid shots from Holt finished the man's journey.

"That was three of the six," Holt told himself. Time to move again. The storm was picking up its intensity, and wind and rain lashed out on the land. He studied the terrain around him. Being near this stream in a downpour was ill-advised. It was time to get out. He figured his next position should be nearer his horse. Then he would high-tail it out of here. He took a first step but loose, wet rock caused him to slip. A rifle bullet whined over his head. A second shot blistered a nearby rock.

The two shots came from behind him!

Suddenly, the riders in front of him unleashed a wild fusillade of gunfire. Bullets and fragments of rocks and branches smashed and caromed, sending damaging shrapnel everywhere. A chunk of rock scraped across the side of his neck. A ricocheted slug slashed across his calf.

Holt was caught in a crossfire. To remain here meant death.

Keeping low, he moved in a zigzag. He did not return fire, not wishing to give his position away. Bullets from the riders in front bit the ground in the spot he had just abandoned. Two shots from a single rifle behind him snapped at trees nearby. Was this attacker by himself or part of the remaining three?

He arrived at the outcropping soaking wet. Rain had only partially reached his horse. It was anxious and alert, its ears turning rapidly. "It's okay, big guy, I don't like this any more than you do," Holt said in a soothing tone. Tag was still tucked under the large shrub, not caring for anything about this night. Holt grabbed the dog with one arm, then tucked him under his other arm that still carried the Winchester. Shots from the group of Thorne riders continued to randomly blaze away as the young Ranger swung into the saddle. He kicked the buckskin hard. The skittish animal, already looking for an escape, was running all out in a few strides.

Bullets pounded away at Holt, but did not reach their mark. He was quickly up and over a ridge, out of the line of fire of the Thorne attackers. He turned north, in a direction away from his friends. He made a quick check. Tag was all right, just quiet and wet. The horse was running smoothly. Holt knew his own body had been hit and was bleeding from his neck and the back of his leg. He was soaked from the hard rain and could not tell how much blood was flowing. He didn't feel a lot of pain, so he guessed these wounds were not serious. He shoved the rifle into its scabbard and concentrated on holding Tag while watching the terrain as best as possible.

From a well-chosen station, Malo Johnson followed Holt's retreat through the sights of his rifle. He fired once, twice, a third time, and again. "Damn it!" he hollered. He saw that Corrigan was upright, and although the Ranger's horse appeared to stumble a little, it kept running, and was now out of range. He thought he had properly judged the windage and elevation. It was not like him to miss. Corrigan's back was a big enough target. He blamed the thunderstorm.

Malo quickly retrieved his horse. Even in the maelstrom of a late-night storm, the assassin stood out—pale skin, long, near-white hair. He jumped into the saddle and followed Holt at a steady trot, leaving the other Thorne men to fend for themselves.

Holt decided the buckskin had run far enough. It wasn't as leggy or rugged as his bay, but muscular and tough enough. He checked the horse down to an easy walk. He looked behind him in a futile attempt to see if he was being followed. The first wave of the storm had passed, taking most of the angry lightning with it for now, but another round was already building in the direction he was headed. Less frequent illuminations lit the ground and sky, but enough to reveal no followers. The horse seemed to be in good shape, not winded, so Holt nudged it into an easy trot. For the moment, the downpour had abated, but there was still plenty of wind and rain to deal with. He noted with satisfaction that this cloudburst would mask his friends' tracks.

He was not sure where he was exactly. He figured to keep this heading until daylight, about two hours away. If he was still clear of Thorne men, he would ride west for the 5 Star. He knew Orion would be operating with the same idea. After they were sighted by Thorne's men, they were supposed to feign heading south, the direction of Holt's town, Wilkon. Holt knew Orion would eventually curl back toward Harold Frederick's massive 5 Star ranch. That had been their plan.

Even though the thunderstorm was still in command of the sky, Holt thought he could smell smoke. Or was it just the sharp smell that lightning sometimes produced?

Abruptly, the buckskin's gait became uneven. "Did you step on something, big guy?" Holt wondered, immediately slowing up to a walk. The horse started tossing its head. Something was obviously bothering it. Holt brought it to a stop and started to climb down for a look when the buckskin collapsed. Tag jumped free. Holt had kicked his feet free of the stirrups before the animal's dropping momentum took him along. Holt hit the soggy ground, but his head hit a shelf of rock.

Blackness that wasn't the storm took over.

Because they were still fresh, Malo Johnson could follow Holt's sloppy hoofprints. It seemed he was closing in on Corrigan. Clearing a hilltop, he found himself approaching cattle milling about. He sniffed at a noticeable smoky smell that permeated, even with the rainstorm. He urged his horse into a slower gait around the herd. He wanted to go faster, but knew better than to spook a large herd. He trotted easily across the grassland pocked with uplifts of rocky shelves.

Lightning lit the world around him. Three silhouettes stood out up ahead, partially blocked by grazing steers.

The sight caught him by surprise. "What the hell!" he exclaimed. Were these his compatriots? Not a chance. They couldn't have tracked down their horses and gotten ahead of him. But who?

As he neared, the shapes turned into people. He readied the rifle on his lap. It was three men, soaking wet, but sooty and filthy. They were gathered around a downed horse. One of them knelt beside a man.

Alerted to Malo's presence, one of the men took hold of the reins of their horses and drew a pistol. A second man watched Malo approach and leveled a rifle in his direction. The kneeling man stood with his double-barreled shotgun also pointed at the noticeably pale man.

Deputy Gus Brooks pulled the hammers back on his shotgun. "Mister, what in hell's creation are you doin' out on a night like this?"

Malo shook his rain-soaked, nearly snow-white hair away from his face. "I'd ask you the same, friend."

The man with the rifle eyed Malo suspiciously. "We live around here. Lightning started a grassfire. We couldn't do much about the flames, but we sure needed to move our beeves away from it all. Fortunately, the rain took care of the flames. Now we're just guiding the herd home."

Gus spoke back up, "Since you di'nt answer our question, you need to turn yourself aroun' an' ride on."

Malo ignored the order and motioned toward the unmoving body of Holt Corrigan. "Is that man hurt?"

Gus hissed, "You already know the answer to that, Malo Johnson. That's why you're out huntin'."

"You have me at a disadvantage, friend. I do not know who you are."

Gus continued, his voice a growl, "I ain't your friend.

Anyone bought by Isla Thorne ain't worth knowin'." He spat his emphasis.

Just then, the three Theriot riders emerged from the hilltop Malo just cleared. The rain and lightning picked up their pace as well. The pale man glanced over his shoulder then grinned evilly at the deputy's group. "It appears you all are outnumbered."

Gus returned the evil grin. "Malo, from this distance, just one of my barrels will blast you clean from that saddle. My friends'll get at least two more of you buzzards before we go down." He raised the shotgun to his shoulder. "Now, get, before I usher you from this world."

Without another word, Malo turned his horse around and loped off, joining the Thorne riders.

Malo did not look back, telling the attackers, "That's Holt Corrigan on the ground back there."

One of the henchmen asked, "Is he dead?"

"Or dying," the pale killer intoned.

"What about the widow an' th' rest of 'em?"

Another henchman broke in. "I saw 'em head south. Riker told us as he was layin' in th' ranch yard that he heard 'em say they was headed for Wilkon."

Malo tugged at his unusual hat. "They're not my problem. I handled my assignment."

CHAPTER THIRTY-THREE

Ranger Captain Laird McCoy appeared once again at Fort McKavett. He had been notified the supply records and action reports he had requested were ready. He had wired ahead, requesting a continuation of his conversation with Major Wooster.

After a brief wait, Captain McCoy was escorted across the post to his meeting. The Ranger captain was led to the major's quarters by a young corporal. McCoy noticed that the young man did not wear a cavalry or infantry emblem, but rather the insignia of the Fifth Military District. Not unusual, but not exactly typical either. He made a mental note of it.

Arriving at the major's personal quarters, they were met at the door by his wife, Celinda, who was always eager to play the gracious hostess. The young corporal announced the arrival of Captain McCoy. "Thank you, Jim, er, Corporal Chase…" she said. "That will be all."

McCoy removed his hat and gave a slight bow. "Mrs. Wooster…"

"Won't you please come in?" She smiled. "I'm

Celinda Wooster. I'm afraid my husband is across the compound. He'll be here shortly."

"Shouldn't I wait in the office? I can—"

"Don't be silly. It won't be long." Celinda did not flaunt her decolletage like her sister, but she was equally skilled in appealing to men. Her smile was warm, and the twinkle in her eyes generous.

The captain couldn't help feeling comfortable around this beautiful woman.

"Please, do sit down." She offered a chair at the dining table set with cups and saucers. She picked up a matching pitcher and poured the captain a cup of hot tea. "I've just made this. You simply must try some. It's my favorite." She poured a cup for herself, then offered him a plate of honeyed biscuits. "And one of these! I make the honey right here."

The captain hesitated.

"Come on, I know you must be hungry."

The captain, ever the gentleman, blew at the hot liquid and took a big sip. He nodded a smile. "You're right." He reached for one of the biscuits.

She motioned that it was entirely proper to dunk the biscuit first.

He did, taking half the biscuit in one bite. Then he enjoyed another sip of tea. One more dunk, and he popped the remainder of the biscuit in his mouth.

"You're right, Mrs. Wooster. This is all delicious. You're very kind." He took another drink and glanced around the room. "Are you sure the major…" He coughed and cleared his throat. "I'm sorry, but we…" He swallowed hard and readjusted the neckerchief at his throat. "We must…w-we m-must"—the room was getting hot, and blurry—"know…about…the connection to…" His words became thick and had trouble coming out. The blurry room went black.

The cup dropped from his hand to the floor, breaking into pieces. The captain toppled from the chair and landed on top of the shattered fragments.

CHAPTER THIRTY-FOUR

Inside the grand and expansive Windmill V ranch house, Calista Theriot anxiously waited for news on the calculated tactics she had launched: unleashing the force of a delusory lieutenant governor, an entrapment of the Widow Whitman, and hiring the assassin Malo Johnson to kill Holt Corrigan. It had been a long night, and morning was creeping toward midday. She restlessly roamed around the massive house, sipping on a crystal glass of rum.

She tried focusing on other matters, like the décor of this manor. Previously belonging to the outlaw Viklund family, the furnishings were—to her—decidedly Swedish and excessively masculine. A Garden District Tudor it was not. Still, it had its charms and comforts. Besides, she would not be inhabiting it for very long. Once Isla Thorne's name was on legal deeds and documents, she would be part of the railroad cabal. She would have her pick of where to live—certainly not in this house or in Stebbins, for that matter.

She was tired of pacing and entered the ranch house's

magnificent study. She poured more rum and tried to settle into one of the room's overstuffed chairs.

Ames Wooster sat in a leather wingback chair by the huge stone fireplace, attempting to stay interested in a thick volume about the animal kingdom. Business kept him in town last night. He rode to the ranch this morning with news that her land purchases over in Kirkland, Wilkes, and Rieger Counties had gone through. Those large parcels, plus her holdings here around Stebbins, now gave her a prominent stake in the swath of Texas vying for railroad development.

Her cook had prepared her favorite breakfast, pancakes, but even with Ames's good news about her property acquisitions, Calista had no appetite. And despite Ames's urging, she also was not hungry for more seductive ways to ease her tension.

Ames finally spoke. "You've created quite a monster in this James Madison Chase. He's certainly coming into his own as *lieutenant governor*." He tried to sound earnest and not the least bit jealous.

"Most people are too afraid to go after big dreams. With him, I can change destinies. I can name my own Rangers. And get rid of some too." She held the amulet at her neck and slowly caressed it. "Soon, Ranger McCoy will be finished. Tomorrow's news will name Madigan as his replacement, a captain of special forces. The widow may have fled the territory, in which case means her ranch is mine." She smiled as she went through her list. "And Malo Johnson is hedging my bet. We need to get all those Rangers, but especially Holt Corrigan."

A knock at the door snapped her out of her soliloquy. She jumped up from the chair and bolted to the door.

An out-of-breath teen stood in the doorway. "Gotta

wire message for Mizz Thorne." He had ridden hard from Stebbins to get out here to the Windmill V.

Thinking it was a note from her lover in Austin, Lieutenant Governor Chase, she looked to Ames. "Pay the lad, will you?"

Ames fumbled for some coins as she turned away to open the envelope, not letting him see it.

Instead, it was a note from Celinda with nonsensical lines about Doll's eyes and Angel's trumpets, and *McCoy Tea Party a Success*. Calista knew the lines referred to poison administered to the Ranger captain. The cryptic wire went on to inform that the articles and wires Celinda wrote implicating Laird McCoy's fraud had been sent.

Calista grinned ear-to-ear.

"Good news, my dear?" Ames wondered.

"Excellent news. We need to celebrate." She retrieved the decanter of dark rum and another glass. Adding to her own glass, she filled one for Ames. He smiled wanly. Rum was not his favorite, particularly this early in the day, plus the telegram had reminded him once again of the rich life Calista led that he knew nothing about.

She raised a toast, and said, "To Celinda and the demise of the Rangers! The mortal beauty of my sister's garden has fated yet another soul to the abyss."

She downed her glass. Her entire body felt warm and alive, so much so that she shed all her clothes and walked back to the study to sit at the large pine wood desk. She sat naked on the leather chair, beaming with energy. She took out a piece of paper and began to write.

There was another knock at the door. Ames went to answer it.

A disheveled Christer Viklund stood there, dirty and not quite dried out from the night's storm.

"I'm here to report to Miss Thorne…about the W Bar L."

Ames began to explain, "She's indisposed at the moment, but you can tell—"

A yell suddenly came from the study, "Have him wait! I'll be right there!"

As they waited awkwardly, Ames and Christer had little to say. The young Viklund looked around the grand entryway. Homesickness and jealousy clouded his thoughts. All of this, the ranch and its beautiful house, had been torn away from him and his family. And now it was hers. He tried not to show his torment.

Finally, Calista appeared, still adjusting her hurriedly thrown-on clothes. "Christer! It's been a good morning, I trust you bring more—"

Just then, someone else knocked at the door.

"A veritable party this morning!" Calista chuckled. "See who it is."

Ames swung the door open. Malo Johnson, as dirty and damp as Christer, stood there, grinning.

Without a greeting, he reported, "Holt Corrigan is dead."

Calista briefly lost her poker face.

Malo continued, "The men sent to capture Lillian and her men failed. But I got Corrigan." He gauged her response. "In the storm flashes, I could see the remainder of the widow's caravan headed south."

Christer awkwardly cleared his throat. "Uh, that's what I was here to tell you." He struggled with keeping eye contact with her. "Uh, not that we failed…the, uh, storm interrupted our trap."

"And Corrigan's one-man counterattack," Malo interjected.

Christer continued, "The man you sent with your final offer was tied up and held by Lillian Whitman and her men. Before they left, he heard them talk about taking the widow to Corrigan's home, in Wilkon. Corrigan said they'd be safe there."

"Is that a fact?"

"Yes, ma'am."

She thought for a moment.

Malo interrupted, "I'd like my money."

Calista licked her lips. Not seductively. More like a hungry tiger deciding it was time to hunt. "First things… Christer, I need you to go to Fort McKavett."

Christer was incredulous. "McKavett? I can't go there. They'll—"

Her look devastated the young man, shutting him up instantly. "I need you there. My sister has work for you, and that is where you will go."

The young Viklund looked at his boots and shook his head in disagreement.

She responded quietly, "When you return, you will be a Ranger, in Captain Madigan's special force."

The young man wasn't even listening. "I-I-I can't. I just can't."

"Can't or won't?" Her words were cold.

"I'll get caught. They'll hang me for sure."

Calista drew a deep breath. With a slight tilt of her head, she suddenly smiled. "There's a box here with some of your family's things. Let's go find it. You should take it."

As she led Christer away, she shot Ames a grave look. It was the banker's turn to stand in awkward silence with Malo.

Calista moved through the spacious house, with

Christer dutifully following. She entered a small keeping room near the kitchen. She gestured over to a table where a large Arbuckle's box sat and said, "I think those treasures should be with you."

He walked over to the table and bent to look inside the box. Calista silently slid behind him, her pearl-handled stiletto in her hand.

He poked around the box's items. "I thought there'd be more—"

His words were cut short by the razor-sharp blade drawing deeply through his throat. As he gasped his last moments, Calista grabbed the young Viklund's collar and pulled him down, making sure he and his lifeblood stayed on the woven rug. He and the box would be wrapped in the floorcloth, taken out back, and burned.

The last words Christer heard before the light left his eyes was, "You had a whole game ahead of you. But you couldn't trust me."

She wiped the blade on his coat and returned it to the sheath in her boot. She looked down at the blond and shook her head. "Your father knew how to play for blood."

Before long, she breezed back to the entryway, rejoining the men. "Where were we?"

"We were talking about my money," Malo answered.

"I'll give you half now. The other half, plus $500 more, when you finish the job." She gestured to a small ornamental bag, stuffed with money and certificates, before picking it up.

"What job? Holt's de—"

"Go to Wilkon," Calista interrupted. "Kill the widow. And anyone else protecting her who gets in your way."

"What if I kill you now and take all of that?" His hand grasped the butt of his Navy Colt.

"Want to think through that call, Malo?" she said dismissively.

Ames stood directly behind Malo. His pistol was aimed at the pale assassin's head.

She slapped three $50 gold certificates into Malo's hand. "Go to Wilkon. Finish the job. Then we'll settle up."

CHAPTER THIRTY-FIVE

Telegrams labeled with the Austin station had been firing off to Stebbins and New Braunfels like a gun. Their messages had been translated into newspaper articles that brought lurid information to Fort McKavett and New Braunfels as well as readers of the *Stebbins Observer*.

The latest issue of the *Observer* featured an article that reported Lieutenant Governor Chase had leveled charges at Ranger Captain Laird McCoy, accusing him of corruption and mishandling money. A secret bank account had been discovered in McCoy's name.

The article went on to tie in the captain's corruption with the fact that the lieutenant governor had also removed Holt Corrigan and Dal Frantze as Rangers, effective immediately. In addition to the two being charged with murder, the warrants for their arrest included aiding and assisting wanted rustler and murderer Lillian Whitman, a Stebbins rancher.

A related story announced that Madigan Sanders had

been appointed to replace Laird McCoy as captain of a special force of lawmen.

In Wilkon, James Hannah read the passage from the same story in disbelief. "*Sanders has been assigned by Lieutenant Governor James Madison Chase to clean up lawlessness in the region from Travis County to Menard County to St. Clair County.*" Recent events had caused Hannah to begin paying for the *Observer* to be couriered to him as soon as it was distributed. This latest issue was only a couple of days old.

He sat at his desk in the office of his own newspaper, the *Wilkon Epitaph*. Atlee Corrigan was seated across from him, listening. "This isn't the first notice that's appeared about Holt being removed as a Ranger, from Stebbins or New Braunfels," Hannah noted. "Holt hasn't responded to my messages. It can't be right, can it?"

"Has Sheriff Wheeler heard anything?" Atlee wondered. She had become more recently involved with Hannah's paper by writing articles and editorials about Texas railroad development.

"No, and that's the strange part," Hannah continued. "If Holt and this Dal Frantze were actually removed as Rangers and wanted for murder, the sheriff here and every other lawman in the region, hell, the whole state, would have been notified. Our sheriff, the Bartle sheriff, the Henion sheriff… None of them have heard a thing!"

"No word about this woman rancher being wanted for murder either?"

"No, there's been no messages from Stebbins—or Austin."

Atlee's face wore a mask of concern. "Something isn't right."

Outside of Stebbins, Calista sat naked at her desk again, re-reading the latest issue of the hometown *Observer*. The takedown of a Ranger captain and the announcement of her own man named to replace the Rangers as head of a special force of lawmen, all gave her an energy that coursed through her body, demanding she shed her clothes.

She savored the passage about Captain Laird McCoy and read it aloud, "*Accused of blatant corruption and mishandling money. A secret bank account in McCoy's name has been discovered and seized.*" She smirked. The secret account was one of Ames's that was filled with rustling funds. He had merely changed the name and taken out most of the money. Although those words were amusing, it was a quote that elated her the most. "*Lieutenant Governor James Madison Chase said, 'He's been doing bad things with Ranger money and it's time the state put an end to it.'*"

And the articles themselves? Written by her own sister, Celinda, and transmitted—by Calista's lover, Chase—from the Austin station directly to the *Observer* editor.

Such a well-planned strike on the Rangers and their captain excited Calista. A bluff? Nonsense. She congratulated herself on such a brilliant concoction.

Back in Wilkon, the whole Stebbins situation was getting the better of James Hannah. "Why weren't wires sent to the entire territory? This is information the region's lawmen should have."

Atlee suggested, "Why don't we go ask the one person who should know?"

They immediately rushed to the Howard's Real Estate, Insurance & Telegraph Office. Soon, the fastidious clerk, Mr. Hayes, was explaining the telegraph operation to them.

"Towns know which telegrams are for them because each message includes the destination town or station." He clarified patiently. "The originating station's name and location is usually included in the telegram's preamble, uh, introduction. This allows the receiving station to know where the message came from."

"So, wire messages begin with the name of the town or station where it's being sent from, right?" Hannah clarified.

"Yes."

"Can you tell if a telegram that says it's coming from, say, Austin, is actually being sent from Austin?"

The clerk blinked. "Why would someone say otherwise?"

Hannah smiled at the man's simple virtue. "Let's just say someone wants to send a message that looks like it's from Austin, but it's really not. Is that possible?"

"The system relies on the trust between the offices and the operators," Mr. Hayes said. "But, no, there isn't a system to verify the true identity or location of a sender."

Hannah nodded slowly.

Mr. Hayes continued, "We handle all kinds of information, some of it *very* confidential. The very nature of that requires a level of trust. If I lose that…" He left the statement unsaid, unsettled at the very thought.

Atlee interjected, "I always thought that operators like you were *sworn to secrecy*."

Mr. Hayes had a small chuckle as though that was a private joke. "I haven't placed hand to Bible, but I have a professional obligation to maintain the utmost discretion regarding the messages I receive and transmit."

Atlee smiled. "My brother-in-law, Holt, would say this is good stuff to know, Mr. Hayes. Thank you for explaining."

Hannah listened to all of this, tapping the roll of *Stebbins Observers* in his hand. Finally, he asked, "If I heard you correctly, there is opportunity for an unscrupulous operator to send false information or misreport where a message is originating from. Is that correct?"

Hannah's reputation as a former lawman and gunslinger suddenly intimidated the clerk. "Why, Mr. Hannah, I surely hope—"

"Oh my god, no, Mr. Hayes! This has nothing to do with you," Hannah assured. "I know you can keep a secret." He looked at Atlee, then returned his focus to the clerk. "We think there is something suspicious going on with transmissions to and from Stebbins. Possibly to and from Austin as well."

Mr. Hayes exhaled a sigh of relief. Composing himself, he said, "That's interesting you should mention that." Both Hannah and Atlee raised their eyebrows and sat up straighter. "After a while, after so many messages, operators like myself can sometimes identify senders by their own fist."

"Fist?" Atlee asked.

"Hand style. Everyone keys Morse code slightly

different," Mr. Hayes explained. "It's a little like handwriting."

Both Atlee and Hannah nodded in understanding.

"It's interesting you say that because the Stebbins operator keys differently now. I'm guessing it's someone new."

"How about the Austin station?" Hannah wondered. "Noticed anything there?"

The meticulous clerk thought a moment. "There is so much traffic there, you know, being the capital and all. Lots of different operators. I really can't say."

"Okay, that makes sense," Hannah said.

"But…" Mr. Hayes began, then paused to collect what he was going to say. "Well, we operators route messages to the correct location based on the destination address. So if a telegram is not destined for a particular station in our routing, we generally ignore it."

Hannah nodded, hoping there was more.

"Although they weren't destined for here or my routing stations, lately I've heard messages out of Austin referring to a lieutenant governor. Someone named James Chase. James Madison Chase." He paused. "I don't know about you, but I don't recall such a man being elected or even named to that office. I make it a point to know who our officials are."

"Me too," Hannah smirked. "And you say these messages went to Stebbins?"

Mr. Hayes bobbed his head. "And Fort McKavett and New Braunfels."

Hannah shook his head, confused.

The fastidious clerk continued, "There has been, however, a lot of wire traffic from Fort McKavett and New Braunfels to Stebbins. Long messages too." He looked around like there were others listening in. “Please don’t tell anyone…” Mr. Hayes then admitted to listening in on long messages not meant for his station. “They seemed to be articles, like for a newspaper.”

“From Fort McKavett?”

Mr. Hayes nodded. “Yes. To Stebbins and New Braunfels. And occasionally one of the messages from this Chase fellow comes from Austin as well.”

“Did you transcribe—”

“Oh no no no no. I would never…I could never…”

Atlee spoke up, “Is there any chance an operator such as yourself could misunderstand what’s being transmitted? You know, make a mistake in transcription?”

“I-I suppose it’s possible, but unlikely.” The clerk shook his head. “If a message isn’t heard or isn’t clear, or maybe the signal isn’t good, the operator always asks to *say again* or *repeat*.”

Atlee exhaled, concern etching into her forehead. “Do you recall anything else unusual about messaging to or from Stebbins? Like, if they sent something that was intended for more than one station, could it be intercepted or just not forwarded?”

Mr. Hayes shook his head. “No. No, nothing like that. Lawmen like Mr. Hannah here or your brother-in-law sent wires all the time asking the region for help or to warn other towns about something bad.”

She bowed her head, worried.

Hannah leaned forward to the clerk. “Mr. Hayes, I have no legal capacity to ask you this, but it involves a legitimate investigation. Do you think you could help?”

CHAPTER THIRTY-SIX

Orion Higbee and Dal Frantze trotted their mounts, both men lost in their own thoughts. It had been a whirlwind few days. First, they staved off an attack on Lillian Whitman's W Bar L, wounding and capturing several Isla Thorne-backed henchmen, killing even more. Bringing those captives into town and locking them up in the face of a corrupt sheriff only stirred the pot.

For their trouble, Holt Corrigan and Dal discovered they had been abruptly removed as Rangers by a lieutenant governor, a politician who has obviously been tainted by Isla Thorne's resources. The two Rangers, Lillian, and her men—including Orion—were accused of murder and other trumped-up charges. Warrants had been issued for all of their arrests.

In order to live and fight another day, they undertook a late-night escape, abandoning the widow's ranch. Their small caravan almost rode into an ambush, which was foiled by Holt's one-man charge. The hardy crew bluffed that they were heading south, hoping Thorne's attackers would believe they were escaping to the protection of the Corrigan compound in Wilkon. All while a Texas prairie thunderstorm hammered at their every move. After a few miles, Orion had curled the small group back west toward the safety of the 5 Star ranch.

Arriving on Harold Frederick's property was a surprise to everyone at the 5 Star. But they immediately understood the reason behind the journey and welcomed the soaking wet travelers with open arms.

Lillian and Frederick became friends during the recent clash with the Viklunds. Both of them felt the heat of Lars Viklund's greed. The widow had abandoned her ranch then as well, but that was to lure the Swedes and their allies, the Carmichaels, into a trap.

Although Isla had yet to clash with Frederick, there was no love lost. The 5 Star rancher had no tolerance for anyone with delusions of grandeur, especially when their wickedness hurt others. He had heard about Isla's designs on accumulating property in order to lure railroad development and its ancillary enterprises. While the wicked Louisianan had not publicly set her sights on his land, he wasn't going to take any chances. His string of riders now numbered nearly sixty men. He had carefully assured that information about that number was planted around town.

"We'd heard that story." Orion grinned when he heard the truth. "An' the one about you buyin' a Gatling gun."

The amused Frederick had said, "Oh my, no. I thought it was a good rumor to start, though."

"Well, it worked." Orion chuckled. "Had me believin'."

The 5 Star owner joined with his own laughter and

said, "I *do* have a cannon. An old smoothbore from Fort Griffin. They're refitting the place, so I pulled a few favors."

"Heckuva souvenir," Orion had said.

"Another good tale for town, too." Frederick winked. "The strength is in the speculation."

Confident that his Lilly and her men were safely squared away in the 5 Star fortress, Orion declared it was time to head back. "We gotta catch up with Holt."

Dal agreed. "Let's ride. Time to bring th' fight to that witch."

They now rode silently through a green Texas valley. Scattered sentries of blackjack, post oak, and juniper hunkered here and there in groups as mesquite shrubs teemed across patches of sweeping grasses. As planned, Orion carried a signed bill of sale to Lilly's ranch, naming him the new owner. Registering this transaction would be the first maneuver against Isla. Secure at the 5 Star, Lilly held another bill of sale, signing the W Bar L back to her. The precaution was something Frederick suggested.

Both Orion and Dal were worn out, mentally and physically. Responsibility to their badges and to their friends compelled them to advance.

Dal's thoughts wandered. He found himself contemplating the war and the daring engagements of his unit. Those experiences felt similar to today—seemingly outnumbered and outgunned. He couldn't help but feel as though he was back in time, his Morgan's Raiders readying for a daring cavalry raid into enemy territory.

Orion focused on Holt and the Thorne ambushers. The attackers should have seen that the caravan was headed south, toward Wilkon. That was too far for their little group to travel safely, but it was a ruse Holt had advised.

The older Ranger told himself the storm likely sent those Thorne bushwhackers scurrying for shelter. But one never knew. They could still be around. He was focused on finding his partner and friend. He exhaled away emotion. Finding the man he considered his brother was what mattered right now.

He was thankful the deluge washed away the tracks of their small group and covered up their trek onto 5 Star land. But the same torrential rain washed out any sign of Holt's tracks, too.

They crossed the stream that had been meant to shelter the Thorne ambush. The waterway flash-flooded in the storm but had since receded.

"Hey! Lookit here!" Dal hollered. He reined up after crossing the stream and was looking down into a collection of boulders and stones along the bank. He pointed at a body driven into the array of rocks lining the channel cut by water. "Don't know how far the current brought 'im, but he ain't been there long."

"That's gotta be one of those mother jumpin' pig thumpers."

"He din't die swimmin'. He's got bullet holes in 'im."

Orion exhaled. "All right. My buddy got one."

"We must be close."

Orion nodded. "Yeah, let's go find that rascal." He proceeded to tell the story of the first morning he met Holt. "The Donegal Hotel in Lodgepole. Been there? Holt comes walkin' in, carryin' himself like a cougar, you know, all coiled-up energy, yet ready to strike with a fury. Well, the Donegal had themselves a service gal…long, thick hair…dimples the size of dinner plates…and very well, uh…"

"Blessed in th' chest." Dal chuckled.

"Yes, blessed indeed." Orion grinned. "This gal was *in-fatch-ew-ated* with ol' Holt. Yessir, infatuated. Rubbed all up against him. Offered him the *Ranger Special*."

"Lots more'n eggs an' steak, huh?"

"You got that right." Orion laughed. "You ain't never seen someone so embarrassed. That Holt turned redder'n your hair."

Both had a good chortle at Holt's expense.

They could tell they should be getting close to the location they were searching for. The world looked different in daylight than in crashing lightning and pounding rain. When Holt left the group to make his headlong charge at Thorne's men, Orion turned the caravan south. At that point, Orion had picked out a gnarled post oak with mesquite bushes circling it, burning it to memory for visual reference on his return. He knew he'd remember it because it reminded him of a teacher at story time.

When they did discover Orion's schoolhouse tree, Holt was nowhere to be seen. The two even split up to scout the position, but found no tracks. No sign of Holt. No sign of Tag Along either.

"Helluva storm," Dal hollered. "We could be a mite off in our calculations."

"No, this is the post oak. Where he took off."

"There's no sign he's been here. Since th' night of th' storm."

Orion silently nodded. "I think we should head off in the direction he went. That's the hill he charged, the only one around. If he's in trouble, it'd be that way."

The two lawmen took off in a lope, up and over the hill where Holt was last seen. They were moving too fast and studying the terrain too hard to have a conversation. Besides, Orion was deep in thought about Holt. His mind carried him to the day he and the young Ranger held off twenty-four warriors in a Comanche raiding party, each of them painted for war, feathers in their horses' manes and tails. It was to be a remembered fight. Holt saved his life that day. The two defended themselves with their rifles and Orion's Ketchum grenades. He still carried a little reminder. A piece of one of his own Ketchum grenade shrapnel had buzzed a little too close. A tiny scar just above his now nearly white beard a memento. Just one of the hurdles they faced while tracking down The Angel…

"There's been cattle here!" Dal called out, breaking Orion from his reverie. "An' a fire! Lookit all that." He pointed to a wide swath of blackened ground before them that spread off into the horizon.

They traveled further, not locating the herd, but discovering plenty of scorched ground. "Ho-lee damn," Orion exclaimed. "Lightning?"

"I reckon so. Imagine what it'd been like without the rain."

They reined up on a small rise to have a look around. The sun had gained control, and with the storm-sotted ground, turned the day muggy and heavy.

In the distance, vultures circled balefully, slow, buoyed by the sultry heat. Orion gritted his teeth. A sign he hadn't allowed himself to think about.

A sign of death.

He spurred his horse hard, covering ground rapidly.

The dark shape ahead came into focus as a downed horse. A coyote and several buzzards were feasting.

Orion skidded the horse to a halt and quickly pulled his rifle from its scabbard, firing four times. Two of the huge birds burst into a scattering of feathers and toppled to the ground. The others cried and flapped frantically away. The coyote yelped in fear and dashed off.

The lanky Ranger could only gaze at the scene in front of him, his mind racing. Dal went on ahead.

"Is…was this Holt's horse?" the one-eyed Ranger asked.

"Yeah. Buckskin. Black legs. Three white socks." Orion's face showed the sadness that was starting to crush his entire body.

"Well, Orion, there ain't no saddle an' bridle. Somebody took all that away." He rode even closer to the dead animal, studying the ground. "There's nothin' of Holt's here. No blood. No sign of a body. An' no sign of Tag Along." He trotted his horse back to Orion. "That's good, Higbee. No bodies."

"Those bastards probably took his saddle."

"In that storm?" Dal challenged. "I doubt it. Thieves are lazy." He took off his hat to smooth back his sweaty, Comanche-long hair. He pulled up the bandanna around his neck to dab perspiration from around his eye and patch. That accomplished, he continued, "Maybe somebody was here to help…an' took him an' Tag Along an' his gear away."

"Yeah. Maybe." Orion nudged his horse and rode a broad sweep around the area of the dead horse, searching for *any* kind of sign. Dal followed. They both hollered for Holt and Tag Along.

Orion finally reined up. "You can tell cattle moved

through here. Headin' north." Dal nodded his agreement. "What's up that way?"

Dal pointed as he spoke. "Well, you got th' 5 Star off to th' west that way. Town is a far piece over yonder to th' east. An' way north of here is th' Flying G."

In a hushed voice, Orion said, "Maybe they took him to town." His mind was reeling. He was getting angry at himself for letting Holt go alone. Overwhelming sadness was building just behind.

Dal answered softly, "Why don't we ride there? To town?" He watched the Ranger he had known for years with concern. "We can check with th' doc. Hell, we can check th' jail."

Orion remembered the other part of the mission—to make enough trouble until real law was brought in. He needed to register the W Bar L bill of sale. He thought of Holt talking about his godfather Silka, saying the former samurai always liked to be attacking. Orion forced himself a short smile at the memory. He pointed his horse east and said, "We need to go. Let's ride."

Hours later, the two Rangers rode into Stebbins. Orion tried hard to clear his mind of guilt, sorrow, and anger. They were riding into who knows what. He had to be able to think clearly, be ready.

He rode past the Blue Sky Inn knowing exactly where he wanted to go. They reined up in front of the building with the large painted letters *DRUGS* on the facade. A weathered sign proclaimed *Physician · Surgeon · Apothecary within*. Orion had spent time here getting patched up after the crooked Sheriff Linus Carmichael sliced the length of his arm with a rapier cane. A wound that only recently healed. "Watch the horses. I'm goin' to check with Dr. Vaughn."

It wasn't long before he returned. Dal could see the answer on Orion's face and didn't ask.

"We're already down by the real estate place, let's get this paperwork registered," Orion said sullenly.

Moments later, they reined up in front of the Charno and Rowe Land Attorneys' office. Orion swung down and marched purposefully inside. Dal was only a few steps behind, studying both sides of the street as he followed.

A stern, bespectacled lawyer looked up from a desk crowded with stacks of papers to see a tall, intimidating man dressed in a black coat and vest entering his office. George Charno removed his glasses, wondering what the man wanted. The bulges under the stranger's long coat attested to the fact that he was armed, supposedly an infraction here in town. The meek attorney was not going to mention that particular ordinance, especially with a second stranger stepping inside as well. This second man was even rougher looking, with an eye patch and a deadly shotgun slung over his shoulder.

"Are you Charno or Rowe?" Orion asked, reaching into his coat pocket to retrieve the bill of sale. Before the man could respond, he continued, "Bought the W Bar L ranch an' need to register my ownership."

The attorney finally answered, gulping, "I-I'm G-George Charno, s-sir." He stared at the paper this tall stranger had presented and gulped for air again. "Are-Are you aware that Lillian Whitman is wanted for rustling? Suspected of murder, too." He could only look Orion in the eye for a moment. "If you've seen her, you should probably inform Sheriff Chapman."

"I'll take that under advisement," Orion responded in

an even voice. "I thought your sheriff was Moose Elkins."

"Oh, he-he, uh, met with an unfortunate accident. He's been replaced."

"*Unfortunate accident*, huh? Tough line of work."

"The new sheriff is seeing to it that things are brought to order. You really should speak to—"

Orion wouldn't let him finish, but still did not raise his voice. "I'll stick to my business. You concentrate on yours. Mrs. Whitman was movin' on. Not sure where. Di'nt ask. She mentioned a problem with a-a-a..." He snapped his fingers rapidly to help remember. "An *Isla*?"

"Uh, that would be Isla. Isla Thorne."

"No one I know."

The attorney cleared his throat and explained that, in addition to their new sheriff, a new Ranger Captain, Madigan Sanders, would be arriving soon to help clean up the crime here in St. Clair County.

"I wasn't aware this was such a rough place."

"Oh yes. Besides Widow Whitman and her men, there are former Rangers on the loose. Holt Corrigan and Dal Frantze. They're wanted for murder." The attorney was proud of the fact that he was privy to all the information he held. "Well, Corrigan isn't on the loose anymore. He's dead. Shot yesterday, resisting arrest."

CHAPTER THIRTY-SEVEN

"Holt? Dead!" Orion roared. "How in the hell… what's wrong with you people?" He wanted to lash out, at someone, anything. The rest of the attorney's information finally dawned on him. "Madigan Sanders? A Ranger? He's a gunslinger! Wanted all over Looisiana."

"Are-are you—"

"I'm Orion Higbee! Holt Corrigan is my friend!" Orion bellowed. "You an' I both know what's goin' on here." He pointed a finger at the attorney. "When all this is over, you better pray you're on the right side of things."

The frightened attorney looked at Dal standing watch by the door. "Is-Is that—"

"He's of no concern to you, Charno. Register this sale. Now."

After the recording of the bill of sale was completed, Orion stormed out of the office and swung into his saddle. Riding down the street, he turned to Dal. "Holt… my god…after everythin' he did for this pissant town."

Anguish and rage were tearing at his soul. "I'm goin' to kill that woman. Her an' the rest of those sonsabitches. Every last one!"

Dal tried to calm him. "Orion, we're gonna find Holt."

"He's dead. You heard the bastard."

"All I heard was some boiled-shirt bazoo with a piece of gossip," Dal said softly.

"They're all in on it," Oron snarled. "I'm gonna get a few of them right now."

"C'mon, Orion…" Dal continued calmly. "Remember New Mexico Territory? Mesilla? We all thought you was dead. That outlaw gang was red-hot tryin' to find you."

Orion was quiet now, taking deep, silent breaths.

"You played possum a good, long time, too," Dal continued. "But we found your ugly butt eventually."

"I 'spose goin' to the jail guns blazin' ain't one of my best ideas. Puts me on their level."

"We even had a funeral for you. Only time I ever saw Cap'n McCoy drunk."

Orion finally shook his head. "That señorita was a fine nurse. An' the mezcal was good. I remember that." A weak smile came to his face.

"I don't believe he's dead, Orion. Maybe he's hurt an' needs our help," Dal said. Long moments passed before he finally spoke again. "You, okay?" he asked.

Orion looked at his old friend. "I'll be better. Thanks, Dal." He sniffed at the air. "Has that Charno fella left to go see the sheriff?"

"Yeah, he's gone. Like someone lit his tail on fire. Definitely headed for the jail."

"That little flug-fisted…" He caught himself. "Let's go to the Blue Sky. See what's new. I gotta a feelin' we'll be havin' a visitor." His grin was deadly. "I feel like chattin'."

They tied up their horses at different hitches and went into the Blue Sky separately. Orion was relieved that Miguel Navarro, the owner, wasn't around. If there was trouble, he would hate that his little pal might get caught in the middle.

Orion stood at the bar and ordered a beer. He dropped a coin next to the mug and tried to strike up a conversation with the bartender. "What's new, friend?"

The barman eyed Orion carefully before responding. "You around for the storm the other night?" he asked.

Orion put on a wry smile. "Sure was. A real frog strangler."

The bartender nodded his acknowledgment at the stranger.

"Seems like Stebbins is growin'," Orion continued. "I'm gonna be doin' some ranchin' hereabouts. You hear anythin' 'bout the railroad comin' through?"

The bartender looked at Orion nervously, like he wanted to say something, then barely shook his head, deciding not to answer.

"How about rustlin'?" Orion tried again. "Any problem with that?"

Down the bar from Orion, Dal shot him a look.

The bartender finally spoke up, leaning in to Orion and talking quietly. He related what he had heard about the widow rancher and her friends being wanted for stealing beef. He said that the word was renegade former Rangers were helping her. One of the Rangers, Holt Corrigan, had been tracked down and killed.

"Madigan Sanders is the new head of a special force

of Rangers," the barkeep confided. "Coming here to track them all down. Keep the peace."

"Madigan Sanders, you say?" Orion brought his mug of beer up to take a sip. His other hand was slipped into a coat pocket. "The only Madigan Sanders I know is *wanted.* In New Orlins. For murder. Besides, I thought Laird McCoy headed up the Rangers in this region."

"Yeah, he was. Newspaper said there was some kind of money problem. Theft or fraud or something." The bartender looked left and right, making certain no one was listening in. "Sanders works for Isla Thorne," he said quietly. "Her friend, the lieutenant governor, kicked McCoy out. Corrigan and Frantze, too."

"I hadn't heard."

"Probably not. You're not from Stebbins."

"No matter," Orion smiled. "I just bought the Whitman ranch, the W Bar L. Bought it from the widow."

The look on the bartender's face was what Orion expected.

Just then, a noise at the doorway announced the arrival of Sheriff Chapman. The sandy brown-haired man wore his nice, but ill-fitting, dark-gray sack suit. Both his eyes were bruised underneath, the result of having his nose broken by Holt days before.

Orion set down his mug and turned toward the door.

"Well, well…" Orion had expected the sheriff, but not who now stood in front of him. "Lewis *Grapeshot* Chapman." The lanky Ranger's voice was thick and even. "You're a long ways off your mark, boy. Shouldn't you be on a riverboat or somethin'?"

At the door, Chapman's face was a study in shock, like he had seen a ghost.

"Good! You remember me." Orion smiled. "Amazin' how your past can come back to haunt you, isn't it?"

"Orion…?"

"How's your ear, Grapeshot?"

Chapman absentmindedly touched his half-gone left ear with his three-fingered left hand.

"No one jumps on a boat of mine an' tries to steal sugar, Lew-wiss. That shovel shoulda taken your head off."

Chapman uncomfortably shifted his stance. "You're under arrest, Higbee."

"What for?"

"You've been aiding Widow Whitman."

"Helpin' a woman is a crime now?"

"She's a rustler. Her men murdered some of my deputies."

"No, Lew-wiss. I was there. They were no-good waylayers. Like you." Orion sneered. "Go play Isla's game somewhere else."

"Knew you turned law dog, Higbee. But you were an outlaw before. An' now you're an outlaw again. You're under arrest."

"Outlaw, hell." Orion's voice was a growl. "I never needed a pardon an' never was on any wanted posters. Been carryin' a Texas Ranger badge for years. Brought down a hundred pig thumpers like you. Hard." He slowly moved closer to Chapman. "Besides, I'm gonna be a rancher now. Just bought the Whitman place." His grin was lethal as he took two more steps. "Do you think there's any man in this town who believes the widow is a rustler? That's just an Isla lie."

Chapman was looking for more courage to stand up to Orion. "The widow has the right to a trial. T-Tell her to come in." He pointed behind the lanky Ranger at the man in the eye patch. "You're Dal Frantze, another outlaw Ranger. You can give yourself up, too."

"And you can go—"

Orion didn't look at Dal but held out a hand to quiet him. Orion had a funny look on his face and a tilt to his head. "*That's just an Isla lie*... Just an Isla lie..." he murmured. "An Isla lie...an Isla lie...an Isla lie..." He repeated the phrase again and again, quicker each time. "An Isla... An Isla... An Isla... An Isla... An..." Realization hit him. "*Calista*."

In three rapid strides, Orion was face-to-face with Chapman.

"She's here, isn't she?"

"She who?" Chapman crossed his arms defiantly.

"You're as bad a liar as you were a pirate, Chapman. You stink as a lawman, too. Crossin' your arms like that. How're you gonna draw on anyone?" His rattler-quick reach pulled Chapman's pistol from its holster. Disdainfully, Orion shook his head as he emptied the gun of bullets. He pushed past the shaken Chapman and out onto the planked sidewalk. In an easy, underhanded motion, he tossed the gun into a water trough.

Dal chuckled and followed his friend outside. Soon they were aboard their horses and trotting down the main street.

"Where to now, hoss?" Dal said, checking their back trail.

"We're payin' a visit to the Flying G," Orion said, eyes slitted in determination. "There is no Isla Thorne. It's Calista Theriot. And the game just changed to blood stakes."

CHAPTER THIRTY-EIGHT

As they rode hard toward the Flying G, Orion filled in Dal on the dangerous creature that was Calista Theriot. While he listened, Dal continually checked behind them, making sure they weren't being followed. When they slowed their horses to a walk, Orion pulled out a folded-up edition of the *Stebbins Observer* and read. He had heard too much back in town that he hadn't known about.

The loss of his friend Holt never strayed far from his mind, but Orion was beginning to channel his grief and anger into tactical action. He had to.

He finally broke the silence, and said, "*James Madison Chase*. Says here he's the lieutenant governor. Who in the hell is this boghole? He wasn't elected, was he?"

"There's no governor, that's for sure," Dal answered. "There's been a military district supposedly runnin' Texas an' Loosiana since th' end of th' war. Buncha blue-bellies callin' shots for this 'n' that. No one knows who's in charge in Austin. It's a mess."

"He was appointed by someone. Hell, maybe even Calista. Wouldn't put this charade past her," Orion grumbled. She was now forefront in his mind as well.

Something clicked inside Dal. "Hey! You just might have somethin' there with that charade talk!" He began to excitedly explain to Orion about his old unit, the Second Kentucky Cavalry Regiment. "You Yanks knew us as Morgan's Raiders," he said proudly.

"You've told me," Orion said. "What you haven't told me before is that you're from Kentucky."

"Why do you think I drink bourbon instead of that Irish rotgut you favor?" Dal smirked. "Anyway, listen to what I'm sayin'...we did more than make raids an' destroy bridges an' stuff. We had spies circulate made-up troop movements. We tapped into telegraph lines to spread rumors. We even sent false orders that way. We made stuff up!"

"But you got caught. Hobson an' Shackelford got y'all in Ohio."

"That's not the point!" Dal rolled his eyes. "The point is *confusion.* We confused th' deuce outta you Federals an' caused all kindsa hell. *With lies*. We routed garrisons in Lebanon, Corydon, Vienna...all over Kentucky, Illinois, an' Indiana. They din't know whether to poop or wind their watches. We got further north than any other Reb unit, Orion. Our lies and deception worked, like it is now."

Orion studied his friend like he was seeing him for the first time.

"Look at these articles," Dal continued. "They only *say* they're from Austin or from this lieutenant governor. Are they really? You said Calista Theriot's a card player, right? What if she's bluffin'? Back when you were privateerin', how many times did your little gunboat overtake somethin' larger because you tricked th' other pilot?"

Orion's face brightened with understanding.

"See? You know what I'm sayin'!" Dal enthused. "What if this *lieutenant governor* is justa made-up someone?" He caught his breath. "I wish I still had that telegram from th' cap'n. It'd be interestin' to take another look at it."

Orion fished into a coat pocket. "I got it. Holt gave it to me around Lilly's table right before we left. He forgot it, so I picked it up. Here." He handed the paper over.

Dal read the message. "I'll be damned," he muttered. "I'll be *gotdammed*!" Handing it back to Orion, he said, "Read it again. Notice anythin' different?" He didn't wait for Orion to respond. "When was th' last wire you got from him where he signed off with his whole name? *CAPTAIN LAIRD McCOY*. That's not right. He always signed off with—"

"McCOY," Orion finished the point. "An' he wouldn't have sent this to *RANGERS HOLT CORRIGAN AND DAL FRANTZE*. It would've just been *HOLT AND DAL*."

"Exactly," Dal declared. "Th' cap'n din't send this."

"Then who the hell did?" Orion thundered. "Who the hell is this Lieutenant Governor Chase?"

"A lot more questions than that, my friend. Like, what's goin' on with th' cap'n? Does he know about any of this? Are me an' Holt really not Rangers? Are those charges against you an' th' widow real?"

"The people wearin' the badges an' callin' the shots right now in Stebbins sure think so," Orion said, rolling his neck to ease tension. "Well, when we head back to town, we're not sendin' any wires. Whoever's in that office works for Calista."

The remainder of the ride to the Flying G was spent pondering their next moves. It was clear to them that Calista was behind everything, but immediate solutions were not handy.

It was nearing suppertime when they got closer to the ranch. Evidence of the wildfire was everywhere. The swath of scorched grass and blackened trees led into the distance.

"*Ho-lee damn*," Orion announced. "I dunno if they lost animals, but this is gonna hurt the herd just the same. Grazing land gone, just like that."

"It'll grow back."

"Not right away. Cows gotta eat, constantly."

They trotted through the open gate of the Flying G ranch house. In the large front yard, Deputy Gus Brooks was preparing a small, one-horse wagon for travel. As the two Rangers hailed the deputy, a dog raced from the porch to greet them.

Orion peered at the gray-and-brown dog. "That sure looks like…" Suddenly, a smile bigger than Christmas crossed his face, and he jumped from his saddle. "Hey! That's Tag!"

The floppy-eared dog came bounding over.

"Hey boy, where you been?" Orion knelt and hugged the dog. "Where's your master?" he asked, patting Tag's back and rubbing his head and ears. The dog couldn't get enough of the attention, and Orion didn't want to stop either. A few drops of happiness leaked from the lanky Ranger's eyes.

Just then, Holt stepped outside onto the porch, setting his narrow-brimmed hat onto his head. He was concentrating on picking up his saddle and didn't expect to see other riders in the yard.

Orion stood and rushed to Holt. The young Ranger saw him coming and dropped his saddle.

Orion wrapped him in a huge bear hug. His words came rapid-fire. "You're alive! What happened? Are you okay?" He stopped and looked at Holt. "Where the hell have you been?"

"Playing dead."

"I should deck you for scarin' the years outta me. Years I can't afford."

Moose's fiancée, Evie, had come out to the porch and witnessed the reunion. "I did that for ya, Orion," she called out. "Smacked 'im good an' proper."

She hopped down and hurried over to Orion, greeting him with a hug. "Th' night of that big storm, we had to move beef away from th' wildfire. Lightnin' set it off. In th' midst of it all, we discovered Holt. His horse had been shot. When it gave out an' fell, it took Holt down too. He hit his head on rock an' knocked 'im right out."

"Thought your head was thicker'n that," Orion teased Holt.

"Stroke a luck we came along when we did. We done scared off some fancy-hatted gunman. That sugar-eater gave me th' creeps," she shivered. "He was white as a ghost. With a stupid hat, by the way. He was movin' in to see if Holt was really dead. Gus an' his shotgun convinced 'im an' his friends to ride on. 'Course, me an' Jak had guns on 'em too."

"So, when did you smack him?" Orion wondered.

"Well, after that ghosty fella an' them rode off, we was able to check Holt's body. Rolled 'im over. He opened one eye, then th' other. Then he smiled an' said, 'Hi Evie.'" She shook her head, and said, "'*Hi Evie*! As though we was havin' tea or somethin'. Scared th' peewoddin' outta me.'"

Orion and Dal laughed.

"I had to lay there," Holt defended himself. "I didn't know who was moving around."

"When Holt stood up is when I smacked 'im. He was a bit wobbly, but I didn't care," she scoffed. "I don't have th' years to waste either, Holt Corrigan!" She smacked him across the shoulder again. Orion and Dal laughed harder.

Holt could only smile and shake his head. "I didn't mean to scare everyone. I had to stay down. I was gonna shoot whoever rolled me over until I heard Gus talk."

Orion smiled. "So, you're really okay, peckerhead?"

"Just a couple of scrapes…my neck and my calf. Damn rock ricochets."

Orion hugged him again.

Dal thumped him on the shoulder. "Sure glad to see you above snakes, Holt."

The appearance of Orion and Dal dawned on the young Ranger. "Wait a minute, you're here! Does that mean—"

"Lily's safe and sound," Orion finished the thought. "She's got Mr. Frederick and the 5 Star crew watchin' over her."

Holt smiled in relief.

Orion said, "If she ain't safe there, no one's safe anywhere."

"I was just saddling up to head to our rendezvous. I needed a new horse, though. Bastards got my buckskin."

"We found it," Orion said. "Made me fear the worst. Your bay is at the 5 Star. The wrangler there, Purd somethin', says to tell that sonuvabitchin' Corrigan hello an' good luck gettin' that fine horse back."

Holt chuckled. "He's a character, isn't he?"

Gus interrupted the welcoming commotion, and said, "Well, I'm headed into town, boys. Time for supplies." He held up a bowler hat and wig from the seat. "Got my disguise. I'm all ready."

"A little late for shoppin', ain't it?" Orion said.

"It's better now if I arrive at dusk. Or later. Holt stirred up a hornet's nest th' other day."

"Sorry for that, Gus," Holt said.

"Nah. It was good them sidewinders tasted some heat. Besides, arrivin' late is good for lil' Navarro too. He sets us up from his Blue Sky pantry. Too obvious to shop at th' general store anymore."

The group could only shake their heads in frustration.

Gus added, "Say, now that you're alive again, Holt, I'll get a message off to Wilkon. They don't need to be thinkin' you're with th' angels."

Dal jumped in. "Gus, we can't trust the wire office. It's under Calista's control."

Gus harrumphed. "Not to worry, that place is easy to get into an' I know how to send a wire. Wait...Calista? You mean Isla, right?"

"Listen, everyone." Orion turned serious. "We just came from town. Y'all need to hear this. You know that new sheriff?"

Holt responded, "Isla Thorne's man, Chapman?"

"That's Lewis *Grapeshot* Chapman. A pirate. One of Calista's river rats. I've tangled with him…before."

"Calista? Theriot?" Holt said. "You sure?"

"Yes. Dead sure." Orion's eyes locked with Holt's. "*Isla Thorne* is Calista."

Holt blinked. The words of Four Shields strode across his mind: *This coyote appears to be a master at causing confusion, lying, and convincing people to believe her*.

He looked at Orion. "You and Boody both said she was capable of anything to get what she wanted."

Orion silently nodded yes. Dal and Gus stood in silence, contemplating this news.

"This game just changed, didn't it?" Holt declared.

CHAPTER THIRTY-NINE

A voice interrupted the solemn meeting out in the yard, "Sawyer says no one else's ridin' out tonight. Come get ya some supper!" Jak Brooks, Gus's brother, summoned the group from the porch with a wave. "There's a big bin of water here, with soap and towels fer washing up."

He greeted Orion and Dal in the yard. "Proud to know ya. Gus's talked about yer exploits alot." He showed the Rangers where they could put up their horses. "They look a bit worn, I'd say. We'll let 'em cool and set 'em up later with some good grain and fresh water."

Sawyer Gates, owner of the Flying G, was a good host. Happy to have a full table, even with the circumstances. He had been a widower only a couple of years, and lost his only son in the war. He had basically adopted Gus and Jak, treating the brothers like family, hiring Jak as his foreman.

Sawyer's daughter, Perla, was a war widow and kept the Flying G house, including the cooking. The smell of her fried chicken and mashed potatoes enticed everyone as they entered the house.

Holt grinned. "We're about to experience the best thing about trail food."

"Yessir, my dear friend," Orion said with an equal grin. "The best thing about eatin' on the trail, is not eatin' on the trail."

Everyone's mood was boosted further when Evie brought a tired-looking, but smiling, Moose Elkins to the table.

Orion and Dal immediately leaped from their chairs in joyful surprise. The cacophony of greetings filled the room. "Moose! Lookit you! Big'un! How're ya doin'?"

They all had huge grins, and even though he didn't need or want it, helped Moose into a chair. He looked around at all of them. "Damm, it's good ta see ya, my friends," he said.

"I warned him before." Holt smiled. "Even though he's so big, he can't just try to swat those bullets away."

The table had a good laugh.

Evie explained, "He's not himself yet."

"But it's gettin' better evry day," Moose added. "I'm startin' ta pull my weight aroun' here."

"You sure, Moose? That's a lotta weight," Orion teased.

The group erupted into more laughter.

The delicious supper left everyone full and contented, especially the three visiting Rangers, and particularly Tag Along. Sawyer and his Flying G ranch hands left after dessert to do some final chores for the day.

Holt and Orion tried to help clean up, but Perla and Evie would not allow them. "Sounds lik' y'all got big plans ta discuss," Evie said.

Holt, Orion, Dal, and Moose settled in around the table, nursing glasses of whiskey.

Orion spoke up first, and said, "Dal, tell Holt what you was tellin' me. 'Bout Morgan's Raiders."

The one-eyed Ranger pulled a piece of paper from his vest pocket. "This telegram forcin' us out as Rangers…? Holt, I din't notice before 'cuz I was mad as a hornet. Lookit how our names is addressed!"

Holt read the wire message again. "Pretty formal. Especially from the captain."

"Exactly! An' th' way he signed off too."

Holt tapped the paper. "You don't think he wrote this."

"No, sir, I do not. Hit me like a locomotive. I been gettin' telegrams from Cap'n for a long time. He *always* used my first name an' signed off with his last."

Holt acknowledged, "Yeah, me as well."

Both Orion and Moose chimed in their agreements.

"We used tricks all th' time durin' th' war," Dal continued. "Rather than tearin' down Yankee wires, we raised all kindsa hell with 'em. We sent false reports, misleadin' troop strengths, lyin' about movements. We got commanders to move their armies just with telegrams. You know, *lies* that caused *confusion*. It worked too, for a spell."

Holt gave thought to what Dal was saying. There was a point there.

"This riverboat pirate likes to gamble, doesn't she?" Dal asked. "Never knew a card sharp that din't like a good bluff every now an' then. You know, set their own odds."

"Then what the hell do we do 'bout it?" Orion broke

in. "How do we find out where this is all comin' from? An' jus' who the hell is this Lootenant Gov-ner Chase?"

"More importantly, how do we stop it all?" Holt asked.

As the myriad of questions sat uncomfortably with no immediate answers, weariness took over. Dal and Moose shuffled off to sleep, leaving just Holt and Orion.

"So, you're lookin' at the new owner of th' W Bar L," Orion announced.

Holt stared at his friend with surprise.

"Yeah, Frederick at the 5 Star recommended it. Said it might take some heat off Lilly."

"Good tactic." Holt nodded.

"She's got my bill of sale givin' it all back once we settle things."

The weight of their predicament closed in. Once again, the two friends were facing a deadly challenge.

"We've got a lot ahead of us," Holt observed, finishing his glass of whiskey. "Calista Theriot doesn't just play for high stakes, does she?"

Orion rubbed at his tired eyes before replying. "When I was in that game, it was for the spoils. She plays for blood. And enjoys it." He exhaled. "That part's no bluff."

Holt borrowed his friend's exclamation and chuckled a response in spite of the situation. "Ho-lee damn."

They slipped into silence, deep in thought.

Orion spoke softly, "When those bogholes in town were practically gleeful at announcin' you were dead, I —" He caught himself and was quiet for several moments before he spoke again. "I'm glad we found you, peckerhead."

CHAPTER FORTY

Word of Sheriff Chapman's run-in with Texas Ranger Orion Higbee spread quickly through town. Whispers of his buying the widow's W Bar L latched onto the town's grapevine.

It did not take long for the news to reach the ears of Ames Wooster in the Stebbins bank. Surreptitiously, he left his lobby office and climbed the stairs to the private apartment. He had spent the night there with Calista and had not seen her leave.

She answered his knock, sleepily. They had celebrated the news of Holt Corrigan's demise through the night. He had left her bed only because there were bank appointments he could not cancel.

After a long embrace and welcoming kisses, he held Calista at arms-length to breathlessly report the news and appearance of Higbee.

"Orion? Orion Higbee?" Her face changed, even softening a bit, running back to a bygone time. She unconsciously reached up and rubbed the bump at her hairline.

A reminder of a night long ago. "He-He was…hmmm… Boody…"

"Calista?" Ames noticed the difference.

She paid no attention to the banker, rummaging through rushing waves of mental images. "That-that was a long—" She caught herself and smoothed the hair over the permanent lump above her temple. Her sinisterly beautiful countenance returned. "So, another Ranger wants to play?"

Ames nodded. "Sheriff Chapman wants blood."

"He apparently had the chance to do so. What was he waiting for?" she sneered, before waving her hand. "No need to answer that."

"I thought you'd want to know." Ames smiled and started to reach for her. She turned and walked away.

At her desk, she retrieved a long wire message. "Get this over to Max Palmer at the *Observer*. Right now. I know it's not Wednesday, but I want his next edition, *with this in it*, out tonight. Understand? Tonight!" Ames bobbed his head in understanding.

As she closed the door on Ames's departure, she cooed to herself, "Orion, my old friend…upping the ante with the W Bar L? How like you." She smirked. "Well, you mangy *carcajou,* here's my raise."

CHAPTER FORTY-ONE

The faint light of false dawn wasn't the first thing up this morning. Ranch duties had the Flying G inhabitants stirring, and restlessness shook the Rangers staying there awake.

After another delicious breakfast from Perla and Evie, the three lawmen helped clean up. They wanted to show their appreciation. Sawyer Gates and his Flying G crew had already set out on their daily chores. There was always work to do on a ranch.

With Orion having more reach than the other two, he was elected to help fix the hinges on a few of Perla's topmost cupboards. Dal shoveled old ashes from the stove's firebox into a bucket. Holt stood on the porch and shucked corn while watching Tag Along stretch his morning legs, racing around the front of the ranch house. The young Ranger was also loosening up his neck and calf—the places where ambush ricochets had caught him.

Just then, Holt noticed a moving speck in the distance. It wasn't throwing much dust or even ash. The moisture from the storm was still keeping things dampened down. Holt's concern level was low. If it was a rider, it was only one.

Before long, he could tell it was a small wagon—Gus. They had expected him to return from his covert visit to Stebbins much sooner, but he wasn't so late as to cause alarm.

Deputy Brooks wheeled into the front yard and set his brake. He hefted a bag of flour from the wagon and trudged up to the porch.

"Morning, Gus! We wondered where—" Holt noticed the man's appearance. Gus's right cheek around his eye was puffed and bruising. There were scrapes along his right jaw, too. "What the hell happened?"

Gus stopped at the top of the stairs and set the heavy bag by his feet. "Chapman happened. An' a few of his... *deputies*."

Orion and Dal heard the commotion and hurried outside.

Dal exclaimed, "Gus ol' boy, who worked on your face?"

"That Chapman fella. Chapman an' his men. They wanted to know where Orion an' Dal went. Even brought Moose up, too."

"How did they know—"

"They don't know. They was just fishin'." He waved off the concern. "There ain't enough people who know my connection out here."

"So how'd they get you?" Holt wondered.

"They grabbed me after I left the telegraph office, sneakin' to my buggy at the stable. I tripped over a damn cat, woke the damn liveryman. He turned me in an' they hustled me to jail. That's where they did all this." He smoothed his mustache. "Chapman's irate as a tromped-on toad since Orion showed 'im up. My face was a handy outlet."

Orion growled, "Those skunk-eatin'—"

"Glad they got me there an' not the Blue Sky. I sure don't want to get Navarro in trouble." They all nodded in agreement. "That new telegraph operator of Isla's is a heavy sleeper. Loud too." He chuckled. "Anyways, I got the wire sent to the marshal in Wilkon, though. I let 'em know Holt's alive, despite what they might be hearin'."

"I appreciate that, Gus. Very much." Holt smiled. "Let's have a look at that eye. You really caught one."

"I'm fine," Gus dismissed the offer. "What else did I hear… Oh! Besides the talk about Orion humiliatin' their sheriff, word was Isla, er, Calista would soon be hostin' railroad men. Big developers. It was in the paper." He reached into his coat and pulled out a folded-up newspaper. "This just came out. Suppertime last night. Lil' Navarro let me have his. I ain't read it yet though."

"So, if Chapman locked you up, how'd you get away?" Holt wondered.

"I used to be deputy, remember?" Gus chuckled and dangled a set of cell keys from his pocket. They all laughed in spite of the situation.

"Let's get this unloaded for you, Gus," Holt offered.

"Hold on…" Dal stopped everyone. He had begun reading the front page of the *Stebbins Observer* that Gus just brought. "I don't believe this!" He pounded the paper forcefully with his finger. "Lookit here…!"

They all gathered around. Next to the top article about railroad developers visiting Stebbins, was another story with a lurid headline, *FORMER RANGER CAPTAIN DEAD*.

They shushed each other to silence in order to read.

"Former Ranger Captain Laird McCoy has finally been brought to justice. Wanted for fraud, theft, and murder, McCoy had only recently been apprehended and incarcerated. McCoy has been killed in a foiled jailbreak.

According to officials in Austin, the escape attempt was led by wanted former Ranger Orion Higbee and other disgraced Rangers. The attempt was thwarted by prison guards, and McCoy was killed..."

The article went on to report that one of the renegade Rangers, Holt Corrigan, had been shot and killed earlier, for resisting arrest.

The three lawmen were shocked and stunned into sadness as they read. Anger soon followed.

Their enraged questions overlapped one another. "Where did this happen?" "When?" "What jail?" "Do they really think we did it?"

The questions came rapid-fire. Answers did not.

Suddenly, Holt stood, pointing at the newspaper. "That's where we start!"

CHAPTER FORTY-TWO

Holt paid no attention to his companions' warnings. He had little regard for newspapers, reporters, or the stories they peddled. His friend James Hannah operated one of the few publications he respected, knowing Hannah's newspaper printed only accurate information, letting readers decide what to think. This latest edition of the *Stebbins Observer* did more than light his fuse. His partner, Orion, could only follow along and hope to keep his friend from harm. Or from harming someone else.

Holt was determined. He was going to ride straight into town. His mission was clear. It was Orion's steady urging that resonated with Holt's *tsét'soyé* bear spirits, which calmed him down. They still rode to Stebbins, except that they held to a side street and back alley, where they tied up their horses.

A young newspaper intern sneaking a cigarette out back tried slowing them down to no avail. Holt charged inside and stormed around the printing press into the publisher's office.

"Are you Palmer? Max Palmer?"

"Yes, I'm Max Palmer, publisher and editor..."

Holt picked up a copy of the latest *Observer,* sitting on the man's desk. He once again read the headline about the captain to himself. He took a deep breath. Orion watched his partner, not certain what was going to happen next. He'd seen Holt this way before, coiling like a panther ready to strike.

"This article, about Ranger Captain McCoy, did you write it?" Holt barked, holding the edition in the man's face.

"N-No, I-I did not."

"You didn't? Then who did?"

"It-It c-came from a trusted source—"

"Trusted?" Holt snorted in derision.

"Yes, it—"

"Silence!" Holt snarled. "You'll speak when I say so." He took a deep breath. "The escape attempt that supposedly killed Captain McCoy...where did it occur?"

"I-I d-don't kn-know..."

"You don't know? Isn't that an important detail?"

"Y-yes, b-but I-I d-don't—"

Holt wouldn't let him finish, battering the man with questions. "Where would you guess this jailbreak happened?"

"I-I d-d-don't know. Austin? Fort McKavett?"

"Interesting choices, Palmer." Holt's eyes were flinty. "Let's say you're right, that it happened at either one of those. How long does it take to travel from here to the fort?"

"I-I don't—"

"HOW LONG, DAMN YOU!" Holt thundered.

"Th-Three days, at-at best."

"Three days," Holt said in a calmer tone. "Even longer to get to Austin, yes?"

The tense and timid newspaperman nodded his head vigorously.

"Your story said this jailbreak attempt was led by Orion Higbee. When did it occur?"

"Th-The wire w-with the article said j-just the day before yesterday."

"Day before yesterday." Holt nodded and looked at Orion. "That's less than two days ago." His Ranger partner grinned back, enjoying the show.

The publisher tried to defend his work. "If y-you have a p-problem with the article—"

"It's a load of crap," Holt interrupted again, his anger rising.

"Now see here—" Palmer started to stand.

Holt reached across the desk and poked his finger into the chest of the publisher of the *Observer*. "Sit down!" he commanded. "You need to hear this."

The intimidating words from the young Ranger put the newspaperman immediately back down into his chair.

"There is no way in hell Orion Higbee led this attempted jailbreak."

"An-And you know th-this how?" Palmer asked.

"This is Orion Higbee." He gestured at the lanky Ranger next to him.

Palmer's eyes got wide.

"Yesterday, Orion Higbee was right here. In Stebbins. Registering his purchase of the W Bar L. You know what he did then? You heard about it, didn't you? What did he do? ANSWER ME!"

"He h-had a st-standoff with Sheriff Chapman. T-

Took his gun. At the Blue Sky." Palmer realized what was being said.

"That's right." Holt paused to glare predatorily at the man. "Do you see wings on this man? DO YOU?" he thundered. "He'd have to have a magical horse to get to Austin, or even McKavett, run a jailbreak, and return." He stopped talking and glared angrily at the man behind the desk.

The newspaperman could only sit, dejected and silent.

"I know you don't write everything that appears in your publication," Holt continued, his voice a bit softer now. "But you do have a responsibility to present information. Factual information. Yes?"

"Well, y-yes, of-of course," the publisher agreed, frightened, not sure where this was leading. "But the wires…the wires came from Austin…they have the capital dateline. They have to be legitimate."

"Do they?" Holt's intensity stared the publisher into silence. "What if it came from someone with criminal intent? Deliberate lying? Someone who purposefully wanted you to misinform your readers?"

"That's impossible!"

"Is it? Is it, Palmer?" Holt hissed. "Did you know Reb troops tapped into existing telegraph lines during the war? They intercepted Yankee communications and sent false information and orders. Think that can't happen now?"

"N-N-No, I didn't—"

"You disgust me." Holt sneered and shook his head with contempt. "You're just like all the other no-account scum. You only care about selling more papers."

Palmer was crestfallen. "I-I j-just print…"

"You just print what?"

"I-I j-just print what I'm told."

"By who?" Holt snarled.

"By…by…" The newspaperman bowed his head in shame. "Her."

"You miserable…" Holt started to lunge around the desk but was stopped by Orion.

Holt blew up. "These good-for-nothing bastards! They print what they want. Miserable liars are what they are…" He grabbed at one of his pistols. "I should shoot you now, you son of a bitch…"

Orion moved beside Holt, one hand gently keeping Holt from drawing his gun, his quiet tone directly in the young Ranger's ear. "We need this town behind us, Holt. We need this man. And his newspaper."

Palmer was in tears, and pleaded, "What do you expect of me?"

"The TRUTH, damn you! Newspapers are supposed to tell the truth!" Holt was roaring again. "Not willingly lie to the people!"

"I t-try to represent the t-truth."

Holt thundered, "Represent… What the hell does that even mean?"

"I-I try…" Palmer was barely audible.

"Not lately, you pathetic—"

Orion silently held up a hand, stopping Holt from finishing. The older Ranger spoke quietly, but firmly at the newspaperman, and said, "It takes courage to stand strong when you know you are right while others are so wrong."

Palmer wiped his tears away with his sleeve.

Holt softened his glower at the newspaperman. "Try harder, Palmer." He picked up a copy of the Observer from the man's desk. His fist crumpled the paper as he shook it at Palmer's face. "Newspapers shouldn't print the crap you've been spreading."

Catching his breath, Palmer found his voice, and said, "I'll certainly report on what we know. What we can verify."

"Start with being your own man. Not Isla Thorne's." Holt gathered himself to leave. "By the way, did you know that Isla is really Calista Theriot, the Louisiana pirate? She is. Try reporting that."

"Wh-What? And who-who are you?"

"I'm Holt Corrigan. A guy you printed was dead." He tossed the edition of the paper in his fist at the publisher's chest and left the office the way he came in.

Walking their horses warily to the end of the back alley, Holt and Orion reined up. Holt had calmed down, but not much.

"So now what?" Orion eyed his partner.

"Calista's holding all the cards at the moment," Holt said.

"You think Cap'n is dead?"

Holt grimaced. "I do. Not from any damn jailbreak, but she's killed him. I'm sure of it."

"I di'nt want to say so, but I got that feelin' too."

Holt nodded sadly. "It's only a matter of time before this Madigan Sanders shows up, sworn in as captain of this ridiculous Special Force of Rangers. Whatever the hell that's supposed to be."

Orion agreed. "An' he'll have a bag of badges. Handin' 'em out like candy to all her men."

"Then they'll be coming after us and anyone who stands in her way."

"Wish we had more men," Orion noted. "Gotta be more than a few angry real Texas Rangers right now. Where are they?"

"I'm guessing they don't even know about the captain or what's happening here."

Silence came between them. Finally, Holt spoke, "I think it's time one of us went to Fort McKavett. There's too much smoke coming from there. You talked with Dal, you know this Major Wooster there is dirty. Who is sending the fake wires from there?"

Orion exhaled. He knew going to the fort was a good play, but didn't want to leave his partner or his friends.

"Okay, Ranger Corrigan. What are you going to do?"

"I'm not a Ranger. I'm an outlaw." Holt grinned. "But that Theriot judge is holding court this week. I'm going to see about getting my badge back."

CHAPTER FORTY-THREE

Inside the Howard's Real Estate, Insurance & Telegraph Office in Wilkon, the operator, Mr. Hayes, was busy translating an early morning message, the dots and dashes coming rapidly. At the request of Wilkon newspaper owner James Hannah, he had been paying close attention to wires sent to and from Stebbins, especially if they involved Austin and Fort McKavett.

He had been up all night after receiving a very unique transmission.

Days ago, Hannah and Atlee Corrigan had come to his office, confused about how transmissions were sent—or not sent. Mr. Hayes had admitted to listening in on a couple of long messages not meant for his station, but for Stebbins and New Braunfels. The wires had originated from Fort McKavett. *"They seemed to be articles, like for a newspaper,"* Mr. Hayes had said then. He also went on to describe similarly addressed messages from someone identified as Lieutenant Governor James Madison Chase.

Mr. Hayes had initially refused Hannah and Atlee's

request to nose around telegrams that were not meant for his station. Once they explained the reasons why, he readily agreed.

Dawn was advancing on the sleepy town of Wilkon. Operating on no rest and very strong coffee, Mr. Hayes peered out his window, vigilant for any stirring at the Wilkon newspaper office. Clicks from his telegraph system grabbed his attention. A wire from Austin. Directed to Atlee Corrigan!

James Hannah arrived at the *Wilkon Epitaph* office way earlier than his usual arrival, even before his editor, Leroy Gillespie, a man who almost never slept. Inside, Hannah set down the packet under his arm and coaxed up a fire from the coals in the stove. Somebody, probably Atlee, had prepared a pot of coffee prior to leaving the day before. He threw a few more pieces of wood into the flames and set the pot in place, hoping it would brew fast. Apprehension over this whole matter with Stebbins and Holt gnawed at him.

He sat at his desk and unwrapped the packet he'd been carrying. Inside was a small stack of newspapers. He selected the *Stebbins Observer* first, noticing its date was just a few days ago. He forced himself to read an article twice. "Oh god… What the hell…" He read the same article that had angered Holt and crew when it first published:

> "*Former Ranger Captain Laird McCoy has finally been brought to justice. Wanted for fraud, theft, and murder, McCoy had only recently been apprehended and incarcerated. McCoy has been killed in a foiled jailbreak.*
>
> *According to officials in Austin, the escape attempt was led by wanted former Ranger Orion Higbee and*

other disgraced Rangers. The attempt was foiled by prison guards and McCoy was killed..."

It was a sentence later in the article that sent his stomach to his throat:

"*One of the renegade Rangers, Holt Corrigan, had been shot and killed earlier, for resisting arrest...*"

"No, Holt, no..." He read the line again, then set the paper down. He took off his eyeglasses and rubbed at his eyes.

His thoughts were interrupted by the sound of Atlee coming through the door, greeting him with a smile.

Hannah looked up hesitantly, dreading having to share the newspaper article with Atlee. She could read in his face that something was wrong.

"What is it, James?"

He couldn't speak, didn't want to speak. She noticed his hands not doing a good job of covering up a copy of the *Stebbins Observer* on his desk.

"It's something about Holt, isn't it?"

As he gathered the fortitude to show her the article, a sharp, insistent rapping sounded at their office door.

Hannah leaped to his feet, taking the paper with him. "Yes, Mr. Hayes, you're up early," he said, answering the door.

The fastidious clerk was breathless, announcing two new messages. "This one came overnight, Mr. Hannah. I wasn't sure whether to wake you, so I waited until your arrival." He handed the first message to Hannah. "It's very peculiar. I haven't shared it with Marshal Freeburg or Sheriff Wheeler yet."

TO THE MARSHAL OF WILKON & ANY INTERESTED PARTY:

NOT MUCH TIME TO SEND THIS.

STEBBINS WIRE UNDER CONTROL OF CALISTA THERIOT.

HOLT CORRIGAN IS ALIVE. REPEAT: HOLT CORRIGAN IS ALIVE.

ALL CONTRARY REPORTS FALSE.

BE AWARE THERIOT MEN MALO JOHNSON, MADIGAN SANDERS.

MAY BE HUNTING HOLT & FRIENDS.

REPEAT: STEBBINS WIRE UNDER THERIOT CONTROL.

NO LONGER TO BE TRUSTED.

SIGNING OFF,

DEPUTY GUS BROOKS

"What do you think of this, Mr. Hayes?"

Mr. Hayes thought for a moment. "Whoever sent this was definitely not the person who has been keying messages from Stebbins as of late." He paused. "It is most peculiar to warn of a station not being trustworthy. I think this is exactly what it appears to be, a warning from Deputy Gus Brooks."

"And you said it just came in the night?"

Mr. Hayes nodded affirmatively, checking his pocket watch. "About five hours ago."

Hannah could not help himself. He whooped with relief and laughter. "He's alive!"

Both Atlee and Mr. Hayes were startled by the outburst.

"I can show you this now," Hannah said, sharing the Stebbins article with her. "That newspaper report is days old. You just heard otherwise, Holt's alive."

Even with the knowledge from the telegram, Atlee's

look was troubled. "I don't like it," she said. "Something is wrong…about all of this. The wire mentions Calista Theriot. She's a pirate from Louisiana."

Hannah remembered Mr. Hayes's announcement. "You said there was another message?"

"Yes. Oh yes." The clerk had to remember as well, caught up in the moment with the news about Holt. "This just came for Mrs. Corrigan."

"That was a quick answer," Atlee said, as the clerk handed her the note. "With the whole tangle of problems they're experiencing in Austin, all of my queries to the capitol are being overlooked or ignored, so I sent a wire to the editor of the *Daily Republican* there," she explained. She turned to hold the note in better light. Reading the message, she nodded. "Says here, *SOON TO HAVE A NEW GOVERNOR, BUT NO ONE CURRENTLY HOLDING THE OFFICE OF LIEUTENANT GOVERNOR EITHER. NEITHER POSITION FILLED FOR NEARLY THREE YEARS.*" She shrugged. "The editor has no idea who James Madison Chase is."

"So who is this Chase really?" Hannah asked. "Does he even exist?"

Atlee nodded. "This is all more than suspicious. I don't like it."

Hannah headed back to his desk. "I'll tell you what's going on. This is crime of a new order, a new way of thinking."

Atlee's stern visage urged him on.

"This is misleading the public on an unheard-of scale. Through their local news. They read it in their newspaper, so it *must* be true."

Mr. Hayes mumbled, "Can they do that?"

"Of course they can!" Hannah exclaimed. "Papers did

it all the time during the war. To throw the enemy off. To appease and pacify the people. And it's carrying over into today's peacetime world." He held up the copy of the *Observer* and popped it with his hand. "Someone's doing it now. Filling people's heads with misinformation. The false wires, the premeditated stories. They do the job of confirming falsehoods, playing on fears… An uninformed public is ignorant. A misinformed public is dangerous!"

"But why?" Atlee was still troubled.

"Answer that, and we can solve this puzzle."

"Maybe we should fight back with some of our own communications," Atlee said. "Break in with our own telegrams. Create our own upheaval. Smoke 'em out. Discover who's doing this."

Hannah smiled. "You sound like your brother-in-law."

"That's my husband, Deed, talking," Atlee corrected with a slight grin.

"Those Corrigans." Hannah shook his head. "I'm glad I'm on their side."

Mr. Hayes had been calculating all of this information silently, and suddenly blurted, "But how can we break in? Sending a wire there looks to be out of the question. Whatever we send will get intercepted. Their newspaper will continue filling their heads with lies."

Hannah stood again. "We send copies of our own *Wilkon Epitaph*! They'll get a taste of facts, what's really going on. I'll get the *Bartle Citizen*, the *Henion Eagle*, and the *Modlin Chronicle* to do the same. We'll all print extra copies to send to Stebbins."

Atlee bobbed her head in agreement. "People will

have to see there is other information. Truer information."

"For now, until we know more, it's how we fight back from here. It's not as sudden as a gun," Hannah noted. "We have to hope, in this case, that the pen is mightier than the sword."

CHAPTER FORTY-FOUR

A day later, it was just before lunchtime when Malo Johnson reined up in the middle of the main street in Wilkon. His trail coat bore the markings of many miles, his near-white hair stringy with wind and dirt, and his coal black Missouri foxtrotter streaked with sweat. It had been a while since he had ridden this far in such a short span.

Calista Theriot had a way about her that made men do things against their better judgment—like sending him all this way to kill a widow. But Calista's money was good and plentiful—and maybe, one day, she would see something in him and offer even more.

The peculiar-looking man, with waxen skin and icy-blue eyes, took in the sights and sounds around him. The sight of this man, who would stand out even in the dark, drew more than a few stares. The handles of Navy Colts protruding from his open dark-gray sack coat made those stares brief.

He stopped at the first saloon he saw that appeared worthy of his business. "The Black Hat…" He murmured to himself, “Hmmm…most fortuitous,” and adjusted his own black, low-crowned John Bull hat with a flashy silver concho band. Some food, a bath, and a nap sounded like a grand plan. Then he would see to locating this W Bar L widow and her men. It oughtn’t be difficult to track them down, he smirked.

He walked through the door of the Black Hat. He was taken aback by the atmosphere, more sophisticated than most he had seen here in Texas. This joint was more suited for New Orleans, he thought. The building looked almost new, with a magnificent bar backed by a huge mirror and shelves stocked with all manner of bottles and libations. As was habit, he observed the clientele. Everyone surrounding him was enjoying all manner of gambling games, as well as billiards and bowling, creating a commotion that was music to his ears.

An open table caught his eye, and he strode to it, repositioning the chair he sat in to face toward the front door.

An attractive woman wearing a day dress of blue cotton with a pleated skirt and fitted bodice came over to take his order. Her blouse’s billowy sleeves were pushed up by work and activity.

He asked for a bottle of rum—dark rum, throwing coins on the table. He eyed her sky-blue eyes and smiled. “Holt Corrigan lives here, does he not?” Her eyes and face were noncommittal. He wasn’t sure if she heard him and asked again, “Holt Corrigan. Where might I find him?” This time, she shrugged and indicated she didn’t know.

She leaned in and spoke over the din of the crowded bar, “I’m new here.” She stood up and headed for the bar. Soon, she returned with his bottle and a glass.

"I'm new here too," he grinned. "Perhaps we can become better…acquainted?"

"I'm working," she said bluntly. She nodded at the bottle. "Is that all you want, or do you want something to eat?"

"It's not *all* I want…" he said lewdly. "But, for now, I'll have whatever you're serving for food."

"We've got roast beef, probably not what you get back home in…" Her face and tone asked the question.

"I'm from Baton Rouge, but haven't been there in a long time," he grinned. "Maybe that's why I need a little gratification."

She spun and walked quickly away.

As she departed, he appreciated her form, thinking to himself she would really be beautiful if it wasn't for that scar along her face. He poured himself a glass of dark rum and murmured, "Still, she would be worthy of my bed."

Another server, a middle-aged Mexican woman, brought him a lunch of roast beef, boiled potatoes, beans, brown gravy, and biscuits. He tucked into the hearty meal and surveyed the grand room, searching for the alluring woman who first greeted him. No matter, he thought, perhaps I'll return for her later.

He smiled at the older Mexican woman, tossing coins on the table and inquired of her where the best bathhouse was. In broken English, she directed him to Norton's, down on the east end of town.

Before he left, he looked around once more for the pretty young woman with the scar. Nearing the door, he stopped to lean on the bar. A bartender soon came over and asked what he was drinking. The pale man responded, "I'm looking for Holt Corrigan. I hear he has horses for sale."

The bartender nodded. "That would be the Rafter C. Bit of a ride out there, though."

Malo smiled and placed a finger on his brim to bid goodbye.

He stopped first at the livery, dropping off his foxtrotter. He squeezed additional coins into the operator's hand to look after his weary mount. Next, at Norton's Bath House, he paid extra for fresh water and settled into the steaming, soapy tub. He thumbed through his copy of Edgar Allen Poe's *Murders in the Rue Morgue* until the water was almost cold. Another small charge bought him a clean towel.

After tucking in his pant-legs to his boots, he pulled a folded black shirt from his saddlebags, similar to the one he had stripped off. Perhaps I'll have my laundry done while I spend time with that saloon girl, he thought.

Behind him, he felt a breeze as the dressing room door opened. He couldn't help but turn around.

Standing there was Wilkon Sheriff, Logan Wheeler. Tall and rangy, a farmer in an earlier time, he had first worn a deputy's badge under Holt Corrigan, then James Hannah. He carried a Henry rifle at his side in one hand, the thumb from his other hand tucked into his belt.

"Yer no horse buyer. Yer Malo Johnson."

"I'm afraid you are mistaken, friend. I'm—"

"No mistake. An' I ain't yer friend," Sheriff Wheeler interrupted. "Luzy-anna state po-lees say they got warrants fer yer arrest from New Or-lins ta Alexandreea ta Shreeveport. Prolly wanted clear ta Memphis an' Saint Looie too. Yer armed an' dangerous. Well, I'll be takin' ya in now."

As Wheeler spoke, the pretty woman from the Black Hat entered the dressing area. Unlike Wheeler's easy approach, she had a double-barreled Greener sturdily tucked into her shoulder, aimed directly at the Louisiana assassin.

Malo put his hands up, waist high, slightly away from his body. A lascivious smile crossed his face as he greeted the woman. "And here I thought we might agree to engage in a little…amorous congress."

The woman's blue eyes flashed like a stormy sky. "There's only one no-good bottom feeder that looks like a ghost and wears such a silly hat," Laudie Kate Hart hissed, as though the words turned sour in her mouth.

"You sound just like that Ranger I killed. What was his name?"

"Holt Corrigan." Her teeth were gritted with wrath and determination. "And the last thing you're going to hear on earth is that *he's alive*."

Malo's eyes widened in surprise and anger. He began to reach for a Navy Colt hidden away in his back waistband.

BOOOM!

Laudie Kate detonated one side of the Greener, hitting Malo in the hips and thighs, knocking him to the floor. As he struggled through the shock of being hit, he tried to recover and grab for his gun. She reset her stance and tucked the gun against her shoulder again.

BOOOM!

Her second barrel blasted, catching the Louisiana killer full in the chest, throwing his body against the wall.

The deafening blasts were replaced by silence that ringed the humid bathing room along with gunpowder smoke that hovered ominously.

Sheriff Wheeler's reaction to Malo's draw had been a split second late. He stood in surprise staring at the torn-apart body. His voice broke the disturbing stillness. "When ya asked us ta wire 'bout Luzy-anna outlaws, I didden think ya'd be doin' th' shootin', Miss Laudie," Wheeler drawled. "But I'm shore glad ya did."

As the smoke cleared, Deputy Bradley Cooke also stormed into the bathhouse, his own shotgun in hand.

Laudie Kate could not take her eyes off the dead man. The deputy, a friend, thought she might get sick. Bradley stepped beside her and eased the Greener from her hands. "You okay, Miss Hart?"

Breathing deeply, but easily, she nodded her head yes.

Just then, James Hannah burst inside. His newspaper office was nearby. Instinctively, he came running at the sound of shotgun blasts, a pistol reflexively in his hand. He was relieved to see that his Wilkon friends were still standing.

"We need to get word to Holt!" Laudie Kate declared to Hannah. "Send a wire to let him know what happened!"

"We can't do that, Laudie Kate," Hannah said.

"We have to! We have to warn—"

"The town of Stebbins is under some kind of outlaw control," he tried to explain. "Their telegraph can't be trusted."

"Then I'll go tell him myself!"

CHAPTER FORTY-FIVE

In Stebbins, a small group had made a determined trip to town from the Flying G. Moose Elkins, his fiancée Evie O'Neill, and their Ranger friend Dal Frantze joined Holt Corrigan on the trek. Holt and Orion's chat with newspaper publisher, Max Palmer, was the first wave. Today's visit was to be the second wave against this woman they now knew to be notorious pirate, Calista Theriot.

Staying behind at the Flying G was Holt's dog, Tag Along. The gray-and-brown mutt had taken a bit of a shine to Gus's brother, Jak, the foreman of the ranch. Tag was quite proficient in helping round up cattle. Jak said he could use Tag's ability as they tried to reorganize their herd after the lightning-induced wildfire. Holt was grateful the dog would be busy and not notice his absence right away. Today's visit to town might get heated.

Moose and Dal climbed down out of the wagon near the jail. Evie hopped out at the Morningside Café, an establishment that doubled as the community meeting hall and courthouse. Holt watched as everyone took their places.

After letting them all off, Gus was to hustle the wagon and himself out of sight behind the livery, where he was to await Holt's instructions, but not before he let a few friends from town know that they should head to the Morningside Café.

Today, the café was serving as the Stebbins courthouse, a handful of small disputes comprising the docket. Inside, the Theriot-placed magistrate, Judge Dugal Ridgely, was conducting the morning's first order of business, a hearing. The inquiry was a dispute that pitted two local businessmen against each other. Unbeknownst to them, the dispute was instigated by Calista. Her hope was that one or the other would sell their business property—to her—following their courtroom defeat.

Evie stepped inside and looked around. The room was nearly empty, save for the people involved and a small handful of townsfolk waiting for their turn in front of the judge. Her appearance interrupted the proceedings.

"This is a closed courtroom, ma'am," Ridgely pronounced with all the arrogance a small man—in stature and mind—could muster.

"That can wait," she said confidently, walking down the aisle between chairs that had been set up for the hearings. "You're goin' to handle somethin' much more important."

A pompous Ridgely, overstuffed with power, tried to dismiss her again, this time threatening to have her arrested. "Someone go get Sheriff Chapman!"

"Put that gavel down, Ridgely." A voice came from the courtroom's rear door, halting the wannabe magistrate's protestations. "Unless you want to wear it where it chafes."

Holt Corrigan stepped forward from the door. Behind him, a small knot of townsfolk followed, hurrying inside to grab chairs.

Ridgely was stunned, first by Holt's appearance, and second, by the number of Stebbins citizens filing into his courtroom. He gathered himself enough to stammer, "Y-You're supposed to be dead!"

"As you can see, Ridgely, I am not," Holt barked. "And these two fellas will be kind enough to postpone their argument, maybe even long enough to figure out that it was your boss who created the quarrel in the first place." He then told the two businessmen, "Isla Thorne caused your beef, go figure this out on your own."

Ridgely tried to feign ignorance. "My boss?"

"Cut the charade, Ridgely," Holt sneered. "You're a puppet. We know who runs things here." The small crowd whispered at the bold statement. Fireworks were already flying.

Ridgely banged his gavel and angrily waved his arms, declaring, "You're not a Ranger anymore, Corrigan! You're wanted for murder!" He banged his gavel again. "Get these people out of here!"

Holt turned and shushed the crowd himself, then gave his attention back to the man at the table podium. "We'll get to that charge momentarily," he said in a quiet, even tone. "But what I'm hearing from you is…if I'm no longer a Ranger, I don't have to abide by any rules a badge represents." He grinned and not in a pleasant way. "Do we understand each other?" Holt's stare was predatory, too intense for the magistrate to continue looking in the young lawman's eyes.

"But first..." Holt continued. "If I *was* wearing a badge and knew *anything* about the law, I'd know that court hearings are generally open to the public."

Just then, the door to the café courtroom burst open further. An even larger crowd of Stebbins townsfolk flowed inside, led by the publisher and editor of the *Stebbins Observer*, Max Palmer, eager to get a front-row seat. Also in the crowd were notable citizens like Miguel Navarro, proprietor of the Blue Sky Inn, and Dory Bywater, owner of the town's fabric and dress shop.

Holt smiled at the appearance of the newspaperman. "Thanks for being here, Palmer. This should open your eyes. Maybe you'll see fit to write about it so everyone can read."

Suddenly, Holt spun, drawing one of his Smith & Wessons and pointing it at the judge. "Ridgely, if those hands come up with anything other than your gavel, your life will be adjourned."

Slowly, the embarrassed magistrate raised his hands from under the table podium. A small derringer was in his left hand.

"Good," Holt said. "Now drop the weapon." Ridgely's derringer bounced twice as it hit the podium, then the floor. "That's the smartest decision you've made in a long time," Holt said as he holstered his own pistol and nodded to Evie.

She stood with a grizzled-looking man standing next to her. She smiled at him in encouragement. The man straightened himself and declared, "My name is Samuel Stockdale, owner of the Triple S. As a rancher in this county, I demand to hear the facts against Lillian Whitman. That charge of rustling against her is as ridiculous as it is false. I also want to hear what this trumped-up case is against these two Rangers. They've done a lot for us around here."

The crowd in the café that had swelled to standing room now broke into a hubbub of remarks and agreement.

Ridgley banged his gavel. "Order! We'll have order here!" He waited for the room to settle. "I've ruled on that already." The magistrate sniffed his disdain. "Widow Whitman is a rustler and needs to give herself up. If you're harboring her, you will come up for charges as well."

Holt shook his head side-to-side. "Lillian will not be giving herself up to you or to any of Isla Thorne's lackeys. Her whereabouts are currently being concealed due to death threats. But you already knew that, Ridgely."

"How can there be a hearing with only the defense present?"

"The same way you held the hearing that brought the charges in her absence?"

"There is no prosecution either," Ridgely carried on. "This is a mockery—"

"No, Ridgely," Holt interrupted. "The mockery has already been committed. Your boss isn't here. You're going to hold a hearing with real facts. Not that crap you pulled before."

"Now see here—"

"Enough!" Holt hollered, his quiet tone gone. "Understand this, Ridgely, we know that Isla Thorne is a pirate. She is a wanted woman whose real name is Calista Theriot." Audible gasps and murmurs shot through the room. "She's been stealing land and buying people left and right, including you. As of now, that's over."

The magistrate hemmed and hawed. "Sheriff Chapman will have to testify on the rustling charge. So will Madigan Sanders. He's a Ranger captain now."

"We'll take care of Sanders when he gets here. He's no Ranger."

"Chapman's not here," the judge persisted. "Someone from the prosecution must be here."

"You pick interesting times to pretend you know anything about law," Holt scoffed. "Get going with this hearing, and you can leave town a free man."

"Are you threatening an officer of the court?"

"No, I'm promising a crook, an employee of a known pirate, that his time in Stebbins is over. You're nothing but a flunky for Calista. She pays for the very thoughts in your head."

Judge Ridgely looked as though he might vomit.

"As for your prosecution witness, he's on his way." Holt turned and called to the door. "Okay, bring in our guest."

Moose Elkins shoved Lewis Chapman through the door. Chapman's new, ill-fitting suit looked even more rumpled. His empty holster and badgeless chest made a silent statement of a *just-lost* dispute. Moose swiftly led the reluctant man to the front, near the judge.

When Chapman saw Holt, his jaw dropped. "Malo Johnson said you was dead. Saw you lyin' in the field, dead, kilt by his bullets."

Holt chuckled. "There seems to be things all you Louisiana bottom feeders have in common. You all wear nice, new suits, and you all lie like snakes. Malo's a back shooter, and in this case, an effective horse assassin." The crowd tittered at this revelation.

Chapman looked up at Ridgely. The two matched

stares, trying to convey messages neither understood. Were they still to lie? Cover for their boss? Or should they just protect their own skins?

Holt interrupted their moment. "Chapman, you're what passes for law in Calista's world, so you're going to be witness for the prosecution. This isn't a trial, but we still expect you to tell the truth. Understand?" He waited for a belated nod from the Theriot-bought sheriff. "Like the rustling charge you concocted about Lillian Whitman. And the tale you told about Dal Frantze and me murdering men sent to attack the W Bar L."

"I-I n-never said…I-I didn't…it-it wasn't my idea." Chapman looked around the room and saw what felt like the entire town of Stebbins staring at him. He gulped for air. This dry land mission was falling apart before his eyes.

Holt called out to Moose, who now stood in the back of the room. "Dal okay?"

Moose nodded affirmatively. "He's in th' jail, watchin' Chapman's *deputies*. They'll all be leavin' when this is over."

Ridgely fiddled with his black robe, figuring out what he should do next. Isla guaranteed that everything would be fine. Now, in the harsh light of a true public hearing, he realized she would never bear the responsibility. That was on him. And Chapman. And all her other followers.

Holt walked to the front of the room, just in front of Ridgely's table podium. He ran his fingers through the cardinal feather in his hatband, then slowly removed his hat. He looked around the packed café and proceeded. "Thank you all for being here. This is an important day. I know it's been a rough time for your town, but we are gathered here, now, to begin the process of returning Stebbins to where it belongs—to you good people."

A wave of quiet murmurs rolled across the crowd.

Holt continued, "Although a hearing doesn't require a jury, the law-abiding citizens among you decided the town deserved to hear the truth." He spoke these last words, looking directly at the newspaperman.

The woman who owned the dress shop stood. "Thank you for this, Mr. Ranger. In case you didn't know, Calista Theriot has men over in Bellinger's. They're there all the time. They're there now."

Holt smiled. "Thank you, ma'am. We'll be dealing with them next." He turned to face Ridgely. "You ready? Start by telling us what a preliminary hearing is supposed to be."

Ridgely took a moment to find his voice. Speaking in a tone weaker than when Evie first interrupted him, he said, "The purpose of a preliminary hearing is to determine if sufficient evidence exists for the accused to stand trial." He paused and declared the first case he would hear was the charge of rustling against Lillian Whitman and her employees at the W Bar L. "The accuser is the Windmill V ranch."

"Just to clarify, Ridgely," Holt asked in a loud voice, "would the *Windmill V* be Calista Theriot?"

Ridgely cleared his throat. "Uh, um, y-yes. Yes, that is true."

Holt requested to question the witness. Ridgely nodded.

"Chapman, you were the one who *presented* a number of cattle that supposedly had their brands changed. Is that correct?"

"Yes. The cattle wore W Bar L brands that were originally Windmill V marks."

Holt ignored the last part of Chapman's answer. "So it was you, Chapman. You, not Madigan Sanders, who saw the cattle and brought the charges, is that also correct?"

"Yes."

"So, we really don't need Sanders here." Holt then focused his remark on Ridgely. "Other than having another Theriot lackey present."

Neither Chapman nor Ridgely could maintain eye contact with the young Ranger.

"As you've already pointed out once, these brands were allegedly changed from Windmill V marks to W Bar L brands. Did I hear that correctly?"

"Yes."

"Chapman, for my own knowledge, and for everyone here, I'd like for you to describe what the Windmill V brand looks like."

"Um, uh…"

"Loudly, so everyone can hear, please."

Chapman looked to Ridgely, confounded.

"C'mon, Chapman, you're a man who carries a badge. You're supposed to have an eye for detail. What does Calista's brand look like?"

Chapman stared at the floor, seething in a moment of embarrassment and growing irritation. Mutters from the crowd bounced here and there.

Holt kept on. "Well then, how about the W Bar L? What does Lillian Whitman's cattle mark look like?"

"It-It…uh…"

"No? How about the revised brand on these *stolen* cattle?"

"I dunno…"

"You don't know?"

"I dunno, you could just tell!" Chapman erupted, again looking at Ridgely for help. But Ridgely was silent, unmoving.

"So, Chapman, you presented these *stolen* cattle and made the formal accusation, yet your only evidence is something you can't truly describe or prove?"

"I-I dunno…uh, no…I was just…"

"You were just what, Chapman?"

The Theriot sheriff mumbled an answer.

"Speak up!"

"I was just following orders!" Chapman exploded. "She said they were stolen and I believed her!"

The packed room burst into a din of comments and chatter.

Ridgely banged his gavel, and the clamor of the standing room crowd dwindled to silence.

Without missing a beat, Holt asked, "By *she*, you mean…"

"Calista! You know who I'm talking about, you fool!"

Holt smirked. "I'm still my own man, Chapman. Not sure who the fool is here." He turned and addressed the magistrate directly. "Well, Ridgely, amazing what happens when facts are introduced. Seems like the main part of their case, *their only part*, just disappeared when the glare of truth was shone on it. Just like rats scattering in the light." He paused. "Should I continue?"

The magistrate looked disgusted. He banged the gavel and cleared his throat. "There is no basis for the rustling charge against Lillian Whitman and her men. The warrants are dismissed." He banged his gavel again.

The room exploded into claps and whoops and cheers.

"We'll be sending wires everywhere rescinding the charges," Holt said above the din, before he walked over to the newspaperman.

"Have enough to write a story, Palmer?"

"I can't accuse Calista of all this. The case against the widow was different. That can be an article. The evidence against Calista is just say-so."

"Is that how you reconcile things so you can sleep at night?" Holt asked with a sneer. "Is that what you'll tell her when she shows up?" He leaned into the man's face so he could be heard. "You had no problem reporting that Orion, Dal, and I were renegades. And that Captain McCoy was a fraud. There was no *alleged*. You declared all of it as fact."

The newspaperman could only stare at his pad of paper.

"Operating on the say-so of a telegram from someone who doesn't exist is pretty bad, Palmer. Texas doesn't have a lieutenant governor, hasn't for about three years now."

"Holt, I—"

"You have plenty to go on. Be a man, Palmer. Do your job."

CHAPTER FORTY-SIX

Someone from the crowd hollered, "What about the murder charges?" Shouts of agreement followed: "Yeah!" "Those Rangers helped our town!" "They're not guilty!"

Outside the courtroom, along the planked sidewalk, Ames Wooster was curious as to the commotion that had grabbed the town's attention. The hubbub had reached the bank, excited whispers, people hurrying out to join the crowd at the café. He left his office to discover just what was happening. He was stunned to see the presumed murdered sheriff of Stebbins, Moose Elkins, filling the doorframe, rifle in hand.

It took a moment to gather himself over the surprise of seeing the huge man. Calista assured him that all the Stebbins lawmen were dead, dispatched by Christer Viklund. Elkins wasn't alone, standing outside the door with him was a small knot of townsfolk, people who could not fit inside the café's large room. Inside, raucous clamoring was being stilled by the hammering of a gavel.

"This isn't right," he muttered and turned to cross the

street. His haste almost walked him into the path of a large freight wagon. Yells and curses from the teamster snapped him out of the fog of his confusion. Instincts took over and told Ames it would be a good idea to gauge what was happening at the jail. Besides the bank, the jail was basically the in-town center of operations since Calista took control.

Watching more carefully as he traversed the rest of the main street, Ames snuck a look through a side window of the jail. He pulled himself back out of sight. That menacing Ranger! The one with the Comanche hair and eye patch! He peeked again. Dal Frantze sat at the desk, his sawed-off shotgun lay on the desktop along with a coffee mug and a newspaper he was reading.

This is not good. This is not good, he repeated to himself. No sign of Sheriff Chapman. And those looked like Chapman's deputies locked in the cells. Something was dreadfully wrong.

Ames straightened his suit coat. He knew there'd be Calista's men at Bellinger's. Always were. For difficulties such as this. He would inform them of the situation and that would be that. The way he'd kept his hands clean as banker and as mayor.

Even if he wasn't acquainted with them, it was easy to recognize hired guns employed by Calista and Madigan Sanders. Their dirty, trail-worn hats and oft-used guns combined with their new, store-bought suits were a contradiction between genteel and barbaric. A quick word, and their mission was made clear.

Three Theriot gunmen left Bellinger's in a hurry. Ames waited in the pool hall until they were gone and ducked out the door, headed in the opposite direction. He would go to Calista's apartment above the bank. She was not there, but it didn't matter. He had a key. It had been his apartment until she took over. Besides, he needed a drink, even if it was rum.

Inside the jail, Dal warmed up his coffee and continued reading the newspaper. Three of Chapman's deputies sat quietly behind bars. The Rangers, Corrigan and Frantze, had promised them the opportunity to ride away after the hearing, but they were still unsure of their fate.

The three gunmen from Bellinger's fanned out as they advanced on the jail. One of them tucked in behind a parked buckboard, watching the door of the courtroom. A huge man carrying a rifle stood sentry there, the man the fancy-dressed banker had warned them about. Ames had told them there was an attempt to take over the town going on in the courtroom.

"Calista has been expecting this and wanted everyone alert for just this situation," the banker had told the gunmen inside Bellinger's. She hadn't said that, but Ames assumed they would act more decisively, thinking she ordered it.

With only one guard inside, the three gunmen decided they would assume control of the jail first before knocking off Ranger Corrigan and the huge man at the door. There was only one way to go about this—overwhelm and not give the man guarding the jail a chance.

The gunman behind the wagon sent the third colleague around the back of the jail. He now stood just below a small barred window that provided air to the cells.

"Jed! This is Teddy." He whispered loudly enough for the deputies in the cells to hear. "Is the guard nearby? Is he watching?"

The prisoner whispered back, “Naw, jus’ readin’ and drinkin’ coffee at th’ desk.”

“Here’s a gun.” He held up a pistol to push it between the bars.

“What’s next?”

“We’re comin’ to th’ door in a few minutes. Catch that guard in a crossfire, but be sure not ta hit us!”

The Bellinger’s gunman snuck back around to the front. They waited for the proper moment to unleash their attack.

Suddenly, from inside the courtroom, a huge wave of cheers erupted.

“That’s it!” the man from the wagon urged. “Let’s go.”

KNOCK! KNOCK! KNOCK!

Someone from the outside pounded on the jail door. “Sheriff! There’s trouble in the courthouse!”

Dal easily called out, “Sheriff’s not here. Sorry.”

“Thorne men are attacking! You’ve gotta help!”

Dal ignored Holt’s orders not to unbar the entrance for anyone but him. He grabbed up his sawed-off shotgun and swung open the heavy door.

Three men charged at him from different positions on the street, guns blazing. Dal grimaced and fired both barrels of his weapon before diving for the safety of the desk. One attacker sprawled awkwardly in the dusty street. Dal noticed his hand was trembly and bloody as he broke open his gun to feed in two more shells.

Shots rang out behind him at his exposed back. He arched in pain as bullets found their mark. He squeezed off one barrel into the cell before spinning away and firing the other barrel at the men appearing in the doorway. One of the men in the cell screamed in pain and went down.

"Hurry up! Get us outta here. We need ta ride!" The caged deputies hollered at their rescuers. The cell doors shrieked their opening as if reacting to the past few moments. Two imprisoned deputies clamored to freedom, and one lay on the floor, unmoving and unseeing.

Two of the original gunmen followed the escaping deputies as they made their way to the door. One was limping, his hip and leg peppered by buckshot. Dal, lying on his side in a growing pool of red, pulled and fired his pistol twice. The gun became too heavy and fell to the floor. The slow-moving gunman dropped on the planked sidewalk.

At the door of the courthouse, Moose heard the firing. He leaned into the room and hollered, "Holt! Shots at the jail! Dal needs us!"

Holt immediately ran to the door. "Stay here, Moose. Keep Chapman and Ridgely covered."

The street had emptied rapidly. Firing anywhere meant trouble, but especially gunshots that left bodies in the street. Pistol in hand, Holt reached the jail in a dead run and saw that the door was wide open. Two men in nice suits lay sprawled and bloody in the street and on the boardwalk. Sharp kicks with his boot confirmed his suspicions about the two bodies out front. He drew his second pistol and cautiously eased to the opening.

Gunsmoke was willowing away in the cramped jail office. In front of him, by the desk, lay the unmoving body of Dal Frantze. The Ranger's long hair was now sopping up the gory crimson puddle forming around him.

Dal was riddled with holes. It was obvious that he had been ambushed from outside and inside. Someone had managed to get a weapon or weapons to the imprisoned deputies.

Looking at a third body lying dead in an opened cell, Holt exhaled and muttered, “Well, my friend, you managed to get at least three of them.”

Just then, heavy steps clumped behind him onto the boardwalk outside the door.

He wheeled and saw the large form of Moose Elkins filling the doorframe.

“Moose! I—”

Before he could finish, Moose was shoved the rest of the way inside. Standing behind the huge man, was Theriot Sheriff Lewis Chapman, holding Moose’s rifle.

CHAPTER FORTY-SEVEN

"You're under arrest, Corrigan, you sonuvabitch," Chapman snarled. "Now, drop your guns."

The two just-freed deputies entered the jail behind the sheriff. They had quickly found weapons and helped get control of the courtroom.

Chapman sneered, "We'll get you locked up and have Ridgely overturn his rulings. You'll still be wanted for murder, and that widow'll still be wanted for rustling. You can't beat our hand."

"What am I bein' arrested for?" Moose asked.

"You shut up. We'll think of something." He motioned with the rifle. "Corrigan, you and this mountain move that body out of the cell."

"Do it yourself," Holt barked. "You've got lackeys right there." There were four guns pointed at him. Chapman had a rifle, one deputy had two pistols, and the other had one. The young Ranger tried calculating how to neutralize these men, but didn't care for how the equation always seemed to end.

As Holt and Moose sat in separate cells, the undertaker was summoned. His helpers assisted with cleaning the floors and taking the bodies away. As this was going on, Holt carefully noted that his matching Smith & Wessons with the panther silhouette handles were thrown into a large Arbuckles box by the desk. Dal's pistol and sawed-off shotgun were tossed there as well.

At suppertime, Ames dropped by the jail in his capacity as mayor. "Just checking on the prisoners who caused so much trouble today," he quipped. He then commended Chapman on locking them up instead of immediately dispatching them.

"Miss Thorne will want to make a grand show of hanging them, create an impression on just what happens to those who dare try to call her at her own game."

"Don't you mean, Calista the pirate? Calista Theriot?" Holt said with derision. "You might as well use her real name."

CHAPTER FORTY-EIGHT

Gus Brooks now stood watch at the Flying G.

Earlier today, he had heard the shooting in the jail from his hideaway at the town livery. When the Theriot deputies broke out of jail and stormed the court proceedings, he had stealthily made his way to the back alley of the Morningside Café. In the havoc, the deputies rescued Judge Ridgely and arrested Moose Elkins, but also caused a storm of panic among the townspeople crammed inside. The stampede of citizens allowed Gus to spirit Moose's fiancée, Evie, away from the deputies. The chaos also provided cover as they bolted from town.

It was well past sunset, but Gus patrolled the grounds around the ranch yard. He did not think anyone saw him leave with Evie, but could not be sure. Just in case, Sawyer Gates ordered all his men to begin working their chores carrying a sidearm or rifle. The Flying G had managed all this time to escape the glare and wrath of Calista Theriot. They held their collective breath that it wouldn't start now.

Especially with Holt and Moose behind bars.

Gus did not know the fate of Dal Frantze, but the amount of gunfire and subsequent escape of the deputies led him to come to conclusions he did not want to think about.

Squinting at shadows in the darkness, he decided that he would travel back to Stebbins and sneak in to determine just what was going on and what was happening next.

He was awake and gone well before the Flying G's usual pre-dawn breakfast. Gus knew his brother and the others would be dead set against his plan. He also knew just hunkering down wasn't livable. They had to know what was being planned, what was coming. And he was the one to find out.

This time, he did not take the small buggy, choosing one of the swifter Flying G mounts instead. Riding a horse would be simpler to move about, easier to conceal than a buggy, and faster to escape if need be.

He did take the time to stuff extra disguise materials into his saddlebags—the bowler hat and wig from his previous visits, a woolen brimless cap, eyeglasses, two additional bandannas, a small pillow to stuff under his coat, and even an old, long cotton dress. He also packed more than the usual boxes of ammo for his shotgun and pistol.

Upon arriving at the holding corral and pond that marked the western boundary of Stebbins, Gus noticed that the main street seemed emptier than usual. The relative absence of wagons and foot traffic concerned him, so he skirted around to the eastern end, the part of town where Holt had snuck in to meet up with Dal not so many days ago. This quarter of town would be a good place to blend in, with a grain mill, lumber mill, and wool factory providing plenty of comings and goings. Other bustling warehouses and three seamy saloons down on this end contributed enough activity that he could practically hide in plain sight.

He left his horse tied up at a hitching post outside the scruffy Grainger's Saloon. There were several other mounts there, all quietly waiting. Gus picked out a freight wagon that was plodding its way down the main street. Throwing his saddlebags over his shoulder and carrying his shotgun, he walked next to the back wheel of the wagon to blend in. He sauntered along until it reached the bakery and then he peeled off to the side of building, hurrying to the back alley.

Two doors down was the rear door of the Blue Sky Inn, and hopefully, sanctuary. Gus waited patiently for someone he knew—and trusted—to appear. He waited a while. A new cook stepped outside, someone Gus did not recognize, so he remained in his place of concealment. Finally, the Blue Sky owner, Miguel Navarro, appeared in the back alley.

"Miguel, my friend, it's Gus Brooks," the real Stebbins deputy said in a low voice. "Are there lots of people inside? I'd like to talk."

The diminutive hotel keeper was more nervous than normal. He looked up and down the shaded alleyway before beckoning Gus to hurry inside. "Let us go, my office," he whispered.

Once tucked inside the little office, Navarro locked the door and pulled a chair up next to it. "We must be eben more careful dese days," he cautioned in a low voice.

"That's why I'm here," Gus said in a matching tone. "What happened after…after the courthouse?"

Navarro looked around anxiously, apprehensive to talk, even within his own haven. "Dat sheriff, Chapman? He angry. Gave badges back to deputies in jail. Dey went to businesses of peeple suspected of being at de hearing."

"Visited businesses?"

"Yes. To warn about any more, uh, resees-tance. Dey said de next hearings would be for peeple not loyal to Mees Thorne."

"Are they still trying to have people believe she's not Calista Theriot?"

"*Sí.* It feel like you be punished eef you use her real name."

Gus puffed out his weathered cheeks and let out a lungful of breath. "That's not good, Miguel. Have those bastards talked to you? Have you been threatened?"

"Not yet. I tink maybe I was not seen at de hearing. Being *pequeño* perhaps helped dis time."

"My friend, you're a big man in my eyes. I know Holt thinks that way too." He paused. "Speakin' of him, have you heard anythin'…from the jail?"

"No. Noteeng. Señor Holt and Meester Moose still dere. I tink dey wait for return of Mees Thorne and de one called Madigan."

"Any word on when they's comin' back?"

"Any day now. We do not know. There eez only dread for dat day."

"That's no way to live."

"Is much fear. No joy. Peeple stay home, only veesit town when needed."

"Is everyone at the hearin' set on surrendering to this Theriot woman?"

"Many peeple would rise up, but how?"

"I ain't sure, right now, Miguel. I really dunno. But we'll be fightin' somehow. Bet on it." They sat in silence for a moment before Gus spoke again, and said, "I'm gonna stick around, at least until this woman returns. See what she's gonna do. Find out what her plans are for Holt an' Moose. Any ideas on where I could stay?" He showed his friend some of the disguises he brought along. "I don't plan on bein' *Gus Brooks* while I'm here."

Miguel looked around again and brought a finger to his lips. "I show you sumtheeng. No one ever to know. I did not tell eben Señor Holt when he hiding." He stood and walked behind the chair where Gus sat. Against the back wall was a nearly floor-to-ceiling cabinet crammed with a few books, cooking pans, bags of coffee beans, a coffee grinder, decorative pottery, a stack of nice chinaware, and other knick-knacks. The cabinet sat on a nice, thick, handwoven rug.

The little hotel owner put a finger to his lips once again. Grasping the heavy piece of furniture securely, he carefully pivoted it with its rug across the pinewood floor. "In here," he whispered with a motion of his hand and disappeared through a man-sized hole in the wall. Gus heard a match strike and saw a glow of lantern light from the opening.

Stepping through the hidden entryway, Gus couldn't help himself. Stifling a chuckle, he said, "Lord a-mercy, Mr. Navarro, you be a man of many surprises." In the illumination, Gus saw a cozy room with a bed, a night-stand, a simple table and chair, and a small dresser. Two shelves on the wall held cans of fruit and Mason jars of jams, pickles, and peppers. The room was not stuffy or musty at all.

"Dere was too much pantry, more than needed. Thees became my *escondite*." He smiled. "De builders did not know what all dis for. I added door into office later." He was immediately serious. "Dees is where I go sometimes when my *suegra* visit. You know, for quiet."

"I'm sure your *mother-in-law* can't be all bad." Gus chuckled again. "But I can't...I can't let you do this, Miguel. It might be too dangerous—"

"Now you know, so now you must stay." Navarro smiled. "I bring you food and newspaper. Let you know when safe to move about."

Gus shook his head. "I can't thank you enough, my friend."

"You stay safe here. Feegur out way to free Señor Holt and Meester Moose."

"That I will, Miguel. That I will."

———

The arrangement at the Blue Sky was perfect. Gus had a secure spot to sleep and hide. Navarro gathered up Gus's horse and took it to the livery. The gracious hotel owner also brought him meals, occasionally eating together in his office. This gave Gus the opportunity to skulk around town, keeping his eyes and ears open.

As much as he wanted to go and visit, he avoided Bellinger's. The favorite spot for Calista Theriot's hired guns was fraught with danger. Too many people knew who Gus Brooks was and might recognize him, even with a disguise. He did, however, chance a walk near the jail, risking a quick peek in a side window. Moose was snoring on a cot too small for his frame. Holt sat on his bed, reading a book. Gus was relieved to see them alive, but did not dare try to communicate with them.

———

Another peaceful night passed. In the late morning quiet, Gus was sitting in Navarro's office, reading a copy of the *Wilkon Epitaph*. The hotel owner had excitedly brought it to his office. His enthusiasm was dampened with concern, however. The front page of this out-of-town newspaper was filled with articles about who Isla Thorne really was and how the town of Stebbins was being horribly misled. He wanted Gus to read the paper before he burned it in one of his stoves.

"Deese are all ober town," the little hotel owner explained breathlessly. "I tink de stage brought dem. Dere were some at de general store and a few of de shops." He was jittery at the prospect of news attacking Calista and her men. "It eez good for peeple to read, but dangerous to do so."

"This paper is from Wilkon," Gus noted quietly and assuredly. "Wilkon is where Holt is from."

Comprehension slowly came to Navarro's face, calming him a little. "Are you hungry, my Gus? Let us have an early lunch." He sprang up to head to the kitchen.

Before long, he hustled back to the office, a tray with stew and biscuits, and a pot of coffee. He was even more agitated than before. "Oh my, oh my stars…!" He carried the tray directly to the little hideout before emerging again. "She eez coming! Dey say Mees Thorne…Mees Theriot weel be here soon! Today!"

"Is there anyone upstairs, Miguel? Can I have a look?"

Navarro's eyes widened. "Eet would not be a good idea."

Gus's eyes were convincing. So was the brimless woolen cap and eyeglasses he donned. "How about this, too?" he said, stuffing the small pillow into his coat. "No one will recognize me."

Navarro wasn't completely convinced, but enough to reluctantly nod. "Room three. Eet is open and unlocked."

Gus cautiously, but quickly, made his way from the back hallway through the large room and up the stairs. The Blue Sky restaurant was not too busy, but busy enough to be preoccupied and not notice a pot-bellied, near-sighted teamster crossing the room to the stairs.

Satisfied his disguise worked, Gus closed and locked the door to room three behind him. The one large window in the room offered a wide view of main street Stebbins.

It wasn't long before he could hear the rumble and jangling of a horse-drawn wagon and lots of horses. He peered through the curtains as a grand coach pulled by two matching gray horses came into view and reined to a flashy stop in front of the bank across the street. Gus scowled at the sight of the driver, a man in a new tailored suit with ammo bandoliers crossed over the shoulders of his coat.

Reining up alongside the coach was a fat man, also in an expensive suit, riding a big, sturdy mule. He looked more like a riverboat gambler, but the pistols gaping through his open coat were not there for show.

Madigan Sanders. With a bright silver badge pinned to his lapel.

Gus shook his head. *What kind of devil would give him a badge?* He knew the answer as soon as he thought of the question.

Fifteen men wearing flashy Special Force badges reined up as well, each looking more vicious than their fresh new suits could hide. These gunmen did not dismount. Instead, they responded to something hollered by Madigan and spurred their horses farther down the street.

Gus watched the bank president, Ames Wooster, come outside wearing a broad smile and open the door to the coach, helping Calista from the passenger compartment. Gus whistled softly in spite of himself. Even from this distance, he had to agree that she was amazingly beautiful. He admitted quietly, "Hard to say no to that. For anythin'."

Before she headed toward the bank, she gave instructions to Madigan. She and Ames disappeared into the bank. Madigan gave his mule a light touch from his heel and headed toward the jail.

Darkness found Gus back in Navarro's office. He had spent most of the afternoon and into dusk lurking around a few of the eating and drinking establishments. There had been no sign of Calista, but hushed rumors of her abounded. Most were fantastical tales of her exploits. No words on what she was planning next.

There did not appear to be as many customers or Theriot men inside Bellinger's, so Gus decided to chance a visit. He rechecked the pillow stuffed into his coat, ensuring it looked normal.

He nursed a mug of beer and pretended to watch a game of billiards as he leaned on a post, his back to a table of Theriot men. Listening in, Gus could hear that these four hired guns were not as lively or boastful as usual.

"I ain't seen her like this befo'."

"She's lik' a swan on th' water most times."

"I believe the Bible would call it *wrathful*."

"I think folks'll get th' message."

"I'm jus' glad we don't havta take this first watch."

Gus was not sure what they were speaking of, but clearly, they were speaking about Calista. She was riled up, and even the underlings knew, probably at receiving word of Holt's attempted takeover in court.

They scooted their chairs back and stood, each tossing coins on the table. They tramped out the door into the night. Gus decided it was time to slink back to the Blue Sky as well.

As soon as he stepped outside, there was trouble everywhere he looked. Heavily armed Theriot men, each wearing bright silver star badges, had stationed themselves all about town, even the east end.

Gus was proficient at creeping around, using the shadows and counting on lapses of attention from people out and about. He had used the skill well during the war and afterward, when he had been a petty thief before discovering there was a better life living on the right side of the law. That ability would be put to the test tonight.

The men now patrolling the town wore crisp new suits, each cradling a rifle. Gus shook his head sadly. These men were on guard, but more importantly, they were meant to be seen, to be noticed.

If townspeople didn't feel confined before, they surely did now. Stebbins was bottled up.

As he prowled through the inky night, Gus noticed the lights were on late at the *Stebbins Observer* office. One of the few places of business, other than saloons, showing any kind of life tonight.

Suddenly, swinging lanterns marked the approach of several people to the newspaper's building. Gus flattened against a stack of pallets in a side alley as the small group approached.

Calista! The dapper banker and the fat gunman with her were easy to spot. The door slammed after they entered the *Observer* office. Gus could see commotion through the office windows and hear her raised voice, but could not clearly make out exactly what she was saying. Something about *all over* and *in the morning*.

Almost as soon as she arrived with her little entourage, they departed. Calista and Ames headed back toward the bank. Madigan waddled across the street, directly toward Gus's position.

Gus held his breath and crouched even lower behind the pallets, only watching the feet of the fat gunman. To be found now would be death.

Just before stepping onto the planked sidewalk, Madigan stopped to light a cigar. In the murky night, the flame from his match seemed to light the surroundings like midday. Gus did not budge, even an inch. He began calculating his first move, his first shots, and subsequent options for retreat.

The cigar lit to his satisfaction, the rotund killer exhaled smoke onto the match, returning the world to comforting shadows and secrecy. Madigan stepped up onto the sidewalk and ambled right by the stack of pallets, so close that Gus could smell the portly man's cologne and cigar. Through slats in the wood, he watched Calista's man and his shiny black boots walk away in front of the line of storefronts.

Gus exhaled his relief and waited extra moments before continuing his quest for safety and the Blue Sky. The rest of his journey was unremarkable. There had been a couple of Theriot men to avoid, but they weren't professionals, just men accepting money to look tough. He smirked at the number of lawmen he knew who had been outlaws…Holt…Orion…his murdered friend, Marshal Baxter Hollings…James Hannah over in Wilkon…and others, including himself. *Boy, wouldn't we be a band to contend with*, he thought as he chuckled.

He finally arrived in the back alley of the Blue Sky and waited patiently for the appearance of his friend. Navarro knew that Gus planned on moving about until well past dark. They agreed that Navarro would check the alleyway on the half-hour throughout the night.

Before long, the diminutive Mexican opened the back door and gazed at the sky. Experience had taught him to gauge time by looking at the stars' movement in comparison to the rooftops.

A word whispered from deep shadow, "*Suegra*."

Navarro grinned. Because he was letting Gus use his special hideout, they agreed a good password would be *mother-in-law*. Navarro removed his white apron, the all-clear signal, and returned inside, leaving the door slightly ajar.

Finally, in the safety of Navarro's office, Gus relayed his discoveries of the day, including the heavily armed Theriot men wearing badges patrolling the streets and Calista's nighttime visit to the *Observer* office.

"I been chewin' on what I heard her say," Gus related. "'All over' an' 'in the morning.' It has to be something about Holt an' Moose."

Navarro shook his head quietly, worried and afraid for his friend, Señor Holt.

Gus expressed the thought out loud, "What if it means it's all over for them in the mornin'?"

CHAPTER FORTY-NINE

Early the next day, Theriot men were still fanned out all over town. This morning, however, they weren't carrying rifles, but armfuls of papers, boxes of tacks, and hammers and mallets.

Everywhere, on posts and storefronts, and on stacks left inside shops, were handbills emblazoned:

CELEBRATION!

To celebrate the town of Stebbins, this Saturday has been set aside for a citywide party.

- Horse Race
- Foot Races (for young & old)
- Spelling Bees (for young & old)
- Cake Contest
- Box Supper Auction
- Dance
- Hanging

Navarro smiled weakly at the man with the big shiny

badge who left a stack of the handbills at his lobby desk. He watched the man leave and disappear down the sidewalk before starting to breathe again.

Hidden under his apron was a copy of the *Henion Eagle*, another out-of-town newspaper calling out the charade occurring in Stebbins. The dressmaker, Dory Bywater, had brought this copy first thing. Her eyes had been wide—with fear or excitement, he couldn't tell.

Wordlessly, she pointed out to him the main story: An article clarifying that the state of Texas was currently without a governor or a lieutenant governor. It read, in part, "*Whoever James Madison Chase is, he is not an elected official. He and anyone else posing as such is a fraud.*"

Not long after Dory left, the Theriot man appeared in his hotel lobby. Navarro was certain this man with a badge was coming to arrest him for possessing such a scandalous publication. Certainly, Calista or Sheriff Chapman or Madigan Sanders had deemed these newspapers illegal.

Realizing his panic was unfounded, Navarro grabbed the first flier on the pile the man delivered and hurried to his office.

He knocked on the back wall and shoved the cabinet open. "Gus! Gus! Look here!" He handed the paper to the just-awakened deputy. "Dese are eberywhere!"

Gus read it several times. His anger and dread heightening each time.

"Hellfire an' damnation! A hangin'!" He stuffed the flyer into his coat. "The Flying G. I've got to get to the Flying G! Maybe we can get some of the 5 Star riders here. This is terrible!"

CHAPTER FIFTY

"You've never held Ranger Cap'n Laird McCoy as a prisoner here?" Orion Higbee was not certain he heard the man's answer correctly. He had ridden as hard and fast as he dared in order to arrive here at New Braunfels as quickly as possible. Leaving Holt behind was a difficult decision, but this investigation was necessary and unavoidable.

He hoped to find answers and return to Stebbins as soon as possible.

A sharp-dressed man with a goatee sat at the desk inside the roomy sheriff's office within the New Braunfels jail. "No, Ranger Higbee. I know of Captain McCoy. I can't imagine why he'd be arrested, much less held here."

Orion was stunned. "But…we received telegrams." This sheriff's news left him confused. "We-We saw a-a newspaper report…" Orion stammered. "It said he was arrested an' killed in an attempted escape." He took off his hat to smooth his hair and to help curb all kinds of conflicting emotions. “What the hell’s happened to Cap’n McCoy?”

“I don’t know, Ranger. I really have nothing for you.” The sheriff paused. “I hope to heaven it’s not true.”

“So, he ain’t a prisoner here. An’ never tried to escape…”

“No, sir. Not here. Maybe Fort McKavett? Have you talked to the officer at their stockade?”

Orion expelled a sharp breath of frustration. “If that was true, wouldn’t you have heard somethin’ about it?”

The goateed sheriff looked sheepish. “Well, yes, you’d think so…”

“Still, it’s worth checkin’ into.” Orion scratched at his beard. “You familiar with the telegraph operation at the fort?”

“Very much so.”

“Who usually sends and receives the wires there?”

The New Braunfels sheriff nodded. “NCOs handle that department.”

“You got names?” Orion inquired.

“That would be Corporals Brock, Mosby, and Chase. They’ve been there a while.”

“Chase?”

“Yes. Corporal Chase. Corporal Jim Chase. I know who he is.”

Calista paced angrily in her apartment above the bank.

“Look at these! What is this?” she bellowed. Strewn on her desk and the floor below it were many newspapers. Publications from places like Wilkon, Henion, Bartle, and Modlin. Her men discovered them while distributing Celebration flyers. Lots of out-of-town newspapers. They all reported similar stories.

There was no lieutenant governor.

Stebbins was under control.

Stebbins was being tricked.

And the worst—she picked up a copy of the *Bartle Citizen* and read from it, "*Isla Thorne is the notorious pirate known as Calista Theriot*! Dammit, Ames! Isla Thorne is Calista Theriot! Written right here!" She wadded the paper and threw it at him.

His weak reply was to walk stiffly to the small fireplace and toss the offending publication into the flames.

"What the hell is happening here! These newspapers! These stories!" she fumed at Ames. "Tell me!"

Ames was stunned to silence.

"How did they know to write these articles? And send them here? How?"

He had no words to help. "I don't know how the papers are getting here, my love. I'm sorry. They just appear."

She poured herself a healthy glass of rum.

"People are reading them too," he added.

"Oh, really?" she snarled sarcastically.

"I think that's why preparations for the celebration are at a standstill," Ames continued. "No one's come forward to build the grandstand. Or the gallows."

Calista exploded, setting the drink down before taking a sip. "*Come forward?* You're waiting for people to come forward?" She paced harder, wanting to throw or punch something, anything. "My god, man, you don't ask for volunteers. You put someone in charge! Someone who will *compel* people to work. And if that doesn't work…force them!"

She sat and rubbed at the bump on her hairline. She began stroking the silver-and-brass amulet at her chest. Her seething slowed. After a few moments, she barked, "Since you can't think and act like a mayor, here's what you do. Have Madigan order his men to comb the town. Confiscate and burn every newspaper that isn't the *Stebbins Observer*." She paused. "If anyone objects, drag them through the street and throw them in jail."

Ames swallowed hard.

She picked up the glass and took a sip before continuing in a more controlled voice. "Get Sheriff Chapman to drum up workers to build the scaffolding for the gallows. It's his hanging. Have him take charge. There's not much time left."

Ames tried to linger for a moment, but she snapped, "Get on it! Now!" He left, and a look of concern crossed her face.

Orion stood in the headquarters at Fort McKavett. Using his badge to gain passage on a snag boat and a small tugboat, he made the journey from New Braunfels quickly, giving his horse a much-needed rest.

A captain, identifying himself as *Officer of the Day* Nissen, presented the older Ranger at the fort's telegraph office. A youthful, almost too-young-to-shave corporal stood at attention, awaiting orders.

"I'm lookin' for telegraph records, son," Orion explained in a serious, but not stern, voice. "I'm 'specially interested in wires sent to the town of Stebbins while Corporal Jim Chase was on duty."

The young blond corporal blurted, “Is he…is he in trouble?”

“You will see to this Ranger’s request, Corporal!” the captain barked.

“Yessir,” the corporal immediately responded.

“By the way, where is Corporal Chase now? Is he here?” Orion wondered.

The captain answered straightaway, and said, “Corporal Chase is a courier for the military district. He currently is not on the base. He’s in Austin.”

A wry smile crossed Orion’s face. “Austin? You don’t say.” He mulled over his next question. “Captain, would you….would the fort have records of visitors?”

“Yes, we do, Ranger, sir.”

“Could you tell me when other Rangers, like me, visited? I’m only talkin’ within the past coupla months.”

“Those would be up at the main office, Ranger.”

“Well, while this good lad is searchin’ for the wire records, can we take a look at the visitor rolls?”

“Follow me, sir.” He then called to the young man, “Corporal, keep at it. Bring what you find to the duty desk, post-haste.”

It was not long before Orion and the officer of the day were studying the ledger of activity at the fort.

“Here we go,” Orion noted. “This visit here by Cap’n Laird McCoy an’ Dal Frantze.” He used his finger to carefully draw down the page column. “Here again. ’Nother visit by Cap’n McCoy, just a coupla weeks later.”

He looked up at the captain. “Does this next column say both visits were to see Major Wooster?”

“Yes, sir, it does.” Something dawned on the officer. “We have the quartermaster paperwork and action reports requested by Captain McCoy. Right over here." But then a look of confusion and concern crossed his face. "If he was here, why did he not take these records with him?"

The captain looked again at the ledger.

Carefully.

"Hmmm. This is…most irregular," he noticed.

"Whattaya got?" Orion wondered.

"Something peculiar." The officer studied the record closely. "This last visit by Captain McCoy was never logged out."

"What's that mean?"

"I'm not sure. It wasn't noted when he left."

"That's usually somethin' that's kept good track of, ain't it?"

"Yes, sir. It's a standing order. Regulations. I can't explain why his departure isn't noted, though."

"Captain, I need to speak with Major Wooster. Right now."

CHAPTER FIFTY-ONE

Like a force of nature, Calista Theriot bustled through the door of the *Stebbins Observer* once again. Immediately behind her was Sheriff Lewis Chapman, desperately trying to keep up while struggling to carry two overstuffed, leather stagecoach bags.

"Here are more of those outrageous papers from towns that don't know any better," she announced. She instructed Chapman to set the cases down by the main desk and paraded further inside the office, nodding at Ames Wooster and Madigan Sanders. The two men had been *talking* with *Observer* publisher Max Palmer for a few hours.

This evening's meeting was not going well for Palmer. Although none of it had been his doing, Palmer bore the brunt of Calista's outrage over the appearance of so many out-of-town newspapers revealing her massive deception campaign.

The publisher was sweating as he hunched fearfully over the type cases. A large bruise was mousing on the cheekbone under his left eye. The right side of his face was inflamed, the color of the red bandanna he used to mop the perspiration from his brow.

As ordered by Calista, Madigan came here to deliver his own brand of editorial. Ames was to see to it that Palmer readied a new issue of the *Observer* for immediate printing and delivery.

Palmer apprehensively lifted his gaze toward the commotion at the office door. When Calista strode through the entryway, his hands tensed around the composing stick. His grip tightened to keep from shaking. He did not want the pieces of type to fall off before he could transfer them to the composing frame. He was already, literally, under the gun and did not want anything to cause his having to start over.

"How are things looking?" She smiled sweetly. The tone of her voice may have sounded syrupy, but her eyes were far from genial.

Ames declared brightly, "We have an interesting biography of Lieutenant Governor Chase. Quotes from him, too." He was eager and anxious that the news would be acceptable to her. Giving her exactly what she wanted might put her in a better mood, for later.

Palmer added shakily, "Y-Yes, ma'am, th-that piece is the lead article, p-plus another front-page article about the g-glorious future of Stebbins." He then looked at Madigan, steeling himself for any swift corrections. Seeing the fat gunman's affirmative nod, he added, "Th-The article t-talks about railroad development an-and the expected growth of the county."

Madigan's tilting head and raised eyebrows urged more information. The publisher continued, "Oh! There's a complete summary of what the recent court hearing *actually* proved, refuting all the gossip and hearsay."

Ames smiled, adding, "There's an advertisement for the Stebbins Celebration right on Page Two!"

"Ames th-thought it would be good to include a story next to it listing the reasons why your *special guests* are to be hanged," Palmer said.

"Excellent!" She beamed, the twinkling truly reaching her eyes this time. "And how fortuitous to be able to add a third *guest* to the gallows!"

"Yeah, fortuitous," Madigan interjected. "We caught that former deputy sneaking out of town. He'll look good up there with a rope." He chuckled evilly. "A Ranger, a sheriff, and a deputy. Holt, Moose, and Gus. A real three-of-a-kind."

Just then, a messenger from the telegraph office arrived at the door, panting and out of breath. "Sheriff Chapman! Sheriff Chapman! They said at the jail you'd be here." He then noticed Calista. "Message for you too, ma'am!"

Not expecting a telegram at this moment, Calista stepped briskly to the door to retrieve the message. Without taking her eyes off the note, she gestured to Ames with her head toward the lad. "Tip him."

The youngster started to speak to Sheriff Chapman, but she immediately called out to him, "Wait!"

She read the note again, unable to completely maintain a poker face as she read.

ISLA:

> RANGER NAMED ORION CURRENTLY AT THE FORT.
>
> LOOKING FOR CORPORAL JIM.
>
> MERRY BEING QUESTIONED RIGHT NOW.

I KNOW HE WILL CONFESS.

MCCOY TEA PARTY WILL BE DISCOVERED AS WILL ALL ELSE.

LEAVING AS SOON AS I SEND THIS.

YOU SHOULD DISAPPEAR TOO.

SEE YOU AT PAPA'S FAVORITE SPOT.

CEE.

Calista kept her composure, her poker face returning. The only tell, a hard swallow and a quick lick of her lips. "I need to send a return," she said to the young messenger.

"I-I-I'm n-not sure that's p-possible," the youth stammered.

"What do you mean?" she barked.

"S-Something's going on there. Th-There's men… with guns—"

A fusillade of gunfire out in the street interrupted the messenger's explanation. Sporadic firing continued after.

Startled, they all looked in the direction of the noise, and the lad tried again. "Th-That's wh-why I was looking for Sheriff Chapman. Mr. Holley gave me her note and told me to run and find her. An-And tell the sheriff."

"Why run? What for?" She glared.

"Three men came into the telegraph office."

"Three…what three men?" she demanded. Sheriff Chapman ran to the office window and peered out, gun drawn.

"The men in jail," the youth explained. "The ones that are supposed to hang. They're in the station, said they were going to dismantle it. The one with the long hair and scar on his face told me I shouldn't be there. To go be safe."

"Corrigan!" she hissed.

More shots rang out. Then there was silence.

Calista rubbed her hands down her body, starting at her amulet and progressing down to smooth out her dress. Her instincts were right. This game was unwinnable. She was glad her earlier telegrams had gone out and been answered. That truly would have been a bust, a catastrophic one.

She knew it already, but her sister's telegram was the signal. The time to regroup was here. But she remained calm and issued her orders.

"Ames, you stay here. Finish getting this edition out."

She moved toward Sheriff Chapman, still at the front window, and whispered, "Lewis, grab those cases and follow me out back."

She turned to Madigan and ordered, "You and your men keep this town under control. You know what to do. Those escapees are to die."

Closing the back alley door behind them, Calista turned and halted Chapman face-to-face. He wasn't certain what was happening.

As she took the heavy bags in her hands, she said in a hushed and even tone, "No questions, Mr. Chapman. You have ten minutes to grab your things. Talk to no one. Meet me behind the saddle shop. My carriage is there, ready. You're driving."

"But—"

"I said no questions!"

"Ma'am, I was only going to ask about your money. If we're leaving, I'm assuming we're not coming back."

"You're a good man, Lewis *Grapeshot* Chapman." She grinned. "Yes, we are folding the game here. It's time to vanish like we do on the river."

"Won't they be looking for you? We can't—"

"We're headed north, to Tozier."

"North?" The realization made Chapman smile.

"There's a New Orleans broadhorn waiting for us there. We'll ferry down the Clear Fork to the Brazos. You'll be aboard the *Hollyhock* before you know it."

"And you...?"

"I'll be jumping off. Headed for Austin. Business to settle. Accounts to close."

"But...your money?"

"What do you think you've been carrying around this evening?"

CHAPTER FIFTY-TWO

The night had started in a frenzy, beginning with prisoners Holt Corrigan, Moose Elkins, and Gus Brooks making their escape from the Stebbins jail. The three lawmen were scheduled to be led to the gallows, but they were not about to allow this travesty of justice to stand. Their only offense had been to pose a huge threat to the pirate, Calista Theriot.

The three falsely accused lawmen were making up their escape plans as they went. It had taken a couple of days, but finally, only one man had been left to guard them. Their *break* from jail had been the easiest part. Gus, being the Stebbins deputy until the Theriot takeover, had a set of keys. He had already used them once to escape Theriot lawmen. Holt still had the set he acquired from when he locked up Madigan Sanders, Malo Johnson, and others. None of Sheriff Chapman's deputies thought to check their boots for anything but guns or knives.

Holt and Gus had quietly joked about which set of keys they would use to free themselves. Out of the cages, they easily got by the one guard. There were plenty of guns stored in the jail office to arm themselves as they escaped, including their own weapons. Lots of ammunition too.

Outside the jail, they had walked calmly in plain sight toward the telegraph station. Their first goal was having Gus send out messages to the surrounding region, asking for help and warning everyone about Calista. Riding free from this town was something they would look forward to later.

At the outset, they had taken the telegraph operator, Mr. Holley, prisoner. A young telegram messenger and a customer had been allowed to go. Their warnings had alerted everyone and started the melee.

Holding the clerk hostage did not keep the hired guns masquerading as Special Force Rangers from trying to attack. Three separate assaults by Theriot men had only resulted in the building's front windows being shot out and six dead Special Force assassins lying in the street.

After a third assault attempt, Gus shook his head. "Stars and garters, we got a solid, fortified position here. Do they like gettin' shot?"

Moose had scoffed, "Them order takers is either well paid or stoopid. Or both."

Holt nodded. "You're right about the money part. They're Calista's men, they're afraid to buck orders."

Gus jested, "We just gotta aim at those flashy silver stars."

Since midnight, there had been no more attempts by Theriot men to rush the building. Gus had been firing from the upstairs vantage point, so it was natural that he took the first turn at trying to get some rest. After a couple of fitful hours, Moose changed places with Gus and was in the loft attempting to sleep. Their hostage, in an effort to placate his captors, showed them the office cache of coffee and hard biscuits.

"We finished the last of the apple butter, or you could have some of that too," the clerk offered nervously. When the shooting started, he had cowered under his desk, afraid to move.

"Thank you, Mr. Holley," Holt said. "Hopefully you won't be caught up in this much longer."

"Any-Anything I-I can do t-to help." The clerk smiled edgily.

"I'm sure you were just following orders."

"Orders?" The man gulped.

"Surely you know by now that Calista has been running a bluff on this entire town," Holt said quietly, but sternly.

"I-I d-don't—"

"You're telling me you aren't aware that Texas is currently without a governor or lieutenant governor?" Holt smiled, but not with his eyes. "And Special Forces run by a fat, greasy gunslinger? Or do you just follow everything that slick banker Ames Wooster tells you to do?"

Holley could not match the young Ranger's gaze and looked down at the floor.

Gus spoke up, "You ain't even the real operator. Is he dead?"

Holley's silence gave them the answer.

Holt continued, "Calista Theriot...does she even know your name?" The clerk looked up blankly. Holt shook his head. "Following her orders blindly and she doesn't even know who you are. For what? A little extra money?" He brought his face closer to the telegraph operator. "There's jail time or worse at the end of this, Holley. Was it worth it?"

The clerk gulped, looking like he might be sick. Holt walked away, letting the man sit with his regret.

The night was soon coming to an end. A new pot of coffee Gus fixed was almost ready. As they awaited the hot brew, Holt and Gus looked from the safety of the telegraph office out through the blasted away front windows.

"Any response from all your messages?" Holt asked.

"Nothin' yet," Gus said quietly. "I did send 'em overnight, though. Not everyone sits at their stations round-the-clock. Plus, they could just be downright confused, not sure what to believe is bein' sent outta Stebbins. A lot've bunk an' twaddle been comin' from here for months now."

Holt nodded grimly.

"I know it ain't trouble with th' wire," Gus continued, pouring mugs for the two of them. "We've received a few relays, just nothin' that responded to us. No offers to help."

Holt blew on his hot coffee and resumed his watch out the front. Gus took his cup to the back of the building where he guarded the small, barricaded entryway.

Holt was mulling over ideas. His panther spirit probed what he knew was arrayed in front of them. This standoff was not going to last forever. No telling what would happen in the light of day. Theirs was not a position that would hold. They could not count on outside help.

The upper floor of this building was more of a furnished attic, with the cot, a small dresser, and boxes of supplies for the telegraph office. This loft had four small windows which, all together, gave an effective panorama of the town. The vantage point provided a good field of fire except for targets that may already be at the doors directly below. The western-facing window up there also looked out onto the rooftop of a fabric shop.

Holt realized he could squeeze through one of those windows. He was used to guerrilla fighting. He could take the fight to the Theriot gang while Moose and Gus were bunkered here. There were horses tied up two buildings down. He wondered what was available in the back alley.

"I've got an idea, Gus," Holt said and broke the silence as he brought the pot of hot coffee to warm up the deputy's mug. "I'd like to hear your thoughts." He topped off his own mug and took the pot back to the stove, away from the listening ears of their hostage.

"You was readin' my mind." Gus smiled as he followed Holt. "We gotta do somethin'. We'll be easy pickin's if they get organized."

"Right. This isn't a position we can defend for long," Holt said. "We need to even the odds."

"I was comin' down on that same notion. You got a plan?"

Holt looked back outside onto the street, gauging the situation once again. "That western window upstairs looks out onto the dress shop. I was thinking I'd climb out, before it gets light."

"An' then what, Holt Corrigan? Gawdamighty, I'm almost afraid ta ask—what'll you be doin'?"

Holt's eyes narrowed. "Thinning the herd. I could create a lot of havoc with those boys out there. Be like old times." He blew on the steaming contents of his mug. "What do you think?"

"Not much of a plan," Gus shook his head. "I don't like it, Holt. That's a tall order—"

"I'm used to sneaking around this town, Gus," Holt interrupted. "Remember, after I returned from being shot, I hid from the Viklunds, skulking around unnoticed for several days."

A voice from the stairwell joined in. "But there wasn't a whole pack of rabid gunmen lookin' ta skin yer hide then." Moose walked the rest of the way toward the two. "I don' like th' idear either, Holt."

"Takin' the fight to them is one thing, we need help," Gus noted. "How 'bout I join you goin' out that window? I could sneak across the rooftops to the Blue Sky. Our friend, Navarro, could scare me up a horse—"

"An' ride to th' Flyin' G fer help?" Moose finished the thought.

Gus nodded affirmatively.

Holt grimaced at the idea. "If you're caught, Gus, you aren't going to get any safe conduct. They'll just shoot you."

"If I thought I'd get shot, I wouldn't go."

Holt smirked at the stubborn deputy. "Well, we didn't have much of a plan after holing up here. I guess we'll play this out."

Gus and Moose nodded their agreement.

"Moose, you'll cut loose at any movements," Holt instructed. "Spread out your shots from different locations. Make it appear we're all still here, ready and on guard."

"Got it," Moose agreed. "I'm gonna ensure this one stays quiet an' occupied first." He bobbed his head toward the hostage. "He's bin gen-rous with his coffee an' biscuits, but he's bin lyin' on Calista's behalf fer months. I don' trust 'im."

"Good idea, boss." Gus smiled at his friend. "Here's a kerchief to shut 'im up."

Moose grabbed a small coil of rope and went to the back of the building to tie up the telegraph clerk.

By Holt's count, the next moments lasted forever. In addition to his Russian Smith & Wessons and rifle, he stuffed two more pistols into his waistband. Like during the war, he could squeeze off a lot of shots before needing to reload. He held his medicine pouch briefly over his heart, asking the spirits for courage and guidance.

Gus shimmied through the window first, followed by Holt. The young Ranger stayed crouched outside the window and watched Gus slink his way across the rooftops and drop out of sight at the Blue Sky Inn.

A few minutes after Gus disappeared, Holt reported to Moose through the window, "No alarms raised out here."

"No sudden movements out front either," Moose acknowledged. "I think he made it."

"Now all he needs is a horse and some luck getting out of town." Holt grinned as he ran his fingers across the cardinal feather in his hatband. "Watch yourself, Big'un."

"Find sum of that luck yerself, Holt Corrigan," Moose said. "Keep yer head down."

CHAPTER FIFTY-THREE

THUNKH! WHAKK!

The man wearing the shiny silver Special Force badge had been too preoccupied with rolling a cigarette to be aware of the figure advancing stealthily upon him. It had been a long, quiet night. The cigarette would have to do in place of hot coffee.

Holt rammed the butt of his Winchester into the back of the gunman's skull, then immediately recoiled to swing the other end of his weapon like a blunt axe. The barrel of the rifle crashed across the side of his target's head. The combination of blows knocked the outlaw senseless.

Holt tossed the man's wide-brimmed hat onto the laid-out body's midsection. Grabbing the unconscious man under his arms, he lifted the dead weight out of the dirt and quickly dragged the mercenary inside a storage shed. The outlaw's long duster coat helped brush away the odd trail of tracks. Holt wanted no sign of a scuffle or concealment.

Working quickly inside the shed, Holt tied the man's

neckerchief across his mouth. If he came to, there would be no cries for help. Securely tying the outlaw's legs and wrists ensured no getaway either.

"That ought to hold you just fine, just like your friends," Holt muttered under his breath. He stood up and admired his work.

Three unconscious Calista gunmen laid in a neat row before the young Ranger. The unconscious mercenaries were supposed to have been guarding the back alley in this section of town. Holt's catlike movements enabled him to prowl noiselessly within this corridor behind the main street buildings, allowing him to approach his prey undetected.

The whole strategy for hunting this morning was to rely heavily on surprise and ambush. The long night had left the guards sleepy or inattentive. He had literally dropped on top of his first victim. Each of these hired thugs had met the butt-end of his Winchester, then been dragged inside the storage shed. The outbuilding, with its inventory for the hardware store, presented an ample supply of rope for his captives. The shed itself would provide a secretive hiding place while he continued to reduce the number of guns arrayed against him and his friends. He had to bust the lock to gain entry, but he would pay to replace it later.

He made sure the neckerchiefs tied around their mouths were secure, then disarmed each man. One store down from the shed in the alleyway, a nearly full rain barrel supplied a good depository for the outlaws' guns.

A plan was evolving just like the day itself was coming to light. There were horses tied up in the alleyway, likely the mounts of the men now lying out cold in that shed. If he could capture or otherwise dispatch the men guarding the station's entrance, it could maybe give Moose an opening to leave the building. The horses in the alleyway would be their ticket for a running fight out of this town, and an opportunity to regroup.

His next move would be to stalk the prey massed in front of the telegraph station.

Led by his keen senses, he would lurk further down this alleyway and get across the street. The strong predatory drive that had been instilled in him—his panther spirit—would allow him to steal unseen around and behind the men ringing the front of the telegraph office.

He inhaled and exhaled deeply, gathering himself.

It wasn't a great plan. But he could make it work.

CHAPTER FIFTY-FOUR

Dawn was slow to arrive in the uneasy town of Stebbins. High, thick clouds kept the sun from mustering its full light, as though it was afraid to show its face. Last night had been especially long and taut, not unlike a hangman's noose.

The sun's apprehension matched the overall mood—a nervous citizenry unsure of whether their town was a short-fused powder keg, with three innocent lawmen escaping jail and barricading themselves in the telegraph office, and a twitchy band of hired guns with flashy, fake badges looking for any excuse to execute their authority.

The fear of Calista still held the upper hand in Stebbins. Her Special Force lawmen retaliating against anyone who crossed them was the lid clamped tightly on the town.

With daybreak nudging the dark into gray, Calista's right-hand man, Madigan Sanders, set out from his boarding house quarters to walk the street. A dawn patrol of sorts, to consider his own options. The portly man with a groomed mustache and tailored suit looked neat as a new pin, even this early. He looked at his pocket watch, then continued his trek through town. As was his nature, Madigan's face this morning was unreadable. He was making the point to check on his men, the ones with the shiny new badges. Made of real silver at Calista's insistence. As he walked, the man readjusted the pistols strapped around his immense belly.

His stroll this morning had purpose, more of an inspection after so many things went wrong last night. He hoped to see Sheriff Lewis Chapman out doing the same. The Louisiana gunman wanted to know what the hell happened with their prized prisoners.

Was Chapman investigating this? Madigan's mind grinded on this question. Surely that has to be a priority, he thought.

The three former prisoners—each of them seasoned peace officers, two of them former Rangers—had barricaded themselves inside the sturdy telegraph structure with rifles and a seemingly limitless supply of bullets. Madigan had lost a half dozen men early in the night, the result of an unorganized response against the telegraph office. The charge had not been ordered by either Madigan or Sheriff Chapman, who, at the time, were both still in the *Observer* newspaper office with Calista and banker Ames Wooster. With no leadership, similar attacks by Madigan's men only resulted in disaster and four more dead members of the force.

Madigan had left the newspaper office and immediately reported to the sorry scene of the standoff. He ordered a stop to the futile frontal assaults, instead instructing his men to circle the telegraph office, in front and behind. During the night, pallets had been stacked for concealment and protection across the street from the station's entrance. Madigan's thinking was, if his men couldn't fight their way inside to grab Corrigan and his friends, they'd make damn sure they remained sealed inside the telegraph office, until Calista ordered otherwise.

Although the town had been quiet for hours, a new set of worries was confronting Madigan. As the dreary morning light chased away the night's shadows, he was discovering that, in addition to all the men killed by the fortified prisoners, several Special Force men were not on duty as expected. The number guarding the front of the telegraph station was not quite half what he had ordered. There had to be an explanation for this.

His mind raced with concerns.

He had not heard from his friend Malo Johnson in a long time. Just last night, Calista had asked about the pale assassin. She had sent him to kill the Widow Whitman and any of Holt Corrigan's friends protecting her. It was not like Malo to go this long without reporting in.

Also bothering him right now was Sheriff Chapman. Besides letting the three prisoners escape, the sheriff and his deputies should be sharing in the responsibility of maintaining vigilance. He had yet to see one Stebbins lawman this morning, including Sheriff Chapman.

Madigan kept his irritation below the surface as he made his way to the jail. He would find out where Chapman and his deputies were, then look into his own men who were, for some reason, not on duty.

He used his own set of keys to open the heavy jail door. At least the door had been locked, he grumbled to himself. He hollered from the opened entryway, "Must be rough, sleeping in!"

"M-Madi…er…Mr. Sanders!" A groggy-looking deputy with a wispy mustache stammered himself awake from the desk chair. Another deputy quickly roused himself from a cot in an open jail cell. His squatty, plump frame waddled quickly to the desk.

Madigan thundered, "Where's Sheriff Chapman! Where's the rest of you deputies?"

"Dunno about the sheriff, sir. The rest of the deputies are…uh—"

Madigan interrupted, "Three men escaped from here last night and you're just lying here!" He shook his head in exasperation. "What are your orders from Sheriff Chapman?"

"Or-Orders, sir?"

"Yes! Did he not give orders or instructions on what you should be doing? Maybe to, I don't know, see about rounding up those escaped prisoners? Keeping watch on the town?"

The two deputies looked at each other in hesitation, not knowing how to respond. And not wanting to respond at all.

"Well, Mr. Madigan, sir… we-we…don't have any orders, sir."

"No orders?!"

"N-N-No, sir. We haven't seen the sheriff."

"What do you mean?"

The taller, skinny deputy decided to be the spokesman and said, "He-He left here after supper yesterday. With Miss Thor—Miss Theriot. S-Said they were meeting you and Mr. Wooster at the *Observer* office."

"And…?"

He looked sheepishly at his compatriot before addressing the fat gunman. "W-Well, he left me here. To guard. The prisoners. I had stayed up overnight patrolling with some of your men." He looked down at his boots. "I-I g-guess I fell asleep at the desk. When I woke up, the big prisoner, the one named Moose, had a gun in my face. The long-haired one with the scar was pullin' his pistols out of the coffee box. The other one was tyin' me up."

"You don't know how they got out?"

"N-No, Mr. Madigan, sir. They was in the cells. Then they wasn't."

Madigan sighed in frustration. "Then what happened?"

"I-I dunno how long it was before two other deputies came in an' found me tied up. We immediately ran to the sound of the guns." He took a deep breath. "The prisoners were already holed up in the telegraph station. We helped yer men to try an' force 'em out."

"But those Rangers are pretty good shots," the other deputy completed the story.

Madigan was getting impatient. "So, what about Sheriff Chapman?"

The tall deputy stared at Madigan, then at his friend, then back at the huge Louisiana gunman. "I g-guess I should a-ask you that. He left here last night, with Miss Theriot. They were gonna join up with you. We ain't seen him since."

"He never came back here?"

"No sir. Not that we saw."

The other deputy chimed in, and said, "We were at the telegraph office til late. With the Special Force men. Just came back a little bit ago."

Madigan did not want to hear anything that sounded

like an excuse. "How many deputies does Chapman have?"

"Uh...seven, sir," the short, chubby deputy reported.

"Track down the other five and bring them here. Then all of you will wait until I return."

The unmistakable sound of a man running hard toward the open jail interrupted their exchange. Thudding footsteps on the dirt-packed main street became hard clopping on the planked walkway outside. A redheaded fireplug of a man wearing a Special Force badge appeared out of breath in the doorway.

"Yes? What is it?" Madigan snapped.

The man tried to find his breath to speak, finally gasping, "Corey said ta find you," he rasped, still fighting for air. "He said ta tell you the three men who was supposed ta be covering the alley ain't there."

Madigan blurted, "*Ain't there?*" Gathering himself, he spoke calmly, "What do you mean?"

The redhead was still finding his wind. "Yeah, not there. Not standing watch. Corey said they was nowhere to be found."

Madigan's face tightened. Still controlling his rising temper, he barked, "Where is Corey now? Did he put more men in the alley?"

"I dunno, Mr. Madigan. I was running ta find you."

Madigan cleared his throat and took a deep breath, collecting himself. Inside, his mind was whirling. What the hell was going on? Where was Chapman?

He pointed at the redhead. "You seem good at tracking people down. I need you to find Sheriff Chapman. Even if he's in bed, drag him out. Tell him Madigan wants to see him, now!"

The first deputy wiped at his wispy mustache and spoke up, hesitantly, "Mr. Madigan, s-sir?"

"What is it?!"

"Uh, w-word is, uh, that, uh…that—"

"Come on, spit it out, boy!"

"Uh, Sh-Sheriff Chapman, uh, left town."

"Left town. Is that so?!"

Finding his courage, the deputy explained, "Yessir. With all the news coming out the past week about Miss Theriot. You know, who she really is. Well, it got people thinking. Then last night, the Ranger and the other two escaped from jail."

Madigan scoffed, "So…?"

"Some are saying they saw the lady and Chapman leaving. Last night." The skinny deputy paused and wiped again at his thin mustache. "So they left too."

"Left? Town?" Madigan thundered. "Employed men with badges? Left town!"

The second deputy broke in, "Y-Yes. S-Some of the men from her force are gone too." He quickly dropped his head, unable to look the fat Louisiana gunfighter in the eye.

The first deputy added, "A group left in the night. I don't know who they were. Another six or seven took out about an hour ago."

Madigan glared at each of them. He scowled at the out-of-breath Special Force redhead. "Go find Chapman!" Focusing on the tall deputy, he said, "You! You stay here. Anyone with a badge who comes to the jail, stays here until I return. Understand?" Then he grabbed the arm of the second deputy. "You're coming with me."

Madigan stepped out onto the planked sidewalk and took another calming breath. He brushed at one of his lapels. They would look in at Bellinger's first. It was early, but maybe the missing men were in there.

The Louisiana gunfighter strutted confidently down the street. He wanted people, especially any of his men, to see him making the rounds. He hadn't walked far when he passed in front of the bank. The bank president, Ames Wooster, scurried outside and made a beeline toward the rotund gunfighter. The finance man's decorum never allowed him to run. Despite the situation, the sight of this town's banker walking comically fast gave Madigan a moment's humor. He knew Calista favored Wooster with the company of her bed, but could never really understand why.

"Madigan! There you are!" If the Louisiana gunman's demeanor was stony in a fight or a poker game, the preening Wooster was a complete contrast. Alarm and anxiety always seemed to be pasted all over his face. He held papers in his hand as he rapidly strode across the street. Something was always wrong in Ames's world, dreadfully wrong.

"Good morning, Ames," Madigan said coolly. "I was just on my way to roust a few lawmen from their bunks. Maybe find our sheriff enjoying a leisurely coffee."

He gestured to the deputy with him to cross the street and go look inside the shops that were open for business. "Check the bakery and the Blue Sky too," he ordered. "I'll be at Bellinger's."

The banker was nearly frantic. "Have you seen… her?" he asked breathlessly.

The question caught him off guard. His boss was not among Madigan's concerns this morning. "Her…? Calista?"

Ames nodded urgently.

"No, I haven't. Not like her to be up this early, though."

"Well, she is not in her apartment." He looked up and down the street frantically. "Have you seen her, since last night?"

"I guess I haven't," Madigan answered evenly. "You were there. We got word about the escape at the jail and then heard the gunfire. She ordered me to look into it. She told you to finish overseeing getting the newspaper out." He shrugged. "Guess I've been busy ever since."

He was not interested in having this conversation with Ames. Or any conversation with him, for that matter. He looked off and could see a rider approaching the outskirts of town. His instincts told him this person was not a threat, just someone on an early morning visit to town.

He was drawn back into the conversation by the sound of Ames's voice. The banker had started to calm down, but not much. "Calista also told Sheriff Chapman to follow her out the back way. Maybe he knows."

Madigan slowly raised his eyebrows. "No one's seen him either."

"He's gone *too*?" Ames wound up again. He waved the papers frantically. "Do you know what this is?"

Madigan shrugged and shook his head negatively.

"I found this on her desk. It's a copy of a proposal. To Emery and Thayer!"

Madigan could only look and wait for the banker to explain. He didn't know those names, and at this point, didn't care. He noticed that the rider from earlier had entered town. He could see now that it was a young woman. An attractive one at that. No threat there.

Ames continued his whining, "Emery and Thayer are railroad developers! The ones she was trying to partner with!"

"Good for her. Looks like things are progressing. Look, Ames, I need to—"

The banker interrupted, "No! This proposal reads as though they are buying her out. Including depositing the proceeds into a bank, in Austin."

Madigan smiled wanly and began walking away.

Ames cried out, "If she sent this, she's selling it all to them!" He looked as though he would vomit. Or cry. Or both.

"Wooster, you need to settle yourself, you're having an apoplexy."

"Do you know what this means?" Ames wailed. "If she's doing this…it means…it means she's folding her game. Folding and running. Oh god—"

"Now wait…" Madigan broke in, shaking his head. "There's an explanation for all this. She's probably out at her ranch. Have you checked?"

"No. But she was supposed to—"

"Ames! Ames!" Madigan's eyes bore deep into the scared face of the banker. "Shut up and listen. You can never read Calista Theriot. Ever. Don't *you* know that by now? You can't assume you know what she's going to do." He looked around, making sure no one was within earshot. "With the escaped men, she probably felt it was safer to not be here in town. No one's going to bother her at the ranch." Something dawned on him as well. "In fact, that may explain where Sheriff Chapman is at. Protecting her."

The bank president's face registered the logic

presented by the fat gunman. His demeanor calmed. "I suppose you're right."

"Come with me, Wooster. I'm getting coffee. Maybe it'll do you good to have something stronger."

CHAPTER FIFTY-FIVE

On their way to Bellinger's Pool Hall, the rider Madigan had glimpsed earlier passed them by. The young woman was now nearly across from them, slowing down as she approached the front of the Blue Sky Inn.

Her face glowed with hard-riding freshness. Her brown hair was taken up, mostly hidden by a beat-up, misshapen hat. She wore the clothes of an ordinary cowhand, but her trail coat and simple work shirt could not hide her proud figure. It was her eyes that stood out most of all, though. Bright blue eyes that captured the palette of the sky.

Madigan and Ames gave her no more thought and kept their pace toward Bellinger's.

The deputy that Madigan sent to find stray Theriot lawmen had managed to roust two Special Force men. The three approached Madigan and Ames in the street.

Madigan asked, "Any more of our men or Chapman's deputies across the street?"

"I dunno, Mr. Madigan, sir." The squatty deputy

gestured back over his shoulder. "Found Dean an' Jesse in the bakery. Brought 'em with me. They said there's two more down at the blacksmith's, by the jail."

"Wait here," Madigan ordered. "Try to look useful. I'll be back." He frowned and continued walking, disappearing inside Bellinger's Pool Hall.

The three Theriot lawmen sauntered off the planked sidewalk and out into the middle of the street. The young woman in front of the Blue Sky quickly caught their eyes. They closely observed and appreciated her every move.

Just then, hollering from inside Bellinger's cut off their musing. The words from the first expletive-laden sentences were indistinct, but there was no mistaking their tone. Immediately following, a long-haired man in a new, but no longer crisp, suit hurtled through the pool hall door. His Special Force star glistening in the morning's drab light.

"Dammit, Corey!" Madigan's voice bellowed from within. "Get those men replaced in the alley or I'll shoot you where you stand!"

Almost sprawling onto the walkway, Corey gained control of his momentum and caught a glimpse of the three Theriot men in the street. They were no longer watching the young woman, but eyeing him. Straightening his hair and suit coat, he barked, "Madigan wants you guys in the alley, watching the telegraph office."

One of the Theriot lawmen responded, "We heard." Another one quipped, "Seems you left Bellinger's in a hurry." The other two chuckled in response to the teasing.

The one called Corey said, "That lard-ass grabbed me from my stool and heaved me from the bar. Lotta muscle to go with all that fat." He smirked in spite of himself.

Wanting to change the subject, he gestured toward the young woman with his head. "Will you look at that. Anyone know her?"

The squatty deputy leered. "Never seen her, I'd surely remember."

"Let's go an' welcome her to Stebbins," the deputy said.

The other three men grinned, and all four started making their way toward the young woman.

She had climbed out of the saddle and finished tying up her horse. She was giving her tack a quick check before climbing up onto the sidewalk to enter the Blue Sky.

The group catcalled as they approached.

"Howdy, darlin'!"

"We'd like some company. Come on over!"

"Hey! Hold it right there! We're the law 'round here."

"Yeah, see these Special Force badges? Real silver."

The woman finally turned and said, "Are you *real* Rangers?"

Corey declared boastfully, "We's bigger'n better than that." All four chuckled.

She smirked and continued toward the hotel doors.

The obnoxious group was flummoxed at being ignored.

Corey ordered, "Hold it right there, girlie, you're under arrest. Don't move."

Not quite to the Blue Sky doors, the woman turned toward the foursome. A pistol from underneath her trail coat was in her hand.

Her move shocked the four Theriot gunmen and stopped them in their tracks.

Out in the street, Corey held out an open hand. "H-

Hey, lady, I said we're the law here. There's more of us than you."

The deputy spoke up. "Just put that away. Nobody's going to hurt you."

Corey took a small step forward. "You don't want to do this. You'll be in more trouble than you can handle."

Click-Click

The sound was unmistakable. The young woman's gun was cocked and ready to fire.

From across the street, three buildings down, Holt watched this all unfold. He had meticulously stalked his way from the alleyway to here. With stealth and deliberation, he used every bit of available cover to conceal his approach and avoid detection.

He was now in front of the farm supply and hardware store, opposite the dress shop whose roof he had covertly climbed out the window onto. He crouched low and silent behind a stack of fence posts, waiting to continue his assault against the Theriot Special Force mercenaries. Holt had already coldcocked three gunmen in the back alley and left them tied up in a shed, then taken down two more outlaws on his journey to this position. Their morning had come to an end when he dumped their unconscious bodies into empty barrels at the stave mill.

His predatory hunt had brought him here, poised silently behind another group of five more Theriot men. They were all that was left of the patrol ordered to hold siege on the telegraph office, each wearing large, shiny stars. They were huddled in front of him just off to his right, tucked behind pallets that had been stacked to shield them from the expert shots that had come from inside the station. The outlaws were oblivious to his presence.

Holt had chosen this location carefully. A café next to him on the right, the El Matador, had a large outdoor patio. This terrace had fencing that separated the café from the street, as well as the farm supply and hardware store next door. This fence concealed Holt as he got himself into position.

It also protected him from any crossfire from Moose across the street.

In addition to the proximity of these five outlaws covering the telegraph office, Holt was now close to the Special Force's unofficial headquarters, Bellinger's. The pool hall was just one door down to his left. There were likely Calista men in there as well.

His panther spirit bristled. The fight was going to be taken to them from here. His surprise attack was inevitable, but first, he would observe his surroundings patiently and strike when appropriate.

Holt was scheming out his assault when the hostile scene involving the young woman unfolded in front of the Blue Sky and stole his attention.

Holt was stunned.

The woman with the gun was Laudie Kate!

What was she doing here?

His emotions ran the gamut of a fanned pistol as he watched the conflict develop. Excited to see the woman he loved. Angered at her treatment by these bottom feeders. And alarmed.

Laudie Kate was now in a drawn-gun standoff with hired killers!

He ran his right hand across the cardinal feather in his hatband and brought his Winchester to his shoulder. He heard Laudie Kate announce in a clear, loud voice, "It would be best if you all stopped right there."

Despite the moment, her *It would be best* pronouncement brought a slight smile to Holt's face. That's my lady, he thought.

Laudie Kate continued confidently, "I'm tired. It's been a long ride. Go back to whatever you were doing."

From behind the Special Force agent named Corey, the deputy urged, "She's bluffing. Come on."

Corey nodded and resumed his advance. The three men with him followed.

BANG!

A bullet thudded into the ground in front of the men. Laudie Kate recocked her smoking pistol and announced, "The next one hurts."

Although his rifle was aimed at the men confronting Laudie Kate, Holt held off. Out of the corner of his eye, he saw the five Theriot men guarding the telegraph station react to her gunshot. He re-leveled his Winchester directly at them, announcing in a grim voice, "I don't want to kill you, and you don't want to be dead. Make another move, and you won't be around to see how this ends." Although they couldn't see him, the sound of a Winchester cocking and a fierce voice startled them, stunning the five to immobility. They each immediately halted their movements.

Back in front of the Blue Sky, the Theriot gunman, Corey, was nearest to Laudie Kate and her pistol. It appeared she knew how to use it, and he wasn't eager to move any closer. Yet, the deputy and the other two men were undeterred and stepped around him.

In a split second, Laudie Kate fired again, and another bullet spat just in front of the foursome. She quickly drew a second revolver.

"No more talk," she declared and recocked both pistols.

"To hell with this," Corey barked. "We're Rangers. Are we goin' to let her do this?"

From the Blue Sky's side alley just behind Laudie Kate, a dark-haired man with close-cropped hair and clean-shaven face stepped from the gray morning shadows. With a voice as cold as his steel-blue eyes, he growled, "I think you boys are in way more trouble than you know."

He only had one arm, but the hand he did have held a large pistol, aimed directly at them.

Holt was stunned.

Blue!

Blue was here! With Laudie Kate!

The Walch Navy 12-shot revolver in Blue's hand was formidable. Two triggers and two hammers. Weighing two pounds, it was twelve inches long. It was a gun rarely seen in this part of Texas. Blue had taken it from a dead Union officer during the war and decided he liked it, especially since reloading a standard six-shooter wasn't easy one-handed.

The oldest Corrigan brother took steps toward the group. "You aren't Rangers or even lawmen. There's nothing *special* about you other than the paycheck you receive from a no-good pirate." He eyed each of them. "It's time you boys leave your iron. Right where you stand."

"While you're at it," another voice rang out directly across the street. "Drop those silly make-believe badges." The order came from a younger-looking version of the one-armed man. This one had long, dark hair and a full mustache. He stepped from the alleyway on the other side of the pool hall from Holt with his Spencer rifle aimed at the group of Special Force loudmouths.

Deed!

Holt's heart sang. *My brothers are here!*

He grinned. This was no longer a fair fight.

The Theriot men forgot about the young woman. Three strangers with four guns pointed at them was a position they never thought they'd be in.

An uneasy quiet fell across the scene. Nobody spoke, nobody moved.

In the stillness, an unseen dog barked at something it didn't like. A water pump creaked and groaned before gushing forth.

The intensity built, stretched taut like a rope about to give way.

Holt's panther spirit prickled. He repositioned the medicine pouch under his shirt, mouthing soft words to the spirits. For good measure, he ran his fingers across the cardinal feather in his hat.

A low rumble emanating from the warehouses at the other end of town became louder as a freighter came into view. The driver of the heavy, laden wagon was oblivious to what he was driving into as he headed for the general store. The leaden clods of the draft horses' hooves and the wagon's rattling trace chains added an odd syncopation to the edgy situation.

The wagon pulled to a stop at the general store. The

driver set the brake and hopped down. Quiet reigned once more as tension remounted.

Somewhere, very close by, the door to an open shop slammed shut. Hard.

The sharp report startled every living creature in the vicinity.

Holt saw the men confronting Laudie Kate reach for their pistols.

He screamed, "Laudie! Duck! Inside!" as the main street of Stebbins exploded in a cacophony of gunfire.

Holt levered two shots from his Winchester at the Theriot loudmouths confronting Laudie Kate, then caught movement in his periphery. One of the telegraph station guards stood to fire at him, nearly point-blank. Holt twisted in that direction and fired two shots as quickly as he could work the rifle's action, dropping the man. In this instant, as his attention was drawn away from Laudie Kate and toward the station, his head and torso had shifted. The movement saved his life. Three shots blistered the post next to where his head had been.

Holt dove. The dive carried him down between the planked sidewalk and the stack of pallets. It would keep him alive for the moment.

When the firing started, Blue unloaded three quick shots, and Laudie Kate fired both her pistols. All five bullets slammed into the Special Force gunman, Corey, and the squatty, plump deputy, dropping them instantly. Both now lay unmoving in the street. The other two gunmen ran and dove for cover behind the freight wagon. Caught in the middle of this sudden maelstrom, the terrified driver of the wagon crawled frantically away and rolled himself into a ball behind a nearby water trough.

Holt took aim at the orange gun blasts now coming

from under the parked freight wagon. Neither shot found its mark, but temporarily kept the gunmen from firing. He quickly looked in the direction of the Blue Sky door, where Laudie Kate had been. She was nowhere in sight. Four more shots from the Theriot men in front of the telegraph station spit at him, causing him to duck.

From his left, Deed's Spencer boomed several times. Two of the guards at the telegraph station crumpled and were still, joining the body of the man Holt had cut down earlier. The remaining two cowered further behind their pallets, deciding whether to continue fighting.

Holt resumed his attention on a pair of legs visible under the freight wagon and squeezed the trigger. The Theriot gunman screamed and reeled, grabbing at his wounded leg. A shot from Blue's large Walch revolver knocked the man into the open. A final shot from Holt jolted the outlaw backward into an unmoving heap.

The freighter's draft horses, already uneasy from the gunfire and commotion, completely spooked at the smell of blood and the spasmic contortions from the man's body as he was shot. The animals' first instinct was to bolt, but the wagon's brake was holding fast. Reacting to their inability to run, they reared and bucked in terror. It all happened so quickly, the remaining Special Force gunman found himself trapped in his hiding spot underneath the terrified animals. It did not take long for the horses' large, wide hooves to trample and crush his body.

Just then, two quick pistol shots were fired at Deed from inside Bellinger's. One of the bullets careened with a nasty whine off the breech block of his Spencer, knocking it useless from Deed's hands. The youngest Corrigan quickly spun away, seeking safe cover on the side of the pool hall.

Madigan stepped from Bellinger's. Ames cowered just inside, hiding behind the doorframe. The fat Louisiana gunfighter instantly assessed the situation. He fired another shot in the direction of Deed, who had peeked around the building's corner. The shot broke off a small chunk of building, sending splinters that showered Deed and forced him back out of sight.

Several doors down to Madigan's left, two Special Force gunmen rushed out of the bank toward a wagon in the street. One of them carried a rifle, the other had drawn a pistol. A client had left a buckboard unattended out front. One of the men freed the horse pulling the wagon and slapped its rear, sending it away. The two then pushed the wagon over on its side, giving them a secure place from which to fire.

Madigan saw this action and moved quickly to join them, firing a couple of blind shots into the alleyway where Deed had gone. From the safety of this barricade, the three concentrated fire on Blue's position next to the Blue Sky.

In response, Blue ducked back into the Blue Sky side alley, using the corner of the building as cover. His Walch revolver was nearly empty, but two more six-shooter pistols were within easy grasp at his waistband.

Back across the street, Madigan's blind shooting at Deed missed its mark. The youngest Corrigan brother vacated the area next to the pool hall, not liking the vantage point. Instead, he had hustled around to the rear of the establishment, carefully opening the unlocked back door.

Edging through the darkened, smoky saloon, Deed crept his way among the now-abandoned billiard tables. His objective was the front door where banker Ames

Wooster stood snapping erratic shots with a pistol. Deed skulked his way forward. He passed six patrons, all cowering under tables. They watched him, quiet with fear, unable or unwilling to move.

For a moment, it sounded as though the gunfire was ebbing throughout the town. Ames eased himself slowly outside onto the walkway, anxiously looking for targets.

Silently, Deed took off on a dead run, heading for the banker. Two strides away, he yelled. Ames turned toward the sound. His eyes suddenly startled wide, and he tried to bring up his pistol. Deed flew into the air, cocked his legs and straightened them, driving his boots into the banker's face and chest. Ames's head snapped back as he grunted and toppled to the ground. His pistol clattered onto the sidewalk.

Quickly regaining his feet, Deed drew his .44 Remington revolver and leveled three shots in the direction of Madigan and the two gunmen behind the overturned wagon. The blasts made them think twice about concentrating fire in Deed's direction.

Ames was recovering and starting to stand when Deed faced him and emptied his pistol's final three shots into the banker's belly and chest. The force drove Ames backward into the street, where he took his last breath in the dirt.

CHAPTER FIFTY-SIX

Deed crouched low and repositioned himself outside behind a large water trough, bringing him closer to Holt's position. As he reloaded his gun, he sent a signal he knew his brother would understand: *Wh-eeet cheer cheer cheer.*

Deed whistled his version of a simple cardinal call and repeated it.

Holt looked over his left shoulder briefly. He did not see Deed, but answered with his own cardinal birdsong. He smiled, knowing his little brother was somewhere close by.

"Good spot!" Deed hollered. "That café on your right has mighty fine barbacoa."

"I'm partial to their steak and eggs," Holt responded.

"What's your plan till then?" Deed asked.

Holt was also using this time to reload. "There's two of these bastards in those pallets," he called out. "They're what's left of the patrol that was supposed to keep us bottled up in that telegraph station."

"I see they did a real bang-up job of keeping you under control," Deed teased.

Holt chuckled, then added, "Time to flush this scum out. Moose is still in the station. He'll help us get 'em in a crossfire."

"They sure got nice, shiny targets to aim at," Deed called.

Kneeling, Holt eased himself around the corner of the stack of pallets. "Now!" he hollered and began concentrating heavy rifle fire at the barricades in front of the telegraph office. Deed also pumped shots from his Remington at the guard's makeshift shelter. Their bullets crashed through the wood frames, launching a ruinous torrent of fearsome splinters and angry lead.

Any thought the two besieged Theriot men had of scooching closer to the station for safety was dashed. Moose added to the barrage with his own blistering fire from inside the office.

The duress from the withering fire became too much for the Theriot men to bear. They panicked. Suddenly, they stood and ran, trying to flee the onslaught. Bullets from Holt and Deed riddled the first man, keeping his body upright as it jerked a few extra steps before collapsing. Moose dropped the last man in a heap in the street, near the El Matador's patio.

At the other end of town, the Chapman deputy left behind at the jail stepped outside. Too far away to hear, Holt and Deed saw him holler and gesture toward the carriage house and blacksmith shop next door. Two Theriot gunmen emerged from the workshop. The Corrigans saw the deputy motion these men to spread out and begin stalking toward the middle of town.

"They're going to get Blue and Laudie Kate pinned

down. We gotta move," Holt exclaimed. He hollered toward the telegraph station. "Moose! There's more of 'em down the street, by the jail!"

He turned, crouched down, and hurried as fast as possible through the side alley behind him. Deed watched and followed his brother. At the same time, inside the telegraph station, Moose relocated to the upper floor in order to get a better firing position toward the far end of town.

As those three Theriot men crept their way carefully up the street, Madigan raised up from behind the overturned wagon to yell instructions. A bullet from Blue, still sheltered next to the Blue Sky Inn, forced the fat gunman back down.

Rifle shots cracked from the upstairs lair of the telegraph office, throwing long-range lead at the deputy and two Special Force men working their way from the jail. The bullets spat at the ground around their feet, whining away into the distance.

The deputy dove for cover, rolling underneath an empty produce stand. He was now on the same side of the street as the Blue Sky, but was too far away to have an angle from which to shoot at Blue.

The two Theriot gunmen with the deputy halted their advance. More shots bit the street in front of them. They turned and ran back to the safety of the carriage house and blacksmithy, where cover was plentiful.

Holt and Deed trotted down an empty back street, passing behind Bellinger's, behind the newspaper office, and behind a shoes and clothing store. They stopped in back of a large, substantial building. Walls of thick adobe. Heavy, secure back door. Windows with bars and thick frames.

"This is the bank," Holt said, catching his breath. "That fat Louisiana bottom feeder, Madigan Sanders, is out front with two of that witch's men. Behind an overturned wagon."

"There were three more coming from the jail," Deed said, both unaware that Moose had chased them under cover. "No telling where they are by now."

Holt tried the bank's back door. It was locked tight. "It was worth a try." He shrugged.

"We need to move," Deed said.

Holt agreed. "That building we just passed, the one next to the bank, is a boarding house. It's got two floors. You take up position in the alley or try to sneak onto that upper floor. There's an outside set of stairs."

Deed nodded.

"I'm going farther down. There's a saddler and tack store next to that blacksmith shop. I'll root out those three from the street. You've got Madigan and the two at the wagon."

In this part of town, the shots coming from Madigan and his men were louder. Returning fire from the Blue Sky was sporadic, but at least it was return fire. Someone, their brother Blue or Laudie Kate, was still in business.

The two eyed each other. Warriors readying for attack. No words needed between brothers.

Holt took off, continuing down the back street. He stopped behind the saddler shop, more of a barn than a shop building. Its large sliding doors were yet to be opened this early morning. He eased further down, landing now behind the carriage house. Unlike the saddle and tack shop, this establishment had all its doors and windows flung wide open, the heat from the forge necessitating the airflow.

Holt lurked his way around and through the huge back doors, rifle at the ready. He was only three steps inside when he saw a large black man staring right at him.

The man was positioned behind a rack of tools and wore a grimy leather apron over a dirty work shirt with the sleeves cut off. A sweat-stained neckerchief swathed his head. His arms were like the rest of his body, chiseled and heavily muscled.

The Negro slowly raised a hand and put one finger to his lips. He then made the sign signaling *Two* and gestured toward the opening at the front of the carriage house, indicating where two men were hiding.

Holt slipped quickly over to the man, looking around the shop, taking in all the sights—coal bin, forge, anvils, a huge array of hammers, tongs, and other implements, including racks, shelves, and buckets filled with all shapes and sizes of iron and steel.

The man eyed Holt intently and stated quietly, "You're not one of them."

Holt quickly whispered an introduction. "Holt Corrigan, Texas Ranger." He stuck out his hand.

The huge man was a little surprised at the gesture. "Elijah. Elijah Henderson," he answered quietly, shaking Holt's hand. "Heard you were dead, Holt Corrigan. Then you were alive. Then you were going to be hanged. Seems you have many lives. Like a cat."

Holt smiled briefly. "I've heard that."

The man gave a quick laugh. "There's two of them, Holt Corrigan, just out front. Both wearing those big, shiny stars."

Holt's eyes narrowed in determination.

Elijah continued, "A badge doesn't make a man good. Those badges are Theriot stars. And anything connected to her is no good."

Holt nodded. "I wish the town had a few more like you."

"So do I," Elijah acknowledged. "There's talk, but too much fear. Mrs. Bywater at the dress shop has had a shotgun hidden away, waiting for a day like this. Mr. Navarro at the Blue Sky, he is ready to fight, too. There are others. I have urged them, tried to lead them, but…" He looked down at his huge bare arms. "This color isn't from forge soot."

A slight frown came over Holt before he responded, "Well, Elijah, help me here. What do you see from this end of town?"

"They're on either side of the big sliding doors. One is off to the left, crouching behind a bunch of wagon wheels. He has at least one pistol. The other one is off to the right, hiding behind a couple of rain barrels. He's holding a rifle and carrying a pistol."

Holt listened intently.

"There's a third," Elijah continued. "One of that idiot Chapman's deputies."

"We've met. He was on guard when we escaped from the jail last night."

Elijah snorted a quick chuckle. "He's across the street, lying under the vegetable stand out by the grocers. He's got two pistols." He paused briefly. "The three tried to move closer to the action, but somebody with a rifle chased them back here and has been keeping them pinned down ever since. I think it's someone firing from the telegraph office."

"That's Moose Elkins. He was the sheriff here until—"

"That demon woman Theriot," Elijah finished the sentence. "Moose was…is…a good man. Glad to hear he's well. His body was never found. I hoped it meant he was alive."

Holt took a breath and set his rifle down. This job would be better handled with pistols. He checked his Russian Smith & Wessons in their shoulder holsters. He still had two other revolvers tucked into his waistband. A quick check confirmed they were loaded as well.

"Thanks, Elijah. I might've walked right into trouble." Holt smiled and shook the man's hand again.

"It's time we put an end to this. To her and her men," Elijah said. He eyed the front opening carefully before slipping quickly to a work area filled with anvils and tools. From a box, he grabbed a huge handful of shotgun shells and shoved them into an apron pocket. Next, he picked up a sawed-off double-barreled shotgun. "I will help you."

"I think you better leave them for me," Holt cautioned.

"This I know how to use." Elijah raised his gun. It looked almost toy-like in his huge hands.

"Okay. I'm going to peel back outside, off to the left. I'll come around the building that way," Holt said. "I'll hit the ones at the wagon wheels and the vegetable stand first." He drew one of his Russians. "Elijah, how about you take station near the front. Find a protected spot. Keep 'em from escaping and coming back inside. Okay?"

Elijah nodded his understanding. Holt returned the gesture and said, "Thank you again, my friend." He ran his fingers quickly across the cardinal feather in his hat and moved out.

CHAPTER FIFTY-SEVEN

Holt peeked around the corner of the blacksmith's wagon shop. Only a few feet away, one of Calista Theriot's gunmen was hunkered down among a dozen or so old wagon wheels arranged on-end in a neat, organized line. The man raised up only to duck back down when bullets from Moose's rifle clipped the side of the building and the Carriage House sign above his head. Moose was firing at movement. It would take a fortunate shot to hit anything at this distance.

Nonetheless, Holt ducked too. Moose would have no idea he was down here. And bullets don't care who or what they hit.

In addition to the gunman just beside him, Holt could see the deputy kneeling across the street by the empty vegetable stand. It was the same deputy who was on duty when he, Moose, and Gus escaped. "*Lawman.*" Holt smirked to himself. "He can't even grow a proper mustache." Still, he reminded himself, anyone with a gun, especially if scared, was not to be taken lightly.

It was time.

Holt spoke clearly, but in a low enough tone that only the man close by could hear. "You have two choices. You can drop that gun, or you can die. Pretty simple."

He startled the man so badly, it appeared he jumped right out of his soul.

"One more time," Holt said in a low growl. "Drop the gun or die."

The Theriot man was frozen with fear and indecision. He looked around, hoping his friends heard the threat and would come to his aid. The two others were only focused on the action up the street.

"You're gonna shoot me anyway," the Special Force agent trembled.

"I won't shoot an unarmed man," Holt said. "But seeing as how you're still armed…"

"Here…" The Theriot man held out his gun, then dropped it.

Just then, two shots slammed into the siding next to Holt's head. Splinters stung his face and neck. The deputy at the vegetable stand had noticed movement and fired at Holt.

The young Ranger flattened himself against the building, giving him temporary cover. The carriage house yard was littered with wagons and carts of all sizes and conditions. Holt spied the bed of an old buckboard that lay abandoned, its axles and reach braces long removed to repair another vehicle. He sprinted to the barren piece of wagon, squeezing off three quick shots in the direction of the deputy as he ran. He slid into the bed's heavy wooden bed, ducking safely behind it.

Something sensed in Holt to take a look at the Theriot man who had surrendered. He looked over just as the outlaw retrieved his gun and was aiming at Holt. The young Ranger rolled to his right, avoiding the Theriot man's shots, and emptied his pistol of its final three bullets directly into him. He growled at the unmoving body, "I told you I wouldn't shoot an unarmed man."

He scurried back to the cover of the wagon bed. The deputy across the way had taken better cover, too, moving further behind the empty produce stand.

Holt wished now he had the firepower and accuracy of his rifle. The deputy was too well-hid at this angle. Even with three other loaded pistols, he took the time to stuff cartridges into his empty Smith & Wesson. One never knew.

Suddenly, rifle shots smashed into the wagon bed next to Holt. These weren't from Moose's gun. The other Special Force agent was firing at him from the rain barrels. The young Ranger was in a safe spot for now, but the angles and odds could change instantly if the two outlaws firing at him got organized.

Holt was rapidly calculating a plan when he noticed new motion by the rain barrels. The large wooden containers sat on a platform, more of a porch, that served as the entryway to the front desk of the carriage house. This entryway had a standard door for clients. Holt's eye caught the door bursting open and the large figure of Elijah Henderson stepping through.

BOOOM! BOOOM!

With one hand, the blacksmith fired both barrels of his sawed-off shotgun point-blank. The blasts shattered the rain barrels and blew the Special Force gunman off the porch. Elijah smoothly reloaded and looked around for more targets.

The deputy across the street tried to use the opportunity to squeeze off shots at the black man. Not only did he miss, he also left too much of his body exposed. Holt emptied his reloaded Smith & Wesson, hitting the deputy in the chest and leg. The wounded man staggered and tried to stand. Holt drew his other Russian and fired twice more, finishing the job.

Holt darted carefully to the cover of the carriage house and blacksmith shop. Stepping out briefly, he waved his hat over his head toward the telegraph office, hoping Moose would see the signal and understand.

Back inside, he calmly shoved more loads into his pistols and nodded. "Thanks, Elijah."

"Here, I brought this," Elijah said, reaching over to hand Holt his Winchester. "Knew you didn't want to leave it in my shop."

While Holt and Elijah were silencing the three Theriot men at the west end of town, Deed was maneuvering into place.

He assessed the stairs to the second floor of the boarding house. They would provide an obviously advantageous firing position. However, the stairs were too open. He would be seen by the Theriot men in front of the bank. The risk was too great.

He wished he still had his Spencer. It lay damaged and useless over by the pool hall. He still had his two Remington pistols and his formidable hand-fighting skills. It would be enough.

He had heard firing from the end of town where Holt had gone. No time to wonder about that. The objective was ahead of him in the form of a notorious

Louisiana gunfighter and two Special Force mercenaries.

They had yet to be alerted to his presence.

Someone who *was* observant was Blue. The oldest Corrigan with sharp, keen eyes spotted Deed inching down the tight space between the adobe bank and boarding house. The gap was narrow enough that most would ignore it as an area where someone would traverse, much less pose a threat. Unfortunately, there also wasn't room to maneuver. If Deed was detected now, he was a dead man.

Despite the precariousness of his advance, Deed smiled at his brother.

The youngest Corrigan made his way through the tight opening, situating himself behind a sturdy bench on the boarding house porch. The shooting angles of the brothers were such that neither could accidentally fire on the other. Blue signaled to Deed that the reloaded twelve shots in his huge Walch pistol were all he had remaining. Deed nodded. He was running low on ammunition as well.

Deed instinctively touched the small Oriental-looking brass circle on a rawhide thong worn around his neck. A gift from his godfather, Silka, the disk was engraved with a symbol of *Bushido.*

"Touch Bushido...for better luck," Silka had taught him long ago. They both had worn similar disks, except Deed's was connected to a sheathed throwing knife carried under his shirt behind his neck.

Madigan Sanders and two Theriot Special Force mercenaries were staying hidden behind an overturned buckboard wagon. They had momentarily stopped firing. It looked to Deed like they were reloading.

"If we're almost out of bullets, they have to be running low as well," Deed muttered to himself. Now was the time, he decided, and drew both his Remington pistols.

"Hey, butterball! You're in a bad spot," Deed hollered. The three outlaws spun around in surprise. "Seems you're about to be in a bit of a crossfire. Is that pirate witch really worth dying for?"

"You got a better offer?" Madigan sneered.

"You get to keep living, for now," Deed called back. "All I can promise."

"That's not much of a promise. Or a life. I got too many marshals, constables, and Rangers already after me. Which one are you?"

"None of 'em. You tangled with Holt Corrigan."

"What makes him so damn special?"

"He's my brother. You crossed him and got the whole family."

Madigan spoke quiet words to the two outlaws with him.

Deed had enough. "All right, fat boy, no more talk. Drop your guns."

"You go to hell!"

Madigan and one of the Theriot men opened fire at Deed, the other blazed away at Blue. The brothers responded with their own volleys. The combined barrage was one huge eruption of sound.

Deed blasted three shots that crumpled one of the Special Force men. Firing twice more, he missed the other Theriot man, who was leveling rifle shots at both him and his brother. The rifleman moved out to the end of the buckboard, behind the axle and spring, to try and give himself more cover.

The return fire directed at Deed was intense, but so far, the bench and their poor aim were providing enough protection. As he ducked behind his shelter, he checked the remaining loads in his gun. One Remington was down to its last bullet. The other had only two. His gun belt was empty. Any extra bullets were in his saddlebags.

The Theriot outlaw with the rifle moved too far around the end of the buckboard. Bullets from Blue's huge pistol toppled him face-first into the street.

Madigan's firing kept up, though, forcing Blue back under cover before he turned his attention back to Deed.

Both men fired at each other, missing their intended targets.

"Your offer still good, Corrigan?" Madigan hollered.

"Only when you drop the guns and put your hands up where we can see them," Deed answered. He was relieved. Both his Remingtons had just clicked empty.

Madigan stood slowly. He dropped one pistol into the dirt, followed by the other. His left arm slowly raised above his head. "You boys got the other arm. I think it's broke," he said. "This is as far as it'll go," he explained as he only lifted his right arm waist high. The suit coat of his right arm appeared ripped as though he had taken a bullet.

Blue moved out from his hiding spot, his gun trained on Madigan. He stopped out in front of the Blue Sky's batwing doors, wary of the Louisiana gunman.

Deed moved cautiously toward the portly gunman, holding one of his empty pistols on him as he closed the gap between them.

Suddenly, Madigan's right arm flinched to grab for a hidden pistol in his waistband.

In one smooth motion, Deed grabbed the throwing

knife behind his neck and threw it lightning-quick at the fat Louisianan. The knife caught Madigan in the left side of his chest and buried to the hilt. The gunfighter froze. A bullet from his hidden gun thumped harmlessly into the dusty street.

Meanwhile, Holt had inconspicuously crept close to Madigan's shelter. As Deed's knife found its mark, nearly simultaneous shots from Holt and Blue raked the wagon barricade. At least four shots tore into Madigan. His body fell back onto the overturned buckboard, keeping him upright. Another deafening salvo of Holt's bullets crashed into him, finishing the job of knocking him down and ending his life.

An eerie quiet started to take hold of the Stebbins morning. Dead Theriot outlaws were strewn all across town. The blacksmith, Elijah, and the town saddler methodically prowled around the bodies, checking for movement.

Holt was in a hurry to find Laudie Kate when an abrupt shot startled everyone. They all looked to see that the saddler had completed a job that earlier bullets had started.

Carefully ambling his way from the telegraph station, Moose called out to Holt, "I left our prisoner tied up inside. Figured he could wait until we know this is over."

"That reminds me..." Holt stopped in his tracks, suddenly remembering. "Elijah! There are three Theriot men tied up in the storage shed behind the general store. Two more are stuffed into barrels outside the stave mill." He then addressed Moose, and said, "I think the reinstated sheriff of Stebbins could use a deputy like Elijah to retrieve those men. What do you think?"

Moose nodded in agreement. "Elijah, do ya swear ta

follow Ranger Corrigan's instructions an' bring those men in? *Alive?*"

Elijah grinned. "Yes, sir!"

"No badge needed, Deputy Elijah. Ya have yer orders. Thanks fer th' help!"

Next door to the telegraph station, the door of the dress shop flung open, grabbing everyone's attention. A man wearing a Theriot Special Force badge emerged, hands over his head, pleading, "Don't shoot! Don't shoot!" Just behind him, brandishing a shotgun, was shopkeeper Dory Bywater.

"Keep moving, you worthless jackwagon," the woman ordered. "Over there, by those men." The gun was a smaller gauge, more fit for her frame, and she knew how to use it. "I caught him trying to sneak away. Miserable sonofa…" she said as her voice trailed away.

Holt and his brothers tried hard to maintain serious looks on their faces, but the sight of this petite little shop-keeper holding an outlaw hostage was almost too much.

Just then, a crash and a scream from inside the Blue Sky Inn ended the peace.

Holt looked up, horrified, in the direction of the racket. Laudie Kate hadn't been seen or accounted for yet. Everyone standing in front of the hotel drew their guns and moved for cover, not sure of what was going on.

First, the diminutive Blue Sky owner, Miguel Navarro, appeared through the batwing doors. A large cast-iron skillet was in his hand. He was followed by Judge Ridgely, holding one arm in the air. His other hand held a bloody rag to the side of his head. Another Theriot man walked out, both arms in the air. Bringing up the rear was Laudie Kate, pistol trained on the captive, her hat held along her back by its tie-down. Her brunette hair, originally pinned up, was now an abundant mess. Her bright-blue eyes sought out Holt.

She was the most beautiful thing he had ever seen.

Holt hurried to the doorway, ignoring the hotel owner's chattering about the scuffle that had ensued inside. He looked back at his brothers, giving them a silent *Handle this prisoner* look. Finally, he came face-to-face with Laudie Kate.

"Do I know you?" He smiled.

She smiled back.

"You look like someone I know, but—"

"There's lots you don't know about me, Holt Corrigan."

"I guess so, I just—"

"Like you still don't know when it's time to kiss me…"

He grabbed her like he would never let go. The kisses came naturally and lingered until he heard one of his brothers clear his throat behind them. He turned and looked around, his hand finding hers. The morning overcast was burning off. The sky was turning brilliant blue.

CHAPTER FIFTY-EIGHT

Within the city limits of Austin, a lanky, older lawman guided a small patrol of cavalry assigned to accompany him. With the absence of a fort, the city did not have a formal military presence, but it did have state militia and Rangers for frontier security needs. Near the capitol building was a series of neat and orderly bungalows for permanent and temporary housing where such forces could live.

"Men, it's over here," Orion Higbee directed from the head of this pre-dawn patrol from Fort McKavett. With the direction and blessing from the fort's newly assigned commander, the older Ranger was charged with locating and arresting Corporal James Madison Chase.

Jim to his friends.

Lieutenant Governor to Calista Theriot and her henchmen.

According to the fort's records and the capitol's accounts, Corporal Chase was one of the troops bunked in the third bungalow on the eastern edge of this quad.

"Captain, whattaya say we keep three or four men

mounted in case there's a pursuit?" Orion quietly asked his military counterpart.

Captain Nissen, Orion's newest friend from Fort McKavett, volunteered to head up this patrol while deferring command to the older Ranger. "That's sound strategy, Ranger sir."

"Those men can hold the mounts for those of us bustin' inside. They're your troops, I'll let you figger out who's doin' what."

As the patrol was organizing and beginning to surround the temporary housing of Corporal Chase, a short, dark-haired man exited the back door of the bungalow. Shutting the door, the figure pulled on a black, wide-brimmed hat. Walking on a worn path toward a tied-up horse, the figure—dressed in black canvas trousers, black shirt, black vest, and black traveling boots—walked briskly but bent over, coughing and hacking into a bright red bandanna.

Two troopers held their carbines crossed in front of them, not allowing the person to pass any further toward the hitching post.

Eager to get inside, Orion eyed the captain from across the yard, an *Is that Chase?* look in his eyes.

The captain quickly shook his head no, indicating with a hand that the person they were looking for was much taller. The officer then called out to the short man, "Does a James Chase live here?"

The figure paused and pointed at a second-floor window before sneezing and coughing again into his neckerchief.

The captain motioned with his head for the troopers to let the man go on his way. "Nasty stuff," he said. "I hate fighting colds."

Orion was already tromping to the front door, six soldiers hurrying to follow him. Captain Nissen took six more to push in through the back. Once in place, Orion hollered, “Now!” and both groups rushed inside.

Watching from the quad’s dirt road, Calista Theriot tucked her red bandanna into her black vest and spurred her horse into a lope.

Charging up a simple flight of stairs, Orion crashed through the closed door, gun drawn.

A handsome young man lay naked on the bed. His eyes were open but unseeing. Life had left his body. Blood, now drying, had seeped from one of his nostrils. More blood and spittle had drooled from his mouth. Orion eyed the body and the scene with a scowl.

A fancy tea set on a tray lay on the bed next to him. Orion looked at the captain. “Is this Chase?”

The captain nodded affirmatively.

Eyeing the partially consumed snack of tea, biscuits, and honey, Orion said to the troopers that made the ascent, “If you’re thinkin’ ’bout it, don’t touch any of that food.”

The realization just occurred to the captain. “This man’s been poisoned!” he blurted.

“An’ all the answers to all the questions went with ’im,” Orion reflected.

The captain quietly ordered all the troopers but two to go back outside and secure the small yard surrounding the little house.

The loft apartment was sparsely furnished. A tiny, struggling wood stove. A larger-than-usual bed, a beat-up dresser, and a small table that doubled as a desk. Orion looked back at the dead man. Young. Handsome. Muscular. Large bed.

Calista.

He walked over to the desk and bent down to pick up a newspaper on the floor. The *Stebbins Observer*. Weeks and weeks of *Observer* issues littered the floor all around the desk. The small table was more organized, but was reserved for stacks of paper from telegraph offices. Several stacks had been hurriedly shoved into the stove. Scraps of partially burned paper lay below it.

Just then, another trooper announced from the closet, "There's an Army uniform here, sirs. Corporal chevrons."

Orion crossed the small room to the closet and retrieved folded papers from the coat pocket. "I don' see any other clothes, so this must be Chase's uniform." He read one of the papers: "*Corporal Jim Chase. Stationed at Fort McKavett.*" He handed the stack to Captain Nissen.

"These papers are dispatches," the captain remarked. "Chase was a courier for the Fifth Military District. He would travel from here to Fort McKavett and back."

Orion returned to the desk and pored through the wire messages and receipts. Stebbins. New Braunfels. Fort McKavett. Lies about Lilly. Lies about Holt and Dal. Lies about the Cap'n. Lies about himself. He tossed the notes down, one at a time, onto the tabletop, like dealing cards.

He spoke, but it was mostly for himself. "Jus' look at this. All of this. Empty talk. Bullyin' good people. Threatenin' my Lilly. Murderin' the Cap'n." A fiery wrath was rising inside him. "An' ev'ryone believed it! You muddy-runnin', fuzzy-bogged witch!" He shook his head and turned to the captain. "Quite the bluff, dontcha think?"

"So, the corporal decided to play lieutenant governor?"

"No. He was just a chip in the game." The grin on Orion's face was a painful expression. "He wasn't alone."

"There's lip rouge on that teacup," the captain interrupted, pointing at the bed. "Everything on that tray is set for two."

Orion nodded. "Like I said, he wasn't alone." He walked to the window, murmuring to himself, "Found a real mark, di'nt you, Calista?"

The captain exhaled his frustration. "This doesn't make sense."

"Yes, it does," Orion sighed as he looked outside. The short, dark figure with the red bandanna was long gone.

CHAPTER FIFTY-NINE

Back in Stebbins, a morning that had started gloomy—weather-wise and outlook-wise—had drastically changed by midday.

No more gunfire thundered through town. No more Theriot men standing around looking snotty. Since the shootout ended, only one more outlaw with a gaudy silver star had been rooted out. He'd been caught climbing into the saddle of a horse in front of the grist mill, looking to make a getaway. Clapped behind bars, he joined a group of surviving Theriot mercenaries that included the disgraced Judge Dugal Ridgely.

But there was still work to be done. The undertaker was methodically gathering up bodies of outlaws who'd been hired to intimidate and harass. All that was left of Calista's Special Force was a heap of weapons and a small pile of shiny silver stars.

Deed eyed the collection of weapons in the street, reaching into the stack and pulling out a new-looking Spencer rifle that had been carried by one of the thugs.

"Hey, Sheriff! You okay with my taking this?" he

hollered with a grin at Moose Elkins. "Those bastards shot mine all up."

Seated on a bench outside the Blue Sky Inn, Moose called back, "Keep it. The town of Stebbins owes you more than that." The huge man had actually never stopped being sheriff—the ambush that injured him and killed Marshal Hollings only stalled his day-to-day duties. His *reinstatement* was merely a formality. That much had been agreed upon immediately.

As the morning's violent clash subsided, more and more townsfolk began appearing out on the street. Businesses opened. Smiles returned. It was as though a huge, smothering blanket had been lifted. The people of Stebbins were ready to take back their town and resume regular lives.

Moose and Deed watched as the last wagonload of bodies was carted away by the undertaker and his assistants. Holt, Laudie Kate, and Blue had taken the Corrigan mounts to the livery. On their way back, they passed by the telegraph office, now functioning with a new operator. Someone with experience from the war had volunteered after the danger had passed. The Theriot clerk had been allowed to go free, but he had to leave town and not return.

Holt stopped in front of the station. "Wait a minute." He reached into his coat pocket for the small leather pouch of tobacco he kept there. Not a smoker, save for an occasional cigar, Holt often offered small gifts of tobacco as tributes to the spirits, an Indian ritual he admired and used for himself. From the pouch, he spread a handful of shreds in all four directions, silently thanking the spirits for their help and guidance. He placed the bag back into his coat and looked at Laudie Kate, then Blue. "Things could've gone really sideways here." He smiled and reclasped Laudie Kate's hand. "Thankful they didn't."

"You'll have to tell me about that…that prayer, sometime," Blue commented. He knew his younger brother wasn't the most devout, but the preacher in him was fascinated by this seemingly sacred act.

Holt smiled. "Lots of ways to thank the Creator. This seems to suit me."

"Amen." Blue smiled.

The three continued their walk and joined Deed and Moose out in front of the Blue Sky.

"Town meeting still going on?" Holt asked.

"I think they're wrapping up," Moose said. "They've got a town again."

Laudie Kate spoke up, "Now that they know what it's like to lose it, I hope they'll work hard to never let it happen again."

First out the door was *Stebbins Observer* publisher, Max Palmer. He looked at the collection of Corrigans and nodded.

Holt greeted the newspaperman with an icy glare. "Palmer."

"Mr., uh, Corrigan…"

"Not sure why you're still here. Are you planning on publishing your…your *paper*?" Holt's words dripped with disdain.

"Wh-Why, y-yes, yes, I am."

Holt glared at the man.

Palmer gulped. "Y-You c-can't blame—"

Holt didn't give him a chance to finish. "Yes, yes I can. You have to shoulder a huge amount of blame. For what you did, for what happened." He gathered himself, not wanting anger to get in the way. "You have to shoulder a burden of responsibility. The truth is just as hard to fight for as upholding the law."

Palmer nodded. "I am renaming the paper," he said resolutely. "I-I know the *Observer* has lost credibility. I'm thinking the new one ought to be called the *Free Press*."

"The *Stebbins Free Press*." Holt mulled it over for a moment. "A lot to live up to."

The newspaperman started to head to his office.

"Palmer, we're allowing you to go free, but count on competition. You'll never be the only voice in Stebbins again."

As citizens streamed by to resume their lives, the owner of the Blue Sky, Miguel Navarro, stood on its porch and announced to the small Corrigan group, "Time to celebrate! Time to eat!"

"Now that's a great idea!" Deed exclaimed.

Around a big table in the middle of the Blue Sky restaurant, Holt, Laudie Kate, Blue, Deed, Moose, and Miguel sat laughing and talking loudly. Holt convinced his hotel friend that his workers could serve the group, that Miguel needed to join in and relax.

Conversation quickly swung to who had not turned up in the tumult of the morning. There was no sign anywhere of Lewis Chapman. Or Calista Theriot.

"If they were smart, they're high-tailing it for the bayou," Blue said.

"With a truly operating telegraph, I've already sent word out about those two," Holt added.

The group then toasted Stebbins's new deputy

mayor, Miguel Navarro. Hearty wishes of congratulations and thumps on his back followed. In the just-completed town meeting, he had originally won the mayoral vote by a narrow margin. He respectfully turned down the office, citing a wish to concentrate on his hotel. The second-place finisher, Mrs. Bywater, was declared the winner. She only agreed to take the helm if Miguel would be her deputy, a role he eagerly agreed to assume.

"There's something you don't hear much," Laudie Kate said quietly to Holt. "A woman mayor?"

"If this place can change, maybe there's hope elsewhere," he agreed. "She's gonna be good."

The late supper meal turned into an afternoon enjoying the company and lingering over coffee and delicious pies. Business in the restaurant picked up. More and more townspeople joined in the merriment.

The shadows across the Blue Sky's front windows and doors changed as afternoon crept toward dinnertime. Suddenly, Miguel hollered, "Look who eez here!"

A brown-and-gray dog with floppy ears had just rambled into the restaurant and made a beeline for the table, jumping into the lap of his master.

"Tag!" Holt cried happily. "Hi, boy! Oh, I've missed you." The pair smothered each other in a happy reunion.

"Watch his tail!" Laudie Kate yelped as she hurriedly moved a water glass and coffee mug to safety. Then she smirked, watching her man and his dog. "For Tag, this guy doesn't need reminding about bestowing hugs and kisses."

Just then, Evie burst through the doors, followed by Gus Brooks. The owner of the Flying G, Sawyer Gates, was not far behind.

Moose and Evie's reunion was tear-filled and joyous. They moved off to the side to catch up.

"Came as quick as we could," Gus announced. "We could tell th' mornin' was eventful. Not a Special Force badge in sight. People out an' about. Smilin' too! Don' remember th' last time I seen that."

"Eventful is an interesting word, my friend," Holt said. "We had help. Say hello to Laudie Kate Hart, and Deed and Blue Corrigan."

"Nice ta meet you all." Gus smiled, then reported, "We got riders outside from th' Flying G, Triple S, an' Half Moon 6. Some of them rode to th' Windmill V. No sign of that Theriot woman, but we got five of them Special Force idiots tied up in a wagon."

"Well, my friend." Holt smiled. "There's more news. The good folks of Stebbins have voted. If you accept, you're the new town marshal. You know where to lock those bastards up. You already got a set of keys." Both men laughed.

As they guffawed at their joke, the blacksmith Elijah strode through the doors.

"Elijah!" Holt hollered over the din of the restaurant. "Join us!" The big man moved carefully toward them through the tables filled with people.

Holt put his arms around both men. "Gus, I believe you know Elijah, the blacksmith."

"Of course." Gus nodded good-naturedly. "We bend each other's ears on all kindsa stuff."

Elijah chuckled in agreement.

"Well, Elijah is also now known as *temporary deputy* Elijah," Holt explained. "I'm sure Elijah would like to keep his business, so you and Moose both can decide how to proceed if the deputy job becomes permanent."

"Aw hell, temporary nothin'." Gus shook his head. "I'd be proud to have 'im. If he wants the job, it's his. We'll figger out how to juggle it later."

With a nod and a huge grin, Holt said, "Well, lock up those new prisoners, then get back here and pull up some chairs. You've got some catching up to do with this party."

As the dinner plates were cleared away, a runner came into the Blue Sky, looking for Holt. He had a telegram.

The young Ranger began reading. "It's from Orion," he said, grinning. "I know it's really from him. The way he addressed it."

HOLT:

SAD TO REPORT, CAPTAIN MCCOY IS DEAD.

BUT NOT IN A JAILBREAK.

KILLED BY MAJOR WOOSTER'S WIFE, CALISTA'S SISTER, CELINDA.

THE MAJOR CONFESSED. CELINDA HAS DISAPPEARED.

AUSTIN HAS PROMOTED ME TO CAPTAIN.

YOU & DAL ARE AND ALWAYS HAVE BEEN RANGERS.

I INFORMED THE LAW IN FOUR STATES THAT ISLA THORNE IS ACTUALLY CALISTA.

WHOLE THERIOT CREW NOW WANTED FOR MURDER & PIRACY.

I'LL BE HEADED TO THE 5 STAR & LILLY TOMORROW.

HIGBEE.

"What is it?" Laudie Kate asked.

Holt looked at her and handed her the message. He excused himself to respond with a wire of his own:

ORION,

CONGRATULATIONS CAPTAIN P HEAD.

REGRET TO SAY, DAL IS DEAD. THERIOT AMBUSH.

WE GOT THE MEN WHO KILLED HIM.

WE ALSO BROUGHT DOWN MADIGAN SANDERS AND AMES WOOSTER.

LAUDIE KATE SHOT MALO JOHNSON IN WILKON.

JUDGE RIDGELY ARRESTED.

UNFORTUNATELY CALISTA DISAPPEARED, CHAPMAN TOO.

MOOSE IS SHERIFF ONCE AGAIN. STEBBINS BREATHING EASIER.

JUDGE ELSHER NASH ARRIVING HERE SOON TO PUT THINGS IN ORDER.

HOLT.

CHAPTER SIXTY

Stebbins was finally getting its town back. Moose Elkins and Gus Brooks assumed their roles as sheriff and marshal respectively. Dory Bywater took the mantle of mayor. A legitimate federal magistrate, Judge Elsher Nash, was soon arriving and wired ahead for Holt's assistance to help sort everything out.

Blue and Deed prepared for their journey home, but before they went their separate ways, they secured a couple of promises from their brother. First, to keep himself out of trouble for a while, and second, a commitment to a Corrigan family dinner gathering as soon as he and Laudie Kate returned to Wilkon.

"I believe the trouble is past," Holt said to his brothers. "That pirate witch is likely hiding in a Louisiana bog somewhere. And her Special Force is all locked up or buried."

"I heard the blacksmith is making something for the town with all those melted-down stars," Deed said.

"The new mayor, Mrs. Bywater, asked Elijah to make some candlesticks or something," Laudie Kate added.

"Well, that's all good. You, my brother, just lie low. For a change," Blue admonished.

"I think Stebbins is in good hands." Holt smiled, then threw his arm playfully around Laudie Kate's shoulder. "Plus, I have this hellcat to keep me safe."

"Yeah, we never knew she had it in her," Blue said. "I guess we should've known since she shot you."

The four laughed at the mention. Holt and Laudie Kate's eyes locked in an affectionate embrace.

"Ride careful, my brothers. Thank you," Holt said, no more words needed.

Although she wanted to return to Wilkon as quickly as possible, Laudie Kate was not going anywhere without her Texas Ranger. The two—and Tag Along—settled in at the Blue Sky Inn, much to the delight of their friend, Miguel Navarro.

In the days that followed, Judge Nash arrived and set to work right away. After several hearings, he wired for prison wagons to take away the Theriot men without delay. Although a message had been sent in the immediate aftermath, the judge sent his own telegram informing lawmen across the state that Calista Theriot, also known as Isla Thorne, was wanted for murder, fraud, rustling, and robbery. This message was also dispatched across the state line to Shreveport, Natchitoches, Baton Rouge, and New Orleans.

With that, Holt's collaboration was no longer needed. He was disappointed that Orion had yet to return, but Laudie Kate was eager to go home. Holt was ready too and was heartened to see his forever love feeling that Wilkon was *home*.

As they set out for the Corrigan homestead, Laudie Kate asked, "I know that a lot of bad guys were caught and that evil woman was discovered and defeated, but does it bother you that she got away?"

Holt bowed his head and shook it.

"I mean," Laudie Kate continued, "won't she just resurface somewhere, with her pirating, with a new name? Who's going to go after—"

Holt interrupted quietly, "Someone will, but not me. She's vanished, like pirates do."

"But…"

"There are bad people everywhere, Laudie Kate," Holt said softly. "Not going to catch 'em all."

Laudie Kate's deep sky-blue eyes could see that Holt's words did not match his feelings and let the subject pass.

Three days later, Holt and Laudie Kate were tying up their tired mounts in front of Wilkon's Black Hat Saloon when a voice cried out.

Hustling from his office, the fastidious telegraph operator, Mr. Hayes, held a piece of paper high above his head. "Holt Corrigan! It's so good to see you!" Mr. Hayes gushed. "For a while there, we didn't know what to think." He caught himself. "You too, Miss Hart. It's good to have you back."

"Thank you, Mr. Hayes." Holt smiled. "Laudie Kate tells me that you played an important role in seeing through all the chaos that pirate witch created. The town of Stebbins, and I, owe you a debt of thanks."

Mr. Hayes was speechless. Humbled and taken aback by such words from Ranger Holt Corrigan, he almost forgot why he had hurried out into the street in the first place. "H-Here, Ranger Corrigan…this has been waiting for you. Came through yesterday."

Holt accepted the message. "A telegram from Orion again," he noted to Laudie Kate.

HOLT:

LILLY IS BACK HOME NOW.

SURPRISED TO FIND HER RANCH UNDAMAGED.

EXPECTED THE BAYOU FROG SQUATTERS TO TORCH IT.

SORRY I MISSED YOU. KNOW YOU'D BE EAGER TO GET HOME.

DON'T THINK ABOUT THAT HORSE PROJECT WITHOUT TALKING TO ME.

WHEN DUST SETTLES I'LL COME FOR A VISIT.

RIDE CAREFUL.

HIGBEE.

"Well, that says a lot without being in the message," Holt declared.

Laudie Kate just watched him, knew more was coming.

"He was the one retiring, turning in his badge." Holt smiled. "Before…all this started. This says he wants me to stay."

"Is he expecting us to go after that Calista witch?"

"Us?"

"I'm already expecting some kind of reward for what I just helped with," she deadpanned. "And I'll want a bigger one if we take her all the way down, Holt Corrigan."

Holt was dumbfounded and could only chuckle.

"You tell Captain Orion I'll expect wages too."

Holt found his words and stopped her. “How about we get married instead? Raise horses. And a family.”

She sighed. “Is that *all*?”

Holt looked hurt. “I’m *serious*, Laudie Kate. I want to marry you.”

She realized Holt had not taken the joke. “I’m serious, too, Holt Corrigan.” She took his face in her hands and looked deeply into his eyes. “I would have settled for a new dress, but that would be so much better.” She threw her arms around his neck and kissed his cheek, working her way to his lips.

He pulled away. “A dress? Well, maybe that’s what we’ll do inste—”

Another big kiss stopped his words.

EPILOGUE

Blue Corrigan stepped back and smiled. "You may now kiss the bride."

Holt grinned and held his new wife by the shoulders and kissed her, then took her in his arms for the biggest of hugs as she kissed him in return.

Corrigan family and friends burst into applause and raucous cheers.

"The whole thing is over." Holt smiled. "You got the new dress *and* a husband."

"The best part is I get you forever," Laudie Kate gushed.

The yard of the Corrigan family's Rafter C had been turned into a huge spectacle of flowers for the occasion. Bina and Atlee decided that the other family ranch, the Bar 3, was not currently suitable for hosting the wedding of their new sister-in-law. Holt and Laudie Kate's new house was being built there, and in the Corrigan women's estimation, there was too much ugly construction going on to host such a beautiful day.

After supper, everyone was savoring slices of delicious angel food cake. The Corrigan family sat up on the huge porch of the ranch house.

Deed's stepdaughter, Elizabeth, watched her uncle and new aunt laugh and enjoy themselves. She spoke to her parents, but everyone could hear, "If they have children, will they have scars like Unca Holt and Aunty Laudie?"

The sounds of happy laughter rang out. Tag Along and Cooper barked their approvals at the joyful sound.

A LOOK AT: RIDIN' WITH THE PACK VOLUME TWO

A WESTERN SHORT STORY COLLECTION

Saddle up and venture into the wild frontier of the American West with *Ridin' with the Pack: Volume Two,* a gripping anthology that celebrates the timeless allure of Western storytelling.

From rodeo circuits to deadly secrets buried in Montana grasslands, each story unravels a vivid tale of survival, justice, and redemption.

Readers will navigate the trials of a young veteran fighting to keep his family's ranch, a man haunted by his past on a quest for vengeance, a former outlaw struggling to leave behind his crooked life, and a Norse adventurer facing his fate on the shores of a newly established colony. Alongside these gripping tales, the search for a legendary pirate treasure tears apart a man's life, a family legacy built on grit and fortitude is threatened by an old frontier rivalry, and the desperate choices of a woman stranded in Dodge City lead to unexpected salvation.

In every tale, the spirit of the West shines through, each story unraveling like a chapter in the epic saga of the untamed frontier—where freedom, grit, and the unyielding quest for justice resonate like the timeless strains of a cowboy's humble heart.

Written by a talented crew of seasoned veterans and rising stars, Ridin' with the Pack: Volume Two *showcases the enduring spirit of the classic Western tale.*

AVAILABLE NOW

ACKNOWLEDGMENTS

There aren't enough words to express my love and thanks to my wife, Cindy. She puts up with me—well, most of the time. Her patience with the long hours I spend in my office when I'm researching, writing, and surfing funny cat videos and stuff is immeasurable. It will be 30 years together this year, I don't know how she does it, but I'm eternally grateful.

My appreciation to the Lost Boys – my Scouts America buds: JimmyT, Lester, Mr. Hayes, Col. Bill, Mayor Moose, Banker Bill, Dave our Royals guy, plus all the rest of the White House crew. Shenanigators First Class, one and all. Your friendship and warmth mean more than you know.

To my Wolfpack Publishing family – Mike Bray, Jake Bray, Kayla Ireland, the whole pack – many thanks for your continued support.

Finally, to my parents Sonya and Cotton Smith. I feel your love and presence every single day, especially Dad's when I'm writing. Sorry Mom, I would have made an unhappy lawyer, a terrible pastor, and a worse doctor. I think I did all right being me. I miss you both, more than words could ever say. Thank you for everything.

ACKNOWLEDGMENTS

ABOUT THE AUTHOR

Scott F. Smith continues the spirit of the Old West created by his father, Cotton Smith, author of the first two books of the Corrigan series and other wonderful Western adventures, such as *Pray for Texas* and *Behold a Red Horse*.

Vengeance Wears a Star is Scott's debut novel and is rooted in the elements that made Cotton's books great—grand themes, moral conflict, and courage. He grew up with a love of American history, reading, and Western movies and is an Eagle Scout and recipient of the Boy Scouts of America's Silver Beaver Award. He continues to volunteer with Scouting to help develop tomorrow's leaders.

As a youth, Scott was introduced to the ceremonies, customs, and traditions of the Plains Indian. Research for Western storytelling heightened his appreciation for and spiritual connection to the land. For many years, he participated in the Desert Caballeros trail ride, covering a hundred miles in a weeklong trek through the Arizona mountains each year.

Scott is an award-winning writer and producer for corporate clients and relishes the experience of staring at a blank piece of paper or computer screen and creating a story within an easy-to-imagine world. He previously taught high school media and video production, having enjoyed sharing his storytelling expertise as well as helping students bring their own tales to life.

A member of the Western Writers of America, Scott and his wife, Cindy, are global explorers but call Lawrence, Kansas, home.

You can find Scott's work at www.ScottSmithWesterns.com.

www.ingramcontent.com/pod-product-compliance
Lightning Source LLC
La Vergne TN
LV040214110826
46LV00005B/1278